Lily's Dance

A novel by

KAREN STEUR

ISBN: 1981244689
ISBN 13: 9781981244683
Library of Congress Control Number: 2017918710
CreateSpace Independent Publishing Platform
North Charleston, South Carolina

Lily's Dance and the author's proceeds are dedicated to Blue Sky Bridge of Boulder, Colorado. Blue Sky Bridge is a nonprofit child and family advocacy center that helps hundreds of children affected by abuse each year. Blue Sky Bridge has four primary programs: child advocacy, medical treatment, trauma-focused cognitive behavioral therapy, and school-based education. www.blueskybridge.org
May we protect the children and never ignore their cries for help. ·

AUTHOR'S NOTE

This is a work of fiction. All names, places, and situations are fictional and do not reflect actual people or facts. However, the stories of the two traumatized women are very true in our world. Childhood sexual abuse and the terror caused by stalking behavior happens more than we want to realize or know about. But these stories need to be told, and these women, as well as men, need to be heard and supported.

ACKNOWLEDGMENTS

I want to thank Leslie Myers for her time and patience with grammatical assistance. I also want to thank Tracy McDermott for her beautiful artwork on the cover. Thank you to Michele Anderson for her expertise in animal communication and to my professors at Regis University for their support as I was writing and rewriting this novel. I want to thank my editor Heather from Createspace. And special thanks to my family and friends for all their love, encouragement, and support with this project.

TABLE OF CONTENTS

THE DEVIL IN LEVI'S

If you are God fearing,
And accept Jesus,
Live with a good heart,
Are you safe from the tempter?

Is the devil the antichrist?
The polar opposite,
So that if you do wrong,
You go south at your end?

In he walks.
Tan, broad shoulders,
Coal-black hair, expressive dark eyes,
A knowing smile.

Muscles ripple through thin black shirt,
Snug black jeans,
Don't impede his confident stride.
Scanning the room, he nods greetings to those looking on.

Your breath catches as your eyes meet.
He pauses, then moves on.
Is the flutter in your chest
Anticipation, wonder, or fear?

He picks up a toy a crying child dropped,
Hands it to the child as the grateful mom looks on.
Then catches an elderly woman as she stumbles,
Settling her with a smile.

Who is this man?
You meet again,
He knows just what to say,
How to touch, how to kiss.

He knows to hold you until you fall asleep.
He knows your wishes and desires.
How does he know?
Is he too good to be true?

Then his life is not as he disclosed.
His truths are lies.
When questioned,
He retreats.

You leave, he follows.
Possessiveness, rage,
You are frightened.
He is pleased.

Two years,
Stalking, terrorizing,
Then he is gone,
Finally gone.

How to protect yourself,
How to protect your friends,
How to protect your family,
From the Devil in Levi's?

LILY AT THIRTY

Lily waves good night to her last student, Amanda, and Amanda waves back at Lily as she climbs into the car where her mom waits. Lily watches the car pull out and drive away. Before closing the door, she looks both ways down the street. With a shiver, she closes and locks the four dead bolts on the door, pulls down the shades, and dims the lights. Putting on Tchaikovsky's *The Seasons*, she walks slowly to the center of the dance floor in her studio. She stretches and sways to the music, breathing in and out slowly, relaxing her back and neck muscles. Getting up on pointe, she dances, letting her mind relax and flow as her limbs keep rhythm with the beat. The world becomes a blur, and Lily can almost feel the warm glow of the theater lights and hear the intake of breath and the clapping of her fans as she floats across the dance floor. After an hour she stretches, turns off the music and lights, and climbs the stairs to her apartment above the studio.

After she places her clothes in a basket near the washer and dryer, she steps into the shower. Steam rises, and she breathes in the moisture. Backing into the water stream, she lets it run down her sore, tired muscles, washing the ache down the drain. As the water starts to cool, she turns it off and reaches for her fluffy burgundy towel from Macy's—a luxury she afforded herself. It comforts her, giving her a few moments of feeling safe and warm. After slipping into a white cotton gown, she pours a glass of cool white wine and strolls to the window. Unlatching the window, she swings it out and sits on the cushioned window seat. With her eyes closed, she leans out and takes in a breath of fresh air. Lily shakes her red curls loose and lets the wind blow them about. Spring in Lakewood, Colorado, brings cool nights with the possibility of snow from the mountains. It feels good to be back in Colorado, not that she really has a choice. She has no choices at all. She moved back here to get away from him, but he followed. Her mom and dad are not far away. She can sometimes feel them, even though they are estranged from her. They still live on the ranch where she grew up. Lily remembers that it is hunting season on the ranch. Soon her dad and cousins will be getting ready for the families that come to enjoy the ranch in the summer. Lily smiles as she remembers.

She started working on her passion when she lived at the ranch. Her dad built her a studio where she practiced her ballet for hours. Then New York was exciting for school and her first job with the company. She danced for one and a half years as a principal dancer and then four years as a prima ballerina. She smiles at the memory. She was so young, driven, innocent, and happy—until she wasn't. She shudders and tries to shake off the sadness.

With glass in hand, she leans out the window. She looks for him at the lamppost, but he's not there. No sign of him, the light of his cigarette, or the shiny silver chrome of his motorcycle. It's been three days since she's seen him. It's very unusual for him not to keep track of her.

Lily goes to bed, but sleeps fitfully. She rises throughout the night, looking toward the lamppost for the glow of his lit cigarette or his nod of acknowledgment and warning. Once she thinks she sees him, but her eyes are deceiving her—it is only shadows across the moon. She should be relieved, thankful, but she's afraid. Afraid of what this might mean for him, for her. It has been two years of him waiting, watching, and reminding.

As the night sky disappears into the light of day, she falls asleep. The ringing of her phone wakes her at 10:00 a.m. She can't believe she slept so late.

Grabbing the phone, she says, "Hello?"

"Lily, it's Sasha. Have you heard?" Sasha says in a loud, excited voice.

With a start, Lily sits straight up in bed. She hasn't heard from Sasha in almost two years. Not since that dreadful, scary night when she realized that she couldn't have any friends. She couldn't risk him hurting them. He wanted her all to himself. She'd given Sasha her new phone number when she'd moved to Colorado.

Lily thinks to herself, *Sasha, you shouldn't be calling me.* But she says, "Heard what?"

"He's dead."

Not understanding what Sasha's saying, Lily says, "Who's dead?"

"Landers!"

The phone drops, and Lily scrambles to pick it up. "What do you mean, dead?"

"The news said he was hit by a bus, dragged, and died instantly. It happened a few days ago, and it was difficult to identify him." Sasha pauses. "Lily, are you OK? I'm sorry if I was too graphic. I was just excited for you. Your nightmare is over!"

Lily lets the phone drop again and sits and stares out at nothing. She can't hear anymore. Sasha was one of her closest friends before they separated for her safety. Sasha's voice sounds like Christmas bells in her ears.

The next day Sasha calls and leaves a message telling Lily the date, time, and location of the funeral. She explains that the funeral is in Colorado. Lily wonders why. Landers told her he was from Louisiana. He said his mom and dad still lived there. Lily sighs and falls back into bed under the safety of her covers. Landers never told her the truth.

That afternoon Sasha calls.

"Hello?" Lily says quietly as she lies in the dark of her room that she has not left since she heard the news.

"If you decide to go to the funeral tomorrow, I can take you." Sasha waits for a reply.

"Yes, that would help. I need to go. I have to see for myself that it's over, that he's finally gone. I just can't go by myself. Wait, why are you in Colorado? Oh, your dad lives here, right?"

"Yes, my dad lives here. I come now and then with Sam to visit him, but I didn't let you know, well, you know why...sorry."

"No need to apologize. You needed to stay safe. Thanks for the offer to take me to the funeral. I'll see you tomorrow."

Sasha tells Lily when she will pick her up, and Lily ends the call.

Lily drags herself into the bathroom and looks in the mirror. She doesn't recognize the face staring back at her. Her skin is ashen, her eyes and cheekbones sunken into her face. She remembers that she hasn't eaten or had anything to drink since she heard the news. She remembers lying in bed, maybe sleeping, maybe not. She isn't sure of anything. She doesn't know what she is feeling or how she should feel. He has terrorized her for two years, and now he is gone, really gone.

"I don't know how to feel! I don't know what to do with myself," Lily says out loud.

The next morning Lily showers and puts on a dark-navy suit. It's lightly raining, so she holds an umbrella as she stands outside waiting for Sasha. Her body sways in the moist wind. Sasha pulls up in her cherry Mustang convertible with the top up due to the rain. As Lily steps into the car, she sees that Sasha's brown curls are pulled up under a brown hat that matches her slacks and jacket. The two friends smile at each other, and Sasha reaches over and takes hold of Lily's hand. They hold hands during the tense drive to the cemetery.

It takes about an hour to get to Clay Cemetery. Sasha parks her car up the hill from the grave site. Sasha and Lily decide to stand back, away from the group. It's a gathering of ten or so people carrying or wearing rain gear as if they anticipate the sky to cry. A clap of thunder sounds in the distance. The early spring has warmed the ground enough to put someone to rest.

Lily leans into a tree for support or perhaps comfort. The stormy weather brings a chilling wind that blows her red curls and causes her green eyes to tear. She's so glad that Sasha is with her. The two friends huddle together under the protection of the tree.

The minister speaks about the deceased in general terms, as if he really doesn't know him. A gray-haired woman sits alone at the graveside.

Though Lily has never met her, she recognizes Landers's mom from an old photograph she saw years ago. His mom wears no glasses or veil. Her face appears to be lined with age and sadness, yet is without expression. There's no tissue or hanky to wipe her eyes. Her eyes are dark, like Lander's eyes. She sits and stares at the grave. Maybe she's in shock. She's alone. Maybe her husband is no longer living. Maybe it's too much for her to lose her son when she has lost her husband as well. Lily knows all too well that there's no greater loss than that of a child. A familiar pain squeezes her heart. She tries to focus back on the gray-haired woman. Perhaps she has not come to grips with what happened. Or maybe she's heavily sedated. There's a big crack of thunder that seems to startle everyone except his mom. She doesn't flinch. She just keeps staring.

The minister mentions that Landers was a father. Lily gasps and wobbles as Sasha catches her arm and steadies her. Lily's heart aches as she remembers what seemed to be so long ago. He said he hated children and didn't want any. *Hate* is a harsh word, but that's what he said. She scans the group, looking for his children. There's a young man, perhaps twenty, standing next to a woman in her forties. Maybe that's his son and a former wife or girlfriend. The woman's arm is draped around the young man. Both have dark hair, dark complexions. She's a nice-looking woman, smartly dressed in a dark suit and heels. She has short curly hair, fashionably styled. Dark glasses hide her eyes. Her hand touches her face as if to wipe a tear. Her son appears upset or angry. He shifts his weight from one leg to another. The woman leans over and whispers something to him, using her hands expressively.

There are three men. All three look as though they have never missed a meal. They appear visibly sad—perhaps sad at the loss of a friend or the reality of their own mortality. Lily watches the men, wondering if they are personal friends or business associates. She didn't think he had any friends—not close friends, anyway. There was so much she really didn't know about him. The men are dressed in sportswear, not very well matched, and their eyes are red and swollen as if from crying or too much drink the night before.

Off to the left, there are three women. They aren't standing together, but are eyeing each other discretely. Lily notices that they are very pretty; two brunettes wearing hats, late thirties or early forties, and one with coal-black hair, very young, who couldn't be much older than the son. All three women are dressed in black. They seem more interested in looking at each other than in listening to the eulogy. Perhaps they didn't know the deceased well, or perhaps they do not feel much emotion toward his passing.

We're all strangers, drawn here by the deceased, Lily thinks. She tries to remember why she's here. The minister continues to speak, and his words roll over her.

I think I'm in shock. I can barely hear, or feel the wind and rain.

Sasha leans over and whispers to Lily that she's going to run and get their umbrellas from the car. Lily bows her head as in prayer...or is it anguish? As the ceremony ends, she looks up, and Landers is standing in front of her. She sees his knowing grin. He steps toward her. In shock, she stumbles back into the tree. She looks for Sasha and sees she is moving toward her car. No one at the grave site is paying any attention. Lily looks deep into his face. His lips are moving, but the words are muffled by the wind and the rain. And then his smile widens—that smile that doesn't show his teeth. She's so scared she can't breathe. She feels hot. He grabs a hold of her and pulls her to him. Her vision blurs, and then it tunnels into black. She's falling.

Lily opens her eyes and finds she is lying on a hard bed or table. She sees Sasha beside her on a bench. Sasha is biting her nails and frowning. A man in a dark-navy uniform sits at Lily's head and is tugging at her. Lily sees their mouths moving, but hears no sound. She can't move or speak. Then she remembers seeing Landers. In her terror, her breathing becomes rapid, and she tries to call out. Her eyes dart left and right. She tries to get up, but she is strapped down. She fights against the straps.

She yells, but only she can hear her words in her head. *What's happening to me? Is he still alive? Were they wrong when identifying his body? Or is he reaching me from the grave? He grabbed me! What would have happened if I hadn't blacked out? Where is he now? He must have faked his death! I can't let him control my life anymore.*

I can't do this anymore. He has hurt me so badly, and I'm so tired and lonely. I'm all alone. I would rather die than continue this torture.

Lily slips inside herself and closes the door.

LILITH—LILY'S MOM

Lilith gets in her car and starts her drive home. She has just finished her three shifts in the intensive care unit (ICU) at Colorado Springs Central Hospital. She has been working there on and off since she married Roy. It's located an hour and a half from her ranch. She usually goes home between shifts, but she had a special case that needed her critical nursing skills, as well as her psychic ability—to talk with the dead or to patients that are in a coma. Her mind plays back the days.

Lilith was caring for a twenty-three-year-old woman, Amy Lane. Amy was found at home by a friend. She was unresponsive, not breathing, and had no a pulse. The friend called 911 and started CPR. Emergency responders resuscitated Amy and placed a breathing tube. The friend said that Amy had stopped taking heroin a year ago, but when she found she was pregnant, she got stressed and nervous, and a syringe was found near her bed. EMS brought Amy to the emergency room, where she tested positive for opiates. After stabilizing her, the medical team admitted Amy to the ICU for acute poisoning and sixteen weeks pregnant.

Amy was on a hypothermia protocol to cool her organs, including her brain, to give them every chance to recover after cardiac arrest. Amy's parents arrived from New York and moved between the ICU family waiting room and Amy's bedside.

It has been forty-eight hours since the arrest. Amy's vital signs are normal, and the baby has a strong heartbeat, but Amy has shown no sign of waking up. Her electroencephalogram (EEG) indicates minimal brain activity.

As Lilith cares for her patient and her patient's unborn baby, she hears, *Where am I? What's wrong with me? Why can't I open my eyes?*

Lilith knows that she is hearing Amy talking to her from her coma. Lilith says out loud, "Amy, my name is Lilith. You are in the hospital, and I'm the nurse taking care of you and your baby. You have a breathing tube helping you breathe. I will keep you comfortable. You are safe. I am monitoring your baby, and your baby has a strong heartbeat."

What happened to me?

Lilith whispers silently, *Amy, you took some drugs that stopped your heart and breathing. A friend found you and called for help. Your heart was restarted, and you were brought to the hospital. You are in a coma.*

How can you hear me?

I have the gift of clairaudience. I can hear people who are in a coma.

Am I dying?

Amy, your brain is damaged. It does not have much activity. When you took the injection of heroin it stopped your heart and breathing. We don't know how long it was before your friend found you, called for help, and tried to get your heart beating again.

If my heart is beating now, why am I not waking up?

Lilith takes a deep breath. *Amy, when your heart stopped, you were not getting blood to your brain. If the brain does not get blood, it dies.*

Lilith hears Amy scream, *I'm not going to wake up? I'm dying. What about my baby? You have to save my baby! Please save my baby!*

Lilith whispers silently, *Amy, please try and relax. We're doing everything we can for you. Your parents are here, and they're trying to decide what's best for you and your baby.*

What can I do?

Lilith strokes Amy's still hand. *Amy, give your baby love, and give love to your parents.*

Lilith's thoughts are interrupted by Amy's parents, who have entered the room.

Mrs. Lane is wrinkling the fabric of her husband's coat as she clings to him. The two stop and stand several feet away from Amy. Lilith notices that both parents' eyes are wet and tears are dripping down their faces.

Mrs. Lane looks from Lilith to her daughter and says, "How can this be happening? She looks like she is asleep and will wake up." Mrs. Lane weeps into her husband's shoulder as he pulls her to him.

Lilith approaches Amy's parents. She sees that their faces are pale and their eyes are red and puffy. "Did you get any sleep last night?"

"Not much," Mrs. Lane replies. "And please call us Susan and Larry." She smiles at Lilith, but as she turns toward her daughter, her face drops.

"Can I get you some coffee?" Lilith asks.

"No, we're going to get some breakfast. We just wanted to check on Amy before heading to the cafeteria." Susan takes in a slow, deep breath and lets it out.

"I was going to start her bath and work her muscles. I'll do that while you're gone."

"We'll be back in about an hour. I think that's when you have rounds with the doctor. Is that right?" Larry asks.

"Yes, at 9:00 a.m. I'll see you then." Lilith watches as they exit the room and close the door.

"Amy, I'm going to start your bath. I'll clean you with warm soapy water and exercise your arms and legs as I do it," Lilith says.

She slowly lifts Amy's arms and washes and dries them. After applying lotion, she moves them in a passive motion. She moves the washcloth to Amy's belly and pauses as she feels a quickening.

Lilith smiles as she hears Amy say, *That's my baby kicking you. Hello! You have to save my baby. Don't let them end our lives together.*

Lilith's breath catches, and tears leak from her eyes. "Your mom and dad are working with the doctors to do the best they can for you and your baby."

No, I know I'm not going to wake up, but my baby...Save my baby. You have to save my baby.

Lilith's chest vibrates as she inhales. She lets her breath out slowly and says, "We're doing everything we can."

After the bath, Lilith takes a break and walks to the hospital chapel. She touches the holy water and makes the sign of the cross before moving into a pew. Tears are spilling from her eyes before she sits down.

Lord, help me. How do I handle this? I can't tell anyone that the brain-dead patient is talking to me and wants us to save her baby.

Lilith's ears are buzzing with the whispers of angels that comfort and speak to her. But she is so overwrought that she isn't listening to what they are saying.

I know you're there and talking to me. I love and appreciate you, but right now I have to get all this emotion out. It's so hard. She weeps into her hands.

She hears, *We love you. We are with you. You will know what to do. You are helping Amy and her baby.*

"How will I know what to do? What if I make a mistake?" Lilith asks out loud.

Follow your heart. You will know.

The next day, after Lilith assesses and charts on one of her patients, she enters Amy's room and finds Susan and Larry sitting on either side of Amy's bed, talking with her. Lilith got a report that Amy's heart rate increased to 160 beats per minute with a few runs of ventricular tachycardia, and her temperature peaked at 105 degrees overnight. Amy was given a bolus of amiodarone and started on a drip to control her heart rate, and she is now wrapped in a cooling blanket to help maintain her temperature. Her heart rate is now stable at 98 beats per minute.

Susan looks up at Lilith. "It's good to see you."

As she looks from Larry to Susan, Lilith says, "How are you two doing?"

Larry takes off his glasses and rubs his eyes. "This is a horrific decision for a parent to make." He pushes his chair back, and the screeching sound makes Lilith jump. Larry heads for the door and yells, "I refuse to make a decision until I have more time!" He leaves the room.

Lilith approaches Susan, who is weeping into her tissues. "You take all the time you need."

Susan grabs Lilith's hand. "Thank you for saying that."

Lilith notices that it's time for rounds with the care team, and Amy's doctor is outside the room. Lilith steps outside with Susan, and the doctor gives Lilith a nod.

Dr. Hobbs extends his hand to Susan as he says, "I'm Dr. Neal Hobbs, one of the critical care physicians caring for your daughter."

"And her baby too?" Susan asks as she shakes his hand.

"Well, of course, consulting with our chief obstetrics physician, Alice May. We're Amy's care team and will discuss her case. Please let us know if you have any questions." He turns to Lilith and says, "Can you give us a review and an update?"

"Yes," Lilith begins. "Amy Lane is a twenty-three-year-old female, post–cardiac arrest with unknown downtime, and she had hypothermia protocol treatment. She is sixteen weeks pregnant. Amy has remained un-responsive, with fixed and dilated pupils, no reflexes, and minimal brain activity per the electroencephalogram. Her baby has a strong normal heart rate for gestational age. Amy is off and on febrile with peak temperature of 105 degrees. She is now normotensive with the cooling blanket. Her heart rate has stabilized with the amiodarone drip, which is safe during pregnan-cy. Labs and other vital signs are within normal range. Her parents, Susan and Larry, would like a family conference with case management, the eth-ics committee, physicians, and nurses, whenever that can be arranged."

Dr. Hobbs says, "Mrs. Lane, we will set up the meeting and inform you of the time and place."

Susan wipes away a tear. "Thank you." She turns and goes back into Amy's room.

Dr. Hobbs turns to Lilith. "How are they doing? Are they coming to a decision?"

"They're so torn up. Amy is their only child. They're trying to see if it is feasible to fly her to New York and keep her on life support until the baby is born."

Dr. Hobbs shakes his head and rubs his temple with his fingers. "How can they think that the baby will be all right? The baby had to have been deprived of oxygen when the mother didn't have a pulse."

"But the baby has a strong heart beat and is kicking. The body shunts blood to the baby in all kinds of circumstances."

Dr. Hobbs's voice rises several octaves. "Lilith, you're not listening. I'm trying to explain the situation to you. The mother was in cardiac arrest, not to mention the drugs she took. The baby is damaged!"

"But we don't know that for sure."

Dr. Hobbs's face reddens, and he takes in a quick breath as he stares down at Lilith and then turns and quickly walks away.

Tears sting Lilith's eyes, and her head throbs. She hears Amy say, *Thanks, Lilith, for fighting for my baby.*

Lilith whispers silently, *I'm doing the best I can. Give your baby love. And give your parents love.*

I will.

Lilith takes her lunch break and goes to see one of her friends, who knows of her gifts. Lilith knocks on Janna's door. Janna, who works as a case manager in the emergency room, has worked and been friends with Lilith for many years.

Janna answers her door, and when she sees her friend, she opens her arms. Lilith falls into her embrace. Lilith cries, and Janna just holds her until Lilith is ready to be released. Janna closes her door, and the two sit down.

"What's going on?" Janna asks.

After grabbing a tissue from Janna's desk, Lilith wipes her eyes and blows her nose. She takes in a shuddering breath.

Janna touches Lilith's leg. "Take your time."

Lilith looks into her friend's eyes. "This is so difficult. I'm caught between my two worlds."

"You know that your gift is a blessing and a—umm, what do you tell me? Oh, a curse. But I don't believe you really feel that way."

Lilith takes in a slow, deep breath and then exhales. "Yeah, about that."

Lilith tells Janna about her patient without revealing the patient's identity. She then tells her about the conversation with her patient's doctor and how she tried to get him to listen to her without revealing that she could talk with the comatose patient.

"He's known me for years, but he looked at me and talked to me as if I were an idiot. He was so angry."

Janna pats Lilith's hand. "You were challenging him. His ego was probably getting in the way of his empathy about the difficult decision these parents will have to make. But you fought for your patient and her baby. Remember that."

Tears leak out of Lilith's eyes. "I know, but it isn't easy."

"I can't even image." Janna stands and pulls her friend into a hug.

"Thanks, my friend. I appreciate that I can talk to you about my conflicts." Lilith smiles at Janna.

Janna opens her office door and says, "Any time."

Lilith walks back to her unit as she tries to shake off the sadness and concentrate on her patients. The conference with Amy's parents is set for the next day so they can get information on the feasibility of transferring their daughter to New York. Lilith gives her report to the night nurse, Jill, and stops by the waiting room to say good night to Amy's parents. She sees them sitting together as Larry talks on the phone and Susan holds his hand. Lilith waves, and Susan rises and comes over to her.

"I didn't want to disturb you. I just wanted to say good night and see if you needed anything," Lilith says.

Susan reaches for Lilith's hand. "Oh, thanks for what you're doing for Amy and our grandchild. Larry's on the phone with one of his friend who's an obstetrician. We're gathering information for the meeting tomorrow. We'll see you then." Susan squeezes Lilith's hand and then turns and walks back to her husband.

Lilith hears Amy whisper, *They want to save my baby.*

Yes, they do, Lilith whispers back silently.

Lilith leaves the hospital and gets in her car. She realizes that she hasn't eaten since breakfast. Seeing a sandwich shop with a drive-through, she orders a chicken sandwich. Her next stop is her room at the Motel 6. After letting herself into the room and placing her sandwich on the table, she turns on the shower. She kicks her work clothes onto the floor and enters the steaming shower. Lilith faces the flow of warm water. She puts her hands on the wall, lowers her head, and lets the warm water run down her back. She sobs out loud to no one and to everyone. When she is spent, she lathers with soap, rinses, and turns off the water. She reaches for a towel and realizes it's thin and worn. She cries again. She misses her fluffy towel from home, and she misses her husband, Roy. If she were home, he would be holding her in a hug. Lilith remembers her sandwich and hopes for a good night of sleep.

Lilith is awake before her alarm. She lies in bed, thinking of Amy. It reminds her of a time long ago when she was caring for a patient who had a brain aneurysm that caused her to become brain-dead. The patient was nine months pregnant. Lilith had adopted the baby girl and named her Jessica Lily. Her daughter took her middle name when she became an adult. Lily is the love of Lilith's life. Lilith's heart twinges. She has had very little contact with her daughter since Lily married. Lilith shivers as she remembers Lily's husband. There is something about him, but Lily loves him and chose him over her family. Lilith receives cards from Lily but has not seen her in a few years. She hopes she is happy in New York.

Maybe we'll find our way back to each other, Lilith thinks to herself.

Lilith climbs out of bed, wipes the tears from her eyes, and gives herself a little shake. She knows today will be emotion packed.

Lilith enters the ICU and gets a report on her patients from Jill. Jill's hair has fallen out of the clip she's wearing. Her eyes are red, and she can't stop yawning.

"Are you OK? And are you OK to drive home?" Lilith asks.

Jill stifles another yawn. "Yes, I'm OK. It was just a busy and very sad night. I haven't had a patient like Amy before, and her poor parents. I can't even image."

Lilith sighs. "It's a hard one. Make sure you take good care of yourself, Jill. You did a great job. Safe travels home, and I hope you can get some good rest."

Lilith enters Amy's room and finds Susan sleeping on the couch and Larry sitting in a chair next to his daughter. He is holding and stroking her hand.

Lilith's ears buzz, and she hears Amy talking rapidly. *Lilith, I want my baby to stay with me. I don't want to be without her.*

Lilith's stomach knots. She whispers silently back to Amy, *Your parents and the doctors are meeting today. They're trying to see if they can fly you back to New York to a hospital to wait until your baby has grown enough to be born.*

But I changed my mind. Tell them I changed my mind.

Lilith whispers silently back, *We'll do everything we can for you and your baby. Give your baby your love. And give your parents your love.*

The family meeting is scheduled for eleven o'clock. Lilith has asked the charge nurse, Marilyn, to watch her patients while she attends the meeting. After giving an updated report to Marilyn, she heads into the conference room. Susan and Larry are already seated at the table. Susan looks up and motions for Lilith to sit next to her. Lilith moves toward them and clasps their hands before sitting down. Dr. Hobbs enters and sits across from Lilith. The others in attendance are the chaplain, Marie, who is also on the ethics committee, the ICU case manager, Cynthia, who is looking into transfer arrangements, the obstetrician, Dr. May, who is caring for the pregnancy, and Dr. Michael Sound, the neonatologist, who is caring for the baby.

Dr. Hobbs looks around the room, and his eyes land on Lilith. He clears his throat and says, "I will start with a history of the patient. Amy Lane is a twenty-three-year-old female, status post–cardiac arrest with unknown downtime. She has a history of heroin use. She reportedly had not been using, but was stressed and an empty syringe was found next to her. A friend found her and started CPR. She had hypothermia protocol treatment. She is sixteen weeks pregnant. Amy has remained unresponsive, with fixed and dilated pupils, no reflexes, and minimal brain activity per the electroencephalogram. She had a maximum temperature of 105, which is now controlled with cooling. Her vital signs are stable at this time. Her baby has continued to have a strong normal heart rate for gestational age. We have been monitoring Amy for heroin withdrawal, which is detrimental to her and her baby. No signs of withdrawal symptoms at this time."

Dr. Hobbs pauses a moment. He takes in a slow, deep breath and lets it out. "We are meeting to review Amy's case and discuss the feasibility of her transfer to New York, to be near family and to maintain her on life support for the remainder of her pregnancy. Dr. Sound will talk about the condition of the baby."

Dr. Sound looks at both Susan and Larry. "Dr. May and I have been reviewing your daughter's records. We do not have an accurate time frame for when Amy was without her heart beating. What we do know is that the baby has a strong heart rate, and Amy's kidneys are functioning. But Amy has minimal brain activity, what we call brain death. For a young woman to be brain-dead, we have to assume she was deprived of oxygen-rich blood to her brain. There is a good probability that the baby was deprived as well, which can lead to a number of fetal abnormalities. And if there was a chance that Amy used heroin during her pregnancy, the baby could have birth defects and learning disabilities." Dr. Sound pauses as he sees Susan wiping her eyes and taking in shuddering breaths.

"I can't even imagine what a difficult decision this must be for you both. If you decide to move forward with the transfer once Amy is stable, the baby will be monitored closely for growth and abnormalities. I know you have met Cynthia, our case manager. She can go over the arrangements and costs. Do you have any questions?"

Susan swallows hard and looks at Dr. Sound. "What did you mean by 'once Amy is stable'?"

"Amy has an irritable heart that is functioning at a normal rate due to medication, and her temperature is being maintained by a cooling device. We would like the temperature to normalize on its own for the health of the baby and have the heart drug minimized before transfer."

"How long will that take?" Larry asks.

Dr. Hobbs begins to speak when an alert sounds overhead. "Code blue ICU room twelve. Code blue ICU room twelve."

Susan screams, "That's Amy!"

Chaplain Marie moves close to Susan and Larry as Dr. Hobbs, Dr. May, and Lilith run from the room. Susan clutches Larry's coat as they follow Marie into the ICU and toward Amy's room. Lilith looks up and, seeing them, motions for them to join her on Amy's left side, where Lilith is administering medications. Lilith places Amy's hand in her mother's hand.

Dr. Hobbs says, "Let's do a pulse and rhythm check." The staff member who is pumping on Amy's chest stops. "V-tach. Start compressions and charge at two hundred joules."

Lilith turns to Susan and Larry. "Stand in the back with Marie." She moves to the defibrillator and calls out, "Charging to two hundred joules."

There is a shrill sound as the defibrillator charges.

"Ready to shock. Everyone clear. Shocking now."

Amy's body jerk as it receives the shock. Larry and Susan jump. A staff member starts banging up and down on Amy's chest.

Lilith hears Susan howl, "No more!"

Lilith sees Larry look down at his wife who nods at him. Larry touches Lilith's arm. "Please stop. Let her go."

Lilith looks at Dr. Hobbs, who has heard, and they both nod. Dr. Hobbs says, "Hold compressions."

He looks at the monitor and sees a flat line. "Is there a pulse?"

"No pulse," Lilith announces.

Dr. Hobbs moves toward Amy, and after putting the earpieces of his stethoscope into his ears, he places the bell on Amy's left chest. "No heartbeat. Time of death, 12:03 p.m."

Lilith covers Amy's chest with a sheet. She turns to Susan and Larry and motions for them to come to the bedside. The staff back away to make room for Amy's parents.

Lilith's ears buzz, and she hears, *My baby is with me. She's so beautiful. I love her so much.*

I'm so glad for you. Give her love and give your parents love. They released her to you., Lilith whispers silently.

Lilith weeps with Larry and Susan as they say their good-byes to their only daughter and grandchild.

It's a long, sad shift of grieving with Amy's parents, talking with Amy, preparing her body to go to the morgue, finishing charting, and caring for her other patient. Lilith is spent. She drags herself to the chapel and kneels. Looking up at the cross that holds the body of Jesus, she gives her thanks and weeps.

Most merciful Father, please be with Amy and her baby. Bless them as you welcome them into your kingdom. Comfort Susan and Larry and help them in their grieving. Thank you that I was able to be a part of this beautiful family journey. Lilith sobs harder as she feels a warning swoosh through her ears. She looks up at the cross and says, "I miss my own daughter so much. Please help us to find our way back to each other."

Lilith sits back on the pew and takes in some slow, deep breaths and lets them out slowly. She rises, gathers her purse and jacket, and heads out of the chapel, down the hospital hall, and into the cool evening air. She enters her car, a blue Toyota 4Runner, and heads for home. Lilith turns onto Interstate 25, and her phone buzzes.

She picks up her phone and says, "Hello?"

"Mrs. Johnson, this is Sasha. I'm a friend of your daughter, Lily. She's sick and was admitted to the hospital." Lilith's ears are buzzing, her heart is racing, and she starts to shake. She pulls her car over and stops.

"What's wrong with my daughter?" Lilith says louder than she means to.

Lilith can hear Sasha gasp. "I don't mean to upset you. Lily appears physically fine, but she has been going through a hard time and fainted. The doctors are running tests. She is at Colorado Memorial."

"I'm so grateful that you called. I'm sorry I shouted. I'll call my husband and head toward the hospital. Thank you again. I'm so glad Lily has a good friend in you."

"Drive safely, Mrs. Johnson. And thank you. Lily has always been a good friend to me as well."

THE HOSPITAL—LILY

I don't want to be here, but I don't know where to go. There are un-known noises that startle me. There's yelling through some intercom. I just doze off and then someone is near my bed, talking to me and touching me. I want to shrink from their touch. What are they doing? My mind is fuzzy. I try to answer their questions, but nothing comes out of my mouth. What has happened to me? Even sleep is not restful. I have nightmares. He's reaching me in my dreams, reminding me that I belong to him, Lily thinks.

"Help me!" Lily screams.

A woman approaches her bed, and Lily shrinks away. "Lily, my name is Laura. I'm your nurse. You're safe. You're in the hospital. There's no one else in your room."

"I saw him! He's hiding. You can't protect me." Lily tries to get out of bed and leave.

"I'm right here. I'll make sure that you're safe. I'm going to get you some medicine to help you relax."

Lily screams and struggles to get out of bed. "No! No medicine. He'll find me. I have to be able to think so I can escape."

Laura helps Lily back into bed and says, "Please don't get out of bed without one of the nurses helping you."

Lily lies still, contemplating her next move. There's a window. She thinks about escaping out of the window. Even if it's high up, she doesn't care if she falls; it would put an end to this nightmare. Laura leaves the room, and Lily goes to the window. She looks out and sees that it is a couple of floors to the ground.

"Perfect," she says under her breath. Unlatching the window, she pulls it up. But the window only opens a few inches—she can't budge it. Lily heads for the door just as Laura is entering.

Lily's eyes are as round as saucers. She doesn't know what to do. She tries to make a run for it, but she is slow and clumsy. Laura holds her and calls out, "I need some help in here!"

Three staff members enter the room and lift Lily back into the bed. A needle pricks her right thigh. She is held down until she goes limp and the fight leaves her.

Lily's mouth feels swollen as she slurs, "You don't understand. I'm not safe."

Lily's eyes flutter closed, and her mind fogs as she hears echoing sounds. She hears Laura speaking into a phone. "Dr. Ball, she's having such bad hallucinations. Maybe we should change her medication."

Uniform-clad people come and do tests. Lily can't count the number of tests. She hears them as if in hushed whispers, but can't make out what they say.

> *They don't understand. They can't protect me. For years I've lived with this impossible fear and anxiety, waiting for his next move. I'm so tired. I don't want to do this anymore. I can't do this anymore. I won't. I feel myself slipping away. I can't grasp anything. My feelings and senses are dull. I'm here, but I just don't care. What more can he do to me?*

Lily's mind feels foggy as she lies in her hospital bed of white sheets. There's the sound of footsteps, wood against the linoleum, a familiar sound. Dansko shoes, she remembers from what seems like a million years ago. Her mom, Lilith, used to or maybe still does wear those shoes. Her chest hurts as she remembers. She hasn't seen her mom in three years.

Why did we stop talking? Did I do something? Did they do something? Lily touches her head; she feels dizzy. *What happened? I don't remember.* Lily rubs her eyes and takes a slow, deep breath in and out. Her mind clears enough to remember. She sits up and says out loud, "We became estranged because of Landers. Mom and Dad didn't like him, and I loved him so much. I had to make a choice, and it was my husband. I only realized much later that he had planted the seeds to keep me from my parents, to isolate me and keep me for himself. After the divorce I had to keep my distance because anyone, absolutely anyone, that got close to me was in terrible danger."

Lily hears her mom's voice from a distance. She's asking to talk with the doctor. Then she hears her dad's voice. Her heart warms and beats faster. Sasha must have told them she was here.

Lily's mind races and her pulse becomes rapid. *Oh, what do I do? How can I keep them safe if I can't keep myself safe?*

Dansko shoes approach her bed. "Lily, it's Mom." Lilith takes her daughter's hand and kisses her on the forehead.

For a moment Lily is a little girl. It feels so safe and warm. She pries her tired eyes open to look at her mom. She looks the same, soft and yet strong.

Then through the medication fog, Lily remembers and cries out, "No, you can't be here! It's not safe. You have to leave!"

Lilith takes a firm hold of Lily's shoulders. "Lily, you're safe. No one is going to hurt you. Sasha told me what happened." Lilith's voice catches as tears leak out of her eyes. "Sasha told me. I had no idea what you were going through with Landers." Then she looks up to the sky, or God, or her angels. "How did I not know? I should have known. What good is my gift if I can't help my daughter?"

This is too much for Lily's foggy brain. Her eyes flutter closed. She wonders if her mom will leave. But she doesn't.

Patting Lily's hand with some force, as if to wake the dead, Lilith says, "Lily, you do not need to be afraid anymore. Landers is dead."

Lily's eyes pop open, and she pulls her hand away from her mom. She tries to sit up. "He's not dead! He grabbed me at his memorial. Get out of here! He will know!"

Lily's heart is pounding in her chest, a wet, hot film covers her body, and she gasps for air as the room goes black. She hears someone calling for her from a distance or a dream, and then silence.

Lily wakes and finds her mom still sitting next to her in a chair beside the bed. The room is dim, and her mom's eyes are shut. Her hands are clasped, as Lily remembers she does when she prays. Lily watches silently.

Lilith opens her eyes and looks over at Lily. "You're awake. I talked with your doctor, and he said that your bloodwork, head scan, and reflexes are all normal. Baby, you are fine, physically. But you are remembering your trauma. It will take some time to work through your feelings, fears, and anxieties. I love you. I'm here. Your doctor is trying different medicines to help you with your anxiety."

Lily doesn't have the energy to speak. She just stares at her mom, who sits and holds her hand. Lily feels her mom's tears fall on her fingertips. She can hear her mom whispering. She remembers that her mom is probably talking with her angels and trying to find out what she can do to help. Lily is so tired that she lets herself float off into the darkness. Somewhere in her brain, she remembers something her mom had said about medicine. Her eyes pop open, and she looks at her mom.

"No drugs. I have to be clear so I can protect myself."

Lilith stands and moves closer to her daughter. "Look at me."

Lily tries to focus. She remembers this firm voice—it's her mom talking in her nurse voice.

"Landers is dead. You are safe."

Looking right back into her mom's eyes, Lily says, "Landers is not dead. I saw him at his own funeral. He's evil like that. He came right up to me, said something, and smiled his confident smile. He grabbed me, and I blacked out. Don't be fooled. He can hurt us." Exhausted, Lily closes her eyes as her body melts into the sheets.

Lilith takes hold of her daughter's shoulders. "Honey, what did he say to you?"

"I don't know, Mom. The wind was howling, and I was so shocked. When he grabbed me I fainted."

Lilith sits down hard in the chair and lets out a swoosh of air. She trusts the messages that she gets from her angels, but she is confused. "Honey, I get no message except that you're all right. Why can't I understand what is happening? Is this your PTSD, or is Landers really alive?" She puts her face down next to Lily's hand. "We will keep you safe. And I will make sure that the rest of the family is safe as well." She kisses Lily's forehead, and Lily hears her mom's Dansko shoes walking away.

Lily hears the doctor ask her mom to step outside the room and talk with him. She smiles—her mom always has to do her nurse thing. Lily closes her eyes; she is so tired. She just wants to sleep.

There are heavy footsteps coming down the hall. A memory of cowboy boots comes to Lily. Then she hears her dad's voice again, talking to her mom.

Cowboy boots approach Lily's bed. "Hey, sweet pea."

Lily opens her eyes and sees her dad's tanned face and warm smile. It has been years since he called her that. "Hi, Dad."

"Can I hug you?"

"Sure."

Her dad's strong arms are gentle as he lifts her to him. It feels so good to be held. Lily feels herself melt into him and doesn't even realize that she is crying. Her dad, Roy, holds her tight until she starts to pull away.

"You OK?" he asks.

"No."

Roy takes his daughter's hand and says, "We'll help you get better. I'll see you soon. Bye, sweet pea."

Lily gives her dad a hug before he turns and joins her mom in the hallway. She sees her dad hug her mom as her mom wipes tears from her eyes.

"I had no idea she was in such pain." Lilith slams her fists into her husband's chest and yells, "How could I not know?"

Roy holds Lilith tight.

After her mom and dad leave, Lily is left alone with her thoughts. She thinks back on her life and tries to remember happier times.

JULLIARD—LILY AT EIGHTEEN TO TWENTY-ONE

When Lily auditioned for Julliard, she was so caught up in the music while she danced across the stage that she forgot why she was there. When the music stopped, she was astounded to find she couldn't even read the faces of those that held her future in their hands. Each day was agony as she waited to hear if she had been accepted as a student.

The blue sky was vast, and the day warm in late December. The sun reflected off the newly fallen snow from the night before, when Lily slept fitfully, waiting to hear. Lily's boots crunched through the snow as she made her way down the road to the ranch mailbox at the entrance of the property. The box was filled with mail. Taking off her gloves, she carefully leafed through the mail as her heart rate increased. Her breath caught. There it was—a legal-sized envelope addressed to her from Julliard. But it was small, maybe only containing one sheet of paper. It wasn't a packet.

Was I rejected?

Dread seeped into her body and mind. Her knees began to quiver, and she felt light headed. She shook her head and shoulders and took in a deep breath.

Lily ripped into the envelope and read, "Dear Jessica Lily, Julliard is pleased to inform you that you have been accepted for the fall semester."

That was all she read before she screamed and ran down the road to the ranch house to share her news. Her family was so happy for her. Her mom, dad, and grandma tried to hide their sadness that she would be moving to New York and might not ever live near home again. But they knew too well of her dream to become a prima ballerina. Even her brother, John, looked low, but Lily knew he was busy and would soon forget that she was gone.

After finishing high school and a busy summer at the ranch, the family drove to New York with Lily's trunk of clothes. Her dad brought the work truck, which held a rocker from Grandma, linens her mom had bought, books, and more clothes. Lily brought her box of precious old toe shoes. She hadn't saved all of them, just the ones that had done her proud during a performance. She had them tagged with the memorabilia.

There was a boarding house near the school that housed many of the students. Lily rented a room with another student named Julian, which was shortened to Jules by her friends. She was from Dallas, Texas, and had a strong Texas drawl. The girls met in Paris when Lily went there one summer to dance. They had kept in touch and were both excited to be going to Julliard. They decided to decorate their room with their ballet toe shoes. They hung pink ribbons in loops on the walls around the room and tied up their toe shoes on each side of the room.

School was harder than Lily had imagined. She had been an A student in high school and one of the top dancers in her class. But at Julliard, everyone was a great dancer and a good student too, especially Jules. Lily found she had to work harder and harder. But it made her stretch beyond her comfort zone, and she became humbled among all the talent. She didn't get the first parts for which she tried out—she was usually in the chorus. Again, she was humbled in her disappointment, but she watched and learned. Watching the lead dancers, she learned about grace, balance, confidence, and discipline. She realized, though it was a hard lesson, that she had been arrogant and sassy. She took extra dance classes. The classes were taped, so Lily and Jules checked out the tapes. They would watch them in their room, studying the other dancers to get ideas on how they could improve.

Lily's body got stronger and leaner. She was becoming a graceful woman, but as a dancer who did so much exercise, she was lean with very minimal curves. That was what a dancer needed. Jules had the perfect body, and she seemed to eat whatever she wanted. Lily thought Jules might have irritable bowel because she always had to use the bathroom after eating. One day Lily saw some vomit in the toilet after Jules had used the bathroom. Lily confronted her friend, but Jules just responded that she hadn't felt well and solemnly denied making herself vomit. She said she would never hurt herself that way. Lily was saddened when Jules started distancing herself from Lily and her other friends. Lily tried to ask her what was wrong, but Jules just said that she was busy and was trying to keep up with her studies. Lily noticed dark circles under her friend's eyes and heard her pacing late at night when she thought Lily was asleep.

One night Lily reached over to her bedside table and turned on the light. "Jules, I'm really worried about you. You're my closest friend. What's going on with you?"

"I'm fine. Just wound up because I'm so busy."

Lily got out of bed and approached her friend. "You aren't fine. I hear you pacing at night."

Jules paused. "I'm so afraid of failing!"

Putting her arms around her friend, Lily asked, "Failing your studies or dance?"

"Both," Jules sobbed.

Lily's thoughts whirled. Had she been so busy and self-absorbed that she hadn't noticed her friend falling behind in her studies? She didn't remember any problems with her dancing—she had only noticed that Jules looked and acted differently.

Still holding onto her friend, Lily said, "Jules, I love you. How can I help?"

Jules let Lily hold her as she cried. Then she sat up straighter, blew her nose on a tissue that Lily had given her, took a deep breath, and let it out slowly. "I've gotten myself into trouble."

Lily sat quietly and listened.

"I was putting on weight, even though I was dieting. I started taking diet pills, which helped a bit, mostly with water weight, and I got a buzz of energy. Then I found I could eat whatever I wanted and purge afterward. It was exhilarating. I had more energy, I was losing weight, and I felt I was finally in control. But now I can't sleep, my stomach and throat burn, everything I eat comes right back up, and I have started losing my hair." Jules started sobbing again. "I don't know what to do. I have wanted to be a ballerina my whole life. Both my parents were dancers. I can't let them down. I can't fail." Jules paused and grabbed her stomach. "Oh no!" she said as she ran to the bathroom and slammed the door.

Lily followed Jules and heard her vomiting through the closed bathroom door. Tapping on the door, she asked, "Jules, are you OK?"

Jules yelled, "No, there's blood!"

Lily took Jules to a nearby hospital. She was treated for erosion of her esophagus and stomach lining. Jules's vomiting had caused the acid in her stomach to burn the tube between her throat and stomach, and the excess acid had burned the lining of her stomach. The acid had also damaged the back of her teeth. Jules asked Lily to call her parents. Jules's parents came and took her home to Texas to be treated at an eating disorder clinic. Sadly, Jules had to withdraw from school. In mourning the loss of her friend, Lily became more determined to take care of herself as she worked her body to become a strong dancer.

The summer term had a workshop, and Lily was one of the lead dancers. Her mom, dad, grandma, and brother came to see her dance. Her mom was worried that she wasn't eating enough. Her nurse hat was on, and she asked if Lily was eating, making sure she wasn't anorexic or bulimic, like Jules and so many other dancers. Lily knew she had a fast metabolism and when stressed she needed more calories, because she dropped weight easily.

The night of the performance, Lily was so happy to feel her family's excited energy. They were dressed and in her dressing room, all talking at once. Lily had three beautiful costume changes. The costumes were beaded and sequined. She and the other dancers performed a piece that had been choreographed by one of the seniors. It was unique, with a combination of ballet, modern dance, and jazz. After the performance Lily's family stood and clapped. She saw tears in her mom's and dad's eyes, and their smiles were broad and proud. Her dad called out with his loud whistle, and Lily knew that she was following her heart's desire.

The next three years seemed to fly. All Lily did was study and dance. Her dancing and confidence improved, and she was getting lead roles in the performances. Top ballet companies often came to watch the dancers perform. Lily and her friends hoped for an invitation to join one of the companies.

Before graduating, Lily was invited to become a principal dancer in the New York City Ballet. She was so proud. After graduating, her life became dance and the company. She found a small apartment, not far from the company, so she could walk to work and stop by the market on the way home. Her friends were the dancers in the company. She couldn't imagine being anywhere else.

TRANSITIONING

Coming back to the present, Lily sighs as she lies in her hospital bed. *Those were the happiest times of my life.*

Lily hears her mom's Dansko shoes coming across the floor. "I'm going to pack your clothes. You've graduated from the hospital and are going to rehab today. The therapists will help you get strong and well, and they will help you work through your anxiety."

"What kind of a place is it?" Lily inquires, even though she knows she's being transferred to a psychiatric rehabilitation facility where she will be safe from Landers's torment.

Lily hears her mom take in a breath. "Honey, it's a psychiatric facility that has a great reputation for helping patients with PTSD. What I mean is that they will help you heal from your trauma." She pats Lily's hand and says a bit too quickly, "Your dad sends his love. You know he had to work today. It's going to be a busy summer. Your brother, John, is vaccinating the cattle and horses. His veterinary business is keeping him busy."

"Mom, what's PTSD?"

"It stands for posttraumatic stress disorder. It is something that happens to people who are traumatized during some event and experience nightmares, sounds, even smells that bring back the memory of the traumatic event, as if it were happening again. You had a terribly traumatic time with Landers, and you can get help to deal with the pain and anxiety of the trauma."

Lily sits up. "But he's still out there and can hurt me! The trauma isn't over!" Lily lies back, exhausted.

Lily's mom moves closer to her bed and takes her hand. "We will find a way to keep you safe. You'll get better, I know you will. Just be patient." She leans down and kisses Lily's cheek.

Lily feels the wet of her mom's tears. She tries to smile.

Lily's mom is quiet for a moment and then says, "Oh, I forgot to tell you, remember your friend Charles—I think we used to call him Chip, or was it Chipper?" She laughs. "Well, he's working with your brother. How about that? They're both vets."

Lily manages a weak smile. "Chipper. I haven't thought about him in years."

Chipper had been her best friend. He'd helped her dad around the ranch so he could save his money for college. Lily and Chipper went to school together and saw each other almost every day. She knew he had been sweet on her, but she hadn't had time to think about boys as boyfriends. Her focus was on her goal—to be a prima ballerina. She had known it would take sacrifice and dedication. She couldn't let boys get in the way. They were too much of a distraction. Lily had seen what happened to her girlfriends. They would go to mush over a boy, and nothing else mattered.

But Chipper hadn't given up. He was always hanging around. John had enjoyed the company of an older boy, even though he'd known Chipper was just trying to get close to his sister. Lily would tell him to stop following her around like a puppy. She remembered how he'd looked so wounded that she'd socked him in the arm and told him she was just kidding.

Her mom loved Chipper. She said he reminded her of her best friend, Jeremy. Jeremy and Chipper both had the same red, curly, out-of-control hair and freckles. Chipper and Lily shared the red, curly hair, but Lily didn't have the freckles—Lily had an ivory complexion. Her skin never colored much in the sun. Her mom would say it was ghostlike, which was funny to Lily since her mom was all about talking with ghosts. Her mom claimed that she still talked with her friend Jeremy, who had died in a motorcycle accident when she was a flight nurse. The story gave Lily the creeps. Her mom told her that Jeremy came to visit her on Halloween. At the time it had irritated Lily that her parents and brother had swirly spiritual stuff around them, but now she smiles at the memory. She wonders if Jeremy still visits her mom.

Lily wonders what Chipper is doing besides being a vet with her brother. She wonders if he finally found that special girl and was married with a family. It's nice that her mom told her that he is working with her brother. Lily likes thinking of Chipper working with animals.

She remembers that she shared her first kiss with Chipper. She smiles to herself at how awkward it had been, trying to figure out how to turn their heads with noses in the way. It had been sweet. They'd gotten better at it over that summer before going back to high school. They would sneak off together whenever they weren't working and Lily wasn't dancing. Lily would start off her mornings with a run, and Chipper would appear from nowhere and run along with her. As they circled back toward the ranch, Lily would climb on the fence railing that held in the horses and work on her balance, with her arms outstretched in an elegant position and her toes pointed. Chipper would watch and clap, and Lily would pretend not to notice. She would leap off the fence in grand jeté—one leg extended in front and one leg extended behind her. She would land without a sound at Chipper's feet.

"You're beautiful!" Chipper would exclaim.

"That's sweet, thank you. But I have so much to learn."

When school had started, Lily had had to get back to her studies and her dancing. She hadn't had time for a boyfriend. Chip's hurt had prevented him from hanging out with her. It had been too hard for him to be friends anymore. Lily had missed her friend, but had to let him go. She had no time to experience love. She had seen how her parents loved and respected each other. They were affectionate and gushy, really over the top. She had sworn she would never behave like them. Lily knew she loved Chip as a friend, but she didn't feel any romantic love for him. She couldn't allow herself to be in love at that time. She had believed that to be a successful ballerina, she could never be distracted by or dependent on someone. Her love was her craft, and she could not, would not, betray it.

HRC DAY SEVEN

A week after moving to Hope Rehabilitation Center, Lily has settled into the routine of her new life—therapy, therapy, and more therapy. It's time for her physical therapist to work her stiff, weak limbs. Lily's trauma had caused her to be stiff and weak. She finds it hard to believe that just two weeks ago she was dancing in her studio in Lakewood.

She hears a knock at her door—the staff is learning not to startle her. Lily takes a while to recover after being startled. She finds she is always waiting and expecting Landers to come find her. She knows intellectually that he can't get into this facility, but that doesn't keep her mind and her reactions from going right back to the fear and terror. The doctors tried medications while she was in the hospital, but the drugs just dulled her senses. Now she's doing only group and private therapy and practicing eye movement desensitization and reprocessing (what the doctors call EMDR) therapy and tapping therapy. These help, especially after a nightmare or a startle; the therapies calm her nerves, slow her heart rate, and even out her breathing.

Unfortunately, Lily is not yet feeling the benefit from her therapy sessions—she just feels vulnerable. The tearing away of the protective barrier she has spent years building is painful. She feels raw and exposed, like a turtle without its shell. Her room has become her haven. It is cool and dark, and no one enters without knocking and asking permission.

Even though she is always surprised by the knock and will jump, it's not threatening.

There's another knock at the door. "Lily, it's Marc."

"Come in."

Marc enters the room and says, "Isn't it just the most beautiful day to have a workout? Time to wake up your muscles. How are you doing today?" Marc looks at Lily and waits for a response, and he catches Lily's reaction. "Don't you roll those pretty eyes at me! Though I'm glad to see you getting a bit sassy—shows me you have spunk. Now let's put it to work. It's a beautiful day outside. Why don't we work out in the garden?"

Marc watches as Lily stands. She sighs and shrugs her shoulders in response. He walks beside her out into the garden. Lily feels the warm sun touch her face and smells the plants starting to come alive with new growth. She closes her eyes and takes in the sweet scents.

What a lovely, peaceful garden. My senses are alive.

Marc stops and indicates for her to sit on the bench under a big tree. "Now we are going to warm up your muscles and then get you up and walking in the sunlight."

Lily smiles. "As you wish."

Marc laughs. "That's the spirit."

Marc has Lily do some arm and leg stretches while seated on the bench. He then has her stand and walk. "You walked all around the garden. You're getting stronger. You'll be dancing in no time."

Not likely!

After returning to her room, Lily relaxes into the quiet safety the room provides. Her solitude gives her a lot of time to think, to remember, and to dream. She feels she is comfortable in this state because she has always been a loner, especially the last two years. As she relaxes, surrounded by her new protective four-walled world, her thoughts are her companions. She looks to the window near her bed that looks out onto the garden. She is on the third floor, so she can open her window and feel the breeze without worrying if someone can see her. Narrow bars line the outside of the window to prevent residents from exiting, but for Lily it's protection from intruders. The thought of him makes her breath catch and her heart rate increase, and goose bumps make her hair stand on end.

"Stop it!" Lily says out loud. "I'm safe here. He can't get to me."

Lily climbs into bed, snuggles into her fluffy pillows, and clutches her book. She has found she loves to read and will often read deep into the night. She doesn't seem to need much sleep, or so she tells herself. Her heart rate picks up speed. She takes slow, deep breaths to calm herself. It isn't sleep she fears, but the dreams it brings. Being locked away in this psychiatric facility gives her protection from him physically, but he finds her in her dreams. They usually start out as pleasant dreams, yet with an undercurrent of anxiety about what is to come. Lily will awake screaming. This is why she avoids her nightly rest until her body and mind betray her and she slips into sleep.

Tonight she is reading Tolstoy's *Anna Karenina* for the third time. When the book drops, Lily slips into sleep. She is dancing up on pointe in her dim studio, swaying to the music, when hidden hands grab her from behind, choking the breath from her. She tries to scream, but nothing comes out, until it does. Lily sits bolt upright in bed. A fine sheen of sweat covers her body. Her breathing is rapid, and her heart is racing when she hears a knock at the door. She is frozen in fear. Then she remembers where she is, safe in her room. The knock comes again.

Lily calls, "Come in."

The door opens slowly, and a blond young woman in a nightgown peeks in. "Are you all right? I heard a scream."

Lily pulls her covers to her chin. She feels a tingling sensation that dissipates within seconds. "Sorry, did I wake you? I must have been dreaming."

"Some dream! That was a horrible scream. Oh, and you didn't wake me. I was just out for a walk. Well, as long as you're OK, I'll let you get back to sleep."

"I won't be getting back to sleep for a while. My name is Lily, by the way."

The girl moves into the room. She is wearing a long blue nightgown with a high collar of white lace. The gown floats behind her as she moves.

"My name is Katherine Suffisant, Kit for short. I have trouble sleeping and nightmares too. Walking helps me. I love to walk and walk." She moves around the room, using her arms expressively and occasionally touching her stomach. She notices that Lily is watching her and takes her hand away from her stomach. Lily notices that there is a small dark spot at the waist of her gown.

Lily moves closer to the headboard of her bed.

Kit stops. "Oh, I get it. You wonder who this crazy girl is, talking and wandering around your room in the middle of the night. I'm sorry. I get carried away. Not many girls to talk to at night. Who would think that they might be sleeping?"

Lily cracks a small smile.

Kit moves toward the door. "Have sweeter dreams. I'll see you around." Kit closes the door and is gone as quietly as she arrived.

Lily takes a slow, deep breath in and lets it out. She opens her book and turns on her book light. After reading a few pages, she fades off into a dreamless sleep.

HRC DAY EIGHT

Lily wakes, stretches, opens her eyes, and then remembers the young woman in the blue nightgown. Had she been dreaming, or had it happened? Well, whichever it was, Lily feels different. She lies there in bed, thinking about what she is feeling. It is a shift—something is lighter, or maybe less lonely. She feels her face as tears leak from her eyes. She shakes her head and sits up in bed.

Lily thinks to herself. *I don't even know that strange woman. She comes into my room in the middle of the night. I don't even know why she is here."* Lily sits quietly for a while and then thinks to herself, *"I wasn't afraid of her. I'll look for her today.*

Lily climbs out of bed and sees the sun peeking through the blinds. When she opens the blinds, warmth floods her room. In her stocking feet, she pads over to the bathroom. She washes her face, brushes her teeth, and runs a wide-toothed comb through her red curls. After dressing, she heads to breakfast and her day of therapies.

Lily enters the dining room. She scans the room and finds she is disappointed not to see Kit. The breakfast buffet is set out in the corner of the room, and Lily goes over and gets in line. She still doesn't have much of an appetite, and nothing smells or looks good. She understands from her therapist that the pleasure of smelling and tasting will come back in time. Lily doesn't give this much credence, since she is still experiencing her trauma, at least in her dreams. But she knows she needs to provide nourishment to her body. She loads her plate with some overdone eggs, tomatoes, sliced cheese, strawberries, and blueberries. Now, hot coffee with a touch of cream—this she can smell as she did the plants starting to peek out in the garden. The coffee warms her and gives her a feeling of calm.

At the end of a full day of working her muscles and her mind and doing some art therapy, the sun is disappearing behind the mountains, and darkness is allowing a few stars to shine brightly. Lily remembers her grandmother teaching her that the first stars are probably other planets, such as Venus. She smiles at the memory of her grandmother, who lives with her family on the ranch. She remembers that her grandmother had been with her mom, Lilith, who was the nurse caring for her birth mom, at the hospital. Her birth-mom had been unconscious from a brain bleed and died after giving birth to her. Her grandma had asked Lilith to adopt Lily after Lily's birth mom died. After Lilith adopted Lily and married Roy, they all lived on the ranch. Everyone still lives there, except Lily.

"I haven't been back to the ranch in years. I bet it still looks the same. Mom said Grandma will visit when I'm feeling better," Lily says out loud to herself as she walks to her room.

Lily can feel her sensitivity to sound, the pounding of her heart, and the tightness in her chest. It makes it hard to take in a deep breath as anxiety sweeps over her. She finds she is rushing toward the safety of her room's four walls. She enters her room, closes the door, and lowers the blind on the large window. She leans against the wall in the dark and works on slowing her breathing and heart rate. Her shoulders relax, and she breathes in and out slowly. She no longer feels the rapid pounding of her heart in her chest. Lily peers between the blind's slats to the outside. From the third floor she has a large view of the gardens below and the eight-foot wooden fence that surrounds the property. There are solar lights along the paths that wind through the garden. She doesn't see anyone outside. Then she sees a spark—no, a match that has lit a cigarette. Lily's breath catches, and a memory fills her thoughts as terror shoots through her body. She is frozen, staring, when she sees the light shine off his face. It isn't him. It's Ruehl, the nice young man who leads the evening therapy sessions. He's taking a smoking break.

Lily lets out the breath she didn't know she was holding. Stepping away from the window, she knows she needs to do something to help herself relax or she will never be able to get to sleep. She smiles as she remembers the lavender bath beads her mom gave her. Lily draws a bath and sprinkles in the purple beads. Small bubbles appear as the water pours into the tub. A light lavender fragrance wafts through the air. Lily dims the lights and puts on "Canon in D" by Pachelbel. Once the bath is full, she undresses and slips into the warm water as the bubbles envelop her. Her senses float her off into a field of lavender flowers blowing in the wind.

Lily stays in the tub until she feels her digits wrinkle. Pulling the drain plug out, she steps out of the tub, towel dries, slips into her pajamas, and turns off the music. After turning out the light, she lets her eyes adjust to the darkness of her room, which is only lit by the light from outside the window. The barred window casts a shadow of her protection on the wall. Up on her tiptoes, she dances across the room and jumps into bed. In her room she feels safe, but she wishes she could stop the nightmares. She turns on her book light and reads until she begins nodding off. Lily slips into sleep.

Then Lily hears his deep voice: "Lily, you can run, but you can't hide!" He's in her room. She runs to the door, but it is locked. She is trapped. As he approaches, she screams—a scream that no one hears.

Then there is knocking at the door. The knocking gets louder, and the door opens as Lily wakes up.

"Lily, it's Kit. Are you OK? I heard you scream."

Lily opens her eyes to see Kit standing in the doorway, and she realizes she's in bed. She releases her bed sheet, which she is clutching. Her pajamas stick to her damp skin. She moves some wet red curls out of her face as she sits up in bed. "Nightmare again. Do you want to come in?"

"I had my nightmare tonight too, so I walk." Kit floats into the room, pulls the chair out from the small desk, and sits down.

"I tried to find you today, but I didn't see you anywhere."

"Oh, I'm in a different ward." Kit touches her belly as she speaks. "I'm on the fourth floor." She puts her hand inside a hidden pocket in her gown and pulls out a key. The window light reflects off the key and makes it sparkle as Kit holds it up. She puts her finger to her lips and says, "Shush."

Lily's eyes widen. "Where did you get that?"

Kit replaces the key and smiles. "I found it on a nurse's desk when she stepped away on a break. I hid it for a year so they would forget about it."

Lily leans forward, intrigued. "Didn't they look for it? Where did you keep it for a year?"

"I removed a tile from the bathroom wall and hid it inside. I wasn't sure if they'd changed the locks. But to my surprise, they hadn't. I don't have any interest in leaving, but I like to roam and explore."

"How do you keep from getting caught?"

"I move around at night between the hours that the staff do room checks. It's so freeing, yet lonely, until I met you." Kit shrugs and swings her feet back and forth as she sits in the chair and then looks up. "You won't tell, will you?"

"Of course not. We're here to get well, not rat on each other."

Kit smiles and then her expression changes and is softer. "Why are you here?"

Lily's breath catches. "Not yet. I don't want to talk about it. Maybe another time."

Kit nods and touches her belly, rubbing it slowly. She stops when she sees Lily watching her. Clearing her throat, she says, "Well, have you ever been in love?"

Lily lets her breath out in a laugh. "Good change of topic. What about you?"

Kit dips her head and sighs loudly. "I couldn't even try. My father forbade it. Said it was a sin—funny, coming from him. I couldn't date or go to parties. My father monitored my every move. I was sent to an all-girls school during the day." Kit takes a deep breath and lets it out in a huff. "That will change when I become eighteen and get out of here. I'll be in control of my life and maybe fall in love." Kit sits back and smiles. Then she leans forward and says, "So tell me—what's it like to be in love?"

"Really? You want to know how it felt for me?"

"Well, yeah!"

Lily pulls her legs up to her chest and hugs them, placing her chin on top of her knees. "I've only been in love once. I had a guy friend when I was young who was interested in me, but I was too driven with my career aspirations."

"What was the career that you wanted?"

Lily closes her eyes. "For as long as I can remember, I wanted to become a prima ballerina. All I did was study dance and practice."

"Did you become a prima ballerina?"

"Yes, I did." Lily smiles.

"Wow, that must have been groovy!"

Lily smiles again at Kit's response. "Yes, I guess it was groovy."

"So when did you fall in love?"

"It was when I was a prima ballerina." Lily pauses and then begins again.

"After a year and a half of dancing my heart out with the New York City Ballet, I became the prima ballerina. As a dancer, I became accustomed to the ballet aficionados. The crowds came in and out, and I started to recognize some of the regulars. Regulars got group or season tickets. They appreciated the ballet and the music and watched the dancers attentively. As a prima ballerina, I got used to stares from men and women. I knew that I was perfecting my craft and they were appreciating it. It meant the world to me and the other dancers to be appreciated for all our hard work. We loved the lights, the crowd, and the applause. I received flowers from admirers. But it was the lilies with the card that read 'from your number-one fan' that intrigued me. I received a dozen lilies the first time, and then each consecutive time they multiplied by a dozen. I asked Mac, who worked at the theater and would bring the flowers in for the dancers, and he said that they were hand delivered by a stout man dressed in formal attire and a top hat. The next performance, I peeked around the curtain as the patrons entered the theater to try and get a glimpse of this man. There he was, top hat and all, sitting in the second row. He was old enough to be my father—well, maybe not quite, but he was still considerably older than me."

Kit scrunches her nose. "Is he the one you fell in love with?"

Lily laughs and shakes her head. "I went back to my dressing room and found five dozen lilies. The note this time was bigger and inscribed with gold writing. It read, 'Ms. Lily Johnson, I request the pleasure of your company for dinner tonight after the show. I will have a car waiting outside at 10:30 p.m.' And the card was signed 'Arthur Williamson III.'"

"Wow, I wouldn't know what to do about that. Did you go?" Kit is sitting on the edge of her seat.

"No, I didn't. I thought it very presumptuous of him. It made the hair rise on the back of my neck." With a shiver, Lily remembers how it made her feel. She takes some deep breaths and lets them out slowly. "I had to prepare for the performance, so I grabbed the bar as I faced the mirror in my dressing room and started leg stretches. I knew I needed to calm down and clear my head so I could concentrate. I felt my muscles relax as they warmed. Focusing on my art always made me feel better.

"Before I went out on stage, I asked Mac to deliver my reply to the waiting sedan. It read, 'Thank you, Mr. Williamson, for your kind invitation, but I cannot join you. Respectfully, Ms. Johnson.'

"The next performance, I found twice as many lilies in my dressing room. A note read, 'Ms. Johnson, I must insist. You will want to get to know me. Please give me a chance. My sedan will be waiting outside. Looking forward to our meeting. Arthur Williamson III.'

"I was unsettled by this man's insistence. But I knew I had to relax and prepare for the performance. I would deal with the situation later. But during one of my scenes, I caught sight of the man holding lilies in the second row and almost lost my balance. Embarrassed, I became even more determined to push any other thoughts from my head and remain engrossed in my character while I danced."

"How creepy!" Kit says.

"After the performance, the dancers were taking their bows, and then I joined them with my dance partner. I saw Mr. Williamson stand and heard him yell clearly over the clapping, 'Bravo, that's my Lily!'"

Lily takes in a quick breath. "And that was when I noticed a man next to Mr. Williamson. He had a dark complexion, was dressed in black, had black hair, and stood broad and tall. He was a visual contrast, standing next to Williamson. His coal-black eyes met mine, and I was startled when he nodded at me. The dark stranger leaned over and appeared to say something to Williamson. Williamson pulled himself up to try to meet the stranger's height and yelled, 'Mind your own business, asshole!'"

Kit wiggles in her chair. "Is the dark stranger the love?"

Lily smiles, nods, and then continues. "So the stranger smiled and leaned down again and appeared to say something to Williamson. Just as the curtain came down, I saw Williamson slam the lilies on the floor and stomp on them. He then straightened his hat and moved out of the row and up the aisle. The dark stranger nodded at me and smiled without showing his teeth. I felt my jaw drop as our eyes met. I nodded a thank-you and exited the stage." Lily pauses.

"So what happened?"

"Well, I didn't see or hear from Mr. Williamson again. And the lilies stopped coming to my room before performances. I was relieved and grateful but wondered what the stranger had said to him to make him yell like he did. I thought that maybe I might get to ask him someday, since he seemed to come to all the performances. He was there each night in the second row, dressed in black. He would enter the theater wearing a black cowboy hat, which covered his black hair and shielded his black eyes. He removed his hat when he sat down. His skin was dark brown, as if the sun had sought him out. The other cast members noticed him too. He started smiling at the end of the performance. His white teeth warmed his smile and contrasted with his dark complexion."

"Wow, he sounds dreamy."

"The dance troupe went to a cast party after the performance, and I saw him from across the room. He smiled when our eyes met, and then his attention was drawn back to a pretty lady wearing a red low-backed dress. She was touching him as her hand gestured in conversation. I was embarrassed that I was watching them, especially when he looked over and smiled as he saw me. I turned away and could feel the heat rising in my face. I took a glass of champagne from a waiter's tray and wandered toward the buffet table. I hoped that my friends couldn't see the embarrassment on my face. As I reached for a small plate, I saw him approaching. My heart fluttered, and my hands became damp. I thought to myself, *This is ridiculous.* I looked down, and he spoke.

"He said, 'Hello. You were wonderful tonight.' I thanked him without looking up. Then our eyes met. I asked if he was involved with the ballet, and he told me that he was a fan with season tickets. The young woman in red appeared next to him and said, 'There you are. I was thinking you ditched me.' Her red-painted lips smiled at him. Dark eyes turned to me, and he said, 'I'm Adam. It was nice talking with you. Congratulations on your performance.' He grasped my hand in both of his with a warmth and softness that sent goose bumps up my arms. The red-dress lady seemed surprised as she looked at me and said, 'Oh, yeah, congratulations.' The two of them became lost in conversation as I walked away, still feeling his warmth."

"Did you want to scratch her eyes out?" Kit laughs.

Lily smiles. "No, I didn't know anything about Adam."

"But you wanted to know more about him. Didn't you?"

Lily grins at Kit and continues. "I left the party, and as I stepped outside, I saw Adam having a cigarette by the lamppost. He quickly put it out when he saw me and apologized for affecting the air with his nasty habit. He explained that he didn't smoke often, only when nervous. I said that I had a hard time imaging him as nervous. He looked deep into my eyes and said, 'I was afraid I wouldn't get a chance to get to know you.' I smiled, both embarrassed and pleased. Then some of my friends came out and called to me to head home. Adam tipped his hat as he smiled, turned, and walked away."

"OK, next." Kit giggles.

"Oh, and he had a motorcycle, a sleek black Honda. It was fully equipped with a comfortable backseat, leg rests, luggage cases, and radio headgear."

"I always wanted to ride on a motorcycle! Did you ride it with him?"

Lily realizes she is having fun. "Yes. On our first date, he picked me up and handed me a helmet. He took off his cowboy hat and placed it in one of the side luggage cases. He put his helmet on, helped me onto the bike, and made sure our headgear worked so we could hear each other talk. Then we were off. It was exhilarating." Lily raises her shoulders as she giggles behind her hand. "It was also very sexy—the power between my legs and leaning into him with my arms around his waist."

"It sounds so cool."

"He stopped the bike on the top of a ridge. We sat and watched the twinkling lights of the city below us. I was still holding him and resting my head on his back."

"Did he kiss you?"

"No. We saw each other about a week before he leaned toward me for a kiss. Yet he stopped and asked, 'May I?' Melting, I nodded." Lily's hands touch her lips, and she closes her eyes.

"And then what happened?"

Lily is shaken from her trance. "He kissed me. His lips were so soft, and his hand gently touched my face. I became so dizzy I swayed, and he caught me by the waist. I was embarrassed, but I leaned into him. It was a few weeks before we slept together. I was in love."

"Were you a virgin?"

Lily's face reddens. "No, I had slept with one of the dancers, but we didn't really date. Adam was my first real relationship and by far the best kisser."

"I'm not a virgin either. But that's a story for another time." Kit blows out her breath and looks down as she touches her belly. She pauses for a few seconds, shakes her head back and forth, and then looks up at Lily. "Tell me more."

"Well, I don't know how to describe it. It was almost like a silly romance novel, but it was happening to me. It was as if he had read books on how to please his lover."

Kit tips her head to the side. "What do you mean?"

"Well, he knew just the right things to say to me to make me feel special and loved. He was so gentle, and his touch was so soft during our love making, and he always asked what pleased me. After we made love, I would fall asleep in his arms. I'm sure his arm, which was under me, fell asleep, but he never complained." Lily touches her lips again. "Oh, and did I mention that he was the best kisser."

"Yes, you mentioned that. Just rub it in!" Kit laughs.

"Well, his lips were so soft." Lily looks at Kit. "Not that I had lots of kissing to compare with, but it was his kiss that I remember."

"Did you ask him what he said to Mr. Williamson?"

"I did. He didn't really give me an answer. He said that the gist of what he said was that Mr. Williamson's behavior was not fitting for a lady such as me. He said it made Mr. Williamson mad, and he stormed off. I was just so grateful that I thanked him and let the matter drop. It wasn't until years later that I wondered what he had really said."

"So what happened to you two?"

A darkness falls across Lily's face. She pauses and then yawns. "I'm getting sleepy. Maybe continue the story another night?" She slips down under her covers.

Kit jumps off the chair. "Oh, right. I need to get back to my room before the room check. Sweeter dreams." Kit approaches Lily's bed and holds out her arms, palms up. "I'm not a hugger, but I want you to know I appreciate that you feel comfortable sharing with me. The Roman method of greeting was holding out your palms to show you didn't have a weapon. Throughout history, the open palm has been associated with trust, honesty, allegiance, and submission." Kit takes in a ragged breath and lets it out. "I would leave the submission explanation out, because *no one* should be submissive. Oh, sorry, I didn't mean to raise my voice. Just a hate button for me."

Lily looks down at Kit's outstretched arms and open palms and notices the scars on the inside of Kit's wrists.

Kit sees that Lily is looking at her arms. "Yeah, well, that's a story for another night too."

Lily reaches out, shows Kit her open palms, and then places her lower arms on top of Kit's outstretched lower arms. They circle their hands around each other's arms. "I appreciate you too, Kit." And she smiles as they squeeze the other's arms and then release.

Kit leaves the room and quietly closes Lily's door behind her.

Lily sighs and smiles as she thinks of her new friend. It feels good. It's been a long time since she has had a friend in whom she can confide, laugh, and just talk. She closes her eyes and falls asleep.

HRC DAY NINE

Lily wakes to a banging noise. She thinks it's someone knocking, but it's coming from her window. She stretches and climbs out of bed. She peeks through the slats in her blind and sees that the wind is banging the screen against the window. She opens the blind and sees grayish-purple clouds hanging low in the sky. It surprises her that the darkness doesn't scare her—she feels she is experiencing some kind of shift. She sees the trees leaning with the wind as if they are dancing, and she smiles to herself. She thinks back to her conversation with Kit—it feels good to remember falling in love. She wants to hold on to those feelings for a while.

Lily stretches her arms and legs and then heads to the bathroom to wash her face and brush her teeth. She applies a bit of mascara and lip gloss and pulls her red curls back into a bun. She reaches for her navy yoga capris and a navy T-shirt and puts them on and then steps into her tennis shoes. Lily is thankful that Sasha brought her a suitcase of clothes and toiletries from her apartment. A look at her reflection in the mirror satisfies her, and she heads to the cafeteria for breakfast.

Lily has a session with her physical therapist, takes a yoga class, and begins a painting of a mountain scene with clouds of gray and purple, just like she saw outside her window during the morning. She laughs at her lack of artistic talent, and then she realizes how good it feels to laugh.

At her afternoon therapy session, she talks with Soma, her therapist, about her feeling of a shift. Soma has black hair with streaks of gray, which she wears back, and wears long dangling earrings with rainbows, angels, and crosses. Her reading glasses hang from her neck by a string of colored beads. When Lily looks around Soma's office, she sees pictures of mountains, lakes, and waterfalls. The pictures help her feel peaceful. "Did you take these photos?" Lily asks.

"Some of them. The others I bought. I just like looking at them and hope to travel there someday." She smiles. "Now, see if you can describe this shift you feel."

Lily looks out at nothing and stretches her arms above her head. "I don't know. I still have the nightmares and I'm jumpy, but I'm feeling a bit more comfortable, maybe with myself or with this place. I'm starting to get my sense of smell back, with my morning coffee and the new plants peeking out in the garden."

Soma smiles. "That's progress."

The two of them talk about Lily's different therapies and her feelings, fears, and goals, but Lily chooses to keep quiet about her friendship with Kit. She doesn't want Kit to get into trouble for leaving her ward and coming into Lily's room at night.

After dinner, Lily returns to her room. She puts on a pair of pink ballet shoes and turns on Tchaikovsky's "Danse Chinoise." She stretches by going through her ballet position warm-up. She freely lets the music sweep her away in dance. As the daylight gives way to the darkness of night, Lily sees her shadow reflected on the wall from the light that comes on outside her window. Her shadow looks free and happy. *That's how I want to feel.*

Lily showers, towels dry, and puts on her nightgown. She climbs into bed, and as she lies back on her pillows, she realizes how heavy and tired her body feels. The exercise felt good, and she experiences the soreness in her muscles with satisfaction. Her hand feels the pillow next to her, and she takes slow breaths in and out as she remembers her furry companion.

Lily had adopted a white long-haired kitten and named her China. China had had the sweetest meow, which welcomed Lily home after work. Lily had taken up biking on her days off, and China would ride in a covered basket on the front of the bike. She had been a great friend. China had been content to wait for Lily while she worked her long hours and would curl up in Lily's lap when she got home. Tears fill Lily's eyes and her heart aches painfully as she remembers that China died too soon.

"I loved you so much, China," Lily whispers. She wipes her eyes, sighs, and closes them as she remembers the soft white fur. She falls asleep and dreams of China. There are angry words and doors opening and slamming shut loudly. There is the sound of screeching tires and Lily screaming as she sees China's lifeless body in the street. She sees "his smile." She sits bolt upright in bed and opens her eyes, realizing she's dreaming. Then she hears a knock at the door.

The door slowly opens. "Lily, it's me, Kit."

"Come in, Kit."

Kit comes toward Lily's bed and sits down on the end. "I thought you would have sweeter dreams after talking about your love. Did it end badly?" Kit seems to notice as the darkness falls over Lily's face. "Do you want to talk about it?"

Lily sighs. "I was dreaming of my cat, China. She was a long-haired white cat that meant a lot to me." Lily touches her face and then says, "Let me back up to Adam." She sighs again and continues.

"As we were getting to know each other, we talked a lot on the phone, and we met for dinner after my dancing. We never seemed to run out of things to talk about. He seemed to know a little bit about everything. He was bright and well read. We could talk for hours. Adam had his own business—he was a marketing consultant.

"Adam met China, my cat, and seemed to love her. But she was not quite sure about him. He brought her toys and treats, trying to win her over. And it worked. He didn't mind that she slept in bed with us."

Lily pauses and looks into Kit's eyes. "I had never had a best friend outside the ballet, except for one when I was a kid. I had never had someone care about me, listen to me, and want to be with me all the time. I didn't know where he got the time. He worked, but he was always available to watch me practice or perform. And he wanted to have meals with me and cook for me when I was tired from practice. I had never met anyone like him. And he gave wonderful massages to my tired, sore muscles."

Kit wiggles as she sits on the end of the bed. "It sounds wonderful."

Lily smiles. "It was. We dated for over a year and started talking about spending our lives together. At twenty-seven years old, I was considering opening my own studio and retiring from performing. Dancers have a shelf life. With the thought of marrying Adam and having children someday, I didn't want to be consumed with the ballet and risk a failing marriage.

"There was a bakery below my apartment, and I remember waking up to the smell of chocolate croissants. Do you like them?"

Kit nods.

"The bakery closed, and it was an empty space. I decided to buy it and create a studio to teach ballet. The studio had front windows facing the street, and I put in raised wooden floor, bars, mirrors, dressing rooms, a bathroom, and an office. Soon it was complete, and I started classes.

"Life felt good. I had my own studio with fun, eager students and a wonderful man in my life. Adam had a cabin on Lake Chance, an hour outside of town. It was an interesting cabin—very rustic on the outside yet filled with expensive antiques and beautiful paintings. He told me he had been collecting for a long time. We would sometimes spend weekends there in the summer, just hiking, fishing, or water-skiing.

"As I said, Adam was unlike anyone I had known. He was gentle and intuitive. If I was home and thinking of him, he would call. If I had a bad day, somehow he knew and would call to cheer me up. He was always hearing songs on the radio he said reminded him of us. He would send me cards. And did I tell you his kisses were so tender?" Lily giggles.

Kit rolls her eyes. "Yes, you've told me about a million times." She giggles right along with Lily.

"Adam and I planned a trip to Colorado for him to meet my parents. Now, I have unusual parents," Lily says.

"Me too." Kit shivers.

Lily notices a change in Kit's expression. "Are you OK?"

"Yeah. I'll tell you that story later." Kit lets out a loud breath of air.

Lily waits, and Kit nods for her to continue. "My parents live on a working cattle ranch. Folks come to vacation with their families during the summer, and then there are groups that come during hunting season. But the most unusual thing about them is that my mom has a gift that allows her to talk with ghosts, and my father is telepathic."

Kit nearly falls off the bed when she lunges forward and says, "What did you say?"

Lily laughs. "I know. My mom is a nurse, and she can hear and talk with her patients that have died and help them understand what has happened. She also has conversations with her spirit guides. My dad can hear thoughts that you put out to him. Not all your thoughts, but the ones you are thinking about him."

Kit sits back. "Wow, people can really do that?"

"Yes, it's a paranormal gift. I would have trouble believing it if I hadn't seen both my mom and dad do and say things that they just couldn't if they didn't have a gift. And to top it off, my little brother can talk to animals."

Kit rubs her chin. "Do you have any gifts like that?"

Lily laughs. "No, nothing."

"That must have been cool, and also kind of annoying."

"Yes, it was. I had to be careful what I was thinking around my dad. Or I would bug him and make up a thought just to get him."

Kit's mouth opens, and she pales. "Did you get in trouble?"

"No, my dad's cool." Lily smiles. "Well, I warned Adam about them. It was strange. Mom and Dad were both quiet and reserved around him. I got the impression that they didn't like him. Adam was trying hard to engage them in conversation—compliment the ranch, tell them how much he loved me and wanted their blessing. He told them he wanted to marry me. I was so touched by his efforts.

"After a hike and dinner, I was helping Mom with the dishes. She asked if I really knew him. I became defensive. I told her I loved him. We had been dating for a year. I told her I knew everything I needed to know about him. Mom said that she didn't get a good feeling about him. I got angry and asked if this was some of her ghost stuff, and maybe she was wrong. I stormed out of the room. I went to talk with dad and didn't get much encouragement from him. He said Adam was a blank slate. I was so disappointed. I knew they were wrong, even if I didn't have any spiritual gifts. I loved Adam. I loved my parents, but I was going to have to choose. I chose Adam. And I became estranged from my parents."

Lily sighs and then continues.

"We were married the next spring with just a couple of friends in attendance. Adam was estranged from his family as well. After we came back from a week of sailing, we went to pick China up at the vet. While she was there, I had her spayed. Surgery was the day before we were to pick her up. I arrived at the vet, eager to hug my little darling. The girl at the desk looked at me sadly and excused herself to get the vet. Dr. Bare, a young, short, handsome man with dark hair and a mustache, explained China had had a stroke during surgery. China was confused and skittish with no movement on her left side. In horror, I listened. He said that it was an extremely rare occurrence and that he had never had it happen to any of his patients. He said it was up to China now. Dr. Bare had given her steroids and diuretics. The next few days would tell—she would get better and fully recover, or not."

Kit gasps. "How awful!"

"I gathered China up in a blanket and placed her in the cat carrier. Tears of fear rolled down my cheeks as I drove her home. Adam was putting supplies away and looked up when we entered. He rushed over to see why I was so upset. After I told him about China, we gently removed her from the carrier. I sat in the family room chair with China in my lap. She recognized me, but when she lifted her head, it was at an angle. Adam prepared a bed in the bathroom with her litter box, food, and water. We didn't want her traveling very far or trying to jump on things. She had to be lifted into her cat box and lifted to her water and food. That night when we closed her up in the bathroom, I couldn't hold back the tears. Adam held me tightly and told me he knew she would be all right. His tender encouragement, though appreciated, did not extinguish my fear.

"Miraculously, day after day she got a little stronger. Adam and I took turns staying home with her. Soon she could take short walks out of the bathroom. In two weeks she could jump on chairs and beds without falling. And by the third week it was hard to tell she had ever been sick. How blessed we felt.

"Adam seemed to love spending all our spare time together, but he seemed less interested in getting together with my friends from the ballet. He told me I had outgrown them and needed to move on. He had a few friends that he had known his whole adult life that we saw maybe once a year. And though he spoke as if they were so close, he criticized them. Occasionally, we would meet someone and get together, but he would find something wrong with them. He never wanted to socialize with people he worked with, never wanted them to know him outside the office. He seemed to be most comfortable just being with me. He said I was his life and all he needed. And he wanted nothing more than me. After long days teaching my students, I was happy to be alone and just snuggle with him."

Kit sits quietly and then says, "I understand that isolation. You don't realize it when it happens, because that's all you know." Kit looks away as if deep in thought and rubs her belly. Then she notices Lily looking at her. Kit shakes her head and says, "So what happened?"

"Are you sure you want to hear more about me? I think it's your turn."

Kit shakes her head hard as she continues to rub her belly. "No, don't worry, I'll tell you about me later."

"Well, I got pregnant, which was a surprise. But teaching my young ballerinas had made me realize I wanted a little ballerina or ballet dancer of my own. We had been together for two years, so the timing seemed perfect.

"I made a special dinner and lit candles all over the apartment. Adam was so pleased at the dinner surprise and how nice everything looked. His eyes shone as he looked at me. I was beaming with happiness. After we made love and he was holding me, I told him our wonderful news—a spring baby.

"There was silence. I wondered if he had heard me. Then I realized his body was tense. The look on his face...I will never forget. He was so angry. I went to the bathroom and cried and cried. When I came out, he was gone. China and I sat in the dark. I couldn't believe what had happened."

Kit touches Lily's hand. "How awful! Where did he go?"

"I didn't know. He came back the next morning. I had been up all night, and he had been drinking. With dried tears visible on my face, I looked up at him. I asked him what was going on. He said he was very disappointed in me. He didn't want a baby. And he said that if I insisted on keeping it, it would be my baby and my responsibility. I couldn't believe what I was hearing. My world was falling apart.

"He had told me he wanted a family. I'd thought he would be so happy. But he wanted things to stay the same. I wondered, who was this man I had been living with all this time? I couldn't believe the change. Had there been signs? Had I been so blind? Had my parents been right to be concerned?"

Kit squeezes Lily's hand, and Lily looks up at her friend and tries to smile.

After a big sigh, Lily continues. "After that we became more and more distant. He would spend long weekends at the cabin and leave me in town. We had nothing to say to each other. My body started changing, and I couldn't tell if he was repulsed or just purposely avoiding me to punish me.

"I read every book about pregnancy, birthing, and babies that I could get my hands on. I knew my health and well-being was especially vital for the health and well-being of my baby. I continued working with as positive an attitude as I could put forth. I was taking care of myself and silently praying and hoping Adam would come around and love our baby as much as I did.

"I read that pregnancy is not only a big change for the woman, but also for the man, so I hoped the nine months would give him time to adjust. I left my books around, hoping he might pick one up, but he showed no interest.

"My young students were very excited and amazed at my growing belly. Luckily, leotards stretch. I felt so happy and healthy. I was sure Adam would soon realize what a blessing our baby would be for us."

"Did he change his mind?"

"No. At about six and a half months, I started preparing the nursery with a fresh coat of yellow paint and animal wallpaper borders. I bought darling baby clothes and supplies. I found an antique crib and chest of drawers in a cute country store. The shopkeeper loaded them in my car, and I happily drove home. I thought preparing the nursery would get to Adam. He hadn't come to any of the doctor's appointments, hadn't heard the heartbeat, felt the baby kick, or seen the ultrasound. He was missing so much. Perhaps the nursery would do the trick.

"Once home, I found Adam in the study upstairs, down the hall from the nursery. I asked and then begged him to help me bring in the furniture. He refused by turning away and saying that it was my thing, not his. He didn't want any part of it.

"I just kept thinking positive thoughts for the baby. Holding onto all the positive energy I could muster, I pushed the hurt and anger aside. I brought in the crib in pieces and each drawer of the dresser. I lugged them up the twelve stairs, while Adam just sat in the study, listening to music and looking busy. The dresser was not very heavy, but it was tall and awkward. Without the drawers, I was able to grip it fairly securely. I knew I should not be doing it alone, but I had no one I could think of to help me.

"Carefully dragging the dresser stair by stair, I started feeling the strain. I yelled and pleaded for Adam to help me. He turned the music up louder and continued with his back to the door. I had half the stairs yet to do and started again when I felt a pain in my side. Again I yelled to Adam, but he either could not or did not want to hear me. I could not move. I tried to balance the dresser against the wall, but it would not stay. I had to let it go, and watched as it went crashing down the stairs and broke into many pieces.

"As I slowly climbed the stairs, I looked sadly into the study. Adam was oblivious to me, so I went to bed. I awoke with painful cramping and was horrified to find the bed soaked in blood. I went into the study and found Adam dozing in the chair. He awoke in surprise and saw my bloody clothes.

"Adam helped me down the stairs, never looking at the broken dresser, and drove me to the hospital. I spent two days in a hospital bed while doctors and nurses tried to save my baby and keep it from being born too early. I continued to bleed, and at the end of the second day, we lost my baby's heartbeat. An ultrasound confirmed my worst fears, and I was told that my baby girl was dead." Lily pauses as tears stream down her face.

Kit moves closer. "I'm so sorry, Lily."

Lily wipes the tears away with her sheet. "Thanks. It was a couple years ago, but it still feels so raw."

"What happened with Adam?"

"Adam brought me home from the hospital. Surprisingly, he seemed to be grieving as well. He was tender and supportive. I was so torn up inside, I didn't have the energy to analyze or question his feelings or reactions. I didn't even have the energy to blame him. I think I blamed myself for being so stupid and trying to lift heavy furniture when I truly knew better.

"I felt lifeless and dead inside. I could hardly gather enough energy to pull myself out of bed to go to the bathroom or get a drink of water. Adam would try to cheer me up, bring me my favorite foods or drinks, but I wasn't interested.

"One sleepless night, I wandered into the nursery. I was shocked to find it empty: no furniture, no clothes, and no pretty wallpaper border. Nothing of my baby remained. And I hadn't even gotten to hold her. Adam had insisted that I shouldn't see her.

"After three weeks, I went for a walk. February was still cold, and there was fresh snow on the ground. It crunched under my feet, but I didn't give it much notice. My senses were numb. I could not smell, feel, or care. I just didn't want to be. Knowing I probably needed to talk with someone yet not caring, it took me another month before I called and got an appointment to see a therapist.

"I had never been to a therapist of any sort, so I was very nervous. Jeanes had been recommended to me by my obstetrician. I sat in her waiting room after filling out paperwork. Soft music played as I waited anxiously, and she finally came to get me. She was tall with a bronze complexion and long dark hair well past the middle of her back. She wore her hair in a long braid. She was quiet and reassuring. I sat on a couch across from her, my arms folded across my chest for protection. There were tissues on the table next to me. Quiet surrounded us for a few moments before she directed me with a few questions.

"Jeanes's specialty was grief therapy. She helped me understand the stages of grief: shock, denial, anxiety/anger, guilt, depression, testing, and acceptance. She helped me understand the trauma of losing a child, and we worked on helping me learn to forgive myself. She asked about my husband, his role and support. I shared with her how supportive Adam had been. I never mentioned what had happened before I lost my baby. It never came into my mind when I was talking to her. Somehow, I wanted to believe it had not happened, that it was just a bad dream, too horrible to recall. I felt close to Adam, and I needed that closeness.

"I left our session exhausted. I was not really feeling better—almost feeling worse—but then I realized I was *feeling*. This was a relief. I thought I would go to see Jeanes every week or so. I needed to get on track so I could return to work. I was physically capable but mentally numb and drained."

"Didn't Adam want to go with you to therapy?"

"Adam never asked about my sessions with Jeanes, and he never mentioned our baby. He was attentive and loving. It was odd. I could not quite understand him. He was now the man I remembered marrying. But who was that man I'd lived with when I was carrying our baby? I could not trust him, though I would succumb to his charm. I wanted and hungered for the closeness we had shared—the closeness that had been absent for the past six and a half months.

"I stopped going to see Jeanes. I felt better about myself and my life and wanted to believe my life was as it should be and that everything would work out. I could not face any other alternative.

"Time does seem to heal pain, and the world keeps turning, never stopping, so you have to just jump back on. I got busy teaching again in the summer and then had a very full fall schedule. And my ballet dancers and ballerinas wanted to do *The Nutcracker*, so this made the holidays busy. They all worked very hard, even their parents, and it was a success.

"Adam and I had a quiet Christmas with China at the lake. The lake was frozen, and we could skate around the edges. We exchanged nice gifts and talked about plans for the New Year. Neither of us mentioned our baby. I decided it was best to leave that conversation for another time.

"I felt I was turning a page in my life—never wanting to forget, yet desperately wanting to move forward. I knew I wanted another child but didn't know if it was possible. I had a checkup with my obstetrician, and he said there was no reason I couldn't have a healthy baby. I knew I needed to talk to Adam, but I didn't have high expectations. We needed to talk, and talk we did.

"When I told Adam I wanted to speak with him about something, he said defensively, 'All right.' He listened attentively. When I was finished, I searched his face for a reaction, reassurance, approval, but saw nothing.

"He paused for a moment. Without rage, he said he liked our life the way it was and did not understand my obsession with wanting to change it. The he yelled, 'Don't I love you enough? Don't I give you all the love you need? Why do you have to spoil what we have? How could you be so selfish? Didn't you learn anything? If we were supposed to have a baby, the baby would have lived. Don't you care about me and about preserving our marriage?' I backpedaled through words, excuses, and apologies. I felt ashamed, guilty, and bewildered. I didn't understand his reasoning. But it was clear he didn't want a child. He implied that if I did, it would jeopardize our relationship."

Kit slides off Lily's bed and starts pacing across the room. "How awful and manipulative!" She stops and looks at Lily. "Oh, sorry, it isn't my place to judge. I'm probably thinking of my stuff. I just can't believe that someone who loves you would talk to you that way."

Lily shakes her head and sighs. "Well, again we became distant. Adam spent a lot of time without me at the cabin. I wondered if he was punishing me or just didn't care. His work took him out of town. He traveled during the week, returning for weekends. Some weekends we got along fine. We never really talked. I was not myself; I was very guarded. Adam seemed to have changed as well. He was reserved, sarcastic, and often short-tempered. Before we could talk or try to resolve anything, he was gone again. I found it almost peaceful when he was gone.

"Time slipped away. We were both busy. During the week, Adam called less and less. If I tried to reach him, he was always unavailable.

There was no tenderness or intimacy. He seemed to ridicule me. He was never happy, always picking a fight."

"What did you do?"

"I started reading books, looking for any self-help I could find. I gave him one of the books, and he threw it down, yelling that I was the one who needed help. I expressed my concerns for us. I pleaded with him to see a counselor with me. He said again that I was the one who needed help.

"I made an appointment with Jeanes the next day. We talked a long time about Adam. We wondered if he had something happening in his life of which I was not aware. Why was he so unreachable? Why was he unwilling to work on the marriage and so quick to place blame? I thought maybe he didn't love me anymore. He certainly wasn't being loving toward me and never wanted to be with me. He spoke of being frustrated that I was never happy. He accused me of being too needy.

"I finally was ready to tell Jeanes about Adam's reaction to the baby. She showed me that there were many control issues that Adam was demonstrating and that talk of a baby seemed to have brought on this change of heart.

"I was fearful of ending the marriage because I felt the guilt of failure. I wondered if Adam was being unfaithful. When I questioned him, he told me that I was weak and insecure. I couldn't understand this person he had become. He was once so kind and loving and was now hateful. I questioned how his feelings could have changed and what he was thinking.

"Adam started paying our bills when he was out of town. I was nervous that I didn't know what was happening with our money. He would get angry and defensive when I asked him about it.

"One weekend he told me he was going straight to the cabin. He said he needed to get some work done and did not want any disturbances. I pleaded with him to spend some time with me, to work on our marriage. He refused and told me not to call or bother him. He said I had gotten too emotional, and he needed to work.

"The weekend came, and I was miserable. I felt so helpless. He was someone I didn't know. I wondered what was happening, and I feared the worst. Impulsively, I decided to go to the cabin and talk to him, and the worst was there. Through the window, I saw Adam with another woman, drinking, laughing, and kissing. I was paralyzed with disbelief."

"Oh my gosh!"

"I slowly drove home, crying until I had no more tears left. I felt anger, betrayal, and foolishness. If I stayed angry, it didn't hurt so much. Now what was I going to do? I had to have a plan. It was China and me.

"Adam must have seen my brake lights and wondered if it was me. When I returned home, there were a dozen messages from him, asking accusing questions. I couldn't imagine anyone slimier.

"On Monday I went to an attorney and filed for divorce. It seemed pretty neat and simple. I figured he loved someone else, he would want out, and I wanted to heal and get on with my life.

"The next Friday, Adam was served with papers. Then the storm began. He called, demanding the meaning of my actions. I confronted him with the night at the cabin, which he denied. He came home, crying, pleading, and yelling. He claimed he never lied, wanted the marriage, would go to counseling, and would do anything to keep me.

"I agreed. Maybe I wanted to believe he didn't want to hurt me. It was so confusing. We went to see Jeanes. It was a drama fit for the screen. He seemed set on making me out to be insecure, needy, irresponsible, and manic. He made up stories, even flirted with Jeanes, and showed off. I was furious. After the session, he was so proud of himself. He felt it went so well. He laughed at me and told me I was worthless and not worth his time. He said he didn't think he wanted our marriage. He made me feel as if I were on a trial basis, and we would see if I could make the marriage work.

"Then off he went again, who knows where. I was so angry. I started going through old bills and receipts. I found expense reports, credit card receipts for trips, gifts, and wine by the case that I had never seen. The extra expenses dated back a year. Then I found his cell phone bill. A year ago there were multiple calls to the same phone number, then after a year there were calls from that phone number. I called the phone company and got a woman's name. When I called the number, a recording gave both her name and Adam's as living there. The slime was keeping house with another woman in another town. I told my attorney to go forward with the divorce. There was no marriage."

Kit claps. "I'm sorry, but good for you. You stood up for yourself."

Lily rolls her eyes. "Well, my action changed things. Adam began to act desperate. He called and left messages every few minutes. 'Please talk to me. You don't understand. It's not what you think. You have it all wrong. You're the only woman I love. We're meant to be together. Don't throw us away. You'll never find anything like us. You'll never find anyone like me.' Later, his tone changed when I didn't respond. He said, 'Don't even try. You'll be sorry.' And then he would soften. 'You know I love you. God knows I love you.' It was gut-wrenching, listening to all the messages.

"Who was this person who had betrayed me and ridiculed me and had been so angry and mean? I thought he would want out, so why was he saying all these things? Suddenly one night, he was banging on the door because I had changed the locks. I told him he could get a few things and leave—we would have to arrange a time during the day for him to get his belongings. He stayed at the cabin, calling me constantly. I tried not to answer the phone because our conversations went around and around. All he would say is that I didn't understand. He was right about that—I didn't understand. He could never give me a good enough explanation of what he was talking about. What I did understand was that he had betrayed me in many ways, and infidelity was not something to forgive and forget. The marriage, if it could be called that, was over.

"The next week Adam came by while I was downstairs in class. He was supposed to clear out his things from our two years of being to-gether. It was hard to keep my mind on my little dancers. The sadness weighed heavily, and I was embarrassed at the futility and had the sense that I had somehow failed. Maybe I was meant to be alone. So it would be China and me.

"I knew he was packing and that it would take a while. After the last student was picked up, I was locking up when I heard car brakes squeal and a woman yell. I looked out and could not see what she was looking at on the ground. Then in sheer horror, I saw a still, white China, soaked in blood. I flew through the door and into the street. Her body was lifeless—she was gone. I felt my heart break. How could this have happened? I looked up at the apartment to see an open window and Adam looking out. I thought I saw a smirk on his face, a gleam in his eye. Surely he had not let her out on purpose. I yelled to him and he said the window must have blown open, and then he disappeared."

Lily catches a tear rolling down her face. "A neighbor brought out a box lined with a linen cloth, and I placed China gently inside. I got in my car and drove. I did not know where I was going, but then I turned down a familiar path. It was a path China and I had taken on our bike rides. The woods were thick and green with moisture. The smell was fresh, and a warm breeze seemed to touch my face. I felt it must surely be China bidding me farewell.

"There was an old shovel I kept in the back of the car in case I ever got stuck. I dug a hole in the soft, moist earth and laid China to rest. Only China knew what love and pleasure she had brought to my life.

"I hadn't been able to bury my child—Adam had refused, and I had been too distraught to object. So I felt today I was grieving and burying my two dear loved ones. The sky grew dark, and I hadn't been aware of the hours that had slipped by while I sat beside China's grave. I felt my life was in ruins.

"It took all the energy I had left to drag myself to the car and slowly drive home. The word *home* was almost laughable. What was home? Home had been a place I'd shared with a man who was a stranger to me, and now I felt the emptiness of not having China waiting to greet me. As I drove up to my apartment, it was dark—no lights were on. I looked up to the window where I sometimes spied China watching for me. Even in a dark window, I would be able to see my fluffy white fur ball. But there was no China. The sadness squeezed my heart until I almost felt I could not breathe.

"As I entered the apartment, I had almost forgotten that Adam had been there. But I was rudely reminded by the disarray of the entire place. There was trash, boxes, and paper scraps all about. It was as if he had emptied drawers and taken what he wanted and left everything else in a pile on the floor. There were gashes in the walls where he obviously took no care in moving things out.

"The apartment appeared in ruins, and it seemed to reflect my life. The next few months were agonizing. Adam tried to intimidate me out of a fair separation of property. One moment he was loving and reminiscent of the good times, and then in the next breath he was cruel and hateful, blaming and accusing and almost threatening. He had told so many lies; I wondered if he had ever told me the truth.

"Some property I thought we had purchased, he had actually stolen from friends and people for whom he worked. Other property he had sold without my knowledge. He had taken out loans and forged my name as cosigner. I now had debt I hadn't been aware of. There was no easy way to account for where the money had gone. He wasn't truthful. He would not give me financial reports. Nothing made sense; there were so many lies. I could not and probably did not want to know what was truth or lies. He kept echoing, 'You don't understand.' I didn't understand, that I knew for sure. And I had no idea what was ahead for me."

Kit sighs. "What a terrible experience."

"Yeah, well, the nastiness continued. There were months of lawyer negotiations, and it seemed to drag on and on. Adam wrote cards and left messages: 'You'll never find anyone like me. You sure made a mess of your life. What were you thinking? Did you really think you could make it on your own?' I would sit with my hands over my ears, rocking back and forth. My attorney told his attorney to have him stop calling me. After that, he resorted to calling and hanging up. Sometimes he just stayed on the line, breathing or just listening. At first I was angry, and then I came to expect the calls. It wasn't scary or eerie, just sad and irritating.

"Then the day came to sign the papers. He looked at me, and I knew we were strangers. I couldn't see or feel any of the tenderness we had shared. He said something about me wasting years of his life. But they were just words. I couldn't figure him out—I was done analyzing and agonizing. He didn't respond in any way that seemed logical to me. I never got honest, heartfelt answers from him, so it was time for me to give it up. I'd failed at understanding Adam or helping him to understand himself."

Lily pauses and says, "You must be tired of me talking."

Kit smiles, but her face is drawn and sad. "I'm so sorry. But it was good to get him out of your life."

Lily looks at Kit's sad eyes. "I wish it had been that easy. But I hadn't heard the last of him." She sighs. "But it's getting really late. We should talk another time."

Kit approaches Lily with outstretched arms, palms open. Lily smiles and places her arms on top of Kit's with palms open. The women squeeze each other's arms.

Kit heads toward the door and then turns toward Lily. "Have sweeter dreams." She closes the door quietly behind her.

Lily sighs and slides under the covers. She looks up at the ceiling and gives thanks for her new friend.

HRC DAY TEN

Lily gets up and stretches. She has slept in, probably due to the long night talking with Kit. Breakfast is over, so she will have to have cold cereal. She dresses quickly and goes out to get some cereal and hot coffee. Lily leans her elbows on the table. She's tired. She has opened up to Kit more than to anyone else, even her therapists. She has an unsettling feeling within her belly that eating doesn't fix. It's a raw ache and a pulling, as if her energy is seeping out onto the floor. She shakes her head and decides she needs to drink more water. Talking about her trauma is hard, and she needs to take care of herself. Her thoughts go to Kit, and she wonders about her trauma. *Fair is fair, and it's Kit's time to share, if she feels comfortable.*

When evening comes after Lily's schedule of activities, she can't wait to shower and get some sleep. After climbing into bed, she tries to read, but falls asleep with the book on her face. Lily hears the distinct sound of cowboy boots coming down the hall. Her heart flutters and she looks up, seeing her dad coming toward her. His smile against his tanned face warms her heart. She stands to go to him, and her dad envelopes her in a hug. But she is grabbed from behind and swiftly pulled away as her dad looks on in horror. The room grows dark, and a deep voice speaks into her ear: "You are mine! No one else's." Lily tries to scream, but no sound comes out.

Then she hears Kit's voice. "Lily, wake up. It's just a dream."

Lily wakes with a start. Kit is leaning over her and talking softly. Lily's vision clears as she becomes more awake and realizes she has tears streaming down her face. "Oh, another nightmare. Actually, I was reliving the real nightmare."

Kit sits on the end of Lily's bed. "Do you want to talk about it?"

"I was dreaming about my dad."

"I have dad nightmares too," Kit says.

"Oh, it wasn't my dad that I was afraid of. I was so glad to see him. We have been estranged for so long, and I just reconnected with him. But then I was dragged away from him, and I hated the helpless look on his face. It is the same look he gives me now as he sees me struggling with my demons."

"Who was dragging you away?"

"Landers!" Lily yells, louder than she means to.

"Who's Landers?"

"Adam's last name is Landers. That's how I refer to him since he's been tormenting me."

"Do you want to talk about it?"

Lily takes in a deep breath and lets it out slowly. She smiles at her friend. "No, I think you should have a turn, if you want to."

Kit's hand goes to her belly. She takes a deep breath in and blows it out slowly while Lily waits.

Kit puts her hand inside what looks like another pocket of her blue, flowing nightgown with the laced collar that circles her neck and pulls out a small book. "I write. I write down my thoughts, my fears, sometimes in poetry. I told you some difficulties that I had with my father. This will explain more."

Kit opens her book. "This is called 'Mask.'"

Face that she knows
Disappears, peekaboo
Teaches, she mimics
Trusts, follows face

Face that she trusts
Tells her of love
Whispers compliments
Makes her feel special

Face that she knows
Changes expression by night
Is it a mask?
She trusts, but it hurts

Face that she knows
By day, wears no mask
Regards her protectively
Sweetness, smiles

Face that she knows
Encourages yet cautions
Should she go?
But is she ready?

New faces of friendship, romance
Face that she knows
Can you trust, are you good enough?
Will they know?

Face that she knows
Discourages friendships
Keeps her small
Promotes insecurity

Face that she knows
Happy with her sadness
Protector, comforter
No one is good enough

Face that she knows
Has known since a child
Face that she trusted
Face that is sick

Face that she thought she knew
No good for her
Life unravels
Pain, denial, shame, anger, and hate

Questions, therapy
Betrayal, loss, and hurt
Realization of his illness
Healing, hope, cycle broken

Face that she knew
Sad, wasteful, weak, old
Dependent on those
He should have loved better

Dark secret kept silent
Relationship ended
Protection of innocent
Now who wears the mask?

Lily realizes her mouth is open in shock. She closes it and reaches out to her friend, whose face is contorted in sadness. Lily asks in a whisper, "Your father raped you?"

Kit nods. "For eight years. Once I got my period, he stopped but continued to paw at me. He called me Kitten. I was the youngest of three kids. Mom was busy with the older ones and their activities, so my father and I spent a lot of time together. He was my best friend. I loved being with him. He told me he loved me best. I loved the attention. He would call to me, 'Kitten, come lie in my lap.' I would curl up in his lap, and he would pet me. He would whisper, 'I love you the most. It's our little secret. Don't tell Mom.' I didn't know that he wasn't being appropriate. It felt so good to have attention and be loved." Kit hides her face. "It sounds awful, I know. I'm so ashamed."

Lily gently touches Kit's hand. "You have nothing to be ashamed of. You were a kid. What were you, six?"

"No, I was five."

"Did your mom know?"

Kit opens her book again. "This one is called 'The Howl.'"

> Baby for which you wanted
> Suckles at your breast
> Finds nourishment, comfort
> Then the wolf howls
>
> Separated too soon
> Left to her own devices
> She searches with no direction
> Finds no one
>
> The wolf howls
> You run to him
> Come back with excuses
> Respect, loyalty
>
> The wolf howls
> The child is tossed out
> Shivering in the dark cold
> Snatched up, away from you
>
> She clings for acceptance, love
> Confused at being licked clean
> Before devouring teeth
> Tear at her soul

The wolf howls
He is happy, content
The child cries
Approval shines on you

The wolf howls
He beckons
To be served and obeyed
Again you serve up the child

Bitten, discarded
The child crawls away
Shamed, she is dragged back
Sacrificed to the wolf

The wolf howls
There is no right or wrong
No black or white
Just suffocating foggy gray

The wolf howls
Grabbing, clawing
He is losing his grip
His desire out of reach

The wolf falls
With a thud
You can't revive him
Screams pierce the quiet

You weep on his grave
Clawing at the soil
The wind howls at your back
As the child walks away

Lily looks at her friend. "Your mother knew?"

Kit pauses. "Well, I believe she knew on some level. When I was very little, I didn't understand what he was doing. I just loved the attention. He always held me afterward and told me how much he loved me. It felt so safe and comfortable in his arms. He said he loved me the best and even more than Mom. So when I was little, I felt guilty that he loved me more than Mom. But Mom would always tell me how proud she was that I was so good to Dad. It was so confusing. Then when I got older and understood how wrong it was, I told Mom, and she yelled at me. She said I had an active imagination, and I was trying to get attention, and shame on me. She said, 'Don't you dare disgrace the family. Your father is a prominent man in the community. Don't you ever say anything like that ever again!' No one believed me. Not even my brother and sister."

Lily squeezes Kit's hand as she tries to absorb this terrible story. "A child should never be ignored. How dare your mom!"

Kit opens her book again. "This one is called 'Daddy's Favorite Little Girl.'"

> How do you explain a little girl's love for her daddy?
> She yearns for the attention
> To capture his eye
> To hear his voice
> Climbs up into his lap
> Strong arms surround her
> And the softest hands
> With the gentlest touch
> She is warm and protected in his grasp
> She is his alone
> His favorite
> The one that he loves the most
> That he spends his free time with
> She tries to be the good girl
> To remain the favorite

But in the darkness
The smell of alcohol is thick
He comes to her
She feels the soft, warm touch
Then his soft hand pulls at her hair
Touches her face
Then covers her mouth
She is held down
He moves painfully over and in
Thrusts, jerks, and then quiet
He is heavy on top of her
It is hard to breathe
Rolling off her
He pulls her to him
Strokes her hair
Kisses her head
She feels and smells his warmth
The softness of his hands touches her neck
She snuggles into him
She alone is loved

Lily sighs. "What a horrible tale, but your poetry is beautiful. Did it help to write it?"

"I started writing after I got here. It did help. But then the nightmares began, and I started remembering details. I felt so alone."

"I can't even image." Lily wipes tears from her eyes.

Kit looks down at her book and then she meets Lily's eyes. "Here's another one. It's called 'Teenage Questions.'"

You are Daddy's favorite
Don't understand why he ignores your siblings
Happy to be the chosen
Why does he look at you oddly
As his boxer shorts fall away, revealing his privates?

Was it an accident?
You are shocked and try not to look
Curiosity takes over and you peek
Then you see in his face, he is glad
Why does he peek at you when you are dressing?
Why is he hiding in the bathroom when you step out of
the shower?
And he is always touching his crotch
He pats you on your bottom
Tickles your inner leg
He is an affectionate father
Hugs and kisses you a lot
But you don't see him be affectionate with Mom
You think you have the best dad in the world
How lucky you are
He is interested in everything you do
Never thinks you are old enough to date
Never thinks anyone is good enough
Then he changes his tactic
You aren't good enough for anyone
He says, "Don't you think they will know?"
It is years until you understand what this means.

"How awful! I don't even know what to say. That should never have happened to you." Lily takes in a deep breath and lets it out, leaning toward her friend.

"It's more common than you know. Sexual abuse happens to one in ten children. Actually, I think it's even less than that: one in eight. And it's often someone that the victim knows." Kit looks at Lily sadly. "It's so confusing for a child. You feel shame that you have such mixed feelings. I felt love for my father and later hate for what he did to me. And the loneliness was unbearable. No one believed me, and I was stuck."

"Is that why you're here?"

"Partly. I was in a bad way. I felt so alone. Mom, Tommy—my brother—and Sue—my sister—didn't believe me. I confronted my father and told him to stop, but he just laughed. He said, 'You're my daughter. We love each other in a special way. You will do as I say.' So I started some 'unhealthy behaviors,' as my therapist calls them. I felt so much pain, and I had no control. So I started cutting myself. It made the ugly pain go away, and I had control."

Lily touches Kit's arms. "Is that why you have scars on your arms?"

Kit looks down at her arms and rubs the scars. "Yes. They're my badges of courage against the evil. Well, my mother saw my arms, even though I tried to hide them. She punished me by sending me to my room. She took out everything that was sharp, even mirrors. I was so angry, but I found another way." Kit rubs her hand over her belly. "Yes, I started with my belly. My nails were sharp enough to get some skin, and I just kept working at it until it bled."

Lily closes her eyes and swallows. She sees Kit looking at her. "Sorry, I get a bit queasy with blood."

"Oh, sorry."

"Don't be. It's just me. So what happened?"

"I did start doing some writing before I got here. I wrote about how I was going to kill my father by injecting air into his bloodstream with a hypodermic needle." She looks at Lily. "You know that kills someone instantly?"

Lily's eyes widened, and she holds her breath.

Kit laughs. "I wasn't really going to do anything, but it felt really, really good to plan his demise. Well, of course Mom found the writing. And she saw some blood on the outside of my clothes. She stripped me naked and saw the cuts on my belly. They had me committed."

"But it wasn't your fault. Was there no one that listened?"

"I was wild and angry when I first got here. I would scream, hit, and bang and throw things. I tried finding ways to cut myself. I felt like a caged animal that was being abused. I was restrained and sometimes put in isolation."

"You'd been abused and were still being abused. I'm so sorry." Lily wipes a tear from her eye.

Kit dips her head and then smiles up at Lily. "I wrote this just after I arrived. It's called 'Justice.'"

> Demons that haunt us
> And keep us awake
> Taunt us and bite us
> And suck out our fate
>
> Castration and hanging
> Will halt their quake
> And vultures will celebrate
> The remains that they ate
>
> As flesh tears away
> And evil drains out
> Ground turns barren, black
> As 'hallelujahs' shout out
>
> Empty sockets stare out
> At those looking on
> Reminder of evil not tolerated
> Banished and gone
>
> Evil soul
> Who's to blame
> Swept away for judgment
> Retribution and shame

"It didn't seem like anyone believed me. This piece was shown to my parents, who were horrified. Then I got shock treatment," Kit continues.

Lily gasps. "Shock treatment! How barbaric!"

"Yes, it was. It knocked out some of my memory for a while. I didn't remember why I was here. I was pretty numb. Then the nightmares started. So although I didn't remember during the day, I seemed to remember in my sleep."

Lily hears a door shut out in the hall and then hears voices. She looks at Kit in horror. "Oh no, they're doing room checks!"

Kit jumps off the bed. She locks arms with Lily, and they both squeeze. She speaks rapidly. "I'm thankful for you, Lily. Have sweeter dreams."

"Me too, and you have sweeter dreams too. Now hurry!"

Kit slips out the door and shuts it silently.

Lily holds her breath as she listens, thinking she will hear commotion as Kit is caught. All she hears is the quiet conversation of the two staff members. Lily is so relieved. She lies awake, thinking about Kit's horror. Her trauma pales compared to Kit's. She thinks about her wonderful dad and mom. She wonders how a father and mother could be so cruel to their child. It is unthinkable, inexcusable.

"How is Kit OK?" Lily asks out loud. Lily sees Kit as a strong, lovely young woman. Someone at this place has to believe her. Lily doesn't pray much, but she says a prayer for her friend and drifts off to sleep.

HRC DAY ELEVEN

Lily wakes and stretches and thinks about her visit with Kit. It makes her sick to her stomach. Kit was committed to a psychiatric facility when she had done nothing wrong. She wonders how anyone could be so cruel. And was there no one here that could help her? Lily is distressed. She has so many questions.

Lily gets up, turns on one of her favorite ballets, *Cinderella*, with music by Sergei Prokofiev. She puts on her pink ballet slippers and dances around the room, with her nightgown flowing around her. Dancing always relaxes her. She has forgotten how important it is for her to dance almost every day. She is dancing for herself and for Kit.

When Lily concludes her dancing, she feels calmer, but still sad. She walks over to the window as rain pelts against the glass. It has been a dry winter in town, and the earth needs rain so badly. It seems it has been raining off and on since Lily saw Landers. She stops herself as she thinks this—her feelings are not as intense. Has Kit's story affected her that much? She feels tears leak out of her eyes and mix with the raindrops in her vision. She watches the wind blow the tree limbs about as the rain whips up the side of her window. It is mesmerizing, and she just stares as her tears flow like the rain. When she is spent, she washes her face, dresses, and goes out for breakfast. She feels exhausted as she goes to her therapies. Afterward, she takes time to journal in her room.

The buffet dinner includes fried chicken, mashed potatoes, green beans, and salad. Lily smiles to herself. She hasn't eaten like this since she lived on the ranch. How she loved the ranch dinners with her family: the laughing, the bickering, the teasing, and the love. She feels a squeeze of her heart. Taking a deep breath in and letting it out slowly, she prays that she will have those memories in her future. Taking a bite of the delicious-smelling and tasty fried chicken feels decadent and sinful for a ballerina. She has been pretty careful as she has gotten older. She can't eat all her favorite foods as she did when she was young, but she has lost weight in the past months and can afford it. She smiles as she licks her lips and the tips of her fingers.

Back in her room, Lily showers and gets ready for bed. She thinks of Kit and wonders how her day has gone. She climbs into bed and pulls out a book she has wanted to read again. *Taking Flight: From War Orphan to Star Ballerina* is the memoir of an orphan who danced her way from war-torn Sierra Leone to ballet stardom. Lily reads until she falls asleep. She is dancing and leaping across the stage as she hears clapping and cheering. The theater lights illuminate her every move. Then the stage darkens to black, and the theater is empty. Confusion and then fear grip her as she realizes she is alone. She sees the white of his teeth as he smiles in the darkness. A scream escapes her mouth. Then there is a familiar voice reaching out to her.

"Lily, wake up. It's just a dream."

Lily opens her eyes to see Kit approaching her bed. Lily smiles as Kit plops onto the end of her bed. "Did you have better dreams?" Lily asks.

Kit frowns. "No, not yet. Mine woke me up, so I came to see how you were doing. Some club we're in!" Kit shakes her head.

Lily sits up. "I've been thinking a lot about you and what you told me. Didn't anyone here believe you?"

"Yes, Leanne did. She's a wonderful and caring therapist. I was so hurt and angry. It took me a while to tell her. But when I did, Leanne believed me. She reported my story to social services, and there was an investigation. I was interviewed and examined. They found old scar tissue from trauma—you know where. My parents and my siblings said I was lying. They said I was a troubled wild child, seeking attention. They said I was always running away and hanging out with bad kids, which wasn't true. They told social services that they had tried everything, and nothing had helped me. My father, in his righteousness, said I was dead to him the moment I spoke such blasphemy. My family was done with me and made me a ward of the state. There was no evidence, and it was my word against theirs. I was forbidden from speaking of the slanderous matter again. Leanne was furious."

"Are you kidding me?"

"No. My whole family deserted me. They believed and supported him and not me." Kit slams her fist on the bed, and Lily jumps.

"Oh, sorry. It just makes me mad, and sad, angry, lonely, etcetera, etcetera. But the bright side that Leanne keeps reminding me about is that I no longer have to be around my father. He can't hurt me anymore. I changed my name to Katherine Suffisant. *Suffisant* is the French word for self-sufficient. I'm emotionally and intellectually independent. The judge said that I can be released if I'm not a danger to myself and feel strong and well enough on my eighteenth birthday on April 20th. I have three weeks to go."

"How long have you been here?"

"I was committed at age sixteen, so almost two years."

"So why a French name?"

"I hope to go to France one day."

Lily smiles. "I'm sure you will."

Kit takes her book out of the pocket of her gown. "This is what I wrote at that time. It's called 'Broken Glass.'"

> It lies discarded
> Bruised, charred, amiss
> Slinks back if approached or touched
> Can lash out and cut
>
> Rain, like tears, washes away
> Smudges of pain and ambivalence

Out of the darkness a light falls
A prism of colors emerges

Reds of courage, survival
Greens of heart, growth, and love
Yellows of renewed power
Blues of guidance and truth

Brilliance shines forth
With purples of understanding
Whites of hope and triumph
Strength and beauty reborn

"That's beautiful. It's a wonderful description of becoming strong in your adversity." Lily pauses, absorbing the meaning of the poem.

"Is your father still alive? You wrote about his grave in 'The Howl.'"

"No, he died a year ago. I hear it was a heart attack. Fitting—he didn't have much of a heart. I thought my mom or siblings would come see me, but no. I wasn't even invited to the funeral. I didn't want to go anyway. I would have spat on his grave. I guess they just want to live their fairy-tale life." Kit turns to another page in her book. She looks up at Lily and smiles. "I wrote this after he died. It's called 'At Rest.'"

In life you roared aloud,
shame and dominance at me.
Submissive fear and obedience made you proud.
Blind to the damage you refused to see.
Fueled by the power of your manipulation,
ignorant and unresponsive to the life you destroyed.
Was this your plan of contemplation,
such sickness you employed?
Now dead, you are but sick memory of abuse
that feeds no more and sets your victim free.
You are, to me, no one and of no use,

your destiny remains to be.
Your blackened grave, no butterfly will light upon.
Judgment came for you, and you are gone.

"That's so powerful. So with your perpetrator gone, do you feel better?"

"Safer, but not better. He still haunts me in my dreams. Even though he's gone, the fact that my family doesn't believe me or acknowledge me keeps my anger and loneliness raw and exposed. And I have been forbidden from talking about the abuse with anyone outside of this facility." Kit breathes in and sighs loudly. "Not fair, huh?"

"No, it's not fair. But you're making great progress in spite of them. And you can talk with me any time, even when we're no longer here. I'm learning that what happened to us fades a bit but is always part of us." Lily squeezes Kit's hand.

Kit squeezes Lily's hand back. "Thanks. I'm 'The Guardian'—the guardian of the secret." Kit reads again from her book.

I was born a guardian,
Peacekeeper of the family,
Only recipient of the evil
To keep the others safe
And maintain the balance.
Ugly duckling, never a swan,
I'm the guardian of the secret.

I was youngest daughter, sacrificed to my father
Who expressed his sick love to me alone.
The family stayed happy, content.
I believed I was loved.
My father whispered love to me:
"I love you the most."
"It's our little secret."
"Don't tell Mom."
I was the guardian of the secret.

My mother acknowledged the love:
"I'm so proud of you for being good."
"Thank you for making your father happy."
"I love you very much."
This was confusing.
But I loved my family.
I was the guardian of the secret.

As I grew, I started to understand the secret.
And I was told by my father:
"No one can love you."
"You aren't good for anyone."
"Do you think they will know?"
"You aren't smart enough."
"You can't make it on your own."
I trusted and loved him,
So I worked hard to be smarter and better.
I didn't understand his manipulation.
I was the guardian of the secret.

A drunken father beckons for me.
The secret continues.
Love was lost, replaced by betrayal and shame.
I reached out to my mother and siblings,
Asking for comfort and support,
Cautioning them to protect themselves.
No one believed me.
All begged that I remain silent:
To protect our mother,
Preserve our family,
Hide the shame,
For they loved our father.
Ugly duckling, never a swan,
I was to remain the guardian of the secret.

Father showed no remorse.
He demanded my presence.
Mother tried to shame me into obeying.
I refused them both.
I ached, for years.
A lonely journey,
That distanced me from my family,
The family that betrayed me.
But I remained the guardian of the secret.

Now that he is dead and buried,
I am free of him.
There is peace that surrounds me.
But I remain mute.
I am the guardian.
So that they can keep their sweet memories
Protected from the seepage of evil,
I remained the guardian of the secret.

I'm the guardian of the secret,
But it's farther from my mind.
I surround myself with love,
With those that know the truth,
And I don't have to hide.
Someday when Mother leaves this place,
Maybe she will know,
And her learning will begin.
Then she will understand
The guardian of the secret,
As the duckling becomes a swan.

"I think I love that poem the best. You're amazing. How did you come out on the other side? I feel like I'm treading water and not going anyplace." Lily stares at her friend with tears running down her face.

Kit reaches over and wipes the tears from Lily's eyes. "You'll get there. I've been working on my stuff longer. I'm not totally there yet, but close. Sometimes you try different techniques and see what works for you. When I was at the height of my torment with bad dreams, I just wanted to block or buff out my pain. I started imagining my dream behind glass, and I buffed the glass with a color—for me, it was a deep purple. I would buff and buff until I was surrounded in the comfort of the deep purple and I didn't see the images of the dream anymore. My therapist thought that was a great exercise for me. I was buffing out the pain of the memory. There's also this doctor named Shapiro. She's working on this new treatment for trauma. It involves eye movement. I think it's called EMR or EMDR. Leanne is trying it with me to see if it helps with the nightmares."

Lily sighs. "Yes, I use that too. It's called eye movement desensitization. I also use tapping."

"I'll keep you posted on how it works for me. Maybe you could teach me tapping. And I still have to work on this forgiveness piece." Kit smiles.

"Forgiveness! Who do you have to forgive?"

"Apparently, my mother and siblings. Not to expect anything from them, but to help myself. I'll keep you posted on that one too." Kit shakes her head.

"How do we know when we're there?" Lily sniffles and dries her eyes and nose with a tissue.

"I think we'll feel it. At least I hope so." Kit smiles. Then she looks at the door and back at Lily. "I'd better go before the hall Nazis come. That was a close one yesterday."

"I'll say." Lily puts out her arms, palms open, and Kit puts her arms on top of Lily's, and then they squeeze and release. "Sweeter dreams."

Kit smiles. "Sweeter dreams." And she slips out of Lily's room, quietly closing the door behind her.

HRC DAY TWELVE

Bright sunshine streams through the blind slats and plays across Lily's face, waking her up. *A day of sun after all the needed rain.* She stretches and climbs out of bed and then pulls up the blind. The sky is a sapphire blue. The buds of leaves on the trees are wiggling out to touch the sun.

Lily feels a heaviness in her chest. Each time she takes a deep breath and lets it out, tears leak from her eyes. She shakes her head, wondering what to do. Moving over to her bed, she kneels and clasps her hands. Making the sign of the cross, she prays. *In the name of the Father, the Son, and the Holy Spirit. Lord…hi.* She laughs out loud. *I bet you're surprised to hear from me, except for last night. But I need your help. Please help Kit heal from her terrible trauma. Help her with her forgiveness. She is such an amazing young woman. I can't believe what she has gone through. Help the souls of those who did her wrong and didn't believe or support her. I wish for her a happy, healthy life, especially on her eighteenth birthday and after she is free from this place. Now for me. I'm realizing that I've been living so isolated in my terror. It felt as if I were the only one that was trapped. Now I realize that there are others like me. I'm not alone. I can get help and become strong. I see what Kit has accomplished. I can hear it in the words of her poetry. Forgive me for being so selfish and only thinking of myself. My family was hurting too, and probably my friends. I don't think much was gained by staying in my bubble of fear. Help me to understand and become brave enough to stand up for myself. I have not been living fully. Bless Kit, my family, and the therapists that are working with us, and bless me. In the name of the Father, the Son, and the Holy Spirit. Amen.* Lily weeps hard, racking sobs until she has no more tears.

She gets up and goes over to the sink to wash her face and brush her teeth. She then dresses in blue jeans and a pink T-shirt with a matching jacket. She pulls her red curls back in a bun and heads out the door for breakfast.

The doors to the dining room are open to the back courtyard and garden. The sun is warming the day. Other residents are grabbing their food and wandering outside, so Lily does the same. As she enters the courtyard, she feels the warmth of the sun like a hug. She tips her face to the sun, and closing her eyes, she breathes in the smell of the new spring flowers just starting to peek out. They smell fresh, but not yet fragrant.

Then Lily remembers that her parents are coming for a visit this afternoon. After breakfast she is busy with her therapies for body and mind. After lunch, Lily's mom and dad arrive.

Lily hears Dansko shoes and cowboy boots coming down the hall. She smiles as she sees them. She gets up and runs into their open arms, and Lilith and Roy circle her in a hug.

"I'm so glad to see you. I've missed you so much," Lily says.

Lilith kisses Lily's forehead. "You aren't just talking about a couple of weeks ago?"

Lily looks from her mom to her dad. "No, I'm talking about the last few years. I've missed you and the ranch, and Grandma, John, Clark, and Steven." Tears spill down Lily's face.

Her father takes a handkerchief from his pocket and dabs Lily's face. "Baby, we've missed you so much too."

Lily pulls them into the courtyard, and they sit together on a bench underneath a crabapple tree with small buds on its branches. "I want to tell you everything." Lily looks from her mom to her dad. "I'm just not quite ready."

Lilith takes Lily's hand. "Honey, you take your time. I already see that you look better. Take your time, and think about coming to the ranch for a while when you're discharged."

Lily's heart rate elevates, and her skin flushes and becomes moist. She's having trouble getting her breath.

Lilith notices the change in her daughter and pulls Lily into her arms. "You're safe. Nice easy breaths. I didn't mean to upset you. We'll do whatever you need."

Lily starts to sob. She looks up into her mom's face. "I can't have anything happen to you and Dad. Or anyone else in the family."

Roy reaches out and takes Lily's hand. "Baby, we'll do whatever we need to do to keep you and everyone safe. We've already talked about hiring security guards to protect the ranch. When you feel ready to come home, we'll have all that in place. But if you want to return to your home, we'll do the same there as well."

Lily smiles through her tears, and she leans into her dad. "Thanks. I would really like to come to the ranch for a while, when I'm ready."

"Yes, when you're ready," Lilith says.

They sit in silence, hugging each other. Lilith notices that her daughter is spent. She and Roy kiss Lily good-bye and leave for the ranch.

Lily takes her dinner to her room, but she isn't very hungry. So many emotions are flooding her: love, fear, and yearning. There is still work to be done. She finishes dinner, gets ready for bed, and tries to snuggle in to read. She has found a book in the resident library. It's a silly romance novel, but it keeps her attention for a while before she slips into sleep.

Lily is in her studio. It's evening after a dinner with her friend Sasha. There's music, and Lily is pulled into a dance. She laughs and tips back her head as a man swings her around. Then there's a crash and broken glass. Lily screams, and then she hears her name.

"Lily, wake up. It's Kit. You're having a bad dream."

Lily wakes to see Kit entering her room. She swallows and sits up in bed. "Hi. Just give me a minute to let my heart rate settle."

Kit takes a seat on Lily's bed. "Take your time. I understand the terror, but it sure gets old. I would like to dream of flying—flying away from my bad dreams." She looks over at Lily. "You know, I've never been on an airplane. Maybe I'll fly on an airplane or one of those gliders, where you float in the clouds. Sounds dreamy."

Lily smiles at her friend. "Well then, that's what you should do. Do it for your birthday."

"Well, that takes money. But I do have some. Old Daddy dumped some in an account for me when he made me a ward of the state. It's like he sold me off." Kit shudders and looks over at Lily. She raises her shoulders and says, "Oh, well."

Lily reaches for Kit's hand and smiles. "You'll be free soon."

"I know. Can't wait!" Kit wiggles back and forth. Then she asks, "Now, tell me about you. What happened after the divorce from Adam?"

"You can only be depressed for a period of time before the reality of life wakes you up. My money was getting low after legal fees and minimal working. I had to get back to work to survive. This survival was not just monetary, but cathartic. I didn't reach out to my parents because I was ashamed.

"I looked at my small life in contrast to the world and the universe. Do we all have a purpose? Did I take a wrong path? Do I just have too much to learn? Do I make bad choices? Do I jump into things without looking closely? Maybe it's my insecurity and need to be loved and wanted. I got so much courage, renewal, and strength from my audience when I danced. When I gave it up and married Adam, I shifted, thinking Adam fulfilled my needs. And he truly enjoyed the power and control of giving me my self-esteem and then ripping it away. I needed to find a way to pull that strength from within myself.

"Getting back into my work would be a start. I'd been getting calls from the mother of one of my students, Sam. It had been three weeks before I finally returned her calls. Sasha, the mom, answered the phone with an enthusiasm that took me by surprise. She said her daughter had felt I'd looked sad and distracted, and she knew I was going through a difficult time. She asked if she could help. This was so foreign to me. Adam had wanted to isolate us, so we had no friends, as well as no family. She suggested lunch on Sunday."

"How nice," Kit exclaims. "Did you go?"

Lily smiles. "Yes, Sasha and I met in a small deli. She wasn't a stranger to me. I'd seen her at all her daughter's performances and when she picked her up after class. But Sasha and I had never really talked. My shyness apparently didn't dissuade her. She talked and talked. I found myself laughing so hard, even at her corny jokes. She had such a positive outlook and joy of life. She had been a single mother since Sam's birth and knew too well the pain and disillusionment of divorce. We had a lot to share. I left lunch feeling uplifted. I had a friend."

Lily takes in a deep breath and lets it out slowly. "Three months had passed since I'd signed the divorce papers. My classes were full. I looked forward to class and all my eager students. My mornings were busy with my paperwork and my exercise routine. Midmorning I had an adult class, lunch, and then class after class until nine o'clock at night. I had Saturday morning classes with afternoon rehearsals before a performance. Sasha, Sam, and I would enjoy movies and popcorn on Friday nights. Sundays were play days. I often planned something with Sasha and Sam.

"Friendship was challenging for me. I'd put up a lot of protective walls, and I wasn't accustomed to openly sharing my innermost feelings. It took a while to trust Sasha. When she saw me having a bad day, she didn't criticize or make fun. She was supportive and a good listener. We were comfortable with each other, and I realized I had been lonely in my marriage for a long time.

"I hadn't enjoyed the friendship of a girlfriend since I'd danced for the ballet. I'd forgotten how much fun girl talk could be." Lily reaches over and squeezes Kit's hand, and they smile at each other. "There seem to be things that only women understand and experience. With a girlfriend I could be silly and relaxed."

Kit nods.

"I found I could trust Sasha with my secrets. I told her of my fears and insecurities, and we always managed to find something funny to make us laugh. Life didn't seem so serious. Sasha was one of those carefree, nurturing people who baked for others when they were sick or sad. She was always bringing me some new yummy baked good. She taught elementary school and was a participant in all of Sam's activities. She grew up on the family farm in Connecticut. One weekend I traveled with Sasha and Sam to her family farm. Sasha's parents were charming, and the food was wonderful. It was so relaxing to stroll around the farm, taking in all the smells. I felt so fortunate to be sharing this with my new friend."

"Did it make you miss your family?" Kit asks.

"Yes, it did. I thought I would reach out to them very soon. But soon, things changed."

"What do you mean?" Kit's brow furrows.

"The next Saturday morning, the phone rang, and when I answered no one was there. A few minutes later, the phone rang again. Again, no one was there. I wondered if it was a wrong number. It had to be. It was too eerie to make me feel reassured that someone had misdialed. That afternoon I received a postcard typed to me. It contained no message, no return address. The picture was of a ballerina dancing alone in an empty room. Looking at it sent a shiver up my spine. I knew who had sent it. But the creepy feeling eventually passed, and I forgot about the calls and the postcard.

"One week later, Sasha, Sam, and I planned a weekend to drive into the country and rent a cabin. I couldn't wait to go, relax, unwind, and play. I cancelled Saturday classes and was packing a picnic basket when the phone rang. Thinking it was Sasha, I answered, asking if she was ready. There was silence. Realizing it wasn't Sasha, I said 'Hello?' Silence, and then the line disconnected. I caught my breath. It had been six months since the divorce had been finalized. Surely he had gotten on with his life. He didn't want the marriage. He didn't want a family. He had a girlfriend. Why was he bothering me? I jumped when the phone rang again. I answered slowly—still no sound. I hung up. It was so creepy. I found myself pacing the kitchen floor. The phone rang again. I grabbed it and yelled, 'Who is this?' A startled Sasha said, 'It's me. What's the matter?' In relief, I told her I was sorry and would explain later."

Kit hugs her knees and then rubs her arms as if she is cold. "That's too creepy!"

Lily sighs. "Yes, it was. But I tried to put it out of my mind and enjoy the weekend. It was a perfect day. We hiked and picnicked, and after dinner in our cabin, warmed by the crackling fire, we roasted marshmallows. Soon Sam couldn't keep her eyes open. After she was snuggled into bed upstairs, Sasha and I had time to talk. I told her about the calls and the postcard. We agreed it didn't make sense that Adam would want to call or send things. It seemed clear he didn't want to be married to me. But why was he holding on? Was it to try and maintain control? I had trouble figuring it out. It made no sense.

"A week passed with no word or contact. My life went on, and I almost forgot, but then the calls started again. No one responded when I answered. I got notes or cards in the mail, reporting his feats and great doings. He wrote encouraging me to contact him. He stated that it would be great to talk with me. He also said he was remarried, so I wondered why he was contacting me.

"Sasha and I tried to work through any possible explanation, but to no avail. Then life would go on until almost exactly the one-week mark, and there would be the silent calls. It seemed so strange and very pathetic. I kept wondering why he didn't have something better to do with his time. I changed my phone number to an unlisted number, but somehow the calls continued."

"That was a great idea to change your phone number. How do you think he got the new number?"

"I don't know." Lily shrugs and continues. "Well, Sasha and I had been swimming laps at the nearby YMCA and had met two brothers, Bill and John, who owned a clothing franchise. They were fun and loved to dance. And I was finally going out."

Kit claps. "Good for you!"

Lily smiles. "Sasha seemed to enjoy herself as well. We frequented several dance clubs. We even took some dance lessons. I'd been going out with Bill for a few months, and Sasha with John. We decided to fix them dinner at my place and dance afterward. It was a lovely evening. I fixed my homemade pasta and sauce, garlic bread, salad, and tiramisu for dessert. We laughed, told stories, and drank nice wine for hours. Then we moved to my dance studio and danced around on the beautiful wood floor. It was so much fun and so relaxing that it wasn't until about two in the morning that the brothers were heading toward their car for home. In horror, we found all four tires slashed. What a terrible way to end a lovely evening.

No other car on the street was touched. We wondered why their car had been singled out. It was a relatively new car. It was too late to fix the car, so Sasha gave them a ride home.

"I was cleaning up the kitchen when I heard a crash downstairs in the studio. As I ran into the room, I could see glass on the floor from a large hole in the window. I'd never heard that there had been trouble on my street. I put a call in to the police, and they promised to drive by through the night."

"Were you scared?"

"Yes, and then the phone calls began again. I could hear breathing on the other end, but no one spoke. The phone rang into the night. I turned off the ringer, but I could hear my answering machine pick up. There was no message. I had a security system installed with a hookup to a local security company. I changed my phone number again, but the calls continued.

"Then one night my security alarm went off. I awoke in fear, wondering what to do. I picked up the phone, and the line was dead. I grabbed a hammer that was stored in the cabinet and slowly crept around the apartment. Nothing seemed to be disturbed. I then went down to the studio. Again, nothing was disturbed. Doors were locked, and windows were secured. The alarm continued to ring. A banging at the front door startled me. I could see a police car and a policeman. He said the security company had called because they couldn't reach me. He searched the apartment and helped me turn off the alarm. I explained that my phone was dead, and he said that was why the alarm had gone off. He explained that the security system sends a signal to the phone line about 2:00 a.m., and if it can't connect, it sets off the alarm. He checked my phone line and followed it out to the box outside. He told me that it had been cut."

"Oh my gosh!" Kit puts her hand to her mouth.

Lily shudders. "I knew who it had been. I just didn't know why he was doing it. It terrified me. Perhaps that was his plan. I became paranoid and watchful, just waiting for something else to happen. When nothing happened, I relaxed and got back to my life. Sasha and I started going out again. We would go to plays and movies. Then newspaper clippings of the movie or play we had gone to would be stuffed in my mail slot. Someone was watching us and following us. *Him.*

"On a crisp fall Sunday, Sasha, Sam, and I went on a bike ride and a picnic. We talked about books and movies, and Sasha caught me up on how her family was doing. It was light and not too personal. It was great fun to see each other. That night after Sasha dropped me off, a car followed her very closely. She didn't notice at first, until it kept turning as she did. She drove right to a police station, and the car turned away. She couldn't get the license plate or a description of the person because it was dark. And now she questioned if they had really been following her or not. But she was spooked.

"Sasha was getting more than a little nervous. Once, we went to a school production in which Sam had a major part. We were so proud. Sam was so pleased to have us cheering her from the front row. After the performance, Sam went to a party with friends, and Sasha drove me home. I saw something sticking out of my mail slot. Anxiously, I pulled it out and found that it was a school program with Sam's name circled. Sasha was horrified. She jumped in her car without saying a word and sped away. She later called and said she had rushed to see if Sam was all right. Luckily, Sam was fine.

"I didn't see much of Sasha or Sam after that. She made excuses not to come over. I didn't hear from the brothers either. I wondered if Sasha had said something to them. Sasha called one day, crying, and said she was sorry, but she was terrified for herself and Sam. She had a hard time imaging what my life was like, it seemed so unreal. She begged me to forgive her, but said she 'couldn't—no, wouldn't—put Sam in any danger.'" Lily tips her head down and sighs.

"How awful for you, though I can't blame her." Kit pats Lily's knee.

"Yeah, my friend had to move on. She was frightened by my former husband's behavior. The hurt, betrayal, and loneliness were devastating. I was dreadfully sorry for the loss of the friendship but knew her primary responsibility was to her child. This was a selfless move of protection. I was even more keenly aware of the terror and helplessness of my situation. How could I let his sick behavior affect my life?

"Police and counselors were of no help. He kept a safe distance to threaten, but not harm, at least for now. Even with phone taps and police surveillance, he was hard to track. I decided if I moved, he would leave me alone and get on with his life. I put my studio and apartment up for sale. I had a realtor to whom I gave instructions and pictures of Adam so that he would not be allowed in my home if he came to snoop. Luckily, my property sold in three weeks. I had scouted out some property in Colorado. The phone calls continued with no one there, but I tried to ignore them."

"Didn't you think he would know that you would move back to Colorado, where you grew up?"

Lily sighs. "Yes, I knew that was a risk. But I wanted to be closer to family in the hopes of reconnecting with them. I picked a town north of where they lived. I thought, why would he follow me?

"So I found a building with an upstairs apartment and an open space below. I lived in the apartment while a studio was built in the open space. It was located in Lakewood, which is north of here. While I was in the apartment, things were quiet. I advertised and had classes ready for the grand opening.

"My days and evenings were busy with classes. I danced and exercised between classes. The days were long, and when I closed at night, I would sometimes think I saw him, or someone, across the street, standing in the shadows, watching. At first I turned off all the lights to see if the street-light's glow was playing tricks on me. Squinting in the dark, I could see the outline of a tall figure with prominent features. I thought it might be Adam. But why would he be here? Then I would hear a motorcycle screech off, and I suspected it was him. He had followed me from New York.

"Time and again, I would call the police, but he would be gone when they arrived. There's no law against him being on a public street—those words rang in my ears. Was I to have no peace? This continued day after day. I would try not to look for him with his lit cigarette, but I always did, and he was always there. Once it was raining hard, and I found myself looking for him, wondering if he was under a shelter somewhere or had chosen not to come. It became almost as if I missed him."

Lily covers her face with her hands and weeps. "I'm so ashamed, but I missed him. I was so lonely. He was all I had. It's so sick!"

Kit moves close to Lily and puts her hand on her knee. "Lily, you were a victim—traumatized and isolated."

Lily looks up into her friend's face. "And there's more. I've been too ashamed to tell anyone this."

Kit squeezes Lily's hand. "You can tell me anything."

"I missed his touch." Lily searches Kit's face for judgement and sees none. "I missed the hunger in his eyes when he looked at me."

"Victims can fall in love with their perpetrators, especially when they are isolated, as you were."

"But I encouraged him."

"What do you mean?"

Lily closes her eyes and takes a deep breath. "I got used to him always watching me. One night when I retired upstairs, I opened the window and took in the night breeze. I closed my eyes and felt the wind blow through my hair and rustle the collar of my gown. When I opened my eyes, I saw him in the darkness below, looking up at me. He was sitting on his motorcycle. I closed my eyes and leaned slightly out the window. My hand stroked my neck and traveled down to my breast. As I gave an erotic gasp, I was shaken into reality and shrank back into the shadows in horror.

"I sat on the floor beneath the window. I wondered what I was thinking. I was falling under the spell of the man who scared my friends away and was keeping me captive. I was sickened by my behavior and what I had allowed to happen to my life. Yet each night, I would put on my gown and lean out the window to find him. In the cool of the night air, I would touch myself as he watched. I saw the glimmer of his smile as he touched himself." Lily opens her eyes. "I never let him into my place. But I wanted him, missed him. It's so wrong and twisted, but it felt so good. It was as if I had some control. I was playing him. He started leaving lilies outside my studio door."

Kit looks into Lily's eyes. "You have nothing to be ashamed of. You were coping the best way you knew how."

"My life became routine, and I thought I was comfortable in it. It seemed to suit me. Rise in the morning, work, exercise, and dance, and then read until I fell asleep. I was alone, but not entirely, because he seemed to always be there, watching me, almost like guarding me. I came to expect it, not fear it. I think sometimes when I danced at night, I was dancing for him. He kept me from feeling so alone. I wasn't alone. When he had scared me and my friends I started calling him Landers, because he wasn't the Adam I had known. Now the names seem to blend together.

"And then I thought he was dead. It was reported he died in an accident. I went to his funeral with my friend Sasha. But Adam wasn't dead. Adam Landers faked his death. He approached me saying something, and then he grabbed me. I was so terrified that I passed out. He must have run off, because when I woke up, I was in an ambulance. I spent a few crazed days in the hospital and then came here. I just didn't want him to be able to mess with me anymore."

Kit stares at Lily. "Wow. Why did he allow the funeral if he wasn't dead? Well, you probably don't know why he does anything. But how do you feel now that you're away from him?"

Lily thinks a moment. "Well, I feel safer here. I just don't want to be trapped anymore. It isn't fair. And I worry for the safety of anyone that gets close to me. My mom and dad said I should come to the ranch for a while. They will have security there. I think that's a good idea. And I've missed them so much. I have a brother, two cousins, and a grandma. Will you come to the ranch and meet them?" Lily smiles at Kit.

"I...think that would be fun. I have no family to go home to. I've never been to a ranch. Are you sure your family won't mind?"

Lily takes Kit's hand. "They'll love you. I can teach you to ride a horse if you like. And my dad makes the best barbecue."

Kit squeezes Lily's hand. "That sounds amazing. I've never been on a horse. They're so big. Scary!"

Lily laughs. "I'll find you a nice quiet horse. Don't worry. So on your birthday, Mom and I will come and pick you up." Lily claps her hands. "That will be so much fun. I can't wait."

Kit jumps off the bed and faces Lily with outstretched arms. "Well, we better get some sleep." Lily puts her arms on top of Kit's, and their hands clasp. "Have sweeter dreams."

Lily smiles. "You have sweeter dreams too."

Kit releases Lily's arms, tiptoes quietly to the door, and lets herself out.

HRC DAY THIRTEEN

Lily wakes up shivering. She pulls the covers up under her chin. The light of morning is just peeking through the blinds. Lily's whole body shakes, and when she touches her neck, it's hot. Her throat is sore.

She hasn't been sick since she arrived at HRC, and she doesn't know what she should do. On shaky legs, she walks to the door and opens it. She looks out and sees one of the staff members.

"Can you help me? I'm sick."

The young woman says, "Sure, get back in bed, and I'll get the nurse on staff."

Lily drags herself back into bed and curls into a ball. In a few moments, there is a knock at the door, and then it opens.

"Hi, my name is Nancy. I understand that you're not feeling well. I'm going to take your temperature, heart rate, respirations, and blood pressure." Nancy wheels a cart over next to Lily's bed. She takes Lily's temperature across her forehead, feels her wrist for a pulse, and then wraps the blood pressure cuff around Lily's upper arm and takes a blood pressure reading. She takes a look inside Lily's mouth.

"I'm so hot, yet I'm freezing. What's my temperature?"

Nancy smiles at Lily. "One hundred three degrees. Your heart rate is elevated because of the fever. Respirations and blood pressure are normal.

Your throat is red. I'll culture your throat for strep." She pulls out a Q-tip and says, "This will make you gag a bit as I swab the back of your throat."

Lily coughs as Nancy swabs her throat.

"You should stay in bed. It's probably a virus. I'll have your meals sent in to you. Is there anything in particular that you want to eat?"

Lily swallows slowly and makes a face. "I don't want anything. My throat is so sore."

"You must drink liquids. I'll get you some lozenges and Tylenol, and I'll have them bring in soft things and a variety of liquids. I'll be checking on you throughout the day. Do you have any questions?"

"No, thank you," Lily says and snuggles under the covers.

Lily slips into a frightful sleep. She's being chased and can't get enough air in her lungs to run fast enough. She yells and wakes herself up. It takes her a while to remember where she is—it's her room at HRC, but the walls are bubbly and popping. Lily touches her head, and she's burning up. Her door is moving back and forth.

"I'm hallucinating, just like I did when I was a kid," Lily says out loud. She remembers times when she was sick in her bedroom at the ranch. Her mom had given her a print of a Norman Rockwell painting. It was of a young girl in a nursery, and it was framed with colors to match Lily's room. But when Lily was sick, that girl reached right out of the frame and tried to grab her. Now Lily's bubbling walls look like faces. Lily sits up in bed. "It's *his* face," she says.

There's a knock at the door, and Nancy comes in. "Are you OK?"

"Yes...well, no. I'm hallucinating with the fever, and the walls are a bubbly, scary face." Lily laughs at herself. "I know that sounds crazy. I hallucinate with high fevers. Have since I was little."

Nancy laughs. "That's a new one for me. I brought you some lozenges, Tylenol, soup, a milkshake, and a big jug of water. Hope that helps."

"I'm sure it will. Just has to run its course. Hope it's a twenty-four-hour bug, not three days."

"I believe it's the twenty-four-hour virus that's going around the ward. Oh, and your strep swab was negative. Is there anything else you need?"

"No, thanks. I'll eat something and sleep. I'll let you know who else comes out of my walls." Lily tries to laugh, but her throat hurts.

Nancy smiles. "You keep me posted." Nancy puts a rolling tray next to Lily's bed and leaves the room.

Lily is in and out of sleep throughout the day and into the night when she hears a knock and Kit's voice. "Lily, are you OK?"

"Kit, don't come in. I have the plague."

Kit stops at the door. "The what?"

Lily tries to laugh. "I have a virus with high fever and sore throat. I don't want you to catch it. It reminds me of how I felt in the hospital before coming here, minus the fever."

Kit creeps a bit closer.

Lily looks up at Kit. "You're blurry. Don't get close! You don't want this."

Kit laughs. "You know, I haven't gotten sick for many years. I must be immune to germs, or they're scared of me."

"I warned you." Lily curls toward Kit so she can see her better.

Kit pulls up a chair near Lily's bed and sits down. Lily takes a lozenge and pops it into her mouth and then sits up slowly.

"Being sick, especially with a fever, makes me feel so vulnerable. I feel like I did when I was isolated by Adam. I was so glad to come here. I wanted to be somewhere that he couldn't get to me. I feel safe here. And except for the fever, I've been getting my strength back and learning about myself. I don't want anyone to have that sick power over me ever again." Lily wipes her face as tears stream down and onto the sheets.

Kit gets a Kleenex and hands it to Lily. "Here."

"Thanks. You know, you've been helping me feel stronger. When you shared your horrible trauma with me and how you stood up for yourself, I was so proud of you. I want to be proud of myself. I can't have him control me. He's sick. And I have to be able to live my life. I don't really want to live here forever, because then he wins. It won't be easy. But I'm going to be brave like you." Lily touches Kit's hand and smiles.

Kit returns Lily's smile. "You are brave. I'm proud of you too. We're going to be OK. And you'll feel stronger when you're well." Kit gets up and puts her arms out to Lily.

Lily closes her arms on top of Kit's, and they both squeeze. "Better dreams for us, and no germs for you. Better wash your hands good." Lily smiles.

"I always do." Kit releases Lily's hot arms and leaves the room quietly.

HRC DAY FOURTEEN

Lily wakes covered in dampness. Her red curls are matted to her face, and her gown is drenched. She gets up slowly on wobbly legs and heads to the bathroom. Her skin is cooler, and she realizes that her fever must have broken. She climbs into the shower to rinse off. She then towels dry and puts on a clean gown.

Lily is surprised to find Nancy in her room, changing her sheets. Lily feels overcome by weakness and slumps into the chair that Kit had been sitting in just hours ago.

"How did you sleep?" Nancy asks.

"I think I did get some sleep. I'm so weak."

"You need another day in bed because your fever may come back. I'll help you get into bed, and then I'll bring you some breakfast. Is there anything special that you would like?"

Lily is grateful for the help as she gets back into bed. "I would love an egg on toast. It's silly, but my mom used to make that for me when I was sick."

"One egg on toast coming up." Nancy smiles and hurries out of the room.

Lily enjoys her egg on toast, but after breakfast she can feel the heat rising in her body. Afternoon and evening blend together as the fever takes her in and out of dreams. Her walls are closing in, and hands are reaching for her. Lily knows it's the fever, but it isn't pleasant. She tosses, turns, and moans out loud. Then in the dark, she hears a voice, soft and melodic.

> Some say love, it is a river, that drowns the tender reed.
> Some say love, it is a razor, that leaves your soul to bleed.
> Some say love, it is a hunger, an endless aching need.
> I say love, it is a flower, and you its only seed.

Lily opens her eyes and tries to focus. She sees Kit standing in the middle of her dark room. She is magically lit by the moonlight from the window. Lily sees her smile.

"That's a beautiful song. I didn't know where the sound was coming from. You have a lovely voice. I seem to remember the song from somewhere."

Kit comes over to Lily's bed and climbs on the end. "You've had a rough couple of days and nights. I thought it might help you to hear a song that speaks to the pain and carries hope. It's been my theme song. It was written by Amanda McBrown and sung by Bette Midler. When I was wallowing in my despair, I would sing it and feel better—kinda hopeful."

"I'm glad you found something to give you comfort in your darkness." Lily reaches over and squeezes Kit's hand.

"Wow, you're still so hot."

"I sure hope you don't catch this awful bug. I feel guilty not shooing you away, but it's so nice to have company."

Kit smiles. "I don't catch bugs, so don't worry." Kit pulls the notebook from the pocket of her gown. "I wrote something for us."

Lily, who has sunk back into her bed, tries to sit up. "What did you write for us?"

Kit smiles as she looks at Lily and bats her long, dark eyelashes.

"It's called 'We.'"

We
You and Me
Move through, at a crawl
Dining on fresh greens,
Shrinking from predators
Vulnerable and exposed.
Then our larvae forms chrysalises.
Hanging side by side
We grow and change.
A transformation,
Metamorphosis.
Swaying in the breeze,
Warmed by the sun
Waiting, safe
Soon to be free.
Then, I hear you
Moving, cracking
You will be free before me.
You will gain strength
And fly.
You are gone with lithe wings.
Then, I am moving, cracking
Quivering, warming, unfurling.
I take off, floating.
We flutter up and down
Making our way
Colors of glorious freedom
We,
You and Me.

Lily claps. "That's beautiful. And it describes how I hope this recovery is going for both of us."

"I read somewhere," says Kit, "that butterflies are symbolic of transformation because of their impressive process of metamorphosis. The butterfly emerges in her glory. We—you and me—need to keep moving forward in our transitions. The journey is our only guarantee. It's our task to make our way, accept the change that comes, and emerge as brilliantly as the butterfly." Kit hands Lily a piece of paper. "I made a copy for you. You can take it with you and remember where we were and how far we came."

Lily wipes a tear from her eye and looks into her friend's eyes. "You have no idea how much this means to me. Thank you."

The two lock arms and squeeze hands. "Sweeter dreams," they both say together. Kit leaves Lily to get some rest.

Lily lies awake, thinking of Kit. It's an amazing, surprising friendship. She has missed having a friend in whom to confide, and they are helping each other as the friendship grows.

Lily thinks back to a conversation she had with Soma. Soma congratulated Lily on her progress. She felt, and Lily agreed, that she was getting close to being ready to leave. Lily shudders, but then she remembers that her mom and dad said they would hire help to keep them safe and protected. Lily smiles as she pictures being at the ranch and sleeping in her old room with the wallpaper of pink and blue ballerinas. Then she wonders if her room is still as she remembers it. Maybe her mom has remodeled it into a guest room.

"Oh, well," Lily says out loud. "I'll just have to find out." Lily thinks about her brother being all grown up, with a grown-up job. The thought makes her smile.

HRC DAY FIFTEEN

Lily opens her eyes and feels the warmth of the sun's fingers on her face. She touches her face and notices that her skin is cool. Sitting up slowly, she assesses how she feels. She feels tired, but better. She climbs out of bed, showers, dresses, and heads to breakfast.

Nancy sees her in the dining room. "Lily, are you feeling better today?"

"Yes, I am. But I just realized that I'm not twenty-four hours without fever, so I better stay in my room."

Nancy smiles. "Well, you're right. How about I get you some breakfast and bring it to your room?"

"Great. A bit of everything—I'm starved." Lily laughs and turns to go back to her room.

Nancy brings her in the paper and a large tray filled with orange and cranberry juice, coffee, cream, bacon, eggs, pancakes, and a bowl of fresh fruit. She puts it down on Lily's desk.

"Wow. That looks incredible." Lily smiles as she pulls up her chair. "I must be feeling better."

Nancy hands her a booklet. "Soma knew you were sick, so she put a workbook together for you to do. She said you're about ready to graduate soon."

"It's funny that you call it graduation." Lily frowns.

Nancy touches Lily's shoulder. "You've had to work very hard to get well. How is that different than working hard at a course in school?"

Lily gives Nancy a smile. "I guess you're right. I'm proud of the strength I've developed." Lily pours maple syrup over her pancakes and takes a big bite. "Yum!"

"Enjoy your breakfast. I'll have your other meals sent in. If you have no fever, you can resume activities tomorrow. We have a hike the day after tomorrow. I think you will enjoy it." Nancy turns to go.

"Thanks, Nancy," Lily says. "And I'll work on my homework."

Nancy smiles as she closes the door.

After breakfast, Lily pulls out the workbook and a pencil. She sits on her bed with pillows all around. She remembers that she had an extensive work-up when she arrived at HRC. Soma asked her questions, did role playing, and had her write out answers to situations in a similar, yet larger, workbook. The workbook was titled "Surviving PTSD and Management of Symptoms." Lily remembers how she had felt, filling out the previous workbook and answering all the questions. It made her see her situation in a different light. She had gotten used to the routine of being watched, manipulated, and isolated—it was her normal. When she had to crack it all open and talk about it, she felt raw, vulnerable, exposed, and ashamed. It was as if she had been doing something hideous and wrong. How had she let herself get there? Soma had helped her see it wasn't wrong—it was a trauma on which to work toward recovery. And though she hadn't told Soma, Kit had been instrumental in her healing. Soma had taught her EMDR and tapping. The tapping resonated with her. When she had a nightmare or a memory and her anxiety elevated, she tapped on pressure points. Lily found that tapping the middle of her forehead helped her best. Lily used the tapping when she was sick and in and out of dreams. But since she had met Kit, she hadn't needed to do the tapping as much. Kit would show up just as Lily was waking up from the nightmare, and talking with her decreased Lily's anxiety. After Kit left her room and she fell back to sleep, she didn't have any nightmares. She was thankful that she had met Kit.

Lily starts reading the questions.

1. Do you feel ready to resume your previous life?
2. Are you excited to resume your previous life?
3. Are there changes you would like to make with that life?
4. How will you go about making the changes?
5. Do you see obstacles that might prevent you from feeling the benefits of your recovery?
6. What can be done to help you feel safe as you return to your daily routines?
7. What are some of the things you would like to do?
8. Do you have individuals with whom you would like to reconnect?
9. How will you go about reconnecting with them?
10. What will you do if you feel you are sliding back into your anxiety and fears?
11. What and who are your resources if you need help?
12. Are there key things you worked on and will continue to work on after you leave HRC?

Lily puts pencil to paper and starts answering the questions. She realizes that she is excited to return to her life and rebuild it. She has no illusion that it will be easy—it will be work. She will have to work, probably sometimes harder than she has at HRC. Resources—yes, she will need to find a therapist that she trusts. Perhaps her mom knows someone, or Soma, and family will be a huge support. She will continue to do the tapping technique to help with the anxiety when she relives the trauma through dreams or memories. Maybe a month or two at the ranch will assist her recovery and help her decide what she wants to do next. She isn't sure she wants to return to her studio where she felt like his prisoner.

After answering most of the questions, Lily puts her pencil down, takes a deep breath in, and lets it out slowly. *Key things to work on: well, I need to forgive the situation of the trauma and forgive myself. I did nothing wrong, and that's what I need to believe. But I allowed the situation to consume, isolate, and terrorize me. I'll work on trusting my instincts, protecting myself, allowing myself to lean on people who care about me, and living my life.*

Lily picks up her pencil and begins again. It feels like she's writing essays as she answers the questions in the workbook, but she feels a better connection to herself. She's taking control. She has acquired tools to assist her as she takes steps back into her life.

When night comes, Lily gets ready for bed and snuggles in with the book she borrowed from the library. The title always escapes her mind, as does the writing. She reads until she falls asleep.

Lily is dreaming of the ranch when she hears her door open and Kit's voice. She opens her eyes and sees her friend approach.

"Hi, Lily. Were you sleeping? I didn't hear you scream. No bad dreams?"

Lily rubs her eyes and thinks a moment before answering. "No, no bad dreams. I was dreaming of my parents' home on the ranch. I leave in three days." Lily sits up in bed. "And I know I'm ready." She smiles at her friend and reaches for her hand. "Kit, you're a big part of why I'm ready to leave. You helped me heal and understand that I have what I need inside me; courage, perseverance, strength, and love."

Kit laughs. "I didn't have anything to do with all that. You did the work. I just shared your journey."

Lily squeezes Kit's hand. "You did more than you know. You were my honest friend, my mirror. Yes, Soma helped, and I worked hard, but your friendship helped me open up and see my life in a different perspective. Your brave sharing of your story helped me understand mine."

Kit opens her mouth. "But…"

"No buts, and I want you to come stay with me and my family at the ranch when you're released on your birthday. I talked to Mom and Dad. They think it'll be good for the both of us. You can stay as long as you like."

Tears leak out of Kit's eyes. "Are you sure I won't be interfering?" Kit turns away from Lily. "Do they know my story?"

"They only know that you were traumatized like me. And I told them that you didn't have any family support. They want you to come. It'll be fun. I'll teach you to ride. We can hike. And the food is wonderful." Lily bounces up and down on the bed. "What do you say?"

Kit gets off the bed and wanders around the room. "Well, I have some plans, but yes! I would love to meet your family and have some relaxation."

Lily claps her hands. "Great. It's settled. Mom and I will come and pick you up on your birthday. And we'll have a party for you at the ranch!"

Kit can't help crying. "You're too kind. To have a family celebration for me...I don't know what to say."

"You don't have to say anything. But remember, I told you that I have unusual parents."

Kit thinks for a moment and then says, "Oh, that's right, some kind of spiritual gifts."

Lily laughs. "Yeah, Mom and her ghosts, and Dad reading your mind. It'll be interesting. Oh, and my brother, John, he talks with animals."

"Doesn't everyone talk to their animals?"

"Yes, but the animals talk back to him, and he apparently understands them." Lily smiles.

"Wow, this'll be an interesting adventure." Kit wiggles in excitement. Then she notices that Lily has gotten very still.

Tears stream down Lily's face. Lily sees that Kit is moving closer to her. "Sorry. I'm happy about going home, but I'm also scared and ashamed."

Kit holds Lily's hand. "What do you mean?"

"I'm not scared that Adam will get to me—well, a bit—but Mom and Dad are going to have a lot of security to keep us safe. But I'm scared of rebuilding my life. I can't believe what I let happen to me. And I'm so ashamed. I missed so much. And I missed Adam and probably encouraged him. What kind of person am I?"

"You have nothing to be ashamed of. You were a victim. You were lonely in your isolation. You need to—"

Lily cuts her off, shouting, "Forgive myself! I know. I've been working on it. I say it and often feel the forgiveness. But I have trepidation about leaving here. Don't get me wrong—I'm ready. Just not sure what lies ahead." She tries to smile at Kit.

"What lies ahead—that's the adventure." Kit playfully slaps Lily on her leg. "And that's what we're going to do—laugh, play, and have adventures. Now save some adventures for me for when I get there."

"You bet I will. Well, tomorrow is a big day of therapies. And the next day is a hike in the mountains." Lily looks at Kit. "Are you going on the hike?"

"I sure am. That'll be fun. I'll see you in the daylight. In fact, I'd better be going now. I don't want to get into trouble and not be able to go on the hike." Kit slides off the bed and holds out her arms, palms up.

Lily places her arms on top of Kit's arms and they squeeze, and she says, "Sweeter dreams always."

Kit laughs. "I like that—sweeter dreams always to you too." She releases Lily's arms and tiptoes to the door, opens it, and closes it behind her.

Lily snuggles down into her covers and drifts off to sleep.

HRC DAY SIXTEEN

Lily sits upon Sammy, the bay gelding she has always chosen to ride. Riding is her therapy to get away from the ranch and just think. She doesn't care where they go. She lets Sammy decide. She isn't interested in training or directing. She is a passenger, which is why she has chosen Sammy. He knows the routine and does his job. The sun is warm on Lily's back. Sometimes she just closes her eyes and moves with the gait of her horse.

Suddenly, there's a flash of light. Sammy spooks and bolts, throwing Lily into a pile of dry pine needles. Startled, Lily assesses if she has any injuries. She finds she's only bruised and sore. When she gets up, she sees that Sammy is on his way back to the ranch.

Lily looks around to see what spooked him. She sees something shiny in the woods. She approaches and sees the silver chrome of a motorcycle. She freezes, her heart speeds up, and her breath catches, just as he steps out from behind a tree. He smiles, and his lips move, but she can't hear a sound except her scream.

Lily sits bolt upright in bed, wide awake now. "Not again!" she says out loud. "Another nightmare." She had hoped they were gone but knew that was wishful thinking. Her heart is racing, her skin is damp, and she's taking in short, rapid gulps of air. She leans back on her pillows. Taking her right index finger, she taps her forehead as she tries to slow her breathing. After a few minutes, her heart rate slows, and her breathing becomes regular and even. Lily takes in a slow, cleansing breath and lets it out slowly. She smiles to herself and says out loud, "I can do this. I'm ready."

Lily stretches, gets up, and makes her bed. She dances to the bathroom on tiptoes. After a shower, she dresses and heads to breakfast and her day of therapies. This is her last day. She's anxious to see what Soma thinks of her workbook answers.

As Lily starts to knock on Soma's door, it opens, and Soma takes her into a warm embrace.

"Happy graduation day!" Soma exclaims. Looking at Lily clutching the workbook to her chest, she says, "Don't look so worried. Deep down inside, you know you're ready."

Soma smiles as she backs up, allowing Lily to enter the room and sit on the soft sky-blue chair that faces Soma's high-backed pine rocker. Lily hands Soma the workbook, and Soma puts on her reading glasses. Lily sits staring at her as she reads through the responses. After Soma is finished, she puts down the book and lets her glasses hang from the colored beads around her neck. She takes in an easy breath and lets it out with a smile.

"Fine answers. How did you feel when you were writing them?"

Lily pauses and looks around the room at Soma's beautiful pictures of scenic places she has traveled. "I was actually excited. I'm ready to really live my life again."

"What helps you be ready?"

"I've learned tools to assist me. I'll find a therapist to use for support. I'll work on connecting with my family; I know they'll be supportive."

Soma leans forward toward Lily. "Any concerns?"

Lily starts to cry, and Soma hands her the tissue box. After a shuddering intake of air, Lily says, "I know Adam is sick. But I hope he won't bother me or my family and friends. My family has security in place to keep us safe at the ranch, but eventually, I'll have to leave. I know I'm stronger, and I won't tolerate his behavior. I won't let him isolate me ever again. I want to live my life freely. So I guess I'm afraid of the unknown. But I have support and tools to assist me. One step at a time, right?" She smiles at Soma through her tears. "And I thank you, Soma, for all your help and support."

"It's been my pleasure working with you. And you can call me anytime, especially until you secure a therapist for yourself."

Lily's next therapy is art. She is finishing her painting, which is supposed to be a mountain scene she started a week ago. The painting has morphed from realism to abstract. Lily finds she is having fun, even though she doesn't know what she's doing. There's a loud crash from behind her. It makes her jump, and she almost falls onto her easel. Then there's a scream. "I can't paint with these watercolors! I need my oils!"

Lily hears the art therapist explain that the supplies didn't include oils due to the fumes. The unhappy artist throws her canvas down and runs from the room. Lily takes in a deep breath and lets it out. *Seeing the troubles of others makes me realize I'm not the only one.*

Lily is thinking she will take a yoga class when she's approached by the program director, Elaine Hill. Elaine says, "Lily, I understand you're a talented ballerina. Would you mind giving us a demonstration?"

Lily's face flushes, and her heart beats rapidly in her chest. "I don't perform anymore, and I haven't been dancing regularly for almost three weeks." Lily takes in a shuddering, excited breath. "But I would love to do a demonstration. How about after lunch, so I can look at what music I have?"

"That would be great. Shall we clear the room that has the wood flooring for about 1:30?"

Lily smiles broadly. "Yes, that'll be great."

Lily goes through the yoga moves, but she has trouble concentrating or keeping her mind at peace because she is thinking of the dance demonstration. She realizes she's nervous and excited. It's a feeling she hasn't had in a long time. She thinks about the energy she expended on hiding, worrying, and waiting for his next move—she doesn't feel that now. She feels the old energy of excitement and anticipation before a performance.

After class, Lily gets a plate of greens and fruit and takes it back to her room. She wants to try out some music and decide what she wants to use. Then she will decide on which dance she will perform. She has her ballet shoes, but her pointe shoes are back at her studio. *I shouldn't be up on pointe anyway. It's been a few weeks and I don't need an injury before the hike and my graduation. But soon, I'll be up on toes. I know it.* Lily smiles to herself.

Lily looks through her CDs. She pulls out Tchaikovsky's "June: Barcarolle" from *The Seasons* and puts it in her CD player. She has put on a long pink tank top, black capris tights, and her pink ballet shoes. She sits on the floor of her room with her eyes shut and listens to the music as she stretches and warms her muscles. She can't help smiling to herself.

Lily starts the music again and dances around her room. She becomes lost in the music as she dips, twirls, and sways, kicking out her legs with arms outstretched. Her body does not betray her. She thinks of her young student dancers and how they begged her to dance for them. She feels electrical currents flowing through her as she moves. And near the end of the piece, she does a grand jeté, where she leaps into the air doing a split and then softly lands on the front foot and then the back foot. She knows she's ready. And she knows she's not only thinking about the performance, but getting back to her life.

With her CD and player in hand, Lily enters the main room. All the chairs and tables have been removed. The outside doors are open, and the staff and residents, including some she hasn't seen before, are lined up around the walls and in the doorways. Anticipation and excitement fuel her. She finds an outlet for her CD player and puts in the CD.

Elaine steps forward and addresses the crowd. "One of our fellow residents is a retired prima ballerina. She has agreed to give us a demonstration. I present Lily Johnson."

Lily steps to the center of the room and looks at all the faces. "Thank you for giving me this opportunity to do what I love most—dance. I usually dance up on my toes with pointe shoes, but I haven't done that in a few weeks, and my shoes are back at my studio, where I teach young ballerinas. So I will be dancing in my ballet shoes, as you see." Lily points to her feet. "I will dance to Tchaikovsky's "June: Barcarolle" from *The Seasons*." She nods at Elaine, who starts the music.

Lily gets into the position of *croisé devant*, which is left arm up to the ceiling, right arm out and pointing down to her side, right leg out front with toe pointed, and left leg back with turnout away from body. The music begins, and Lily steps onto her right leg and begins to dance. She uses the whole floor to travel around with spins, jumps, glides, and turns. The music has a hold of her, and she is moving with every beat. She ends with a grand jeté as everyone claps, and Lily gives a low curtsy. Lily is smiling from the inside out.

Lily takes a lavender bubble bath that evening, which almost puts her to sleep. She climbs into bed, pulls her covers to her chin, and with a slow sigh falls asleep. She's dancing in the dark, except for a warm spotlight that follows her every move. She sways like the branches of a willow tree. She's laughing on the inside. Then she hears laughing. Is it the audience laughing with her? She hears a knock that is out of place. The knock can be heard over the orchestra. She wonders why anyone would do that.

Then she hears a voice. "Lily, you OK?"

Lily opens her eyes and is startled to see Kit standing next to her bed. "Oh, hi, Kit, you startled me."

"I startled you. You were laughing out loud. I didn't know what was going on in here. Were you dreaming?"

"Yes, I was. It was an amazing lovely dream." Lily closes her eyes as she remembers.

"Wow. Wish I could have dreams like that." Kit plops onto the end of Lily's bed.

Lily smiles at Kit. "You will one day. It takes you by surprise."

"I can't wait. What were you dreaming about?"

"I was dancing on stage. Oh, I had a chance to do a performance for the residents yesterday. It was so much fun. That's probably why I dreamed about it. I've missed it." Lily smiles to herself.

"Would you dance for me sometime?" Kit puts her hands together as if in prayer.

"Of course. I'll show you a bit now if you like." Lily slides off the bed. She puts on her ballet shoes and moves into the center of the floor, facing Kit. "I won't turn on music, so we won't wake anyone, but I'll hum. I'll start with some stretching positions."

Lily starts humming Tchaikovsky's "Waltz of the Snow Queen." After stretching, she's dancing her rendition as a solo dancer. She sways, twirls, and travels around the room, with her nightgown flowing around her. She ends with the grand jeté.

Kit claps as Lily does a low curtsy.

"You're very kind. Do you see why I love it so?" Lily asks.

"Yes. I don't think I really ever saw any ballet. You're so beautiful when you dance. You have to keep that up."

"Yes, I realize that I must." Lily comes over to the bed and climbs under her covers after taking off her ballet shoes. "You know there's the hike tomorrow. Are you still going?"

"Yes, I am. There are a few of us from my ward that are being allowed to go. What fun—we'll see each other outside this place in the daylight." Kit reaches in her pocket and pulls out a piece of paper. "I wrote another poem and made a copy for you. It's called 'Forgiveness.'"

Tired of anger,
Fear exhausting
Not perfect.

Mistake maker,
But stronger than I know.
Can't miss a moment,
Have lost too much.

Forgive the past,
Release the pain.
Possibilities breathe in,
Breathe out resolve.

Don't need to forgive you,
Forgave myself,
For being the people pleaser
At my expense.

Did the work,
Fought back.
Now I'm free.

Lily sighs. "That's beautiful, and exactly how I feel."

Kit hands Lily a copy. "I wrote it for both of us. We've come so far together." Kit smiles at Lily.

"Yes, together!" Lily smiles and holds out her arms, palms up. Kit places her arms over Lily's, and they both squeeze and release. "Better dreams to you, my dear friend."

Kit moves toward the door. "Better dreams to you too." She leaves quietly.

HRC DAY SEVENTEEN

Lily wakes to another sunny day. She does some of her stretches before getting out of bed. This is her last day; she will travel to the ranch tomorrow. Excitement and anxiety bubble up within her. She takes in a slow, deep breath and lets it out. Lily looks through the blinds and sees several yellow buses parked outside the courtyard fence. *Those are for the hike. I can't believe I can do something outside, during the day, with Kit.*

She dances off to the bathroom to wash up, apply sunscreen, and get dressed. Lily puts on jeans, a short-sleeved T-shirt, socks, and tennis shoes. She pulls her red curls back into a ponytail and puts on a visor hat. She places her sunglasses on top of her head for later. She's leaving her room when she realizes she should have layers. It's early April, and even though the weather is projected to be in the upper fifties and low sixties, the weather can change and become cold. She ties a lined rain jacket and sweatshirt around her waist and then walks out to the dining room for breakfast.

As she looks around, she notices everyone else dressed in similar clothes. The room has been set back up with buffet tables and dining tables and chairs. It's a startling change from yesterday's stage where she had danced. She smiles at the memory.

Lily grabs some oatmeal, some peaches, and a cup of coffee. She sits down next to another resident, who looks up as she sits and then stares at his breakfast.

"Hi there, my name is Lily."

The young man looks up at her again and then looks away. He takes a bite of cereal and crunches.

Lily tries again. "Are you excited about the hike?"

He says nothing, but shrugs his shoulders and continues to crunch on his cereal.

Lily realizes that in the weeks she has been at HRC, she hasn't interacted very much with anyone—actually, no one except her therapists and of course Kit. It isn't surprising that this young man has nothing to say to her.

Lily eats her breakfast in silence as she glances out the window at the beautiful day. There's a feeling inside her that she hasn't felt in a while. She smiles to herself—it's happiness.

At 9:00 a.m., everyone boards the buses, and they head southwest toward Golden Gate Canyon State Park. The distant mountains are still covered in snow, but the Canyon is dry, and there are a few signs of spring. As the bus enters the park, Lily pushes down her window. She gets a whiff of pine from the many pine trees. She closes her eyes and breathes it in—it reminds her of the woods around her family's ranch. She sits back and smiles. *I'm waking up.*

The buses pull up to the visitor center, and everyone gets out and files into the log cabin that houses the center. There are maps, bathrooms, and walls of pictures of what is available to see. Lily looks around for Kit and is disappointed not to see her. She wonders if she is still on the bus, in the bathroom, or has wandered off to look around. Surely she is here somewhere.

After ten minutes they are asked to reboard the buses. The buses travel down the road to the Horseshoe Trailhead. After parking and exiting the bus, everyone gathers.

"Welcome, everyone, to Golden Gate Canyon State Park. In case you don't know me, I'm Elaine Hill, the program director at HRC. We're at the Horseshoe Trailhead. There will be three guided tours, with one staff member for each group."

Elaine scans the group. "Your guide will be wearing bear bells."

"Bear bells?" someone cries.

Elaine smiles. "Yes, we don't want the bears to be surprised by us. That can be very dangerous. It will also keep you aware of where your guide is at all times. One of the hikes is up the 1.8-mile trail, and then we have a half-mile hike. If you aren't interested in hiking, there's a walk around the campground. There are picnic tables off to the side of the trail. You'll find box lunches that you can take with you or have when you get back. An outhouse is available south of the picnic tables." She pauses and looks around at everyone. "Any questions?"

"Are there really bears? Aren't they hibernating?"

"Good questions," answers Elaine. "It's early for bears to be out, but due to the warm weather, there have been some sightings of black bears." Elaine looks around the group again. "Well, if you don't have any more questions, we will start out. Jeremy, the art therapist, will be the guide for the 1.8-mile hike. Jeremy, would you raise your hand?"

Jeremy raises his hand. Lily sees Jeremy is wearing jeans, a thermal long-sleeved shirt, and an orange reflective jacket. He jingles the bells that hang at his waist. His smile is shaded by the big-brimmed hat he wears.

"And Anna, one of your physical therapists, will guide the half-mile hike."

Anna raises her hand. She has on a cowboy hat, a down vest over a flannel shirt, jeans, and cowboy boots with thick treads. She smiles as she jingles the bells that hang from the belt at her waist.

Elaine jingles the bells that hang at her waist. "I'll be with the group that walks closer to the trailhead."

Lily looks around and spots Kit at the back of the gathering. Kit puts up her hands and stretches them out wide, indicating that she wants to do the long hike. Lily nods and mouths that she will get two lunch boxes for them. Kit nods agreement.

The three groups disband, and Lily picks up two lunch boxes. She follows the line of about ten going up the trail. Kit catches up with her, and the two smile as they bump shoulders. Lily notices that Kit has a bandana tied around her head. She wears baggy jeans with tube socks and boots, a tie-dyed T-shirt, an extra-large flannel shirt, and a black biker jacket tied around her waist.

"Nice outfit." Lily laughs.

"Thanks, it's one of my favorites. It drove my parents crazy." Kit shrugs and grins. Then she starts singing "Walk like an Egyptian" as she walks with one arm above her head and one behind her, low, in an imitation of an Egyptian painting.

Lily laughs so hard that it fuels Kit to dance all the more. The two friends are skipping and dancing, and the commotion causes some of the hikers ahead of them to stop and stare. But Lily and Kit don't care. They're having too much fun.

As the group continues up the trail, they stop to hear about wildlife and vegetation. They can see beautiful mountain ranges in the distance. A couple of deer graze just off the trail. They walk through groves of aspen trees that are just budding. The smell of pine surrounds them, and a sweet dampness travels in the air from deep in the shadows of the woods, where moisture still lingers.

Lily puts on her sweatshirt. The shade of the trees has caused the temperature to be cooler.

At the end of the trail, they reach a clearing and a lookout. They can see the expansive Continental Divide. Everyone takes a seat on logs or rocks to have their lunches. Lily and Kit sit off to the side so they can talk. The sun warms them as they eat their lunch of turkey-and-cheese sandwiches, a chocolate chip cookie, an apple, and a bottle of water.

Lily takes out her cookie and turns to Kit. "I'm really full. Would you like my cookie?"

Kit grabs the cookie. "I'll eat it before you change your mind. I have a terrible sweet tooth."

Lily laughs. "Then you'll love my mom's cookies. She makes snicker-doodles and puts whatever you like in them—chocolate chips, M&M's, raisins, whatever."

"Chocolate for me!" Kit smiles as she licks the chocolate off her fingers.

After lunch, there is a jingle of bear bells. The guide, Jeremy, steps forward. "How's everyone feeling?" Jeremy looks around and sees shoulders shrug. "Well, are your stomachs full?"

There is a group response of "Yes!"

"Did you get some exercise?"

"Yes!"

"Do you have the best guide ever?" Jeremy smiles and puts his arms up in the air.

"Yes!" A few people giggle.

"Well, let's head back. After we board the buses, we're going to drive up to Panorama Point and get out and enjoy the views. After that, we'll drive back to HRC. There will be a barbecue cookout in the various dining rooms."

The 1.8-mile group saunters back down the trail, with Jeremy in the lead. Kit and Lily bring up the rear.

"Do you know the song "Wind beneath My Wings"? It was sung by Bette Midler," Kit asks.

"Yeah, from the movie *Beaches*. So sad!"

Lily starts singing, and then Kit joins in. "It must have been cold there in my shadow."

Kit puts her arms around herself and shakes with laughter, and Lily laughs too. They sing together. "To never have sunlight on your face."

Kit covers her face as Lily roars with laughter.

Jeremy stops and turns around. "Lily, are you all right?"

The girls stop singing. Lily, embarrassed, says, "Sorry, just singing." She shrugs her shoulders.

"OK, then. Let's continue." Jeremy turns back around and heads for the trailhead.

Kit shrugs. "Serious crowd."

Lily smiles and tickles Kit. "I guess we need to be serious about the hike. We can sing all we want at the ranch."

"I can't wait." Kit bumps Lily behind her knees and takes off ahead, laughing.

When they return to the rest of the groups, they board their buses. Lily waves to Kit, and Kit waves back as she disappears onto her bus. They have agreed to meet again tonight, since it is Lily's last night.

Lily settles into her seat as the bus heads to the panoramic view. She didn't know how exhausted she was until she sat down. *I'm in awful shape— something else to work on at the ranch.* She smiles to herself.

After traveling through the park, the buses park at the lookout point. Almost everyone gets off the buses to look at the snowcapped mountain ranges in the distance. The air is cooler away from the trees and at a higher elevation. Lily puts on her jacket as others do as well. Lily doesn't see Kit—she must have stayed on her bus. Elaine passes out bottles of water as Jeremy points out the different mountain peaks. A medical helicopter can be seen in the distance.

Jeremy points at the helicopter. "The medical helicopter might be re- turning home after a mountain rescue."

One of the residents shouts, "Glad we didn't need a helicopter!"

"Me too." Jeremy sighs.

Lily remembers stories her mom told of when she was a flight nurse and traveled on the helicopter. Lily is amazed at some of the things her mom did. She laughs to herself. *Especially the ghost stuff.*

Soon it's time to get back on the bus and head back to HRC. Lily dozes in the warmth of the sun coming through the window. Once at HRC, she gets a plate of food from the dining room and heads to her room. She's tired. She puts her plate on the table and sits down. The dinner includes barbecue ribs, potato salad, and apple slices. It smells good, but the taste can't compare to her dad's barbecue. She knows she will have to tell him how much she missed his cooking.

After eating, and disposing of her plate in the dining hall, Lily takes a long, hot shower. She lets the water run down her back as she thinks of all she has experienced here at HRC. She smiles when she thinks of Soma and Kit. They both have helped her so much. She lets tension and anxiety wash down the drain. After turning off the water and toweling dry, she puts on her pink nightgown and climbs into bed. Lily picks up the book she borrowed and flips through the pages, deciding not to finish it. She makes a list of things to do in the morning before leaving—returning the library book is on the list.

Lily turns off her light and easily slips into sleep. She is galloping along on Sammy when there is a banging noise she doesn't recognize. Sammy doesn't seem to hear it. Then there's a voice. She recognizes it, but doesn't see anyone.

She calls out, "Who's there?"

"It's me, silly." Kit enters the room as Lily opens her eyes.

"Oh, sorry, I was dreaming and heard your knock in my dream. So when I responded, it was in my sleep."

"Well, at least it wasn't a nightmare. Progress, yes?"

Lily smiles as Kit approaches. "Yes, progress."

"I can't believe you'll be gone tomorrow. Lucky you!"

"Soon it will be you too."

Kit jumps on the end of the bed. "I have something for you."

Lily sits up. "What is it?"

Kit reaches into her nightgown pocket and pulls out two strings of beads. She holds them out to Lily. "I made these. They're amethyst and hematite beads. Good for protection and healing. I made one for each of us."

Lily takes the beads in her hand and turns them over as she examines them. "It's beautiful." Lily puts the bracelet on her wrist. It is strung with elastic twine. "Kit, I love it. How sweet of you. I'll wear it home."

Kit smiles. "I'm so glad you like it. I'll wear mine as well." Kit slips on the bracelet and puts out her arms to Lily.

Lily places her arms on top of Kit's, and they both squeeze. Then Lily pulls Kit toward her and gives her a hug. "Thanks for all you did for me. I can't wait to see you in two weeks."

Kit feels tears spill from her eyes. "I'll miss you till I see you again."

Lily releases Kit, and Kit climbs off the bed and heads toward the door. She turns and says, "Sweetest dreams to you, my friend."

"Sweetest dreams to you too, my friend. See you soon."

Kit quietly opens the door and closes it behind her.

Lily sighs as she watches her friend leave.

HRC DAY EIGHTEEN—HOME

Lily wakes to darkness. She looks at her bedside clock and sees that it's 5:30 a.m. She's excited to get up and pack for her trip home. She stretches and climbs out of bed. With a turn, her eyes scan the bed that comforted her in the safe haven of her room. Taking in a slow, deep breath and letting it out, she says out loud, "I'm grateful for my time here."

After making her bed and washing her face, she gets dressed in black jeans and a long-sleeved black-and-white striped T-shirt. Lily gets her suitcase out from the closet—her few items won't take long to pack. She empties the drawers that hold her clothes and places her clothes in the suitcase. Next, she packs her shoes, toiletries, and the few books that her mom had brought her. After closing and latching the suitcase, she places it by the door. Scanning the room, she spots the library book. Lily grabs it and heads out to the library and then to breakfast.

After turning the book in to the library, Lily gets in the buffet line. She takes a plate and loads it with a sunny-side up egg, bacon, and piece of cantaloupe. She sits at a small table near the window to the courtyard. The sun's warmth reaches through the window and bathes her. She closes her eyes and tips her head back—she can see the golden light through her closed eyelids. In the distance she hears the familiar sound of Dansko shoes and cowboy boots clicking across the floor, coming closer. She opens her eyes to see her mom and dad approaching, full of smiles.

Lily gets up from the table so fast that it unsettles her chair and sends it tumbling to the floor. She doesn't notice as she flings herself into the waiting arms of her parents.

"We're so excited that we had to come early," Lilith says.

"The family is waiting for you," Roy adds.

"I'm not that hungry. Let's go now."

"No, I'll sit with you while you finish. Your dad can take your things to the truck." Lilith beams as she holds her daughter tight.

"OK." Lily sits down across from her mom and picks at her food.

"Now eat. You'll get hungry on the drive. It takes about forty-five minutes."

Lily smiles. "It's so nice to be mothered." Then Lily begins to cry.

"What is it, baby?" Lilith asks as she scoots her chair next to Lily.

Lily's wet eyes meet her mom's. "I was almost a mother, but I lost my baby."

Lilith hugs her daughter. "I had no idea. I'm so sorry. You'll be a wonderful mother someday."

"I hope so. We have a lot to share with each other." Lily leans into her mom.

After breakfast, Lily and her mom head to the front desk to check out. Lily sees Soma waiting for her behind the desk.

"Mom, I want you to meet Soma. She's the fabulous therapist who helped me during my stay here at HRC."

Lilith approaches Soma and takes her hand in both of hers. "Nice to finely meet you. I'm so grateful for all you did for my daughter."

"It was my complete pleasure." Soma smiles at Lilith.

She releases Lilith's hands and steps toward Lily. Taking her into a hug, Soma says quietly in her ear, "I'm so proud of you. You're strong, and you'll do just fine."

Lily smiles and hugs Soma back. "Thanks for everything."

Lily and Lilith walk out of the doors hand in hand. Once outside, Lily sees her dad standing near the passenger door of his truck. It is bright red and shiny—a Dodge Ram with the ram symbol on the hood.

"Nice truck, Dad."

"It's a couple of years old. I washed and waxed it special for your homecoming." Roy smiles as he strokes his truck.

Lily smiles and gives her dad a kiss on the cheek. She climbs into the back as her dad holds open the door. Lily is amazed that she is once again seated behind her parents as they drive toward the ranch.

After getting off the freeway, the truck turns onto familiar roads, and then Lily sees the stone entrance with the wired sign that says "Welcome to Always Summer Ranch." She rolls down her window and smells the pine trees. As they approach the stone entrance, there is a hut and a uniformed guard, who steps out to greet them.

"Hi, Mr. and Mrs. Johnson. Welcome back. I see you have a visitor." The guard peeks in the car.

"This is our daughter, Lily," Lilith says.

The guard smiles. "Hi, Lily, my name is Officer Marcus Lambert. It's very nice to meet you. I want you to know we are here twenty-four hours a day patrolling the property and checking all visitors coming and going. Please let me know if there's anything else you need or if you have any concerns."

Lily is surprised, even though her mom had told her that there would be security at the ranch. She puts on her best smile. "It's nice to meet you too, Officer Lambert. Thank you."

The officer steps away from the truck, and Roy continues driving toward their house. As they approach, Lily sees a banner flapping in the wind. She sits forward to read it. "Welcome Home, Lily" is printed in pink and blue letters. She smiles and squeezes her mom's and dad's shoulders.

"Thanks so much."

Lilith looks over at Roy and says, "There's more." Lily takes in a quick breath, which Lilith notices. Lilith reaches back and touches her daughter's hand. "Don't worry. We just want you to know how glad we are to have you home. It's just family. You can always go rest in your room."

Lily lets out a breath that she didn't know she was holding. "Thanks, I'm just nervous. I've been so isolated."

"I know, honey. Just take it slow. And let me know when I do too much. I can take it." Lilith smiles.

A dog comes running out from around the house, barking, just as Lilith opens her door. Lily pauses, and Lilith says, "Oh, Sky, we're home. You good girl, meet Lily. Lily, this is Sky, our border collie." Lilith rubs the fur around Sky's ears.

Lily steps down from the truck, and Sky runs up, sniffing her up and down. Lily puts out her hand, and Sky licks it. She strokes the soft black and white fur. Sky leans into her leg.

Lilith laughs. "She's taken to you. She's a great guard dog, as you witnessed. And she loves to help herd the horses back in and move the cattle from pasture to pasture. When she's not working or playing, she loves to curl up with us."

Roy gets out Lily's suitcase, and they climb the wooden steps into the log home that Lily shared in her childhood. Sky bounds ahead of them. Once inside, Lily can smell the barbecue.

"We're home," Lilith announces.

Grandma comes from the kitchen with an apron tied around her middle. She has tears in her eyes as she grabs Lily in a hug. "Honey, I've missed you so much. So glad you're home."

Lily hears heavy steps on the stairs. She looks up to see her cousins, Steven and Clark. She notices that they've gotten older and more mature looking. She smiles to herself—she has too. They circle her in a group hug. "Welcome home, Lil."

Lily looks around at all the love. It's overwhelming and also so nice. Then there's a clambering up the front steps, and the front door flies open.

"Sorry, I'm late. I had a late case...Oh my gosh, is that you, big sis?" John runs at her and picks her up off her feet in a swinging hug. He sets her down gently and looks down into her face. "You're gorgeous!"

"Well, thanks, little brother. You aren't so bad yourself." Lily puts her arm around her brother as they all walk into the living room to sit down.

Lily looks around the room at her beautiful family. "Now, what has everyone been doing? Catch me up. Grandma?"

Grandma smiles and clasps her hands in her lap. "Well, let's see. I still live in one of the cabins on Pine Lane. When we have guests at the ranch,

I head the bridge games and bingo. I love to help with the cooking. I still walk around the ranch, but love driving the carts. I think my life is about the same as when you went off to Julliard." Grandma covers her mouth and laughs.

Lily laughs and then turns to Steven. "What have you been up to?"

Steven takes out his wallet and slides out a few pictures. "I still run the ranch with Clark. You remember my wife, Missy, and our three boys, Mac, Ben, and Sam. Mac is eighteen now, and the twins are sixteen. Missy still teaches school in town at the boys' high school. She couldn't be here because the boys had swim practice."

"I bet your life is busy. I'm so happy for you." Lily smiles at Steven and then turns to Clark.

Clark scratches his head. "Well, here's a picture of my wife, Ali, and our daughter, An, who is fifteen now. She's taking ballet and heard about your dancing. She's excited to be able to talk to you. She and Ali will be back from shopping this afternoon."

Lily smiles at Clark. "I'll be happy to talk with her."

Lily looks over at her brother. "Tell me, tell me."

John sighs. "Well, I can't decide which lady to settle down with. There are so many knocking on my door."

Lilith and Roy laugh.

"My veterinary practice is busy," he continues. "I was glad when your old friend Charles joined me. When I was taking care of all the large animals in the area, it didn't give me much time for anything else. So maybe now, you never know."

Lilith loudly clears her throat.

"OK, Mom." John glares at his mom as he blushes and then smiles. "I'm seeing a nice lady named Amy. It's new. We'll see."

Lily smiles at her brother and then yawns. "Sorry, I think I'll go get settled into my room before lunch, if that's OK?"

Lilith jumps up. "Of course, you must be tired. Why don't you rest, and I'll let you know when we're going to eat? Your dad put your suitcase in your old room."

Lily gets up and looks around at her family. "Thanks for sharing. I know we'll have more time to catch up later." She climbs the stairs to her old bedroom. Sky follows and then runs ahead, jumping up on the bed.

Lily laughs. "You sure make yourself at home."

As she enters her room, she's surprised and happy to see that it hasn't been changed. It still contains the white four-poster bed, desk, and vanity with matching chairs. The walls are still covered in pink-and-blue ballerina wallpaper. Sky is curled up on the pink-and-white laced pillows that match the comforter. Lily closes the door and climbs onto her old bed next to Sky. She strokes the soft fur as Sky nestles next to her. Looking around the room, she realizes that it's smaller than she remembers. She stares at the dancing ballerinas until she drifts off to sleep.

In a haze of sleep, Lily can hear a knocking on her door and someone calling out her name. She is about to call out to Kit as she wakes and realizes that she is in her childhood room. It's her mom at the door.

"Come in," Lily says as she sits up, rubbing her eyes.

Lilith peeks in the room. "Did you get some rest?"

"Yes, it feels really good. I didn't realize I was so tired."

Lilith comes in and sits on Lily's bed. "I figured that Sky would be with you. She loves taking naps. You guys slept three hours. "

Lily reaches over and rubs Sky's ears. "I forgot how comforting animals can be. I had a cat for a long time. Her name was China. We were buddies."

"I bet you and Sky will become buddies as well. I hope having the family crowd over isn't too much for you. They just all missed you so much and wanted to see that you were all right."

"I must admit, it's a bit overwhelming. I've been isolated, except for my students and of course the therapy classes. I may have to just start socializing in small increments." Lily smiles at her mom. "Sorry, I don't mean to be a bother."

Lilith takes Lily into her arms. "You're never a bother. You take your time. Just let me know what you need and how I can help. I also want to understand what you went through." Lilith wipes the tears that leak out of her eyes. "I've missed you so much."

Lily cries into her mom's shoulder. "Me too, Mom."

Lilith gives Lily a big hug and releases her. She pats Lily's knee and Sky's head. "Just come down when you're ready. We'll have an early dinner. After, you can take a walk with Sky or just come back up and go to bed." Lilith turns to leave the room.

"Thanks, Mom."

Lily climbs off her bed and goes into the bathroom to wash her face. After drying her face, Lily looks in the mirror. It's the mirror she last looked in when she had brought Adam to meet her parents. She sees herself looking so different. Her face is pale, and her cheekbones are prominent.

Sky whines from the bedroom. "Do you need to go out, girl?" Sky barks. "You understand, don't you?" Sky barks again. "Well, let's go outside and then have some of that delicious dinner I smell. That will help put some weight on me."

Lily opens her door, and Sky races down the stairs and out the open front door. Lily climbs down the stairs and sees her family sitting at the table as her mom and grandma bring in platters of food. She takes a seat between her brother and her dad around the oval oak table of her childhood. After everyone is seated, they clasp hands. Lily grabs her brother's and dad's hands.

"Most merciful Father, we thank you for bringing our Lily back home to us, for the love we share, and for all our bountiful blessings. Bless this food to the nourishment of our bodies and us to thy service. In the name of the Father, the Son, and the Holy Spirit. Amen," Roy says.

"Amen," everyone says out loud.

Lily smiles to herself as she listens to the chatter, the clanging of utensils, and the warm laughter. She's glad to be home. It has been too long, and she has missed them so much. There's no pressure for her to share her story. Everyone just enjoys the food and laughs at all the old stories of Lily and John growing up. They eat heartily on barbecue ribs, corn, salad, and buttery rolls. There is apple cobbler for dessert with a scoop of homemade vanilla bean ice cream. What a wonderful feast. Sky sneaks in while they are eating and lies on the floor between Roy and Lily. Roy reaches down and gives her some gristle from his plate and lets her lick his fingers. Lily looks over, and her dad puts his finger to his lips as Lily laughs.

"Roy, you better not be feeding the dog at the table!" Lilith laughs as everyone joins in.

Roy puts his clean hands in the air. "Who, me?"

Sky joins in the laughter with a bark and twirls around.

The cousins insist on doing the dishes with Roy, so Lilith, Grandma, John, Lily, and Sky go out on the wraparound porch and sit in the many rocking chairs.

Lily sits next to her brother. "I just realized that Clark's and Steven's families didn't join us."

Lilith hides a yawn. "They had dinner together at Clark and Ali's house. They thought having the kids over might be a bit much for you on your first night. You'll see them soon."

Lily yawns. "Sorry, I didn't realize their absence until now. That was very thoughtful of them. I look forward to seeing them too."

The sound of horse hooves are heard on the drive, and a uniformed officer rides up to the porch. He takes off his hat. "Evening, everyone. Just doing my rounds. Most everyone is tucked in for the night."

Lilith stands. "Thank you, Officer Dan. I want you to meet my daughter, Lily." She turns to Lily. "Lily, this is Officer Dan. He and Officer Will patrol the ranch at night. Then we have Officers Simon and Luke who do the day shift. Officers Marcus Lambert and Jessie Townes cover the front gate."

Lily waves. "Nice to meet you, Officer Dan."

"Nice to meet you, Lily. Well, I'm off. Have a good night, everyone." He turns his horse down the road and trots off.

"Do they use their own horses, or are those ranch horses?" Lily asks.

Lilith smiles. "Good question. They could bring their own, but we have plenty. They ride the ones that we use for hunting."

Lily yawns again. "I think I might need to get to bed. Thanks for the wonderful dinner."

"Good night, honey." Lilith rises and gives her daughter a hug. "Let me know if you need anything. Oh, and Sky might want to sleep with you, if that's all right. She loves to snuggle."

"I would like that." Lily leans down and kisses her grandma and then hugs her brother.

When Lily enters the house, Sky is close at her heels. Lily looks into the kitchen and sees her dad laughing as he flicks the dish towel at Steven. "Good night, guys. Thanks for dinner."

"Good to see you, Lily," Clark and Steven call out.

Roy sets down the towel and approaches his daughter. Taking her into a hug, he says, "Now, I hope you sleep comfortably. I heard you met Officer Dan. He'll patrol all night. You have nothing to worry about. But just remember that your mom and I are downstairs if you need us." He hugs her tight.

Lily hugs her dad back—it feels so good to be home. She lets out a slow breath as she releases him. "Good night, Dad. Thanks. I love you."

"I love you too, sweet pea."

Lily climbs the stairs to her room, with Sky close behind. She closes the door to her room, and Sky jumps on the bed. Lily goes into the bathroom and turns on the shower. When the room has filled with steam, she takes off her clothes and puts them in the hamper next to the sink. She ducks under the water as she climbs into the shower. The warm water feels comforting as it cascades down her back. She lathers and cleans herself with the lavender bath soap her mom has supplied for her. She relaxes as the water loosens her tight, tired muscles. After turning off the water, she towels dry and puts on her pajamas.

Sky looks up as she enters the bedroom. Lily climbs under the covers next to Sky and pats the soft fur.

"You do like to snuggle. I usually read before falling asleep. Hope I don't disturb you." Lily continues to stroke Sky's fur. "Oh, and I have nightmares and sometimes scream. Hope I don't scare you." Sky licks Lily's face. Lily laughs and snuggles under the covers. She opens her book but only reads a few pages before turning off the light. "Sweet dreams, Sky."

Lily enters her empty studio. She dims the lights and puts on *Swan Lake* by Tchaikovsky. She stretches, does some barre exercises, and then gets up on her toes and dances around the room. Her body sways to the music, but then the mirrors crack. She stops in horror as she sees his reflection, broken apart in the pieces of the mirror. The air is thin, and it's hard to breathe. Lily tries to take in a breath. Her throat is constricted. She tries to scream. Then she is wet. Something wet is touching her face. She opens her eyes with a startle and realizes that Sky is standing over her, licking her face. Sky is whining.

Lily reaches up and pats her. "It's OK, Sky. It was just one of my nightmares. Thank you for rescuing me." Sky lies back down next to Lily. "Now you get to see what I do to calm myself." Lily begins tapping on her forehead. Sky looks on and then snuggles down next to her. Lily taps until she falls asleep.

MOM AND DAD

Lily wakes as the sun shines through the white-laced curtains. The light beams dance across the pink-and-blue ballerinas on the walls. Sky notices Lily's awake and starts licking her.

Lily laughs. "I'm not going to need a bath if you keep this up." She pats Sky and jumps out of bed. "How about I get dressed and we take a walk before breakfast?" Sky yips in agreement.

Lily washes her face, puts her hair back in a ponytail, and then slips on jeans, a sweatshirt, and boots. She grabs a jacket and opens her bedroom door. She can smell coffee brewing. As she climbs down the stairs, she sees her mom and dad talking in the kitchen. They look up when they hear her.

"Good morning! Would you like some coffee?"

"Good morning to you both. Yes, please. Can I take it to go?"

Lilith stands up. "Where are you going?"

Lily laughs. "Sky and I want to get in a walk before breakfast."

Lilith smiles. "You two sure are getting cozy."

Roy hands Lily a cup. "Cream and sugar in a to-go cup, yes?"

"You remembered. Thanks. We'll be back soon." Lily and Sky step out onto the porch.

Lily takes in a deep breath—the air is fresh and smells of pine. She jumps off the steps and takes off at a brisk walk. Sky races ahead and then runs back. She repeats this over and over, only stopping to relieve herself or sniff out something good. Lily heads down the path to the studio. When she gets there, Sky stops and looks expectantly at her. Lily tries the door, but it's locked. She reaches behind the dome light to the right of the door—the extra key is still there. She unlocks the door and then places the key in her pocket. She decides to keep it with her while she is on the ranch.

Lily enters the studio, with Sky close behind. She does not need to turn on the lights because the room is bright as the sun shines through the skylights. The room is just as Lily left it almost ten years ago. She hadn't shown it to Adam when they had their brief visit. She thought that her family might have used the space for something else until her mom told her they still had it. Lily could tell from the smell of lemon pine that her mom had recently cleaned the mirrors and floors. Lily takes off her boots and dances around in her socks as Sky looks on.

Lily becomes breathless as she twirls around. She laughs at herself. Looking over at Sky, she says, "I need to get in shape. Do you want to help me, girl?" Sky yips.

Lily lets herself out of the studio and locks the door. She hears hoof-beats and sees an officer riding up the road.

"Hello, Miss Lily. My name is Officer Simon. How's your walk?"

"Nice to meet you, Officer Simon. Sky and I are having a marvelous walk."

"I think your brother might be down at the stable. I saw his vet truck."

"Thanks, I think I'll go down and see him." Lily and Sky turn toward the stable as the officer trots off down the dirt road.

Lily smiles to herself. She is so thankful that her mom and dad arranged for security at the ranch. It helps her feel safe, and she hasn't felt safe walking outside by herself for over two years. And Sky is helping her too. She has forgotten what joy and comfort a pet brings.

As they near the stable, she sees her brother's truck. She thinks how it would be fun to see her brother in action. Sky runs ahead into the barn, and Lily can hear barking and yipping.

As Lily enters the barn, she sees her brother leaning over, patting Sky. But as he rises and turns toward her, she sees it isn't her brother.

"Hi, Lily. It's been a long time."

"Hi, yourself. Charles, or is it Chip still?" Lily feels her face warm.

"Actually, it's Charlie. I lost the Chip after high school and tried Charles, but it seemed to revert to Charlie. You look wonderful. Glad you're home for a visit. How long will you be here?"

Lily notices his curly red hair is graying at his sideburns. "I think at least a month."

"Well, then, we'll definitely need to get together to catch up, if you like?"

And he still has some freckles on his nose, but very handsome freckles. Then she answers, "That would be nice. I just got here yesterday afternoon, so I need a few days to get settled."

"Totally understandable. I'll give you a call in a few. Sorry, I just need to finish up with this calf."

"What's wrong with the poor thing?"

"Looks like it stepped in a hole. The leg is just sprained, but I want to check and see if it has any cuts. We'll need to keep it out of the fields until it can walk and run again. Don't want a mountain lion to get it."

Lily takes in a sharp breath of air. "I forgot about mountain lions. I've been a city girl too long. I need to be careful walking around here."

Charlie smiles down at her. "You'll probably be fine around the ranch. Sky will let you know. She's a good scout."

Lily's feels her cheeks warm again. "Well, I better head back for breakfast. It was nice seeing you, Charlie. I almost said Chip—that will take some practice."

Charlie laughs. "You can call me whatever you want. See you soon."

Lily turns as she waves so he can't see the blush running up her neck. She wonders what has gotten into her. But it is fun seeing an old friend. So much has happened since she lived on the ranch. She wonders if she can share her past with him. And would he share his past? She shakes her head and speeds up her walk toward the main house. Sky is running laps, as her breed does. Lily remembers reading that border collies have so much energy. Sky probably needs to go out with her dad and do some work today.

As Lily and Sky climb the steps to the house, she can smell bacon. She closes the door behind her and heads into the kitchen. Her mom is cooking bacon, and her dad is frying an omelet.

"Wow, it smells great in here."

Lilith turns around. "Did you have a nice walk?"

Lily smiles. "Yes, Sky runs and runs. I went to the studio—it looks beautiful—and I danced for Sky. She enjoyed it. We met Officer Simon. We walked down to the barn to see John, but it was Charlie instead. That was a surprise." Lily takes in a deep breath and lets it out. "Mom, Dad, does Charlie know what happened to me?"

Lilith turns, sits down next to her daughter, and pulls her into a chair. "Lily, no one but the family knows what happened. Charlie, just like the officers, knows that someone is trying to hurt or scare you and that's why we have security. They don't need to know anything else. You can tell Charlie whatever you feel comfortable telling an old friend. Of course the officers have details about Adam, but no one else does."

Lily lets out a breath she didn't know she was holding. Tears leak out of her eyes as her mom takes her in her arms. Her mom holds her as she cries, and her dad comes and circles the two of them in a hug.

"We won't let anything happen to you, sweet pea," Roy says.

Lily looks from her mom to her dad. "I love you guys."

"We love you too."

Lilith gets up and takes some plates out of the cabinet. "Now, let's sit down and have some breakfast. Then we can talk about what you want to do today."

After filling the plates, Lilith places one in front of Lily, and she and Roy sit down on either side of her. Lily looks from her mom to her dad. She is so glad to be here with them.

"Looks delicious." Then Lily thinks to herself, *Wow, Dad, Mom must have finally taught you how to cook.*

"What are you saying, Jessica Lily…" Roy shouts, and then he sees the grin on Lily's face. "You punked me!"

"I sure did." Lily laughs.

"What's going on?" Lilith asks as she holds a fork, on which she has speared some egg, in midair.

Lily leans in and bumps her dad's shoulder. "I was just checking to see if Dad still had his telepathy gift."

"Lily, shame on you." Lilith laughs while trying to look stern.

The three eat heartily in silence. When they're finished, Lily gets up, clears the dishes, rinses them, and puts them in the dishwasher as her parents look on.

Roy clears his throat. "Lily, when you're ready, I—well, probably your mom too—would like to know more about Adam. It would help us understand the trauma you went through."

Lily sits back down at the table between her parents. "That reminds me, I want to call some of the names that my therapist, Soma, recommended. It would be good to have a therapist to call if I need one." Lily takes a deep breath and lets it out slowly. "I do want to tell you what happened. But first, I want to tell you how sorry I am for the pain I caused you." Lily bursts into tears. "I can't imagine how you must have felt when I chose Adam and severed ties with you." She cries even harder.

Lilith and Roy lean in and hold their daughter's hands. Lily sees that they are both crying too. Lilith gets a box of tissues as many needed tears are shed.

When they have dried their eyes, Lilith pours a glass of water for each of them. Lilith and Roy wait for Lily to speak.

Lily's breathing becomes quieter. "I was so in love with Adam. I'd never been in love before. It seemed the best choice to be with him. It was wonderful in the beginning. He was smart, attentive, sensitive, understanding, and seemed to have the same goals as I did. I retired from the ballet and bought a studio space below my apartment. I taught ballet classes and danced when I had the chance. Adam's marketing business was doing well locally, so he didn't have to travel too much. Then we got pregnant."

"You have a baby?" Roy shouts and jumps up.

Lilith grabs Roy's hand, pulling him back onto the chair.

"No, Dad. I lost the baby." Lily wipes tears from her eyes. "It was awful."

Lilith reaches for her daughter. "Oh, honey, how terrible for both of you."

Lily meets her mom's eyes. "It was terrible for me, but Adam didn't want children. Losing the baby seemed to make our marriage stronger, until I was ready and wanted to try to have another baby. The marriage broke up, Adam had an affair, and after the nasty divorce, I thought it was over. But Adam stalked me and anyone that got close to me. I got a restraining order, but he stayed on the outskirts of the one hundred required feet and just watched me. I could never prove that the notes, flowers, calls, cut phone lines, and vandalism had been him. I moved from New York to Lakewood to get away from him, but he followed me. I could see him watching from the lamppost across the street from my apartment. He was there every night, until he wasn't. There were three days when I didn't see him, and then heard from my friend Sasha that he had died. We went to the funeral and watched from the hill above. Then he showed up, standing right in front of me, and he grabbed me. I was so terrified that I fainted. I guess I couldn't take it anymore. I just snapped. But I'm braver now. I don't want to be the isolated victim anymore." Lily sits up straighter in her chair.

Lilith looks at her husband and then at Lily. "You're strong. And we'll help you in any way that we can."

"I know you will. You already are. I'm so glad to be here with you at the ranch. I do feel safe. Thank you for the trouble and expense of all the security."

Roy smiles. "It's no trouble. It's kind of like the Wild West, with the sheriff on horseback doing his patrol. I think the officers enjoy the change as well."

Lily laughs. "Well, I'm going to make some calls for a therapist. Then, Mom, how about we go into town and do a little shopping, and maybe have lunch?"

Lilith claps. "Oh, yes, I can do that. But I'll need to make a call and have an officer accompany us."

"I didn't know we could do that. Wow, you guys think of everything." Lily gets up and heads toward the stairs and then turns. "I'll reimburse you for these security expenses, once I get back to work."

Roy stands and approaches his daughter. "No, you don't have to worry about any of that. I have it covered. I haven't been able to spoil my daughter for years. This is my catch up."

Lily falls into her dad's arms, and she whispers, "Thank you. It means so much to me to feel safe right now."

Roy whispers back, "You're just letting me be a dad."

"I love you, Dad." Lily squeezes her dad and then releases him. She looks over at her mom. "See you in an hour?"

Lilith nods. "See you in an hour."

As Lily walks to her room, she sees her dad put his arms around her mom. She hears her dad say, "We had no idea our girl was going through this nightmare. We have to do everything we can to keep her safe."

Lily sits on her bed and takes out her phone. She looks at the business cards for therapists that Soma gave her. She looks around and realizes that Sky has not followed her up the stairs. Then she hears a whine at the door and a soft scratch. When she opens the door, a blur of fur rushes in and jumps on the bed, scattering Lily's phone and papers.

"Hi, girl, I missed you too." Lily climbs on her bed and ruffles Sky's fur. "You know, you'll have to stay with Dad when we go shopping." Sky looks at Lily, whines, and then puts her head down and closes her eyes.

Lily gathers the scattered business cards and puts them out on the bed. She uses her phone to locate the closest therapists to the ranch. One is a male and one a female. Lily feels a tightness in her chest as she thinks about the decision. She decides on the female, Elizabeth Ann Newsome. She calls the number and makes an appointment for the next Monday. She wants to see if she feels comfortable with Ms. Newsome so she can call her if she needs a tune-up. Lily laughs to herself. Those are Soma's words—tune-up. It takes the sting out of saying you need a therapist.

Lily climbs off her bed and takes a look in the mirror. She isn't sure what kind of shopping her mom wants to do. And lunch out in public… that isn't something she has done in a long while. Lily feels a shiver go up her spine. She takes in a sharp breath as she remembers her fear. Sky jumps off the bed and moves close to Lily, leaning into her.

Lily feels herself immediately relax as she touches Sky's soft head. "You're good for me, girl." She opens her door, and the two head downstairs.

Lilith grabs her purse and something red and approaches. "Good, you're ready." She leans down, fastens a red thing around Sky's back, and then clicks on her leash.

Lily watches and then asks, "What's that for?"

Lilith stands up and looks at Lily. "Sky is a service dog. Not only can she help us herd at the ranch, she's trained to assist, protect, and comfort trauma victims."

Lily takes in a sharp breath. "You got her for me?"

"Yes, honey. I told you that we would do anything to help you feel safe." Lilith smiles. She hugs her daughter and pats Sky and then hands Lily the leash.

Lilith opens the backseat of her blue Toyota 4Runner for Sky and asks her to jump in and then buckles the dog in. Lily climbs in the front passenger seat as Lilith climbs in and starts the car. Just as they are heading down the drive, a solid black car pulls up behind them. Lilith checks her rear-view mirror and points at the car. "That's our security bodyguard, Officer Ben."

Lily sighs. "Mom, this must have cost you a bundle. Are you sure?"

Lilith looks over at her daughter. "You bet."

They exit the ranch and head for the interstate that will take them to Colorado Springs. Lily feels so grateful for the love and support of her family. With Sky and the security officer, she thinks that maybe she can relax and enjoy herself.

"Mom, what are we shopping for today?"

"You, of course." Lilith smiles as she keeps her eyes on the road.

"Me!" Lily pauses. "You know, I haven't been shopping in...I don't remember the last time, except for groceries." She smiles and sighs. "This will be very nice. We haven't shopped together since before I went off to Julliard."

"That's right. We have a lot of shopping to do. I thought you might like to get some clothes for riding. You do want to ride, don't you?"

"Oh, yes. I want to take Kit when she comes, so I better practice before she gets here."

"Do you want to take a ride this afternoon before dinner? We could do a short one to get your riding legs back in shape."

"Great idea. Does Sky come along too?"

Lilith looks over at Lily. "Sky goes everywhere you go."

"What if you need her to move the cattle?"

"Well, then, maybe you'll have to help as well."

Lily laughs. "I better start practicing then."

After thirty-five minutes, they pull off the interstate and enter the mall's parking lot. They spend two hours walking, talking, and shopping. They have bags of jeans, shirts, sweaters, shorts, T-shirts, slacks, a couple of dresses, ballet tights, leotards, a skirt, shoes, boots, socks, and some makeup. Officer Ben helps carry the bags because Lily and Lilith are loaded down. Lily is surprised that no one worries about Sky walking with them from store to store.

Lilith gives a big sigh. "That was power shopping. I'm starved. You ready to eat?"

"Sure." Lily is relieved—she isn't used to shopping, and it's all very overwhelming. But she has a lot of nice clothes. It feels like a new beginning.

"I saw a Mexican restaurant as we came in. Would that be OK?"

"Wow, Mom, I haven't had Mexican food in ages. Let's go. Oh, can Sky come in?"

"Everywhere you go." Lilith smiles and heads to the restaurant. Officer Ben is close behind.

They take seats on the indoor patio, and Sky curls up under the table. Officer Ben takes a seat out in the mall across from them to keep a watchful eye.

Lily looks over at Officer Ben. "Doesn't he eat with us?"

"No, not while he's on duty. He'll eat after we get home."

"Can I at least get him something to drink, like lemonade or iced tea? He's been carrying my packages."

Lilith looks over at the officer. "Yes, that would be nice."

Both Lilith and Lily order the fiesta salad and a glass of lemonade. They order a to-go lemonade for Officer Ben. Lily takes it over to him and thanks him for his service, and he gratefully accepts the drink. Even Sky gets a bowl of fresh water.

Lilith sees Lily watching her and looks up. "What? Do I have food on my face?"

Lily laughs. "No. I'm just so thankful for this."

"You're welcome. It's so much fun for me to get to spoil you with some fun clothes."

"Yes, I'm thankful for your generosity, but I'm also thankful for being here with you."

Lilith reaches across the table and squeezes Lily's hand. "I'm thankful too."

After lunch, they load the car with the many packages. Sky jumps in the backseat and is secured, and mother and daughter drive home to the ranch, singing to Carrie Underwood's "Blown Away." Lily doesn't realize that she's crying.

Lilith looks over at her. "What is it, honey?"

"I just can't believe that Kit had to live through the horror of her father raping her."

"Oh, how horrible. You told me there was abuse, but oh, my God. Poor girl!"

"I'm so glad she'll be coming here for a while."

"Me too. I look forward to meeting her. I'm so glad you found such a good friend."

Lily takes a deep breath in and lets it out slowly. "We helped each other heal."

Lily is lost in her thoughts of Kit as they pull into the ranch's drive. Once parked outside the house, they unload all the packages. Lilith takes off Sky's vest, and Sky runs off to look around. Officer Ben waves to them as he circles around and drives off. Lily waves and yells a thank-you.

"Lily, why don't you have a rest, and we can head out for a ride in a couple hours, about three o'clock?"

Lily realizes she's exhausted—going to a mall and shopping was more stimulus than she has had in a long time. "Great idea," she says as she grabs as many bags as she can carry and heads upstairs. Sky rushes ahead. Lily closes her door, places the bags on the floor, takes off her boots, and snuggles up with Sky on the bed. Sleep comes quickly.

Lily wakes at two forty-five. She puts on her boots and heads down the stairs with Sky. She can smell fresh-brewed coffee and sees her mom holding a mug. Grabbing a mug off the shelf, she pours herself some of the rich-smelling coffee.

"I smell vanilla." Lily adds cream and sugar.

"Yes, I love vanilla coffee." Lilith takes another sip and sighs.

Lily looks at her mom. "Do you still have Sammy, the bay gelding?"

"Yes, we do. He's twenty-two years old now, I believe. We don't use him for the guests, just friends when they want to trail ride. He does well for short rides, and he loves getting out. You used to love to ride him. Is he who you want to ride today?"

"I would like that. He'll probably be a good horse for Kit to ride. She doesn't have any experience with horses."

"Then he would be a good one for her. He would take good care of her. Do you want to head down to the barn? We can bring our mugs with us. And grab a jacket—it starts to get cool as the sun moves west."

"Let's go." Lily heads for the door.

"I think I still have your old helmet."

"It'll probably fit. I don't think my head has grown since I've been gone."

"Now, your brother would have a good comeback to that comment."

"I'm sure he would. I hope to spend some time with him in the next couple of weeks. I want to know about his life and his business. And Grandma Catherine, how is she doing?"

Lilith moves in to put her arm around Lily. "She's eighty now. I can't believe it. She's doing very well. She had one scare when she fainted about two years ago. She was home alone and called us when she woke up. It turns out that her heart rate was high and irregular. It made her dizzy, and she fainted."

"What do you mean, high and irregular?"

"It's called rapid atrial fibrillation. The upper chambers of her heart weren't beating normally. They were beating too fast to empty the blood properly. She's on medication, and she had a pacemaker implanted that kicks in if her heart gets too fast. She takes walks, swims, and enjoys her bridge and bingo. We got her a monitor to wear around her neck so she can call us if she needs us. We offered for her to move into the main house with us, but she likes her independence."

"I'm sorry that I didn't know about all of this. You must have been scared for her."

"Yes, we were. But she's doing very well now. And you'll get to visit with her and catch up on her life."

As they near the stable, the horses are wandering in for dinner, and Sky is helping herd them in. Lily enjoys the familiar smell of the horses—it reminds her of her childhood. She sees a bay gelding with white around his face and knows it is Sammy. She grabs a halter from a hook in the barn and heads toward Sammy. With a whistle and a pat, she faces him. He touches her hand and puts his head against her chest. She circles his head and gives him a kiss as she whispers, "I'm home, boy. I've missed you. Will you take me for a ride?" Sammy meets her eyes with his, and she knows he understands her.

Lily places the halter on Sammy and ties him to the fence. Taking a hoof-pick, she cleans out the mud and stones from his four feet. She brushes his soft fur and combs his mane and tail. She grabs a saddle pad and places it on his back, slips the western saddle on, and then cinches it up tight. Lilith hands her his bridle and her helmet. It takes Lily a bit to remember how to put the bridle on and secure the straps, but Sammy is very patient.

Lily pats Sammy. "You're probably laughing at me as I fumble with your bridle. Thanks for being patient. I'm rusty."

Lily puts on her helmet and climbs into the saddle. It feels good to be up on a horse. She had forgotten how wide the horse can be. "I bet my legs will be sore tomorrow."

Lilith laughs as she mounts her gray mare. "This is Willow. She's a rescue from a neglected barn. She was very skittish when she arrived a few years back, but she loves it here now. She is a Trakehner warmblood. She has amazing gates. The family that owned her had started her training when their farm went into bankruptcy. I'm thinking of breeding her. It would be fun to have a baby out here. I'll probably wait until next year, so we can have a spring baby. That will give me time to research a good sire.

"Let's go. Why don't we walk the whole ranch? That way you can see the changes we've made. You probably know your way around, but it's been a while."

"That's fine by me. I need to get my riding legs back. What time do we need to be back?"

"Dad is making burgers tonight, so we can take our time."

Lilith and Lily head down the road. Sky runs ahead and back to check on them and then runs off again. The afternoon breeze is cool, and Lily appreciates that she wore a jacket. Her mom's mare is prancing ahead. Lily squeezes Sammy with her legs, and he trots to catch up. Lily can still see snow on the mountain peaks, and there are some purple-gray clouds coming over the mountains. Lily wonders if they are going to get some moisture. It can still snow in April. The warm days have greened up the grasses around the ranch property. It's familiar and so beautiful and relaxing. Lily's body sways with Sammy's movements.

As they turn a corner, Willow's and Sammy's ears prick forward. Lily looks to see what they are looking at and sees Officer Simon trotting up the path.

"Good afternoon, Mrs. Johnson and Miss Lily."

"Officer Simon, you can call me Lilith."

"Only if you call me Simon." He laughs. "Are you having a nice ride before the weather comes in?"

Lilith looks toward the mountains. "Are we expecting a storm?"

"Rain and maybe snow mix is what I hear. Well, I'm going to finish my rounds before my relief gets here." He tips his hat. "Have a nice evening, ladies."

"You do the same, and thanks." Lily waves.

Lilith, Lily, and Sky finish their ride around the ranch. Once back at the barn, they take off their horses' tack, brush them, and give them some grain. When the horses have finished, they open the gate, and Sky herds them out toward the pasture. Then all three walk back to the main house as the smell of grilled burgers wafts through the air.

BROTHER JOHN

Lily wakes to something banging on her window. She wonders if it is the wind or a branch. She gets up and looks—it is Adam, staring at her. She shrinks away from the window and opens the door. There he is again. She shuts the door and locks it. She waits and doesn't hear anything, so she peeks out. No sign of him, so she runs for the stairs and climbs down. She hears a tap on the window, and there he is again. She runs to her parents' bedroom, but he is standing in the doorway. She screams for them, and then she is shoved and covered with water. She wakes up to find Sky standing over her with a paw on her chest. She is whining and licking Lily all over her face.

Lily reaches up and ruffles Sky's fur. "Good girl. Thanks for bringing me back."

Sky lies down next to her with her head wrapped in Lily's arm. Lily does her tapping to bring her heart rate and respiratory rate back down to normal.

Lily sighs. "Well, I'm awake now. Why don't we go downstairs and get some coffee?"

Sky jumps off the bed and heads for the door. Lily and Sky go down the long wooden staircase, stepping as quietly as possible. Lily smiles to herself when she steps on the familiar step that still creaks as it did in her childhood. Her mom could always hear her. The banister has gotten smoother with indentions where Lily can imagine her childhood fingers gripped the rail. The house is dark, and Lily can see that the door to her parents' room is still closed. She glances at the clock in the kitchen—it says four thirty. Lily knows her dad will be up soon, so she puts on a pot of coffee. Then she notices a wrapped book on the island with her name on it. Opening it, she sees that it is a pink leather journal with an attached pink pen. A note that is enclosed reads, "My dear Lily, journaling my thoughts often helps me sort out difficult times and explore new opportunities. All my love to you, Mom."

Lily wipes a tear from her eye. She grabs a mug of black coffee with cream and sugar and curls up in her dad's favorite soft-brown-and-beige plaid reading chair with matching ottoman. She hugs the journal to her chest as Sky looks on, wagging her tail as she sits next to Lily.

Lily pulls out the pink pen and opens the journal. She starts writing. *I have stepped back in time. Back into the safety and comfort of my childhood, back into my childhood room and being cared for by my mom and dad. But I'm a grown woman of thirty. How did this happen to me? I was so driven and independent. I had my life mapped out. I'd succeeded in meeting one of my dreams.*

Lily puts down her pen and closes her eyes. The curtains open, and a spotlight follows her as she floats on pointe across the stage, swaying and doing pirouettes. Her body relaxes at the memory. Lily opens her eyes and begins writing again.

> *I was so happy dancing. It was the best time of my life. And when I retired and started my studio, I loved teaching the young dancers and seeing their dreams unfold. But prior to retiring, I fell hard into love. I had never been in love. It was an amazing feeling. I got lost in someone else. I still had my studio and teaching, but I was lost in my husband. I gave up my family and my friends. I thought it was the right thing to do. Was that a mistake? How could I have been so wrong about someone? He had me mesmerized—so mesmerized that I gave up everything and everyone to follow him. If he had really loved me, why would he have encouraged me to*

abandon my family? And my baby…And why the obsession with me after the divorce? He wouldn't let go. What kind of person does something like that?

I know there are labels: narcissist, sociopath. But what label am I? I allowed the torment. I didn't think I had any other choice. But is the 24-7 security the answer? I must admit, I feel safe. But what am I going to do—live on the ranch forever? And what must all this security be costing my parents? Would I need to be followed to work and back? I don't know how to stop his behavior. Maybe I can't. Maybe he will wear down after a while and get on with his life. Good thing I am going to a therapist on Monday. I want a life. I want to have a baby. Maybe I do it on my own. But can I bring a child into this mess?

Lily stops writing and weeps. She hears footsteps and looks up as her father approaches.

"You OK, sweet pea?"

"Oh, Dad, no, I'm not. I'm so lost." Lily puts out her arms to her dad, who kneels and hugs her as she cries.

Roy holds his daughter until she starts to release him. "Honey, it will take some time, but you'll find your way."

Lily looks up into her dad's face. "How do you know?"

As Roy brushes his daughter's red curls off her wet face, he says, "I just know it with every cell in my being." Roy takes Lily's hands. "Have you looked outside?"

"No, it was dark when I got up."

Roy pulls Lily up out of the chair. "Come, let's go out on the porch."

Roy opens the front door, and Sky runs out. Lily sees that the world has a beautiful thick covering of snow. Her feet crunch in the snow as she travels down the steps and onto the lawn. The snow is about five inches deep. It is thick and fluffy with a good crunching sound. Lily loves that sound; Sky does too. She is racing about, biting at the new flakes that are falling. Lily lies down on the cold, white snow and moves her arms up and down and her legs in and out, making a snow angel. She breathes in the fresh air. Making a ball of snow with her hand, she whirls it toward her dad, hitting him in the chest.

He bursts out laughing. "You're in for it now, girl." He makes the biggest snowball he can and hits Lily's back as she runs.

"What's going on? It's 5:00 a.m.!" Lilith calls out as she pulls her robe tighter around her.

"Actually, it's five thirty. Good morning, beautiful." Roy grins. "We're just enjoying the snow."

Through the falling snow, car lights can be seen coming up the drive. A Jeep pulls in quickly, and Officer Dan jumps out. "Everything OK, folks?"

Lilith sighs. "Yes, sorry, just my childish husband and daughter playing in the snow in their pajamas." A snowball plants itself at Lilith's waist. "Oh!" she screams as her husband and daughter laugh. "You guys. I'm going in for coffee. Do you want to join me, Officer Dan?"

"No thanks, Mrs. Johnson. I've had my coffee fill tonight. I'll just finish my rounds before my relief gets here. Good-bye." Officer Dan gets in the black Jeep and pulls away.

Snowballs fire at Lilith as she heads for the door. One gets her, and the rest hit the door. She turns and glares out the window at her husband.

Roy turns to Lily. "I guess I'm in trouble. I'd better make it up to her."

"Oh, Dad, she just needs her coffee." Lily laughs.

Sky is rolling in the snow and eating it. Lily realizes that this was just what she needed—a fresh start, like the new-fallen snow. She'd called her brother and planned to spend the day with him. He's expecting her at his house around seven o'clock. She thinks she'd better get dressed and then have some breakfast before heading to his house. She's anxious to hear about his life and the new girlfriend, Amy.

Lily, her dad, and Sky crunch through the snow, climb up the stairs, and step into the house. Lilith hands Lily a towel to dry off Sky. Then Lily and Sky head upstairs. Lily changes out of her wet pajamas and puts on a pair of jeans and a sweater. Meeting her parents back downstairs in the kitchen, Lily sits down to a steaming bowl of oatmeal and raisins.

Lilith is sipping her coffee. "Lily, your brother called. He's expecting you at seven. He has a horse that's having contractions. Sounds like you might get to see a birth."

"Wow, that would be wonderful." Lily finishes her last bite of oatmeal, drinks the rest of her orange juice, and heads to the rack for her coat. "I think if I leave now, I can make it to his house by seven, even in the snow."

"Have fun, sweet pea." Roy waves his spoon.

Lilith picks up Sky's leash and hands it to her daughter. "Lily, you can leave Sky in your brother's truck or take her with you. Just remember that she reacts to your emotions. She's trained to help you. So if things get tense on one of your brother's calls, you need to reassure her that you're OK. You might have to ask her to stay, but tell her you're OK and that she's a good girl. Oh, and remember your brother can help as well."

"I've noticed how smart she is. Thanks for the tips. And I want to hear more about John's gift." Lily gives her mom a hug. "I love you, Mom."

"I love you too, baby." Lilith hugs Lily back and releases her as Lily turns toward the coatrack.

Lily puts on her coat, hat, boots, and mittens. She opens the door, and Sky runs out and down the steps. Lily takes in a deep breath of the fresh air, crunches down the steps, and heads down the drive toward John's house. He had a cabin built on the property once he finished vet school. Lily knows she won't have time to see the inside. She'll probably get there at the time they need to leave.

It only takes fifteen minutes and she is stepping onto John's porch. Lily bangs the knocker twice. John answers the door, holding a big mug of coffee. Lily smiles and gives her brother a hug. John is her younger brother, but he stands ten inches taller than her in his stocking feet.

"Hi, sis, I'll get my coat. The snow and cold may be affecting the mare's labor. I better check her out." He turns, slips on his boots, and puts on his hat and coat. "Mom told me that Sky would be going with us. I haven't had much time with her. How is she working out?"

"I've never had a dog, and certainly not one that was trained like Sky. She senses my moods and even wakes me when I have a nightmare."

John puts his arm around his sister. "I wish I'd known what you were going through. I'm so sorry. I would have liked to break that guy's nose or something."

Lily feels the tension in her brother's body as he speaks, and it surprises her. He is such a gentle soul. "You know, I would have liked that. Well, not really. But I appreciate you coming to my defense. It was complicated. He's so unpredictable that I never know how or who he'll choose to lash out at. I couldn't dare let him hurt anyone that I love." Lily snuggles into her brother's tall body. "I'm so glad to be here at the ranch. Mom and Dad did so much to secure our safety. But I can't live like this forever. I need to find another way."

John gives Lily a hug that pulls her off her feet. "You don't have to worry about that now. Just enjoy the peace for a while." He smiles down into his sister's face and kisses her forehead.

John opens the passenger door to his white veterinary truck and slides the seat forward for Sky to get in the back and then secures Sky's seat belt. He helps Lily up into the truck and shuts the door. Once he climbs in, he starts the engine and turns on the heat. They roll down the drive onto the ranch road.

"Where's the horse? Is it a home or boarding facility?"

"It's a small farm in the mountains west of here. It'll only take us twenty minutes to get there."

"Is this her first foal?"

"Yes, and she's scared. The family, Jameson, had two horses, and the older one died of colic just after the mare, Linda, got pregnant."

Lily laughs. "They named her Linda?"

John smiles. "Yes, their seven-year-old daughter named her. You won't believe the names she has picked out for the foal."

"Let me guess. Tom, Mary, Dick, Jane?" Lily laughs louder.

"You aren't far off. Jack and Jill." John chuckles.

Lily is quiet for a minute. "You said she's scared. Did the owner say something, or is this part of your gift?"

John looks over at his sister. "Do you really want me to answer that? You always made fun of what I said about animals."

Lily frowns. "I'm sorry. I shouldn't have made fun of you. It's wonderful that you, Mom, and Dad have these gifts. I just don't really understand them since I don't have gifts like that."

"You know, everyone has the capability. And the gifts come in different forms for different people. Does the hair ever stand up on the back of your neck for no reason, and it makes you look around? Or you get a tingling feeling?"

"Yeah, that's happened to me."

"How about, do you ever get a sinking feeling in your gut?"

Lily thinks a moment. "Whenever the phone rings—I'm afraid it's Adam."

"Those are things to be aware of. You might be getting a message or a warning."

John pats Lily's shoulder. "Well, anyway, it was distressing for Linda to see her friend die. And the hormones of pregnancy didn't help her either. Mr. Jameson borrowed a goat to keep her company, but she has a lot of anxiety. I've been talking her through everything, and it helps for a while. When she gets wound up, Mr. Jameson calls me to come and check on her."

"Do they know that you can talk with their horse?"

"No, not really. They just hear me talking softly to her. They don't know that I can understand her. But she seems better after we talk, so they're pleased."

"What an amazing gift—to be able to help a frightened animal."

"Thanks. But we might have our work cut out for us. I bet the storm coming in has put her in a spin."

"Would she go into labor early because of the storm?"

"Probably not. The first stage of labor is usually one to four hours. But if a mare feels threatened by a predator or a bad storm, she can delay the labor by hours or days."

"So what happens to the foal in the first stage of labor?" Lily asks.

"This is when the foal moves into the birthing position within the uterus. With the onset of contractions, the mare can become restless, pace, and break into a sweat. That's probably what Madge and Walt Jameson are seeing, and why they called me. The mare can have frequent urination and defecation. She'll hold up her tail and look back at her flanks. This is also a sign of colic if she's constipated. That also might be a reason Walt called me after they lost their other horse to colic. Some mares back up to a wall and press with the contractions. It seems to help the pressure."

John slows the truck down and turns into a drive. Lily can see the barn up ahead, nestled back to the right of the house. The goat is standing out in the front paddock.

"I see the goat. He must not have wanted to be inside with all the excitement. Mom said I would have to see how Sky does. Is it OK if she comes in?"

"Of course. I don't think she would let you go in by yourself." John jumps out of the truck, gets his bag out of the back, and heads into the barn.

Lily and Sky climb out of the truck and head in. Lily speaks softly to Sky. "You're a good girl. You can watch John do his work with the mare."

As Lily and Sky enter the barn, Lily sees the mare, Linda. She is a stout palomino with a golden coat and a silky white mane and tail. She has a sheen of sweat covering her body. Lily can see that the mare is relieved to see John. She nickers as he approaches.

John rubs the mare's neck and face as he talks to her softly. "I'm just going to examine you. You're doing a great job, Linda. You'll have a baby very soon."

John takes out his stethoscope and listens to Linda's belly. He speaks out loud for the Jamesons, Linda, and Lily to hear. "Linda, you have good belly sounds. And I'm feeling another contraction, which is helping your baby foal to move into position. Good girl. Keep up the good work."

John moves around her and says, "Walt, do you know approximately when the labor started?"

"No, we just came out this morning, and she seemed anxious."

"What time was that?"

"About six forty-five, and she was pacing. Georgie, our goat, wanted out of the barn. I was glad you were planning on coming out this morning."

"So, Linda, you've been in labor about forty minutes. We'll just be with you and available if you need us."

Linda backs up to the wall and starts pushing, as John had told Lily she might.

John introduces Lily to Jenny, the Jamesons' daughter, and to Walt and Madge Jameson. He introduces everyone to Sky, who sits closely at Lily's side.

"Why is Linda backing up to the wall? Won't she hurt herself?" Jenny asks.

"Good question, Jenny. When a mare is in labor, there is a lot of pressure as the foal moves around to get ready to be born. Pushing up against the wall helps the pressure. And no, it doesn't hurt her."

"Can I get everyone a cup of coffee?" Walt asks.

"Dad!" Jenny whines.

"Oh, excuse me. Miss Jenny, how would you like a hot chocolate with marshmallows?"

"Yes, thank you, Daddy."

John moves over to check on Linda as Walt walks toward the barn door. Just then, Linda lets out a grunt as water pours out the back of her.

"Walt, don't go anywhere. You're having a baby soon."

John turns to Lily. "Linda will probably lie down soon. Once the foal's head and shoulders emerge, the mare will stop pushing for a while before the hips and hindquarters slip out in about forty minutes. This is important to help prevent the umbilical cord from breaking before the last blood supply from the placenta flows to the foal. This also may protect the mare's uterus from infection."

"How is she looking?" Lily asks.

John lifts Linda's tail. "I see a foot." John puts on long gloves and turns to Lily. "Put on some gloves because I might need your help. Linda, you're doing great. We might help you deliver this baby."

Walt comes forward. "Is everything OK?"

"The baby is big and long," John says. "We just may need to help a bit." He gives a small smile.

Lily has a sinking feeling in her stomach. She feels that John is worried. She leans down and speaks to Sky. "You're a good girl. I have to help John, so you need to stay here. You're such a good girl. I'm proud of you. Now, stay." Lily puts on the long gloves and moves in close to John.

He leans over and whispers to Lily, "The foal is big. We need to help guide the foal out. It might take some pulling. If I pull, you guide." Lily nods.

"OK, Linda. Let's deliver your foal. One foot is out." John puts in his hand to direct the other foot. "Second foot is out. And here comes the muzzle and the head. Lily, guide!"

Lily takes hold of the feet as John reaches for the chest. He takes a deep breath and pulls as Lily pulls and guides the legs. Linda grunts as John lands on his backside with the foal's head in his lap. The foal takes a breath. Linda's body relaxes, and she gives a big sigh. Both Lily and John laugh in relief.

Walt moves in close. "Why is the rest of the baby not coming out?"

"This is normal. She rests a while and it gives time for the foal to get the blood supply from the placenta."

Lily strokes the foal's head. After a while Linda gets restless. She raises her head and tries to stand, as the foal's hips and hindquarters slip out. She stands, and the umbilical cord breaks. Linda starts to have contractions, and she expels the placenta. John holds it out for Lily to examine with him. They don't see any holes.

Lily smiles at John. "No retained placenta."

John smiles back. "You learn fast."

Lily leans into John and realizes that she has tears streaming down her face. "That was amazing."

Linda moves next to her new foal and licks her clean. She doesn't seem to mind that John is examining her baby. Lily watches as John examines Linda and the foal. Linda tucks her head around John, as if giving him a hug. John strokes Linda's neck and speaks to her quietly. The two lean together and touch heads, and then John stands and looks at the Jamesons.

"The foal is a filly—a girl!" John shouts. "Jenny, her name is…?"

"Jill!" Jenny yells and jumps up and down.

Sky gives a little yelp, and everyone laughs.

They gather inside the Jamesons' house for coffee and hot chocolate. Madge brings out some chocolate cookies she made the night before. Lily and John wash up before enjoying the coffee and cookies by the roaring fire. Sky has a dog bone, which she is happily chewing in front of the fire. Jenny kneels next to Sky and pats her.

Madge whispers to John, "Jenny sure wants another dog. She misses Billy. Animals just don't live as long as we would like."

"You gave him a good life. You found him before Jenny was born, didn't you?" John pats Madge's shoulder.

"Yes, he was our first child." Madge seems to shake off the sadness. "Well, having little Jill will make a difference for Jenny. She's been mourning Billy for a couple months, but when she could feel the foal kick in Linda's stomach, she got so excited."

John sighs. "Madge, I hope you know how happy Billy was with you. You gave him a great life, and you helped him have a peaceful death. He didn't suffer."

Madge quickly wipes a tear from her eye and leans toward John. "Thanks for that. I didn't want him to suffer, but I also didn't want him to think we'd given up on him."

"He was ready to go."

"Thanks for helping him and me." Madge smiles as she looks at her daughter talking to Sky.

Lily and John put on their coats and call to Sky.

"Thanks for the coffee and delicious cookies," John says.

"You're welcome. Thanks for your care of Linda and Jill." Walt walks them to the door.

Once they are in the truck and heading home, Lily turns to John. "Thanks for letting me see what you do and letting me help. I saw you talking to Linda. What was she saying, if you don't mind my asking?"

"No, I don't mind. I'm pleased. Let's see…she wanted to know if the filly was OK, because it had gotten stuck. She thanked me for helping her, and she said she'd been very frightened. I told her she did a great job, the filly was healthy with no injuries, and that she only needed my help a little bit."

Lily looks at her brother. "How does she tell you those things?"

"Well, it's not like you and me talking. I talk to her in my normal voice, and I think it as well. I hear her thoughts and feel her emotions."

"You hear her speak?"

"I don't hear it out loud—I hear her in my head. I hear the voice, feel the emotions, and sometimes see pictures and get scents. Sometimes it takes a bit to figure out what the animals are saying. The information doesn't come in sentences like when we speak. It might be fragmented. And if the animal is hurt or scared, its emotions and pain are mixed with the message."

Lily claps her hands together. "That's unbelievable and amazing."

"It certainly helps me in my business."

Lily pats John on the leg. "How's your love life? And does Amy know about your gift?"

"Very subtle, sis." John takes in a deep breath and lets it out as he stares at the snowy road ahead. "Amy and I have been dating for a couple weeks. I haven't told her anything yet. I haven't had good experiences with sharing my gift."

"I'm sorry to hear that. You're such a catch, gift and all."

"Thanks, but you're my sister. It's hard to find someone with like beliefs or who can accept even if they don't believe."

"What happened?"

"I met her at CSU—her name was Joanne. We were so in love. I told her about my gift, and she was excited about it. We visited psychics and read books on mediums and the various psychic gifts. We both went to vet school and were going to go into practice together. Mom and Dad loved her. They were so excited. She seemed to fit into our weird family. Then we started our veterinary rotations. I couldn't help it that my gift was part of my practice, but it bothered Joanne. She said she wasn't jealous, but she felt she didn't believe in the gift anymore. She said things like it's the devil at work, it's my overactive imagination, my ego, mental illness, and another one—a cult at work. I think she couldn't have us being different. Also, you know I'm a vegetarian and have been one since I was little."

"I remember. Mom and Dad weren't happy, at least initially."

"Well, they came to understand. Joanne adapted to being a vegetarian when we were in undergraduate school. I didn't ask her to—it didn't matter to me. It was just a decision I needed to make. But she went back to meat when we were in vet school. I didn't care, but she didn't like it that I wouldn't have meat with her. I guess she just didn't love me for me." John sighs.

"So you're afraid if you tell Amy, she'll hit the road?"

John looks over at his sister. "Something like that."

"But if she's going to react the same way Joanne did, don't you want to know sooner rather than later?"

"You have a point. I just hope she'll get to know me, and then the gift won't matter. I like her a lot."

"Then you should tell her. You deserve to be happy. And if she isn't the right one, you should be free to find someone else."

John looks at Lily. "Seriously, are you taking your own advice?"

Lily takes in a sharp breath and scowls at her brother. "We're talking about you."

"You deserve to be with someone who will treat you, and love you, like you deserve. I'm so sorry for what Adam did to you. I hate that I didn't know and lost contact with you for so long."

Lily sighs. "I just couldn't tell anyone. I was frightened that he would hurt the ones I love."

John squeezes Lily's hand. "You'll see the other side of this, when you least expect it. There are nice men out there."

"I'm not ready yet. Maybe someday."

John's pager goes off, and he pulls over and looks at the message. As he opens his phone, he nods at Lily.

"Sully, I'm twenty minutes out. Keep him up, walk if you can, and don't let him kick his stomach. See you soon."

John turns to Lily. "A colic—common with a change of weather."

"Let's go, doc." Lily looks out the window. The snow has stopped, and the sun is peeking out from behind the clouds. "Is Charlie working today?"

John looks at Lily with a big smile on his face. "No, he's off today. When we're both working, the pages go out to both of us, and whoever isn't busy takes the call. It works pretty well. He's a great partner and a really nice guy. And he's single—probably never gotten over you."

Lily punches John in the arm.

"Ow!" John rubs his arm. "Think about it, at least as a friend. He's one of the good ones."

Lily puts her finger to her lips in a thoughtful expression. "OK, I'll think about it."

John pulls the truck onto a wooded drive and continues as the sun blinks through the trees. At a clearing, Lily can see a couple barns, an outdoor arena with jumps that are still covered with snow, and a large stone house with a wraparound porch. A stone carved with the words "Meadow Stables" is to the left of the entrance to the stables. As the truck pulls up, Lily sees someone motioning for them to come to the front barn. John pulls up and gets out his bag, a syringe, and glass vial and then runs for the barn. Lily and Sky follow him in.

They find the horse lying in the indoor arena. "I'm Sue Hampton. This is Raisin. He went down, and I can't get him up."

John rushes over to the big bay thoroughbred gelding and strokes his neck. "How long has he been uncomfortable? And how was he acting?"

The horse tries to lift his head and then tries to kick his belly.

"He didn't finish his breakfast and then didn't touch his lunch. He was pacing, rolling, and pawning the ground."

"I'm going to give him something for pain and to relax his gut. Then I'll examine him and see what we have here."

Lily and Sky stand back as John fills the syringe with the liquid from the vial. He talks to the horse as he works. The horse doesn't react much when John pokes for the vein and gives him the medicine. John takes out his stethoscope and listens to the horse's heart and abdomen and then counts his respirations. Lily sees that he takes the horse's temperature under the tail.

John stands and talks to Sue. "He has no fever, his heart rate is up, and he's in a considerable amount of pain. He has no lower bowel tones.

I'm going to do a rectal exam. The medicine I gave him should make him more comfortable."

John runs to his truck and returns with a bucket, tubing, and a bottle of solution. He puts on a long glove and greases it, and then he asks the horse to stand. After the horse is standing, he inserts his hand and whole arm. He empties out some stool and reinserts his hand and arm. After taking his arm out and taking the glove off, he approaches the owner.

"Raisin's bowel is twisted. Now, it might relax and untwist, but he has no bowel sounds in his lower colon. I recommend taking him to the hospital so that surgery can be done if needed."

Sue bursts into tears. "I don't think I can drive him myself."

"We can hook your trailer to my truck. We'll take him to Littleton Hospital. My sister can drive your truck if you don't think you can drive."

"I'll just go with you guys, if that's OK. I'll call my husband to meet me there."

"Show me where your trailer is. We need to go now."

After the trailer is hooked and secured to John's truck, he pulls it around to the arena. John talks softly to Raisin as he walks him to the open trailer. Raisin stops, and John faces him. John strokes Raisin's neck as he whispers to him. Then John faces the trailer, and Raisin slowly enters. John secures him and shuts the trailer door.

He turns to Lily. "Can you make sure my rear lights on the trailer are working? I'll have Sue and Sky get in the truck. Just stand here and I'll try the brakes and then the turn signals."

"Sure, I'm ready."

John gets in the truck and starts it. Everyone can hear Raisin moving around in the trailer. John puts his foot on the brakes.

"Brake lights work," Lily yells.

John tries the left and then the right turn signals.

"Signals work," Lily yells and then heads to the passenger door and gets in.

They head down the drive and out onto the road toward the animal hospital. John can hear Sue crying in the backseat. He opens the middle console and pulls out a box of tissues.

John looks at Sue in the rearview mirror. "Sometimes the movement of the trailer relaxes the gut and untwists the bowel. That's what we'll hope."

Sue tries to smile through her tears. Lily says a prayer for Raisin.

In forty-five minutes they pull into the animal hospital. John had called ahead to let them know they were coming and so the surgical team is available if needed. John pulls up and then backs the trailer up to the horse entrance. The ground is covered in rubber mats to keep the horses from slipping. John turns the truck off and places the emergency brake on. He opens the doors to the trailer as the door to the hospital opens. The floor of the trailer is covered in solid, soft, and liquid stool.

John slaps his leg and laughs. "Looks like the trailer therapy may have worked." He approaches Raisin, talking to the horse in a low, soft voice. "That's right, Raisin, you did a great job. We're just going to take you into the hospital and listen to your gut and maybe take a picture of your belly."

John unties Raisin and walks him out of the trailer and into the hospital. Raisin snorts as they enter the hospital.

John turns to Sue. "He's feeling better—a great sign."

The hospital team approaches them, and John gives an update on Raisin. He takes out his stethoscope and listens to Raisin's belly and then indicates that he can hear some bowel sounds in the lower intestines. The other vets concur that it would be a good idea to keep Raisin for observation. Sue is relieved and thanks John with hug. John pulls the trailer into a parking spot and unhooks it from his truck. He and Lily go back in to check on Raisin as he settles into his temporary stall. John steps in and talks softly to Raisin as Raisin lowers his head and licks his lips. John gives the beautiful horse a strong stroke across his neck and exits the stall.

He turns to Sue. "He's much more comfortable. Call me if you need anything or come up with any questions." He hugs Sue again.

When John and Lily are back in the truck, Lily says, "You're amazing. Your animal clients are so lucky you can talk to them and help them understand what's happening to them."

John smiles to himself and squeezes Lily's knee. "Are you hungry? We missed lunch."

Lily laughs. "I forgot all about food. Yes, let's get something to eat."

Sky barks agreement, making John and Lily laugh.

"And tell Amy. You both deserve it."

John looks over at his sister. "OK, I will." He smiles as he pulls the truck out of the hospital drive and onto the street.

After filling their bellies, John, Lily, and Sky head back to the ranch.

"I need to do some paperwork, and I have a prepurchase exam at four o'clock. Do you want to stay with me, or should I drop you at the main house?"

"I'm tired. You've already shown me your busy job. Yes, please drop me at the main house. Actually, drop me at the main gate—I know Sky needs to get some exercise, and so do I."

"Front gate it is."

When the truck pulls in the drive, John and Lily wave at Officer Townes. Lily and Sky get out, and John drives off. Sky chases the truck up and out of Lily's sight, and then she runs back to Lily.

Lily laughs. "You're fast, girl." Lily ruffles Sky's fur and pushes her off. "Now go get John again." Sky shoots off like a rocket.

Lily smiles as she watches Sky. The sun is warm on her face as she strolls down the drive. Sky runs back to her and then takes off to the right and then back and to the left and then back. When they reach the main house, Sky is panting happily.

Lily opens the door and removes her coat, hat, gloves, and boots. Sky runs into the kitchen to get some water. Lily joins her, gets a glass from the cabinet, and fills it with filtered water.

There is a note on the kitchen table: *Lily, we're out doing some work on the property. If you get home before us, we'll probably have dinner around five thirty. Love you tons, Mom and Dad.*

Lily writes a note at the bottom: *Sky and I are upstairs napping.*

Lily and Sky climb the stairs, and Sky jumps on the bed as Lily closes the door. She picks up her journal and slides out the pink pen. Fluffing the pillows, she sits down next to Sky and opens her journal. She opens the drawer of her bedside table and pulls out the two poems Kit had written and given her: "You and Me," about their journey to healing, and "Forgiveness," something they both were working on. She runs her hand over the written words her friend had put down on paper. Lily folds the poems and puts them in the back of her journal.

> *What a day! John's work as a vet and animal communicator is amazing to me. I feel so blessed that I'm getting to know my little brother. And he's such a nice young man. There are nice men out in the world. How did I choose so wrong? I feel so disconnected with the world. I can't live here forever with guards. That would just be another isolation. Come to think of it, when John and I went out, we didn't have security with us. I'll have to ask Mom. Maybe it was because he's a male. But you know, Adam didn't ever hurt me or anyone else. He did vandalism, and threats—many threats. So maybe I'm looking at this the wrong way. If I can't be intimidated, maybe he'll stop. I know it's a risk. He had me convinced by his actions that I was in danger if I had friends or dated. He just watched me if I was by myself. He didn't vandalize when I was by myself—oh, except the phone lines. I just can't imagine that I'll have security around me all the time. Maybe Sky would be enough to help me feel safe. Will I ever be able to go back home? Do I want to? Do I want to start fresh somewhere new? Can I open my heart again? I can't wait for Kit to get here. She'll be sorting out her life too. We can sort out our lives together.*

Lily closes her journal, snuggles next to Sky, and falls asleep.

There's a knock at the door, and Lily calls out, "Is that you, Kit?"

"No, it's Mom. Can I come in?"

Lily opens her eyes and realizes she's in her ballerina-papered childhood room, not at HRC. "Yes, Mom, come in."

Lilith opens the door slowly. "You OK?"

"Yes, I just forgot where I was. Kit would come and knock on my door at night, and we would have long, wonderful talks. I thought it was her when I heard the knock. She always came when I was having a nightmare. It helped so much to talk to her about them. She had nightmares too."

"I can't wait to meet her."

Lily smiles at her mom. "I told her about your gift and Dad's too. She's excited to meet you. She'll probably have questions about your gifts."

"I'm happy to answer anything she asks."

"With her dad being dead now, she might have questions about him."

"I might not know the answers, but I'll do my best." Lilith pats Lily's leg. "Are you hungry for dinner?" Lilith sees the journal on the bed and touches it.

"Thanks for the journal. I'm filling it up."

"Journaling always helped me." Lilith smiles and heads downstairs.

Lily takes a deep breath—she can smell something. She's trying to place it. She takes in another deep breath. Bacon, yes, and brussels sprouts—not her favorite, but she will do her best. She makes a face and laughs.

She climbs off her bed and heads downstairs with Sky in the lead. "Smells great. How can I help?"

Lilith grins at her daughter. "I know you don't like brussels sprouts, but they're great cooked with bacon. Why don't you set the table?"

"I'm on it. And I'll eat anything you prepare. You're both spoiling me. How about I cook tomorrow night?"

Roy turns from the stove. "You, cook?"

Lily bumps her dad as he laughs. "I love to cook. I know I've probably been acting like a lazy little girl around here. But I can sure chip in and help."

Lilith approaches her daughter. "Honey, I know you're a grown woman. You just had a terrible trauma and need to heal. Be gentle with yourself. Before long we'll have you working on one of the tractors."

Lily laughs as she tries to picture driving a tractor. "I can do that. Might take some practice."

Roy places a platter on the table—roast duck with orange sauce. Lilith puts down a plate of wild rice. Lily pours water with slices of lemon in the glasses and brings in the brussels sprouts and bacon. They all sit down.

The three hold hands as Roy says grace. "Most merciful Father, thank you for the blessings of this day, and especially the blessing of having

Lily here with us. Bless this food to the nourishment of bodies and us to thy service. Amen."

"What a feast. I have a lot to live up to when I cook tomorrow night."

Roy laughs as he carves the duck. "You sure do. What are you going to feed us?"

"Roy, stop that. Lily, you can make whatever you want."

"I'll have to give this some thought; maybe campfire goulash." Lily giggles.

"Take whatever you need from the garden, and we have a large supply of different meats in the freezer. If you need anything else, we can make a trip to the market," Lilith says.

"Thanks, Mom."

There is silence, except for audible chewing as the three enjoy their meals. Lily finds the duck so tender that it melts in her mouth. And she loves her dad's orange sauce. The brussels sprouts are surprisingly good when cooked with bacon. Lily smiles to herself and thinks how anything tastes good with bacon.

Lilith puts down her fork. "Lily, your grandma would love to have a visit with you tomorrow. What do you think?"

Lily swallows her bite of food and takes a drink of the lemon water. "I would love that. And could she come over for dinner tomorrow night?"

"Of course. She would probably love to help you cook. And she makes amazing pies, if you're interested," Roy says.

"Oh, that reminds me, Mom. I told Kit about your delicious snicker-doodles and all the things you put in them. She loves chocolate."

"I'll be sure to make her some when she comes. Maybe we should do a family trail ride together?"

"And a picnic?" Lily asks. "I loved our family rides in the mountains and stopping by a stream for lunch. And of course John looking for toads."

Lilith laughs. "I don't think he does that much anymore."

"No, I guess not. But he sure is good with his animal clients. And I don't just mean medically. He's amazing—a whisperer of sorts."

"Did you have a fun day with him?" Roy and Lilith ask together.

"Yes, I helped him deliver a filly. Her chest was stuck. It was unbelievable. And he just whispered in the mare's ear and helped her feel so comfortable."

Lilith smiles at Roy. "Yes, he has a special gift."

Lily looks from her mom to her dad. "And he's such a nice young man. My little brother, all grown up." Lily smiles.

Roy takes Lilith's hand and smiles at Lily. "Yes, both our babies are all grown up."

After dinner, Lily clears the plates. She brings out some raspberry sorbet and chocolate chip cookies.

Lily takes in a deep breath and lets it out. "This is probably premature, but I want to talk to you guys about something that's important to me."

Lilith and Roy exchange looks, and Lilith says, "Honey, you can talk to us about anything."

Lily takes in another breath and lets it out slowly. "Well, I know I need to get well and heal. I'm working on that."

Lilith smiles. "Yes, you are."

"I have to figure out my life and work situation. I want to teach still, but I'm not sure where. But what I do know is that I want to have a baby."

Lilith and Roy both take in sharp breaths.

"I can see this surprises you. But I'm thirty years old. I would like to have two children someday. I don't know if I'll find a partner, but I know I want to be a mom. I know I'll be a good one." Lily pauses.

"Honey, you're young. You still have time," Lilith begins.

"Sweet pea, this reminds me of someone I know." Roy smiles at his wife.

Lilith leans into him. "Yes, that's true. I was in my early thirties and didn't know if I would be getting married, so I was looking at sperm donors. That's when I met your mom and grandma. You were, and are, my—our—blessing." Lilith looks at Roy. "We'll do anything for you. You have our support."

Lily finds that she is crying. "That means the world to me. I have some work to do first, but thanks for your support. And thanks for your constant unconditional love."

Lilith and Roy move in to hug their daughter. After they release her, Lily asks them to take Sky for a walk. As they leave, Lily takes the plates and platters into the kitchen. She turns on the radio to a country station. As she wraps the food, puts it away, and washes the dishes, she sings to Martina McBride's "Anyway."

> You can spend your whole life buildin'
> Somethin' from nothin'
> One storm can come and blow it all away
> Build it anyway

The door opens and Lilith dances in, grabs a dish towel, and sings along.

> This world's gone crazy and it's hard to believe
> That tomorrow will be better than today
> Believe it anyway

Roy claps when they finish singing, while Lily and Lilith bow. Everyone is laughing, and Sky is running around them, enjoying the energy.

Lily realizes she's exhausted. She hugs her mom and dad and dances up the stairs. Once she's in her room, she runs a bubble bath of lavender, lights a vanilla candle, and, after undressing, slips under the bubbles. Sky snaps at the bubbles, making Lily laugh.

"You're the best, girl."

Sky loves the praise. She lies down on the thick pink bathmat and seems to smile at Lily.

When Lily finds she is nodding off, she lifts the drain plug and climbs out of the tub into her thick, fluffy white towel. She smiles, knowing her mom bought new towels before she arrived. After dressing in her night-gown, she slides into bed and opens her book, *The Notebook* by Nicholas Sparks. She reads a few pages and finds the book keeps dropping on her face. She turns out the light and slips into sleep.

GRANDMA CATHERINE

Lily is in a canoe, methodically moving the paddle from one side of the canoe to the other as she glides across the lake. She has sweet memories of being on a lake as a child with her family. The breeze blows her red curls, and she sees two red-tailed hawks floating on the breeze above her. She tips her head back and closes her eyes as she feels the easy rock of the canoe in the water. She is startled by the sound of a man's voice—she thought she was alone.

"What made you think I would let you come out here by yourself?"

Lily opens her eyes. Adam is sitting in the boat in front of her. *How did he get there? Has he been there all along? Is he always going to be there?*

Adam answers her thoughts. "You don't have to worry, Lily. I'll always be here. You can't be by yourself. I have to protect you. You'll see." He laughs out loud.

Lily wakes to Sky licking her face. Her heart is racing, and her chest feels tight. It's hard to breath. Lily starts tapping her forehead as Sky continues to nuzzle her. Soon her heart rate normalizes, and her breathing becomes regular.

Lily hugs Sky. "We'll be fine by ourselves. He can't intimidate us. At least I'm going to work hard on not allowing it. Right, Sky?"

Sky yelps a response. Then the two snuggle together and fall back to sleep.

Lily wakes to the smell of coffee. *Note to self—get a coffeepot with a timer. It's wonderful to wake to the aroma of coffee.* Lily stretches and climbs out of bed and then looks out the window. It's partly overcast, with gray clouds over the mountains. "Maybe some more snow today, Sky."

Lily puts on jeans, a flannel shirt, and wool socks. She and Sky climb down the stairs. She puts on her boots, coat, and hat. Opening the front door, she gets a blast of cool air. She lets Sky out and walks down the drive. She didn't bring her gloves, so she stuffs her hands in her coat pockets. Sky races around, chasing a rabbit, and then she is up the drive and out of sight and then back, rolling in the snow as it crunches under her. Then she jumps up and runs off again.

> *How will I give Sky this kind of exercise in the city? Maybe tossing a ball at the park. I've seen those long-handled sticks that you toss the ball with and it sails through the air. I'll figure something out, wherever we live.*

Sky comes barreling back, and the two walk back into the house. Lily sees her dad in the kitchen—he is pouring two mugs of coffee.

Lily takes the mug that her dad hands her. "Thanks, and good morning. Where's Mom?"

"She got a call that the hospital was desperate for staff. She knew you were spending the day with Grandma, so she agreed and went into work."

"That was nice of her. I know she loves the work. I can't imagine doing the things she does with her nursing." Lily grimaces.

Roy smiles as he stands up straighter. Lily knows he's proud of her mom. "Yeah, it doesn't seem to bother her. She likes the messy emergencies, and she's good at her job." He takes a sip of his coffee. "She'll miss dinner, since she won't get home until eight thirty or nine, unless the patient census drops and they don't need her for the whole day."

"I'll make enough for the four of us with Grandma. And if Mom doesn't make it, she can eat when she gets home or save it for lunch tomorrow."

Roy wiggles his shoulders. "What are you going to make for us? You mentioned goulash, but I didn't know if you were kidding."

Lily smiles. "Well, something along those lines. I'll see what we have in the freezer. I want to make a crockpot meal with cornbread. And I'll try to talk Grandma into making a pie."

Roy laughs. "I bet she's already made one in anticipation of your visit."

"Can I look for a recipe on one of the computers?"

"Sure, I think your mom's tablet is in the kitchen drawer. You don't need a password to get on."

"Thanks." Lily finds the tablet in the drawer with her mom's lip balm and gum. It makes her smile that some things don't change. She searches "slow cooker goulash" and finds a great recipe.

"Dad, do we have chuck roast in the freezer?"

"No, but we have sirloin, cut up in pieces. That would be even better. Do you want some breakfast?"

"I'll get out the sirloin, thanks." Lily takes a sip of her coffee. "I think I'll make some oatmeal this morning."

"That sounds good to me. I'll put a pan on for both of us."

"Thanks, Dad. You're spoiling me." Lily smiles as she writes down the goulash recipe on a piece of paper. "Would you prefer cornbread or biscuits?"

"Cornbread, please." He smiles.

"Cornbread it'll be. I'm going to run out to the greenhouse and get some vegetables. Is the sirloin in the kitchen freezer or in the freezer in the garage?"

Roy opens the freezer. "Let me check." He rummages around, taking packages out and reading the labels. "Hm." He digs deep into the freezer. "Found it." He hands it to Lily with a big smile.

"Thanks." Lily puts the meat in the sink in a bowl with lukewarm water and then grabs a basket from the shelf above the cupboard. After putting on her coat and boots, she and Sky head to the greenhouse.

The greenhouse is set back behind the house. Lily hears hoofbeats on the drive, and she turns but sees it isn't Officer Simon. She waves as the man approaches.

"Hi, you must be Lily. I'm Officer Luke. I'm just out doing my rounds. Are you two out for a walk?"

"We're getting some vegetables from the greenhouse."

"How nice. Well, have a great day." He tips his hat, turns, and trots away.

Lily and Sky follow the path to the door. Lily opens it, and they step inside, closing the door behind them. It's warm and moist inside the greenhouse. Lily remembers that her dad carefully watches the temperature and moisture levels to make sure they're prime for growing. Lily takes off her coat and hangs it on a hook by the door. She takes in a deep breath and smells all the greens and flowers. She remembers that she loved to play in here in the winter when she was a kid, and she and John would play hide and seek. And they'd planted some of their own seeds that they had bought with their own money. It was fun to watch them grow. She smiles at the memories. Then she remembers how she would dance down the railroad ties that separated the beds. She never shared that with her parents, and John didn't rat on her. Once she fell into one of the flower beds, and she and John had to fix the plants. She laughs out loud, and Sky looks over at her.

"It's OK, girl, let's get to it." Lily and Sky walk down the rows as Lily collects onions, garlic, bell peppers, tomatoes, carrots, potatoes, parsley, bay leaves, and even some roses. She places them in the basket that hangs from her arm. Sky grabs a mouthful of parsley, and Lily laughs. "Is that good, girl?" Sky happily chews. "I guess so." Lily puts on her coat and closes the door behind them, and they head toward the main house.

Once inside the house, Lily takes off her boots and hangs up her coat. She can smell the oatmeal cooking, and she thinks she smells a hint of cinnamon and brown sugar. "Smells good in here."

Roy turns from the stove and smiles. "You have a nice basket of supplies. Oh, I smell the roses."

"I thought it would be nice to have flowers on the table." Lily takes them out and cuts the stems at an angle. She gets out a vase from below the sink and places the roses in the vase, with lukewarm water and a touch of sugar. She puts them on the kitchen table so they can enjoy them during their breakfast.

Roy spoons the oatmeal into bowls and puts a pitcher of cream on the table. The two eat in happy silence as Sky eats her food in the corner. After they are done, Lily collects the bowls, rinses them, and puts them in the dishwasher. She takes the slow cooker out of the cabinet and turns it on low. She browns the sirloin with the onions and garlic. She adds the broth, the browned sirloin, and onions and garlic to the slow cooker. Then she washes and chops the parsley, tomatoes, potatoes, carrots, and bell pepper. She adds the chopped ingredients and three bay leaves. She sprinkles in some paprika, salt, pepper, and caraway seeds. After placing on the lid, she checks that the temperature is on low.

Lily turns and sees her dad watching her. "What?"

Roy grins. "It's just so nice having you here."

Lily goes over and gives her dad a hug. "It's good for me too."

Lily calls to Sky and heads for the door. "I'll make sure to check on dinner in seven hours. Is Grandma still in the Pine Street cabin?"

"Yes, same one. Do you want me to drive you?"

"No, I prefer to walk. And Sky needs lots of exercise."

"I noticed that. Have fun."

"Hey, Dad, what book are you working on now?"

"You're sweet to ask. I have some great ideas that I would love to talk to you about. We'll sit down sometime soon."

"I'd love that. Bye, Dad." Lily buttons her coat and puts on her hat and gloves. She and Sky leave the house, closing the door behind them.

Lily notices that the clouds are coming in, so she pulls up the collar on her coat and picks up her pace. Sky is running back and forth, having a great time. When they get close to Grandma's cabin, Lily can see smoke coming from the chimney. She is glad she'll have a fire to sit by. She can feel the temperature dropping with the extra cloud cover, and the air smells of moisture. Lily and Sky climb the stairs to the small cabin. It has an evergreen wreath on the door with a sign that says "Welcome." There's a knocker in the middle of the wreath, and Lily bangs twice.

Grandma throws open the door and grabs Lily up into her arms. "My goodness, I couldn't sleep. I was so excited that you and I were going to have the day together."

Lily hugs her Grandma tight. She smells of cookies, chocolate chip, and a perfume she is having trouble recognizing. Then Lily remembers it is Rosewater. She hadn't looked at her grandma closely when she first arrived at the ranch because she was so overwhelmed by the stimulus of so many family members. But she notices her grandma is shorter, like herself. She is also a bit rounder and softer. Her hug feels so good. And her curly gray hair—Lily can't help herself, so she reaches up and strokes her grandma's soft curls as her grandma smiles at her. Lily looks into her grandma's green eyes, which mirror her own. She's a reflection of herself. She gives her grandma another tight hug.

"You smell delicious, Grandma. I smell cookies and your Rosewater."

"What a memory you have. I've worn Rosewater for as long as I can remember. I'm glad I can still get the cologne." She moves out of the doorway for Lily to enter. "Come in and get warm. The temperature is dropping. Let me take your coat."

Sky has been standing behind Lily, but once Lily enters the house, Sky shoots in and runs by Grandma.

"My goodness, I forgot about the dog. Her name is Sky?"

"Yes, Sky. Is it OK that she's here? I remember that you don't like dogs."

"Oh, honey, it's not that I don't like them. I'm afraid of dogs. I was badly bitten when I stepped between your mother and a dog when she was little, and I got twenty stitches. So I haven't preferred to have dogs. Your folks didn't have dogs while you were growing up because of me and also the many guests. But I understand the value of Sky for you. I'll just have to get used to her."

Lily calls Sky to her side. "I'm sorry that happened to you. I know it's hard to get over a trauma. Sky is very intuitive. Tell her your fear is from your past experience, not her, and think calm thoughts. She has the softest fur. She wakes me up with kisses when I have a nightmare. I can't believe how amazing she is."

Grandma takes a deep breath in and lets it out slowly and then sits down on the couch. "Come sit with me and help me get to know her."

Lily sits beside her grandma and hugs and kisses her. "I'm so glad to see you." Tears leak out of her eyes, and she sees that her grandma is crying too. Sky comes over and puts her head on their hands. Grandma pets the soft fur and talks softly to Sky. Sky licks Lily's hand and then Grandma's, making them both laugh.

Grandma looks at Lily. "Would you like some hot chocolate and cookies?"

Lily smiles. "Yes, please."

Grandma gets up and goes into the kitchen, and Lily follows her in. The kitchen is decorated in gingham of reds, greens, and blues. The colors flow from the curtains, dishtowels, rugs, and knickknacks. Her dishes and mugs match the colors. Grandma has pictures of her daughter, Lily, John, Mom, Dad, and a black cat. There are also pictures of the cousins, their wives, and their kids. Then she recognizes a picture of herself in costume. It is the playbill from her ballet *Swan Lake*. But it's the picture of her birth mom that holds Lily's attention.

Grandma sees Lily looking at the picture of her biological mom. "You look a lot like her," Grandma says as she sees tears in Lily's eyes. "Honey, how can I help? You've been through so much."

Lily lets her grandma take her in her arms. "I'm lost. I don't know who I am. I'm not even sure of my memories—they're darkened. Sometimes I think I made them up to comfort me. Can you tell me everything? I'm not sure I remember what I've been told."

"Honey, I'll tell you anything. Why don't we go sit on the couch and have some hot chocolate and cookies? I'll get some albums out. I think that will help. It helps me."

Lily goes over to the couch and sits down, and Sky lies down on the rug at her feet. Lily takes in a deep breath and lets it out slowly. Then she prays out loud. "Lord, I don't talk to you often, but I need you. Help me sort through my life to understand what is real and what is not. Help me heal and get strong. And thank you for the blessings of my family, which includes Sky."

Grandma comes back into the room, weighed down with four albums. She sits down next to Lily and places the albums on the coffee table in front of them. Then she grabs a box of tissues and sets it near Lily. "You might need these. I know I will."

Grandma hands Lily the first album, and Lily opens it. The first several pictures are black and white. There is a curly-haired young woman with a nice-looking man with short hair, combed back. He is standing behind the woman, and the two are smiling. In one of the pictures, the man is in a service uniform and is holding the woman tightly.

Lily looks over at her grandma and sees tears glistening in her eyes. "Grandma, is that you and Grandpa?"

Grandma nods and grabs a tissue. "Yes, that was my love, and your mom's dad. His name was Samuel. He went to Vietnam and never came back."

Lily puts down the book and hugs her grandma. "Oh, Grandma, I'm so sorry. I knew this happened, but I don't ever remember seeing the photos."

"No, I don't bring them out very often. I just look at them when I'm missing him."

Lily turns the page and sees her grandma pregnant, with a smiling dad-to-be behind her. He has his arms around her and is touching her big belly. He has on a suit, and she's wearing a flowered dress with a sash tied above her belly. "You guys look so happy."

"Yes, we were."

"Did Grandpa get to see mom when she was born?"

"Yes, he came back from Vietnam and was there for the birth. Though in those days, dads had to wait in the waiting room. I was told he paced a track in the floor. After your mom was born and was taken to the nursery, they let her dad come see her through the glass. He came into my room with tears in his eyes. He hugged me and was so happy." Grandma looks at Lily and sees she is crying. "Lily?"

Lily looks up into her grandma's face. "I wish Adam had wanted our baby." She covers her face with her hands and cries hard.

Grandma puts the book aside and takes Lily in her arms. "Shush," she coos. "Tell Grandma what happened."

Lily leans into her grandma and tells her about Adam: their courtship, marriage, pregnancy, loss of the baby, divorce, and the stalking. Grandma listens as she holds Lily.

Grandma continues to hold Lily in her arms. "Oh, honey, I had no idea you were going through all that. I'm so sorry for the loss of your baby." Tears are streaming down her face and landing on Lily.

Lily looks up at her grandma. "You're thinking about Mom?"

Grandma grabs a tissue and wipes her eyes. "Yes, I miss her so much. I wish you could have known her." She cups Lily's face in her hands. "You'll have a child someday soon. It's the most wonderful experience— so filled with love, challenges, adventures, and worries, but pure love."

"I hope so. And if I don't find a man that treats me right, I'm going to have a baby on my own. I'm just going to wait until I have my life straightened out." Lily smiles at the thought.

Grandma gives Lily a squeeze as she reaches for the album. "You're more like your mom than you know."

Lily helps open the album again. She sees the picture of Grandma holding her mom and Grandpa leaning in, touching his new baby girl. The baby is wrapped snugly in a blanket.

"I know you can't tell the colors from the black-and-white snapshots, but your mom had bright-red curly hair. She was wrapped in a pink blanket that probably clashed with her red hair, but she was the most beautiful thing we had ever seen. My hair was bright red and terribly curly, especially after sweating during the arrival of your mom. But Grandpa said I was so beautiful. He always said that." Grandma smiles as she remembers.

"You are beautiful, and so is Mom." Lily leans down to get a closer look at the old photo.

She turns the page and sees picture after picture of the baby, her mom, with notations at the bottoms of the pictures: Jessie in the bath, Jessie crying and making her desires known. Then there are pictures of Lily's grandpa: pacing with Jessie, patting her on the back, trying to get her to burp, and exhausted, asleep in the recliner with baby Jessie. There is a picture of Grandma, Grandpa, and Jessie, all dressed up. They all have hats on their heads. The caption reads, "First family trip to church." Then there are pictures of her mom lying on the floor, looking at toys, reaching for toys, and then sitting and playing with toys.

Lily turns the page, and there is a big photo of her grandpa in uniform. He has his arm around Grandma and is holding her mom. There's a sadness in their eyes as they smile for the photo.

Lily looks at her grandma, who touches the picture ever so slightly. "Is this the last picture you have of Grandpa?"

"Yes. Isn't he handsome?" Grandma strokes the picture.

With a sigh, both women turn the page. There is picture after picture of Jessie as she grows up. Then there are colored photos. There's one with her standing in front of an easel covered in colored handprints. Jessie is turned toward the camera and smiling as she holds up her painted hands.

Lily laughs. "She has my hair."

"Yes, she does. And she hated it. She straightened it when she got older. Do you remember me telling you that when you were begging your mom to let you straighten your hair? You were so mad that she said no. You were so defiant. You said you were going to straighten your hair when you became a famous ballerina. And you did."

Lily grins. "I did. But I haven't felt like it since I was pregnant. I didn't want to put any chemicals in or on my body."

"Did you know your mom was an artist? That was her first painting, but she kept drawing and painting. I have more pictures."

Lily turns the page and sees pictures of her mom with her paintings and awards, vacation pictures at the beach with her mom sitting on a rock, sketching, roller-skating, prom pictures with funny-looking boys that looked ill at ease, high school graduation, and another beach picture.

Grandma points. "That was a graduation trip to Acapulco. That was really fun. And your mom did some beautiful pictures of the water crashing against the rock. Here's a picture of one of her paintings."

"I know that one," says Lily. "You have it on the wall in your bedroom. I forgot all about it. You told me that Mom had painted it." Lily sighs. "I guess I was pretty self-absorbed." Lily looks at her grandma. "I'm sorry."

"You have nothing to be sorry about. You were a busy, driven child with a loving mom, dad, and grandma." Grandma laughs at Lily. "Your mom, my daughter, wouldn't have wanted it any other way. I knew there would be a time when you would want to know more about her."

"Yes, I do. I feel so lost and confused about my choices and what I've let happen to me."

"Lily, you were a victim of circumstance. Remember all that you accomplished as a ballerina and opening your dance studio. You loved, and Adam failed you. I'm sure you've heard in your therapy sessions all the labels that apply to Adam."

"Oh, yes, narcissist, sociopath, controlling egomaniac, and pathological liar, just to name a few."

"All you did was trust and love someone. You have nothing to be ashamed of. This was probably your growing journey."

"Well, I'm about done with growing."

"Lily, we should never stop growing. That's what this life is all about. It's our learning ground. "

Lily looks at her grandma. "So when I don't need to learn anything else, I'm done?"

Grandma smiles. "Maybe. But, honey, there's something new to learn every day. That's the beauty of this life. Even at my age, I'm learning new things all the time—about people, relationships, the environment, history, politics, and on and on."

"I never thought of it that way. In my growing, I've realized that bad things happen to people, but we, meaning me, are responsible for how we move through and get on with our lives."

Grandma smiles and hugs Lily. "That's very wise." She turns the album page. "Now, here's a picture of your mom the day she went off to college. She got a scholarship to study art at Bennington College in Bennington, Vermont. She did very well in school. Here are some pictures when she came home and brought friends home and some of her outlandish art projects." Grandma laughs as she looks at the pictures. "Sometimes I didn't know what her message was in her artwork. But that was her freedom of expression. Oh, this is graduation day. This is your mom with her friend Lydia. They both got jobs in Denver. I guess I knew she wouldn't come back home. She had to stretch her wings." Grandma looks at Lily. "Sound familiar?"

"Yes." Lily smiles.

"Jessie got a job at a design firm, and she got an apartment with good lighting so she could still work on her art. She would attend the art fairs around Colorado and show her work on weekends in the summer. She made some money selling her work, but her job paid the bills. Here are some pictures of some of her paintings, and of course that's Jessie holding her work."

"They're beautiful scenes of Colorado. She was very talented. I can see she liked painting flowers and birds."

"Yes, she did. And she wanted a baby but hadn't found a relationship that she wanted to maintain. So your mom went to a sperm bank, researched the best donor, and got pregnant. Here are pictures of her at different stages of her pregnancy."

Lily sees the smile on her mom's face as she touched her belly in the photos. She notices that as her belly got bigger, her face became rounder looking, and she had abandoned her straight hair for curly hair. Then there was a picture of her grandma and her mom having what looked like tea and sandwiches in a café. They were leaning toward each other for the picture and had big smiles on their faces.

Lily hears Grandma take in a sharp breath. "That's the last picture I have of your mom. I had come to Denver for a visit before her scheduled C-section. She had too narrow a pelvis for a vaginal delivery, so her only option was a C-section. We had lunch that day and picked up a few things for the baby. Jessie was so excited, but the weight of the baby tired her out. We had an early dinner at Jessie's apartment, and she went to bed. She said she had a slight headache. I was staying in her guest room, which had an adjoining bathroom. Before I got ready for bed, I checked on Jessie. I couldn't wake her, and her breathing didn't sound right, so I called 911."

Lily squeezes her grandma's hand. "That must have been so scary."

"I was petrified. Later, while she was lying in the hospital bed, I worried that there was something I should have done to help her. Your mom, Lilith, helped me so much."

"What do you mean?"

"She explained the physiology of your mom's aneurysm, the bulging blood vessel that broke, and how I did everything I could. It was a nightmare. And once I accepted that your mom, Jessie, couldn't be saved, I worried about you. Lilith was wonderful, every step of the way." Grandma looks at her granddaughter. "You know that Lilith was able to talk with your mother."

Lily's jaw drops. "I knew she talked with her patients, but I never asked her about Mom."

"Your mom was one of her patients."

"What did Mom say to her?"

Grandma looks at Lily. "You could ask Lilith."

"You tell me, Grandma, please." Lily's eyes are wet with tears.

"Well, your mom, Jessie, was in a coma for a while before she died. She could talk to Lilith because Lilith can talk to her patients that are in comas or when they have died. Jessie asked what had happened to her. Lilith told her she'd had an aneurysm that had burst and that she had no brain activity. Your mom was worried about you, and Lilith told her you were healthy. She had a lot of questions and was trying to get used to her situation. Lilith was very helpful to your mom as she transitioned to death. But Jessie was worried that I couldn't raise a baby at my age. She wanted Lilith to do it so I could be a grandma. Lilith wanted to have children, but she tried to help me feel comfortable with the thought of raising you by myself. After you were born, your mom died, but she continued to talk to Lilith." Grandma pauses for a moment to let Lily absorb the information.

Lily swallows hard. "What happened next?"

"After you were born, checked over, and cleaned, the nurse put you in my arms. You were so little and beautiful. I carried you over to talk to your mom. I told her that she had done a great job, and you were perfect. I kissed her and told her how much I would miss her. I assured her that her baby was going to be taken care of—that Lilith and I were working it out."

"Tell me more."

"Did you know that your mom and Lilith's mom had the same condition?"

"No, I didn't."

"That night, Lilith went home to think about what to do. I stayed in the hospital with you, helped give you your bottles, and changed your diapers. They had a room for me to sleep in that was near the nursery where you stayed. The next morning, Lilith came in and saw me rocking you. You could see the love in her eyes—she was already attached to you. Your mom's spirit was still hanging around, making sure you were all right and talking to Lilith. I didn't know at the time about Lilith's gift. She told me later and helped me have a conversation with your mom. Anyway, I handed you to Lilith to hold. I remember telling Lilith that the two of you looked like it was meant to be. Your mom and I truly thought Lilith was the best choice to raise you. And I was lucky enough to get to live nearby and be a continual part of your life with your new mom and dad."

"Grandma, did Mom suffer?"

"No, she didn't feel anything except the initial headache. And Lilith helped her understand what was happening—to grieve and to mourn the loss of life and the loss of being able to raise the baby she loved so much."

Lily sniffs. "Grandma, why didn't you want me?"

"Oh, honey, I did, and I was right there always. I just felt it was better for you to have a young mom and dad and a forever grandma. I lived with Lilith until I bought a condo down the street. I saw you almost every day. And when your mom and dad got married, I moved to the ranch with them and you."

Lily sighs. "I remember you always being there and coming to all my performances, no matter how small." Lily smiles at her grandma.

"You bet I did. I'm so proud of your hard work. You became an accomplished dancer." Grandma hugs Lily. "Honey, I always wanted you, and so did your mom and dad. And we still do."

Lily's tears stream down her face. "But why did Mom have to die? Was it my fault? Would she have lived if she hadn't gotten pregnant with me?"

Grandma hugs Lily even tighter. "Lily, your mom had an aneurysm that no one knew about, and it just started leaking and then burst. There was nothing anyone could do. And because Lilith could communicate with your mom, she knew that your mom's main concern was you. She wanted to make sure you were taken care of."

Grandma sighs and touches the picture of her daughter. "Your mom wanted kids as far back as I can remember. In her teenage years, she had painful menstrual cramps, and she was diagnosed with endometriosis. She had to take birth control pills to prevent her menstrual cycles and cause the endometriosis to go into remission. She had laparoscopic surgery to see how the disease had progressed, and the physician used laser to burn as much of the endometriosis as he could. He told her that she had so many endometrial lesions that she might not be able to get pregnant. He told her that if that was a goal, she had better try getting pregnant sooner rather than later."

"I've heard of endometriosis, but I'm not sure what it is."

"When someone has endometriosis, not all the lining exits the body. It attaches inside the body to organs, muscles, and nerves. Then with each menstrual cycle, more attaches, and the tissue that has already attached becomes stimulated and grows, bleeds, and causes pain."

"Sounds awful."

"It is. So your mom decided she was going to try and have a baby. She was twenty-five years old. And as I told you, she got pregnant with the help of her doctor and donated sperm. She had a healthy pregnancy and was so excited for your arrival." Grandma looks closely into Lily's face. "You have two mothers that love you."

Lily smiles at her grandma. "I am lucky. I just need to believe that I'm worthy of the love my family gives me."

"You are worthy. Now, look at all this security everywhere."

Both Grandma and Lily laugh. "It's a bit ridiculous. But I appreciate how safe it makes me feel."

Grandma looks at her watch. "My goodness, we've been sitting here for hours. You must be getting hungry. I made some chicken salad. Would you like some?"

"That sounds delicious. I just want to freshen up in the bathroom."

"Of course, it's the second door on the left."

Lily and Grandma rise from the couch. Lily turns and embraces her. "Thanks, Grandma. I love you so much."

"I love you too, honey."

Lily starts down the hall and then turns. "Grandma, I'm making dinner tonight at the main house. I would love it if you came."

Grandma's smile gets even bigger. "I'll be there. Thank you."

LILITH—DAY AT THE HOSPITAL

Lilith wakes up next to her husband and kisses him on the shoulder. Then the phone rings. She reaches for it, knowing it's the hospital.

"Hello?"

"Lilith, this is William. We're short today and wondered if you would like to come in and help us out. We'll send you home early if the census drops. What do you say?"

"I'll jump up now. With my drive, I might be about fifteen minutes late."

"That would be great. See you soon. Thanks."

Lilith hangs up the phone as Roy rolls toward her. He takes her in his arms. "Nurse to the rescue!" He kisses the top of her head and releases her as she climbs out of bed.

"I don't know if I'll be home in time for dinner."

"Don't worry. Lily and I can figure out something to make, and we'll save you some." Roy climbs out of bed. "I'll pack you a lunch and get you a cup of coffee and a protein bar to go."

"You're the best, honey." Lilith smiles.

Lilith washes her face, brushes her teeth, puts on a small amount of makeup, and pulls her blond hair up into a bun. She slips on her scrubs, grabs her work bag, and heads for the door. After she puts on her Dansko shoes, coat, and gloves, Roy hands her the lunch, coffee, and an egg sandwich.

"I thought you were going to give me a protein bar. This smells yummy."

Roy kisses her cheek. "I thought something warm would be nice. Have a great day. Drive safe."

"Thanks, honey." Lilith opens the door and closes it behind her as she heads down the steps to her car.

Lilith listens to NPR on her way to the hospital. The roads are clear of snow and almost dry, and traffic is light this time of morning. She yawns as she sips her coffee and nibbles on her egg sandwich. She smiles as she thinks of Roy. *Such a good guy.* She didn't look in on Lily before she left. *It's nice thinking of her sleeping in her childhood bed.* She knows it'll be nice for Lily and her dad to have some time together. Lily also plans to see Grandma Catherine today. Lilith can almost smell Grandma Catherine's cookies, which she knows she's baking for Lily's visit.

When Lilith arrives at the hospital, she parks and heads inside. She goes down the hall, stops in the chapel, touches the holy water, and makes the sign of the cross. *Lord, may I heal and do no harm. Please be with me, my patients and their families, the staff, and my home family, especially Lily.* Lilith touches the holy water again and makes the sign of the cross. The she turns and heads to the ICU.

The nurses are giving reports at their patients' bedsides. Lilith checks the board and sees that she has one patient and one admission coming at 8:00 a.m. She puts her belongings in her locker and joins Georgia, the night nurse, for a report. Georgia is a sweet, young, experienced nurse. She has long red hair that is pulled back in a ponytail. Her nose and inner cheeks are sprinkled with freckles.

"Hi, Lilith, thanks for coming in. I'll give you a report on your first patient. She's an eighty-year-old with congestive heart failure. Your second one is a forty-nine-year-old female, lower gastrointestinal bleed, hypotension—her blood pressure is low at fifty-eight over thirty-eight; receiving fluid with blood ordered."

Lilith joins Georgia for a report in her patient's room. She receives a report on Mabel Saxton, who is responding well to her medication and is breathing better. Lilith also speaks with the family. She then checks her chart, gathers her medications, and goes into her patient's room to do a head-to-toe physical assessment. Lilith checks Mabel's neurological status, skin, and movement and then listens to her lungs, heart, and abdomen. She assesses the patient's pain and delivers the medications. Lilith returns to the nurse's station and reviews her new patient's chart. As she is finishing up, the patient arrives on a stretcher with the emergency room staff.

Lilith touches the patient's hand and says, "Hi, Mrs. Fischer, my name is Lilith. I'll be your nurse today. We're going to help you move off the stretcher to the bed and get you comfortable."

A young nurse that Lilith doesn't recognize is pushing the stretcher. "Hi, Lilith, my name is Nadine. I gave my report to Georgia. Did she pass it along to you?"

Lilith smiles. "Yes, and it's nice to meet you, Nadine. Any changes since the report?"

"Yes, Mrs. Fischer received one unit of blood. She tolerated it well, and her blood pressure has risen to ninety-two over fifty-eight with a heart rate of one hundred ten. Dr. Sims with gastroenterology is being consulted, and he'll be in early this afternoon for a scope. He would like Mrs. Fischer to have the bowel prep as soon as possible. I put in the order. Prep items should be arriving soon."

Lilith and Nadine help Mrs. Fischer to scoot over to the ICU bed, and they hook her up to the monitoring system at the bedside. Lilith sees that her patient's heart rate, blood pressure, and pulse oximeter level are stable. Lilith covers her up and helps Nadine remove the stretcher from the room. Lilith gives Mrs. Fischer the nurse call button and tells her she will be right back. Nadine, using eye and head movements that the patient can't see, has indicated that she wants to talk to Lilith outside the room.

Once outside the room, Nadine says, "Lilith, something's bothering Mrs. Fischer. She's scared to death. When she heard about the scope, she started shaking and her heart rate went up."

"Does she have any family? I read that she's a widow."

"Yes, she has a daughter who lives in Pueblo. She's on her way."

"Thanks, Nadine. I'll try and see if I can find out what's bothering her."

Nadine leaves the ICU, and Lilith returns to her patient's room. She sees Mrs. Fischer crying when she enters.

"Mrs. Fischer, I see that you're upset. Is it OK for me to come in, or do you need a moment alone?" Lilith can see that her patient's heart rate is elevated.

"Please call me Mary. You can come in. I'm just so scared."

"What is it that scares you? I can explain the whole procedure to you and answer any of your questions."

"It isn't, well, it is the procedure." Mary puts her face in her hands and cries hard, racking sobs.

Lilith gives Mary a box of tissues and moves a chair closer so she can sit down. "I understand from reading your history that you've had a lower gastric bleed before, and it resolved and didn't need treatment. You've a history of hemorrhoids. Is that accurate?"

Mary dries her eyes and blows her nose. "Yes, and that's what caused the bleeding before. But I don't know this time." Mary starts to cry again. "I don't know if I can do it."

Lilith leans toward Mary. "You won't feel a thing. You'll be given a sedative so you're comfortable during the procedure."

"No, I can't have any medication. I can't."

Lilith doesn't remember any allergies to medications in Mary's chart, and there's no indication that she has any addictions. Lilith is perplexed. "Mary, why can't you have any medications?"

Mary sniffs and looks at Lilith, with tears welling in her eyes. She takes in a shuddering breath and lets it out. "I'm a rape survivor. My father raped me for years during my childhood. I had suppressed the memory until five years ago. When my husband died, my father came to comfort me. He said nasty, vile things to me, and the suppressed memories returned."

Lilith reaches out and takes Mary's hand. "How very awful for you. Did you get some support?"

"Yes, I had lots of therapy and friends that helped. And I have a loving daughter. My father drove his car into a tree after I confronted him and told him to stay away from me. He died at the scene."

"That must have affected you as well. I hope you know that his accident wasn't your fault."

"I do know that. And I'm glad he's gone. But I have PTSD from the trauma. My dreams haunt me. If I drink alcohol, which I don't anymore, or if I receive sedation or pain medication of any kind, I have PTSD. I go right back to being that child—held down and raped. I scream and fight. So how can I have medication for the procedure, especially when it will be invasive to my lower body? I know I'll scream and fight them. That's what I did when I had the last scope. It was awful, and I ached all over from fighting them."

Lilith takes her other hand and puts it on top of the hand that Mary is squeezing tightly. Mary loosens her grip. "I'm sorry. I didn't mean to hurt your hand."

"Don't worry. Now I have an idea. I do think it's important for you to have this procedure to see where the bleeding is coming from, but you don't have to do it alone. We can verse the team so they know your history. I can be right there with you. You can listen to my voice. I'll talk you through the procedure."

"For some reason, I believe that you can help me. I'll try if you promise not to leave me."

"Mary, I'll check with the charge nurse and make sure she can watch my other patient while you have the procedure. I'll be right back." Lilith leaves the room.

Lilith finds Cynthia, the day charge nurse. She fills Cynthia in on the status of her patient and her needs around the colonoscopy, which is scheduled for 1:00 p.m. She asks if it's possible for her to be with the patient for the procedure and to have someone watch her other patient.

Cynthia looks at her assignment board. "Lilith, I don't think that will be a problem. I know you have a special gift in the comfort and compassion department. And I see that your other patient has transfer orders. So after you transfer her, you can stay with Mrs. Fischer until after the procedure. And I might send you home then if we don't get any more patients."

"That would be great. I could have dinner with my daughter. She's home right now."

"How wonderful for you. I'm sure you've missed her. I'll do my best to get you out of here."

"Thanks, Cynthia." Lilith returns to Mary's room.

"Mary, I'll be here for the procedure. I'll be talking you through it and answering all your questions. If you have a flashback, I'll remind you that you are safe, and I'll never leave your side. The procedure will take place right in your room."

"Thanks. I apologize ahead of time for any bad behavior on my part. I don't know what I'll do."

"Don't worry. Now, I'm going to see if your yummy bowel prep is here. Emptying your bowel helps the doctor see better during the scope." Lilith grins and leaves the room.

Lilith's day is flying by. Mabel, after eating her breakfast and cleaning up for the day, has walked around the nurse's station without any difficulty in her breathing. Lilith is catching up on her charting, calling reports to the cardiac floor, and getting Mabel ready for transfer.

Mary's daughter, Melissa, arrives and is at her bedside. Mary has a breakfast of lime-flavored bowel prep. She's drinking it slowly, but without any ill effects of nausea or vomiting. She's making many trips to the bathroom.

After completing her charting and transferring Mabel, Lilith checks in with Mary before her lunch break. As she enters the room, she sees Mary's daughter still sitting at the bedside. "How are you doing, Mary?"

"Oh, hi, Lilith, I'm getting lots of exercise going to the bathroom over and over again. My stool still has a bloody look, but not as much as when I was at home." Mary looks over at her daughter. "Sorry, Melissa, this must not be too much fun for you."

"Oh, Mom, I'm here for you. I just want to get you patched up so you can go home." Melissa touches her mom's shoulder as she speaks and smiles at her.

Lilith can tell by Mary's scowl, the wringing of her hands, and the tapping of her foot that she's nervous. "The prep makes you go often to clean out your colon. And your skin color is pink, and your heart rate and blood pressure are normal. Your bloodwork shows your hematocrit has risen from 29 to 35 percent. The lab will be in to check another level in a few minutes. I'll be taking a break, and Nancy, one of the other nurses, will look in on you and get you whatever you need. How are you feeling about the procedure?"

"I'm scared. I don't like not being in control. That's how I feel when I get medication. And once I feel I've lost control, I slip right back into PTSD. I don't know what will happen."

"I'll be right there with you. You'll feel my touch and hear my voice."

"Thanks. Melissa will wait in the family lounge. I don't want her to hear me babble nonsense."

Lilith turns to Melissa. "Dr. Sims and I will come and talk to you after the procedure. He'll explain what he found and if he did any interventions. And I'll tell you how your mom did during the procedure. Then I'll bring you back to see your mom. Do you have any questions?"

"No. Thanks, Lilith."

"I'll see you both in about thirty minutes." Lilith turns and heads to the nurses' lounge to eat her lunch.

The lounge is empty. Lilith opens the refrigerator and takes out her lunch bag. She sits down at the table and pulls out a chicken, basil, and spinach sandwich. There's a small container of vinaigrette. She dips the sandwich in the vinaigrette. "Yum," Lilith says out loud. As she chews, she looks out the window at the snow-capped mountains in the distance. The sun is starting to melt the snow that surrounds the hospital parking lot. Lilith wonders what Grandma Catherine and Lily are talking about. She smiles as she remembers how excited Catherine was when she heard Lily was coming home to the ranch.

Once her lunch break is over, Lilith returns to the ICU. She sees that Dr. Sims's nurse has arrived with the equipment and is entering Mary's room. Lilith washes her hands and enters the room. She smiles at Mary and Melissa. Joan, Dr. Sims's nurse, has introduced herself to Mary and Melissa and explained that she is going to set up the equipment for Dr. Sims.

Lilith adds, "Melissa, you can stay while they set up, if you like."

"OK, I will." She squeezes her mom's hand.

Lilith opens the computer that's next to Mary's bed. She clicks on the lab tab to see if the results of Mary's hematocrit are posted. "Your hematocrit is 34 percent. It only dropped one point."

"Is that good?"

"Yes, you don't need any blood at this time." Lilith smiles.

Dr. Sims enters the room and sits down next to Mary and Melissa. "Hi, I'm Dr. Michael Sims with gastroenterology." He shakes hands with Mary and Melissa and then asks questions about Mary's history and symptoms. He does a belly exam and explains the sedation, procedure, and possible interventions he might do. He has Mary sign the consent form. Mary explains her past experience with rape and her PTSD with sedation or pain medication. She tells him that Lilith is going to coach her through the procedure.

Dr. Sims smiles at Lilith. "I'm sure that Lilith will help you feel comfortable. I'll answer any of your questions and explain everything as we go along." He pats Mary's hand. "Are you ready?"

Melissa rises and kisses her mom on the forehead. "I'll be in the family lounge."

"OK, sweetheart." Mary tries to give her best smile as she grabs for Lilith's outstretched hand.

Lilith nods at Melissa as she leaves and closes Mary's door. She moves in close to Mary. Lilith has an oxygen mask and oral suction available for Mary. Joan asks Mary to turn onto her left side with her knees bent. Dr. Sims asks Joan to deliver a prescribed amount of Versed for sedation and fentanyl for pain.

Lilith knows that she must speak plainly and clearly so that Mary can understand while she's sedated, so Lilith whispers into Mary's ear. "Joan is giving you some sedation and pain medication. You'll feel heavy, so just sink into the bed and relax. I'm with you, and you're safe." She strokes Mary's head as she speaks.

Mary's voice is slurred. "I feel it. I'm sinking."

"Just squeeze my hand. I'm here. You're safe."

"Mary, I put warm gel on the tube and will be inserting it into your rectum. Try to relax. You may feel some pressure as it follows the curve in your intestine," Dr. Sims says.

Mary squeezes her buttocks and yells, "No, you're not doing that to me! Don't touch me! It's my body!"

Dr. Sims stops and looks at Lilith as she leans down and says, "Mary, it's Lilith, your nurse. You're in the hospital, and we're putting a tube in your rectum to see where you're bleeding. We'll give you a little more sedation and pain medication. You're safe. I'm with you."

Mary is given more medication, and she relaxes and closes her eyes. Dr. Sims tells her he is inserting the tube further.

Mary suddenly opens her eyes and tries to sit up. She fights with her legs. "Damn you! You're not going to rape me! Help! Help! Leave me alone! You can't do this!" Mary's heart rate is elevated, and she is hyperventilating. Lilith and Joan hold onto Mary so she doesn't fall off the bed as she fights.

Dr. Sims stops. He has beads of sweat on his brow, and his eyes dart toward Lilith. Lilith puts her arms around Mary and holds her tightly. Lilith knows that Mary is confused because of the medication. She changes her conversation to imply she is placing the tube so as not to confuse and frighten Mary. "Mary, it's Lilith. I'm here with you. I'm just putting a tube in your bottom to see what's causing you to bleed. You're not being raped. Your rapist is dead and buried. You're safe. It's just a tube. I won't let anything happen to you."

More sedation is given to Mary, and Lilith places an oxygen mask on her face. Mary's body relaxes—she is asleep. But Lilith hears, *Where am I? What's happening to me?*

Lilith knows that Mary is talking to her in her drugged sleep. She sees on the monitor that Mary's heart rate is elevated. Lilith whispers silently, *Mary, this is Lilith. I am your nurse. You are at the hospital, because you were bleeding from your rectum. I am putting a tube in your rectum. It has a scope to look and see what is causing the bleeding. You are safe. I won't hurt you. I am with you.*

Why can you hear me? I don't even hear my voice.

Lilith whispers silently, *I have a gift to be able to talk to patients when they are in a coma or asleep from sedation. Mary, you are safe. It is just a tube to see why you are bleeding from your colon. I won't let anything happen to you.*

Lilith sees on the monitor that Mary's heart rate has normalized. She knows that the medication will cause Mary to forget what she tells her, so she repeats herself over and over. She leans in close and whispers in Mary's ear, "Mary, this is Lilith. I am your nurse. You are safe. I put a tube in your rectum to find out why you are bleeding. You are safe. I won't let anything happen to you."

"Ah, here's the problem—a torn hemorrhoid. I'll band it, and we'll be done," Dr. Sims says.

Lilith continues to whisper to Mary. "Mary, my name is Lilith. I am your nurse. I put a tube in your rectum to see what was bleeding in your colon. You have a hemorrhoid that I will place a band on to stop the bleeding. You are safe. I won't let anything happen to you. You are safe. Just relax and let the medicine help you sleep. I am holding you and you are safe."

Dr. Sims bands the hemorrhoid. He then washes the area and watches through the scope to see if there is any bleeding. When he sees that the bleeding has stopped, he withdraws the tube and covers Mary.

Lilith continues holding Mary and whispering, "Mary, this is Lilith, your nurse. The procedure is over. You are not bleeding anymore. You are safe. I won't let anything happen to you."

Dr. Sims looks over at Lilith and mouths, "Thank you." He wipes the sweat from his brow with his arm and whispers, "I'll go out and tell her daughter we're done, and she can come in." Lilith nods as she continues to whisper to Mary. Joan gathers the equipment, nods her thanks to Lilith, and leaves the room.

Melissa peeks in and sees Lilith holding her sleeping mom. She moves close to the bed. "How is she?"

Lilith looks up and says to Mary, "Mary, this is Lilith, your nurse. You are safe. The procedure is over and went well. You are fine. Just rest—you are safe. I will let Melissa hold your hand until you wake up. I will be next to your bed, charting on the computer. You are safe. I won't let anything happen to you."

Thank you, Lilith.

Lilith speaks silently to Mary, *You are welcome, Mary.*

Lilith completes her charting as Mary wakes up gradually by listening to Melissa read a story. Lilith comes over to Mary. "Mary, do you know where you are?"

"Hi, Lilith, I'm in the hospital."

"Do you remember why you're here?"

"I was bleeding, you know, down there." Mary points down toward the end of her body. "I had a colonoscopy done. Oh, that's right. Did Dr. Sims find anything? The reason I was bleeding?"

Melissa leans toward her mother. "Mom, I told you."

"But I don't remember."

Lilith sits down next to Mary's bed. "Mary, the medicine affects your memory, so it's normal to forget. Dr. Sims found a torn hemorrhoid. He banded it, and it stopped bleeding. You're going to be fine."

Mary grabs Lilith's hand and whispers, "How was I? Did I make a scene?"

"You did get confused as to where you were and what was happening to you. You were frightened. I was right there with you, and you did a great job."

"I remember your voice and that you were holding me. Thanks so much."

"It was my pleasure, helping you feel safe. Now you rest. I think they might be sending me home soon. I'll let you know."

Melissa stands and approaches Lilith. She reaches out and takes Lilith into a hug. "Thanks for what you did for my mother. You have no idea what that meant to both of us."

Lilith releases Melissa and smiles over at Mary. "I'm thankful that Mary trusted me with her personal tragedy. I'm so glad that I could help."

Lilith leaves Mary's room and sees Cynthia, the charge nurse, heading toward her. "Lilith, you can report off to Mike and get out of here early."

"I just finished my charting. I'll do that now. Thanks, I'll be home in time for dinner with my daughter."

Lilith finds Mike, and the two go to Mary's bedside. "Mary, this is Mike. He'll take good care of you until the night shift gets here. I'll give him a report now, and you let me know if you have any questions or anything to add."

Lilith gives her report and says good-bye to Mary and Melissa. She goes to her locker, gets her things, and heads for her car.

She calls Roy's number. When he answers she says, "Honey, they let me leave early. I should be home by five."

"Great. Lily made dinner, and Grandma Catherine is joining us. So glad you can make it. Did you have a good day?"

"Yes, but emotionally draining. I'll tell you about it when I get home. Bye for now." Lilith ends the call and climbs into her car. She takes a long drink of her water, which she didn't have much of during the shift. She thinks of Mary and her trauma, and then she thinks about Lily and Kit. She knows with trauma, no matter what it is or how much you work on it, when you are in a vulnerable state, it can come back to haunt you. She shudders, takes a deep, cleansing breath in, and lets it out slowly. "God bless them," she says out loud and then starts her car and drives toward home.

Once home, Lilith parks and exits her car, climbs the stairs, and opens the front door. She can smell something delicious. "Yum, what am I smelling?"

Lily comes around the corner and says, "It's beef goulash, and the corn bread is almost ready. Grandma's setting the table. Are you hungry?

"You bet. I'll just shower, change, and be right out." Lilith says hi to Roy, Catherine, and Sky before going to her room.

Lilith comes out of her bedroom with wet hair. "Oh, I feel better, and hungry." She approaches Lily and takes her in her arms. "Honey, I love you so much." She squeezes her tightly.

The squeeze makes Lily's breath escape. "Mom, you OK? Did you have a tough day?"

"Yes, but I'll tell you about it later. I'm just so sorry for the trauma that you and your friend Kit have gone through. You're amazing, honey. Do you know that?" Lilith looks into her daughter's face.

"Well, I don't know about that. But I'm getting there. Thanks, Mom, I'm so glad to be home. And Kit will love it here too. Now let's say grace and eat."

There's plenty of laughter and chewing as the food disappears. Roy sneaks a piece of meat to Sky, and Lilith catches him as Sky grabs it.

"Roy! No feeding the dog at the table."

Roy grins. "Lily told me to."

Lily laughs. "Dad, I did not." She smiles. "But good idea. She's such a good dog. I just love her."

Sky goes to Lily's side as if she knows Lily is talking about her. Lily pats the soft fur around her eyes and the top of her head.

Lily remembers that tomorrow is Sunday. "Can we all go to church tomorrow? And does Sky get to go too?"

Lilith smiles. "That's a great idea. And yes, Sky goes wherever you go."

FRIENDSHIP RENEWAL

Lily wakes and stretches, and so does Sky. Sky gives her a wet kiss across her cheek as Lily ruffles her fur. The sun is bright as it shines through the white lace curtains. Lily rises and goes to her closet.

She touches the new clothes that her mom bought her. *What should I wear to church today?* She looks over at Sky. "You're lucky you don't have to worry about what to wear." Sky gives a yelp. "OK. I guess you need to go out. Give me a moment. It's been so long since I went to church. I think I remember it's pretty casual, but just in case." Lily pulls out a brown corduroy skirt, a cream silk shirt, and a brown-and-navy pullover sweater. She grabs the tall brown boots. "Nice." She's a bit excited to get dressed up. She hums an old hymn, "Ave Maria," as she gets ready.

Lily and Sky descend the stairs with the click of Lily's boots. Lily opens the door for Sky. She's out like a rocket, running this way and that, doing her business and looking for something to chase. Lily stands on the steps and breathes in the fresh air as the cool wind whips her red curls around her face. She smiles to herself as she thinks back to the night and realizes she didn't have any nightmares. She dreamed, but the dreams were a fuzzy conglomeration of color, family, and activities. She sighs and thinks, *Progress.*

Sky runs back and rubs up against Lily. "Let's go, girl, and get some breakfast."

Lily finds her mom and dad in the kitchen, making breakfast. They turn and smile at her as she enters. Lilith is wearing a long skirt in a wild-flower print and tall boots. She has a white shirt under a red cardigan. Roy has on nice blue jeans and a pressed western shirt that's covered by a brown leather vest.

"We thought we heard you coming down the stairs and going out the front door. My, you look nice. Those clothes are a perfect fit for you," Lilith says.

"I love them. You guys are spoiling me. I know it has to end, but not yet." Lily grins. "Can I help?"

"Why don't you set the table," Roy says.

Lily nods and goes to the island, opens the drawer, and takes out napkins and place mats. She gathers the silverware and fills the glasses with orange juice. She puts a stack of plates next to her dad, who is making omelets. Lily leans in and gently bumps her dad. "That smells wonderful." Roy smiles in response.

Lily grabs Sky's bowls and fills one with fresh water and the other with a scoop of organic dog food. She places them on the rubber mat at the end of the kitchen counter. "Here you go, girl."

Lilith and Roy watch Lily and Sky. Lilith winks at Roy and asks Lily, "Is Sky too much trouble?" She gives Lily a serious look and then breaks into a smile.

"Mom, you know I love her. She's great for me. You know, I didn't have any nightmares last night."

"I'm so glad, honey." Lilith leans into Roy, who gives her a hug as they smile at their daughter.

Lilith gathers the berries she washed and places them in a bowl with a spoon. Roy puts the omelets on the plates. Lily pours coffee into three mugs and puts the cream and sugar on the table. They all sit down.

Roy says grace. "Heavenly Father, bless this day, bless this meal, and bless us to thy service. In the name of the Father, the Son, and the Holy Spirit. Amen."

Lily and Lilith chime in with "amen" and make the sign of the cross.

They all eat heartily. Lily cleans the dishes and puts them in the dishwasher. She runs upstairs to brush her teeth and comes back to put on her coat. She steps outside with Sky, as Lilith and Roy wait in the truck.

They drive down the road to Grandma Catherine's house. She's waiting on the porch, wrapped in a camel-colored wool coat with a matching hat. Her gray curls can be seen curling up over the rim of the hat. She smiles and waves as they approach. She comes down her steps, holding onto the rail. Roy climbs out and helps her up into the truck, where she sits next to Lily and Sky.

St. Agnes Catholic Church is a fifteen-minute drive. One of the security guards pulls up behind them and travels along toward the church. The fifty-year-old stone church is set back from the road down a long driveway that ends in a parking lot. It's nestled among thick blue spruce trees with evergreen bushes along the front. Roy parks next to his nephew Clark's SUV, and they climb out of the truck. Lilith puts Sky's working vest on Lily's dog, and Sky moves in close to Lily. Ben, the security guard, follows them in and sits at the back of the church.

Roy leads his family up to the middle of the left side of pews. They sit next to Steven and his family, including Missy, Mac, Ben, and Sam. Lily notices that the three boys are dressed in nice shirts that are tucked into their jeans. Missy has on slacks and a long sweater, and Steven wears jeans and a western shirt with a leather vest like his uncle. Sitting up one row is Clark and his family, Ali and An. Ali and An wear dark lace veils on their heads. Lily had forgotten that very traditional Catholic women, like Ali and An, wear veils to Mass. They kneel to pray before Mass begins and rise to sing as the priest enters and proceeds down the aisle. Sky maneuvers back and forth over the kneeling rail and finally lies across it.

As Lily is singing next to her Grandma, she notices from the corner of her eye that someone to her right is looking in her direction. Her face flushes when her eyes meet Charlie's. He is standing next to his mom and smiles right at her. She smiles back. Lilith catches the look, nudges Roy, and whispers in his ear.

Five minutes later, John arrives, and they make room for him in the pew. He says he just finished an emergency call. He tickles his sister, and she scowls at him and then smiles.

At the traditional giving of the peace to each other, Lilith whispers to Lily, "We're going to have a family dinner tonight. Would you like to invite Charlie?"

"Mom!" Lily whispers a bit too loud. Then she smiles. "That would be nice."

After the service, they exit the church and shake hands with Father Rod. He's a tall, broad-shouldered young man who came to St. Agnes three years ago. Lilith told Lily that she is very fond of him and that he visits his parishioners at her hospital.

The parishioners gather outside the church, while the sun warms the air. Lily has a chance to say hi to Clark's and Steven's wives and children. As Lily is talking with her brother about his emergency, Charlie joins them.

"How's the steer?" Charlie asks as he nods at Lily.

John looks from Charlie to Lily and smiles. "Oh, the steer. Yes, silly boy was trying to get at the cows and got cut up in barbed wire across his chest. Twenty-five stitches. He'll be all right. I gave him an antibiotic, and I'll have to go out and check on him later."

Charlie looks down at Lily. "How're you today, Lily?"

Just then, John's pager goes off again. "Excuse me, guys, I have to call on this page."

John leaves Lily and Charlie standing alone, with Sky sitting next to Lily, looking at Charlie.

"I'm fine, *Chip*." Lily laughs, waiting for a response.

Charlie laughs and then looks away as if remembering. Then Charlie looks deep into Lily's green eyes. "How's your visit been with your family? I know they were so excited that you were coming home."

"It's really nice. Hey, tonight we're having a family dinner. Would you like to come? Mom wanted me to invite you."

"Since your brother is on call, I can come. Thanks. I was going to go for a horseback ride on the ranch this afternoon. Would you like to join me?"

Lily is surprised by the invitation. "Um, I haven't ridden much. I had a ride with Mom around the property. Well, I'd like to go up into the mountains a bit. Sky will come along."

"I know this is none of my business, but I've noticed the security since you came home. Is it OK for you to ride up into the mountains? Will one of the security guards come with us?"

"Yeah, I know. I don't mind telling you what happened, but maybe later. I suppose a guard will ride with us. And Sky never leaves my side. Is that a problem for you?"

Charlie lets out a breath. "No, I don't mind. I would love a chance to catch up. How about we meet at the barn at one thirty?"

"That'd be nice. I'll check with Mom and find out how it works with the guard. I'll call you if there's a problem. How's your mom doing? I saw you sitting with her in Mass. And I was so sorry to hear about your dad. He was a great man."

"Thanks. We miss him. Mom struggled for a while, but she's pretty great now. She misses him all the time, but she stays busy. She disappeared with her church lady friends. I think they're in the basement serving coffee and donuts. She'd like to see you while you're here."

"I'd like that. I'll be here a month or so." Lily sees her mom waving. "I need to go. I'll see you at one thirty. Bye, Charlie." Lily turns and heads to the truck. She can feel the smile on her face, and she realizes that it'll be nice to talk with an old friend. *He's so darn sweet and polite and easy on the eyes. He reminds me of the country gentlemen in those romantic Hallmark movies.*

Lily and Sky climb into the backseat of the truck and sit next to Grandma.

Grandma pats Lily's knee. "That was a nice service. So glad you were there with us, Lily." She smiles and touches Lily's face.

"Me too. It's been a long time since I went to Mass."

"Lily, did you invite Charles to dinner tonight?" Lilith calls from the front seat.

"Yes, Mom, and he likes to be called Charlie."

"Oh, OK, I'll call him Charlie. I think it's because John always refers to him as Charles. Maybe that's just for business." Lilith looks at Roy, who shrugs his shoulders.

"Oh, and he invited me to go riding with him this afternoon. Will security go with us?"

Lilith looks back at Lily. "Will you be going up into the mountains?"

"Yes, we were thinking about that."

"Then yes, you'll have security going with you, just as a precaution. I'll arrange it. When are you planning on going?"

"I'm meeting him at the barn at one thirty. Which horse does he ride?"

"Charlie has his own horse, Silver Knight. He's a dark-gray Arabian. He keeps him here and allows us to use him on group trail rides. The wranglers enjoy riding him. He's smart, steady, and very good at herding horses or cattle."

Roy pulls his truck into the ranch drive, and he waves at Officer Marcus in the security hut. Officer Ben honks that he is continuing after they are on the property.

They drive to drop Grandma Catherine off at her house. As she climbs out of the truck, she turns and says, "See you at six for dinner. I'm bringing three pies." She smiles in delight.

"Yum," Lilith calls back.

As the truck turns toward the main house, Lily asks, "What can I contribute to the dinner?"

Lilith turns back toward her daughter. "Everyone brings something. Your dad's smoking barbecue brisket—he started it this morning. John's not included, since he's on call and we don't know if he'll make it. Steven's family will bring a vegetable dish and potatoes, and Clark's family brings this wonderful sweetbread. That leaves a big salad. Can you help me with that and set the table? All the ingredients are in the refrigerator and in the greenhouse. I'll make some lemonade and homemade ice cream to go with Grandma's pies."

"I'll do the salad and set the table. I'm hungry just thinking about all the food."

Roy parks the truck in the driveway, and everyone gets out. Lily takes off Sky's vest, and Sky takes off to run up and down the drive. Lily can smell the meat smoking.

"I'm going to make a sandwich before going on my ride. Can I make you guys a sandwich?"

Roy jingles his keys. "Sure, that would be nice." He looks at Lilith, and she nods.

Lily goes into the house as Sky zooms past her, and the two go upstairs. Lily takes off her boots and sets them in the closet. She hangs up her shirt and skirt and folds the sweater and puts it in the chest of drawers. She takes out a pair of jeans and puts them on. Looking in her closet, she chooses a tank top and a flannel shirt. Lily goes to the mirror and combs through her red curls. She puts them in a ponytail, adds a bit more mascara to her long lashes, and smiles to herself. She realizes that she's excited to have a ride with her old friend—she knows he still likes her. *We'll see.* Lily grabs her red cowboy boots and heads downstairs.

In the kitchen, Lily gets out some bread, and pops eight slices into the large family toaster and pushes the lever. Opening the refrigerator, she takes out a package of deli chicken slices, pepper jack cheese, mustard, mayonnaise, fresh basil, and a couple of tomatoes. Lily slices the tomatoes thinly. She cuts up two apples and three oranges and mixes them in a bowl. After turning the oven to broil, she sets the toast on a baking sheet. She dresses each with mustard and mayonnaise, two slices of chicken, a slice of cheese, tomato slices, and sprigs of basil. Then she places the baking sheet in the oven. Lily puts out some plates, napkins, silverware, and water glasses. She knows it won't take long under the broiler, so she checks the sandwiches frequently. She can smell the basil cooking.

Roy and Lilith come into the kitchen as Lily is taking out the sandwiches. She looks up at their smiles of surprise. "Are you hungry?" She laughs.

"Are you kidding?" Roy asks. "And I see you made me two open-faced sandwiches."

"Looks amazing," Lilith adds.

Roy looks at his wife and nods.

Lily sees the silent exchange between her parents. "Are you guys doing your telepathy thing?" She pretends to frown. "I could use some tools like that in my toolbox."

Lilith and Roy smile and nod at their daughter. The three eat in silence.

After lunch, Lily gives her parents a hug, grabs three water bottles, and puts on her red cowboy boots and matching jacket. Lilith told her that Officer Luke will be going with them. Lily and Sky head toward the stables.

Sky runs ahead and then runs back to Lily, and Lily smiles at her excited dog. Sky jumps, yelps, and wags her tail back and forth.

When they arrive at the stables, Lily sees that Charlie has two horses tied and is brushing a beautiful, dark gray. The other horse is Sammy, the bay gelding Lily rode with her mom.

Lily approaches Charlie. "Is this your horse? He's beautiful."

"Thanks. He's a fine boy. I love it when I get a chance to ride him. I caught Sammy for you. Is that who you wanted to ride?"

"Oh, yes, he's such a good boy." Lily grabs a brush and strokes Sammy's neck and back. He leans into her as she brushes. With a hoof-pick, she picks the dirt out of his hooves. Lily places a saddle blanket and saddle on Sammy and cinches him up. She puts on his bridle and then puts on her helmet.

Charlie has his horse ready as Officer Luke rides up.

"Hi, there, I'm Luke. You must be Lily and Charlie. I'll just ride behind you guys if that's OK."

"Hi, Luke, that's fine," Lily responds, and Charlie waves. Both Lily and Charlie get on their horses, with Sky in the lead, and they head down the road to the west toward the mountains. Lily notices that Luke has water in his saddlebags. She gave a bottle of water to Charlie and has two for herself and Sky. Luke rides several yards behind them so as not to intrude on their conversation.

Lily looks over at Charlie, who is riding next to her. "It's weird having security around all the time. I hope you don't mind."

"I'm just glad to have some time to talk with you. I want you to have whatever makes you feel safe."

Lily takes in a shuddering breath. Sammy's body tenses, and Sky looks back at Lily. Lily realizes that not only is Sky attuned to her, but Sammy is as well. She leans down and strokes Sammy's neck. "It's OK, boy." She then looks down at Sky. "I'm OK, girl." Sky holds her gaze for a minute and then darts off.

Charlie looks over at Lily. "Are you doing OK?"

"It just comes in waves."

Charlie's eyes follow the sway of her body as she keeps rhythm with her horse.

Lily catches him staring at her. "What're you looking at?"

Embarrassed at being caught, Charlie smiles and recovers with, "I was just remembering that I have a secret."

Lily's eyebrows arch. "A secret."

"Well, more like a confession."

"Now you have my attention. Pray, tell. What could you possibly have to confess?"

Charlie takes in a deep breath. "I came to New York to see you dance in the ballet."

Lily pulls her horse to a stop. "You did? Why didn't you tell me?"

Charlie nods for them to keep moving. "Oh, come on. I just wanted to see you dancing your dream. And you were splendid." He smiles.

"When? What ballet?"

"I don't remember the dates. But one Christmas I saw you in *The Nutcracker* as the Sugar Plum Fairy, and then as Juliet in *Romeo and Juliet*, and again in *Swan Lake*."

"You came to New York three times and didn't tell me?"

Charlie's skin flushes. His legs wrap around his horse, and Silver speeds up. Lily does the same and catches up with him. She stares at him until he meets her eyes.

"You know I pined for you in high school. And when I heard from John how proud he was that you were a principal dancer for the NYC Ballet, I had to see you."

"I never saw you when my family came."

"They didn't know I came. I haven't told anyone. I just wanted to see you. I was so proud that you'd reached your dream after all your hard work. Oh, and I don't mean you stopped working hard. I can't even imagine how hard you worked." Charlie looks ahead and then turns to Lily. "I guess that sounds kind of stalkerish."

Lily flinches and then shakes off the feeling. "Well, at least you were a benign stalker."

Charlie sees Lily flinch. "I'm sorry, Lily. I didn't mean to upset you. I just didn't know if you would want to see me. You were the girl that got away."

Lily frowns. "I never meant to hurt you. I was consumed with my goal."

"I know. That was a long time ago. But I guess I should have told you I was there. I was too embarrassed to even tell John."

"It's OK. I'm glad you saw me. I'm proud of that part of my life."

Heaviness hangs in the air between them as they ride on in silence. They reach the ridge that overlooks the ranch, and the view is majestic. Lily remembers that this was where her parents had gotten married. They love reminding her.

Lily dismounts and takes some large swallows of water from her water bottle. Sky comes up close to her side and sits down. "Are you thirsty, girl?" Lily tips the bottle on its side, and Sky drinks the rest. Sky gives a yelp. "You want more?" Sky yelps again. Lily opens the second bottle and drinks half and then gives the second half to Sky. She notices that both Charlie and Luke are taking a water break while still sitting in the saddle.

Lily looks out again toward her childhood home. *Lord, help me to move on with my life without living in constant fear and anxiety. I want to live. And thank you for my supportive family, human and furry, the security, and old friends.* Lily turns and smiles at Charlie, and he responds with a quizzical look.

Lily leans down and gives Sky's fur a ruffle and then leans in and kisses her. She nuzzles Sammy and gives him a kiss and then climbs up in the saddle.

Charlie asks, "Ready to head back?"

"Yes, I have to help with dinner." Lily grins.

"What can I bring?"

"I think everything is covered."

"How about wine?"

Lily thinks a moment. "That would be great."

"Now you won't believe this, but I bought shares in this winery in Grand Junction. I have cases of the wine in my basement. It's pretty good too. Is your dad making barbecue?

"Yes!"

"Oh, boy, I have a Cabernet that'll be perfect. I'll bring several bottles."

"I can't wait to try it."

An afternoon spring breeze follows them as the horses prance home. Lily feels her body relax into the saddle—she feels good in the company of her old friend. They chat easily about Lily's work with the ballet and her friends and about how Charlie chose veterinary medicine and then partnered with John.

Back at the stables, Officer Luke waves good-bye as he turns his horse to ride the perimeter of the property. Lily and Charlie thank him, and then they unsaddle their horses, brush them, give them some grain, and open the gate for them to rejoin the other horses. Sky shoots out to herd them through the gate and onto the path toward the other horses.

Lily laughs. "Sky has so much energy. She's so good to me, so I must remember to let her have her time."

Charlie looks after Sky. "I think you're doing just fine by her." He grins and then turns to Lily. "I enjoyed the ride. I'll see you tonight."

"I enjoyed myself too. See you soon." Lily whistles, and Sky comes running. The two head toward the main house.

Once inside the house, Lily showers and changes. She puts on a pair of dark-green slacks and a cream blouse with a pattern of little holly berries. She puts on one of her favorite pairs of slip-on black shoes. Lily, with Sky at her side, heads into the kitchen to see what vegetables are available in the refrigerator and makes a note of them. Then Lily grabs a basket and goes out to the greenhouse. Sky runs along with her. Lily fills her basket with green onions, radishes, beets, romaine lettuce, tomatoes, carrots, and cucumbers, and then she grabs some daisies for a centerpiece.

As Lily gets ready to leave the greenhouse, she calls to Sky, who's enjoying sniffing all the different plants. "Come, Sky." Sky runs to her side. "Good girl." Lily rubs Sky's head.

The house is busy with activity. Grandma has come early to help, and she sets her three pies on the kitchen island. Lily makes the salad with almost every color imaginable: red, light and dark green, yellow, purple, orange, and white. She adds pumpkin seeds and dried cranberries. After tossing the salad, she covers it with a damp paper towel and places it in the refrigerator. She joins Grandma, who's setting the table.

"Your pies smell delicious. I think I smell cherry and blueberry. What's the other one?"

"Peach," answers Grandma.

Lily smiles in surprise. "That was my favorite when I was young. I forgot that."

"Honey, you're still young." Grandma chuckles as she looks at Lily over the top of her reading glasses.

"Yeah, but I don't feel that way."

"You will soon enough." Grandma gives Lily a hug. Moving back to the table setting, she says, "Oh, I heard your young man is coming for dinner."

"Grandma! He's not my young man. We're old friends."

Grandma winks at Lily, and Lily grins back.

Soon the cousins and their families arrive. Lily notices the sweet aroma of the bread as Ali hands her the basket

Lily smiles up into Ali's kind face. "This smells so good. And I look forward to getting to visit with you, Ali.

"Me too, Lily. And I'd be happy to give you the recipe. It's an old family favorite."

"I'd like that. Thanks." Lily puts the bread on the table next to the butter.

Steven and Missy carry in the green bean casserole and potatoes au gratin. Their boys, Mac, Ben, and Sam, come in holding board games and move to the family room to set up a game. Clark and Ali's An follow the boys in, and they all sit around the big coffee table, ready to play.

Lilith comes into the room, dressed in a mocha-print skirt floating about her legs. She wears a cotton cream-colored sweater with a horse brooch that Lily remembers her dad had given her. As usual, she has on wool socks that match her skirt.

Lily smiles. "Feet cold, Mom?"

"Now don't make fun of me. You know I get grouchy if my feet are cold." Lilith kisses her daughter on the top of her head.

Charlie enters the house carrying a case of wine.

Lilith looks up. "Hi, Charlie, what did you bring?"

"I brought some wine from my vineyard. I'll open a couple of bottles."

"That's right. John told me you had a vineyard."

"Well, it's a share in a vineyard in Grand Junction. I like the wine. Hope you will too."

"It's so nice of you to bring it. I'm sure we'll like it. I'll get you a corkscrew."

Charlie opens two bottles and puts them on the table. He joins Lily as she's tossing the salad. "Can I help?"

Lily smiles at Charlie. "No, thanks, I think everything's done."

Roy comes in, holding a platter filled high with barbecue brisket. He's still wearing the clothes he wore to church, except instead of the vest he has a brown bolo tie with a silver eagle that Lily remembers her mom gave him.

Roy looks over at the kids getting ready to play a game. "Dinner's ready. Can everyone take a seat at the table?" Roy sets the platter down on the dark-oak oval table that has been in his family since he was little.

Lilith pours lemonade in the glasses. Lily brings out the salad, which she has dressed with a vinaigrette dressing. Grandma puts out the casserole and potatoes.

Everyone sits down. Roy takes a seat at the head of the table and asks everyone to hold hands. Charlie sits next to Lily. Roy begins. "Most merciful Father, we are thankful for the gathering of family and friends. Bless us, bless this food to the nourishment of our bodies, and bless us to thy

service. In the name of the Father, the Son, and the Holy Spirit. Amen."
Everyone makes the sign of the cross as they say "amen."

There's laughing, talking, and lots of chewing. Lily loves hearing the exchanges between the cousins. Before they're finished, John comes in from work. He washes his hands at the sink and pulls up a chair next to Charlie.

"You missed a good one, partner."

"I left my pager at home, so I didn't see what you went out on."

John winks at Charlie. "I'll save the story until after we eat."

Lily looks over with a smile and says, "Thanks for that, brother."

Charlie leans toward Lily. "Do you like country dancing?"

Lily swings her head toward him in surprise. "Yes, but I haven't done it in years."

Charlie takes a sip of his wine and swallows and then looks at Lily. "There's a new bar in the next town that has great burgers and a country band on Thursday night. I have that night off. Would you like to go?"

Lily looks at him as she thinks. "That'd be nice. I'd like that."

Charlie looks down at Sky, who's sleeping on Lily's foot. "Sky, you're invited too."

Lily touches his arm. "And security will have to go as well. Are you sure that's OK?"

Charlie smiles. "Of course, but I get the first dance."

Lily laughs. She realizes that she's finally relaxing and truly enjoying herself.

NEXT STEPS

Lily's having so much fun with her family that she doesn't notice the silence that falls over the table. Then she hears footsteps coming toward her. She looks, and there he is. Sky is at her side, growling.

Lily shivers. "How did you get in here?" She looks from her dad to her mom, but they are silent and far away. She looks for her brother and Charlie, but they are gone.

"You knew I would find you. You're mine. Now everyone will have to pay!" Adam yells.

Lily stands and faces him. "I'm not yours! Get out of here!" She moves toward him as Sky barks. He backs away and out the door, into the rain. Lily and Sky follow him onto the porch. Lily wipes the rain from her face—it's hard to see. She tries to see where he is, but he's gone.

"Damn you! Leave us alone!" Lily screams into the dark.

Lily wakes up to Sky licking her face and yelping. She wipes her face on the covers. "It's OK, girl. I'm awake now. We scared him off, you and I." Lily takes a deep breath as she snuggles with her beloved companion and does her tapping to slow her heart rate and breathing.

Lily stretches and climbs out of bed. She walks to the bathroom and washes and dries her face. She remembers that she has an appointment to see the new therapist, and she sighs. She knows that it's always hard to tell her whole story to someone new. *It's like ripping the bandage off a wound that's healing—tearing the skin and making it open and raw all over again.* She shudders and then dresses and heads down the stairs.

After letting Sky out for a while, she gives her some fresh water and food. Lily makes herself a cup of coffee. Her mom is at the hospital, and her dad is meeting with a new group of turkey hunters. Lily makes herself some scrambled eggs with tomatoes. She opens her journal and writes as she eats. She feels better than she has in months—actually, years. She knows her family has a lot to do with it. Sky and all the security also help her feel safe. She isn't having as many bad dreams, and the dream last night was awful, but better. She stood up for herself. *Kit would be so proud.* She will tell her all about it on Friday when they pick her up on her birthday.

Lily calls security and gives them the time she needs to go to her appointment. She writes in her journal for another hour and then makes a list of the things she wants to discuss with the new therapist. Lily runs upstairs and brushes her teeth and then heads back downstairs and grabs her journal and the list of discussion topics for her therapist.

She hears a car pull up in the drive and pulls the curtain back from the window to peer out. It's Officer Ben. He waves as he sees her.

Sky is up and at her side. Lily puts the service jacket on Sky, slips on her cowboy boots, and grabs a jacket from the coatrack. Her dad left his keys in the bowl on the table next to the door. Lily grabs the keys and heads out the door, with Sky at her heels. She opens the back door of her dad's big red Dodge Ram truck, and Sky jumps in. She secures Sky with a seat belt, and then she climbs into the truck.

She lets out a big sigh. "Oh, boy, it's been years, like ten, since I've driven a truck, and a month or so since I've driven at all." She looks back at Sky. "Here goes!"

Lily's surprised at how easy it is to steer the truck—the turning radius is sharp, and the ride smooth and quiet. "Wow, they've sure improved the truck. I could get used to this." Lily notices in her rear-view mirror that Ben is close behind her. This is her first adventure away from the ranch by herself. She lets out a slow sigh with her breath. She's glad that Sky and Ben are with her.

She pulls up to the small row of log office buildings, and Ben's car slides in next to hers. Lily unbuckles Sky and puts on her leash. They approach the office.

"How're you today, Miss Lily?" Officer Ben asks.

"I'm good. Thanks for asking. Glad you're here."

"I'll just wait for you in the waiting room. Is that OK?"

"That'll be fine. I'll let you know if I need anything. Thanks again."

"You don't need to thank me. I'm here for you." Ben nods and smiles as he grabs a magazine and sits in the waiting area.

Lily approaches the receptionist and receives some paperwork to fill out. She answers the questions and hands it back. Within five minutes, Lily and Sky are taken to an office, where she meets Elizabeth Newsome. The receptionist hands Elizabeth the paperwork that Lily filled out.

Elizabeth approaches Lily and offers her hand. "Hi, Lily, I'm Elizabeth Newsome. You can call me Liz. It's nice to meet you."

Lily shakes her hand. "It's nice to meet you too. This is Sky, my service dog."

Liz moves out of the way and motions toward a small navy suede couch. "Please have a seat."

Lily notices that the room is bright with lots of windows and that the shades are pulled up halfway from the bottom. Lily suspects it's for privacy, since they're on the ground level. Whatever the reason, it makes Lily feel safer. There are fresh yellow roses on Liz's desk. Lily catches a hint of the rose smell. She sits down, and Sky curls up at her feet. Liz takes a seat across from Lily, in a chair with the same upholstery. There's a box of tissues and a pad of paper with a pen on the table between them.

Liz clears her throat and leans forward as she looks at Lily. "We have an hour for our meeting. To make the most of the time, could you think of three goals that you would like to work on? You can use the pad and pen to write them down or the notebook you brought. While you think about the goals, I'll review the paperwork you filled out."

Lily nods and opens her journal. *1. Tell Liz what happened and how it's affecting me. 2. Share the tools in my toolbox. 3. Come up with next steps to get on with my life.*

They both finish about the same time, and their eyes meet. Lily shares her goals with Liz.

"That sounds like a good start," Liz says.

Lily tells Liz about Adam and the phone calls, notes, cut phone lines, slashed tires, and broken windows after the divorce and what led to her stint at HRC. Lily covers it so fast that she stops to take a deep breath. She doesn't realize that there are tears streaming down her face. Sky has risen to a sitting position and has her head on Lily's lap. Lily has been stroking her head without knowing it.

Liz hands Lily the box of tissues. "Your dog—Sky is it?—is very intuitive."

Lily looks down at her sweet dog. "Yes, she is."

"Were the police involved when Adam did something tangible? For example, the cut phone line?"

"Yes, I reported everything, even the phone calls that just had someone breathing on the line. I have a restraining order." Lily sighs. "The police take down the information but tell me there's no proof that he did the tangible things. And when he stood across the street watching me every night, he was outside the restraining order area and was on a public street. The police would patrol by my place, but he would just move when he saw them and come back when they had gone."

Liz is silent for a moment and then says, "Did he ever physically harm you, or did you suspect he might?"

"No, but I know he was responsible for allowing my cat to be hit by a car, and he was glad. And he followed my friend's little boy, which felt terribly threatening. He destroyed property, and grabbed me at the funeral. But it's his words and actions that make me fear for myself and anyone that gets close to me."

"Have there been any sightings of him since you've been home at the ranch?"

"No, but the security my family provided and Sky allow me to move around without fear or anxiety."

Liz leans forward. "You mention fear and anxiety. Is that what you're working on?"

"Yes, and by alleviating the fear and anxiety I hope to become independent again."

"Well, you've been through a lot. Now tell me about the tools in your toolbox."

Lily wipes her eyes and blows her nose. "While I was at HRC, my horrid nightmares and panic attacks continued. The panic attacks would occur from a smell, a sound, or a word someone used. I had no control over when they happened or how to avoid them. When I was living in my home, I had real reasons to be afraid. I was safe at HRC, but the panic found me. I realize it is PTSD. And I learned some EMDR techniques that help relax me and slow my heart and breathing. I use the tapping technique on my sternum or forehead. It helps when I wake from a nightmare. Since I got Sky, she wakes me from nightmares and then I do the tapping, after I thank her."

"That's quite a dog you've got there." Sky looks over at Liz and wags her tail.

"Yes, she's the best."

"What're some of your other tools?"

"I've also been journaling. I had a good friend at HRC. We shared our traumas, and it helped to talk it out. She was so brave. It encouraged me to be braver. She's coming to the ranch on Friday. I also worked on forgiveness. I forgave myself, and I forgave the situation. I feel I'm stronger now. In my nightmare last night, I fought back. I'm trying to take back my life." Lily takes in a slow, deep breath and lets it out. "And I made an appointment with you, so that I would have a therapist if I have the need."

"Those are good tools. Can you tell me how your life now is different than it was before HRC?"

"I was so isolated before HRC. I felt I had to stay to myself because Adam threatened anyone who got near me. So with the security and Sky, I've been able to get out for hikes, horseback rides, and shopping at the mall, and I'm reconnecting with my family. I have a large family who all live at the ranch, and we go to church together. We just had a Sunday dinner, and I wasn't as overwhelmed by the crowd as I was when I first arrived. I've been dancing in my childhood studio. Ballet was my life, and it feels good to get back to it. I reconnected with an old friend who works with my brother. We went on a horseback ride and are going out for dinner and dancing Thursday night. I've had a night or two without nightmares. I'm not back at work yet—I have to figure that out. I'm not sure I want to go back to my Lakewood studio." Lily takes a breath. She is trying to tell everything all at once. "I know that the security can't last. I'm sure it's costing my parents a lot of money."

Liz checks the time. "Let's talk about next steps."

"I want to have some fun with my friend," Lily says. "She'll be staying with us for a couple weeks or so. I need to dance more and get back in shape if I'm going to start back to teaching soon. I need to figure out if I should sell my old place and start new somewhere else or return to my old studio. I had a studio where I taught ballet, with an apartment upstairs. I need to figure out how to live without twenty-four-hour security. So I need to work on myself: trusting my instincts, trusting people, working on bravery, and continuing to forgive myself for getting into the mess."

Liz smiles. "That's quite a list of next steps. You could make a timeline and start with the simple things, like working on your ballet, enjoying yourself when you go out with your friend, and enjoying your friend who is coming on Friday. And keep journaling, if that's helping you. We can set up a next appointment to check in and see how things are going for you. Would you like to come back in a week or two?" Liz opens her appointment book.

Lily thinks about Kit's visit—she doesn't want to interrupt the first week with Kit. "How about two weeks from today?"

"Same time, nine a.m.?"

"Yes, that'll work." Lily rises, with Sky at her heels. She shakes Liz's hand. "Thanks."

Liz pulls her into a hug. "Be gentle with yourself. You've been through a big ordeal. Take your time to heal." She releases Lily, steps to the door, and opens it.

Ben sees Lily approach. He puts down his magazine and rises to open the door for her and Sky.

Ben gets into his car as Lily secures Sky in the back of the truck and then climbs in. She takes in a deep breath and lets it out slow, and then she starts the truck and heads toward the ranch. Raindrops fall on the windshield, and Lily finds the control for the wiper blades. She lowers her shoulders—she had not realized she was holding them up. She feels tight and exhausted. But she likes Liz. "Step one. Right, Sky?" Sky yelps in response. As she enters the drive to the ranch, Ben honks and waves, and Lily waves back. She waves at Officer Lambert in the hut as she drives under the sign that says "Welcome to Always Summer Ranch."

Lily parks and lets Sky out to run. Sky runs up and down the drive, and then she joins Lily on the steps to the house. They enter and find Roy in the kitchen.

"Hi, Dad, you sure have a nice truck. Thanks for letting me use it."

"Sure, sweet pea, any time. I made vegetable soup and sandwiches for my hunt team and have some left over. Do you want some?"

"I get to enjoy the perks of your job." Lily laughs as she sits down at the counter. Sky curls up at her feet.

"Well, I usually make enough for myself and your mom if she isn't working. But you never know how hungry those hunters will be. Sometimes they eat everything, and I have to come home and figure out something else for lunch. Today one of the group members got the flu and couldn't come, so there's more food for us." Roy gives Lily a turkey-and-cheese sandwich on whole wheat and a bowl of the vegetable soup and then sits down next to her.

Lily takes a sip of soup. "This is delicious."

"Glad you like it. How was your therapy session?"

"You know, I liked her a lot. She was very organized, and we covered a lot of ground in one hour. I'm going to start working on my next steps right after lunch."

Roy furrows his brow. "What next steps?"

"Oh, those are things I'm going to work on before I meet with her again. One is to get back to my dancing so I can be in shape to teach. I've only been to the studio twice since I've been home." Lily takes another bite of her sandwich and then eats a spoonful of soup. "Thanks for keeping the studio. It brings back so many fond memories."

Roy tips his head and grins. "I just couldn't get rid of it. Maybe I was hoping you would come back and dance in it."

Lily gives her dad a hug. "I love you, Dad. I'm pretty self-absorbed right now. I'm sorry I haven't asked you about your work at the ranch or talked to you about your ideas for the next book you're writing."

Roy takes his daughter's hands in his and looks her in the eyes. "Honey, you're processing a lot while you heal. There's time for us to catch up on me later. But not much has changed."

The two clean up the kitchen, and then Lily and Sky go upstairs. Lily takes out her pink tights and black leotard and puts them on and then slips on some jeans, a flannel shirt, and a pair of socks. She puts a towel and her ballet slippers in a bag and hangs it on her shoulder. She and Sky head downstairs, where she gets her coat and boots and opens the door.

Lily sees her dad at his desk in the study—he is looking down at his computer. "See you later, Dad. Thanks for lunch."

"You're welcome. Have fun. Oh, your mom and I are driving into Denver tomorrow because I'm meeting with my publisher. We wondered if you would like us to stop by your place and get some of your things."

Lily gives a shudder and sighs. "I'm not ready to go back there, so that would be very nice. I'll make a list today and give you the keys and directions. And you know my black Honda Civic is there in the parking lot. Can you check on it? I think I want to sell it. It isn't worth much."

"Do you want me to see if I can sell it? You could leave me the title, and I could check while we're in town."

Lily sighs. "Actually the title is in my file cabinet. I'll leave the directions for that too. Thanks so much."

"No problem. Happy to do it." Roy waves, and his eyes travel back to his computer.

Lily and Sky start down the road to the studio. Sky runs up and back, getting her exercise. Lily calls to her, and Sky races back. Lily laughs and ruffles her fur and sends her back off. Sky takes off at a full run. It makes

Lily laugh to watch her having so much fun. *That sweet girl sure makes me happy.*

With a skip in her step, Lily continues down the road to the studio and unlocks the door with her key. Once inside, Sky lies down on the floor next to a chair, where the sun casts a warm beam as it shines through the skylight. Lily looks through the old CDs next to the stereo. She picks out *The Nutcracker* and Marco Sala's "Plies (Barre)." She takes off her coat, shirt, and jeans, and slips on her ballet slippers. Goose bumps cover her arms. She wonders if it's excitement or the chill in the studio air. After turning on the heat, she puts Marco Sala's CD in the player and moves into position to start her warm-up. She goes through the ballet positions where she moves her arms down and up and out with her feet moving in different positions with her arms. Then she does some barre positions and stretches, holding onto the barre or putting her leg on the barre. She moves to the middle of the floor and sits down. She stretches out her legs in front of her and then to the sides and leans down with arms outstretched. After she feels her muscles are warmed up, she stands and tries some spins and a couple leaps.

Lily sighs. She realizes that her balance is not as it was. *Trauma affects so many things.* She knows she'll have to be careful and go slowly. She doesn't want an injury to slow her down. She changes her mind about trying to do one of her old ballets and puts on a CD with a combination of classical music with Bach, Beethoven, Chopin, and Tchaikovsky. She moves into the center of the floor and lets the music envelop her. Her arms and head sway with the music, and she lets it lift her up on tiptoes as she moves across the floor. She does slow, easy moves with stretches. She then does an arabesque, where she stands on one leg with her other leg and arm stretched behind her. Her other arm stretches high to the ceiling. She pauses and holds her position. Then, back on tiptoes with legs straight, she moves across the floor, swaying with her arms in positions at her side, out, and over her head. She ends with an arabesque as she reaches the wall and turns and moves in the other direction. She feels stronger and more balanced the longer she works. After about an hour, she is damp and spent.

Lily does some stretches to cool down. When she finishes, she calls to Sky. "Come, girl." Sky jumps up and joins Lily with licking and wagging of her tail. Lily laughs as Sky's big tongue wets her face. Lily towels off, puts on her clothes, coat, and boots, and then races Sky back to the house.

The house is quiet. Lily thinks her dad must be off with the hunting team, so she goes upstairs and showers. After changing, she lies on the bed. Sky is already there. She sleeps and dreams of dancing. When she wakes an hour later, she realizes there were no nightmares. With a smile, she gets up and goes downstairs to let Sky out. After coming back inside, she finds there's meat marinating in the refrigerator. She decides to get some vegetables from the greenhouse, but the basket is missing. Sky follows her to the greenhouse, where she finds her dad with the basket, picking out vegetables.

"Hi, Dad."

"Hey, how was your workout?"

"It was great. I'm a bit out of shape."

Roy laughs. "You'll change that, I'm sure."

"Are you gathering vegetables for your hunting group or just the family?"

"Oh, I already got the hunters' dinner set up for them. They were starving. This is for us. Are you in the mood for anything in particular?"

Lily thinks a moment. "Green beans. I love them freshly picked."

"Then green beans it is. How about some tomatoes?"

"That'll work. I sure eat well while I'm at home."

Roy grabs a few tomatoes and looks over at his daughter. "Healing food for the soul."

Lily sighs. "Yeah, if only it were that simple."

"Sweetie, you're getting there." Roy puts his arm around his daughter, and they walk back to the house. Sky runs around them.

Lily laughs as she looks down at Sky. "She gets her exercise and still stays close to me."

"She's a smart one, like my daughter."

Roy and Lily eat dinner with Lilith when she returns from work. Sky has eaten before they do and has already been outside for a walk. Lily volunteers for dish duty before heading to bed. She stops by the study, where her parents are sitting and reading.

"Mom and Dad, thanks for going to my place tomorrow. I left the keys on the table by the door with a list of things to pick up and the address, along with my car key. You go through the studio and then up the stairs to my apartment. I also wrote in which drawers to locate the items. I really appreciate this. I know I'm not ready to go back there. It's messy. I haven't been back since I went to the funeral."

Lilith sighs as she sees the frown on her daughter's face. "What do you mean, keys? Is there more than one door to go through?"

Lily takes in a slow breath and lets it out. "No, I just have the front door, but I have three separate locks on it and another dead bolt on the inside. That was my extra security. I tried a security system in New York, but Adam found a way to sabotage it."

Lilith rises and hugs her daughter. "Oh, honey, I'm so sorry for what you went through."

"Thanks, Mom," Lily says quietly in her mom's ear. She hugs her mom and then releases her. She says good night and goes upstairs with Sky to bed.

SHADOWS

Lilith brought Lily's ballet toe shoes from the apartment. Lily hugs them to her chest, remembering better times. She puts them on and then slips a skirt over her leotard. As she gets into position, the music starts. Her arms and legs move as she follows the music. She rises on pointe and glides across the floor. After moving forward and back and then side to side, she does pique turns—turning on one leg while up on her toe, with the other leg bent and the toe behind the knee and her arms following, traveling on the diagonal. She then does four double pirouettes; she turns on one leg up on her toe and ends with a stance of one leg in back and her arms out to side.

Then her partner dances onto the floor. She dances on pointe toward him, and as she reaches for his outstretched hand, their eyes meet. Her breath catches—it's Adam. She lets out a scream and falls to the floor. The room goes black.

She's being shaken, and there's a loud noise. She must have fainted because someone throws water in her face. She shakes her head and opens her eyes—Sky is rocking her body with her paw and licking her face. Lily's heart is racing, and she's finding it hard to take a deep breath. She puts one hand on Sky and starts tapping her sternum with the index finger of her other hand. Soon her heart beat slows and her breathing becomes easier.

Lily ruffles Sky's fur. "That was a bad one, girl. Rats, I thought it was getting better. I feel I'm going backward."

Lily jumps out of bed and shakes herself. She turns on the shower, and when it is warm, she climbs in. As she stands under the warm water, she weeps, hard, racking sobs. Then she bangs the wall with her fists.

"I'm so pissed at you. You haunt me in my dreams. I'm not going to let you control me."

Lily gives the wall one last bang. She washes herself, turns off the water, dries off, dresses, and makes her bed. Then she grabs her journal and stomps down the stairs, with Sky following at a safe distance. Lily lets her out and goes to get a cup of coffee. Her mom and dad have already left. She's glad to have the place to herself. She hears Sky whimper at the door.

Lily opens the door. She reaches down and pats Sky. "Sorry, girl, I should have stayed out with you. I'm sorry. I'm just mad. Time to do some journaling."

She curls up in the chair near the front window. She takes a sip of her coffee, sets it down, and opens her journal. She starts writing feverishly. Her hand begins to hurt, and she notices that she is pushing down hard with the pen. She moves her hand over the words and feels the indentation. She can feel that she is seething, so she keeps on writing. Lily fills the pages with her pent-up anger—she lets it all out.

"No one, especially not Adam, is ever going to mess with me again," Lily says out loud and then lets out a loud sigh. She looks over at Sky, who's sitting and looking at her with her head tipping left and then right.

"Am I worrying you, girl?" Lily reaches out and strokes Sky's head. "It's OK. I'm getting into the anger phase of this process. I'm going to scare away those shadows. I'm not going to allow them to cover my sunshine." Lily takes in a slow, cleansing breath and lets it out slowly. "Let's get some breakfast." Lily and Sky walk into the kitchen.

Lily's glad that her parents are getting some of her things—she doesn't want to go back to her apartment, maybe ever. Lily sets about journaling for two hours after breakfast. She then goes for a long walk with Sky around the property. They stop at the stables, but all the horses are out in the fields. She hears hoofbeats and turns to see Officer Simon coming up the drive.

"Hi, Miss Lily, how are you today?"

"I'm fine, Simon. How's it going for you?"

"Pretty quiet. Are you thinking about a ride?"

"You know, I was just out for a walk, but I would like to ride. Would you mind if I join you on your rounds?"

"It would be my pleasure. I'm going to finish this circle and then come back. You should have your horse ready by then." Simon trots off.

Lily sends Sky out to herd in Sammy. She whistles, and Sammy answers her with a low nicker. Sammy doesn't seem surprised to see Sky heading his way. Sky brings Sammy toward the barn, where Lily puts on his halter and ties the lead to a post. She brushes him, cleans out his feet, sets the blanket and saddle on his back, and cinches the girth. She puts on his bridle and then puts on her helmet and fastens the strap under her chin. As she gets in the saddle, she hears Simon approach.

Simon pulls his horse to a stop near Lily. "All set?"

"Yes, thanks. I'll just follow your lead."

Simon heads down the left road. Lily rides next to him, and Sky darts around while keeping her eye on Lily. Lily feels that Simon senses her need for quiet, so the two ride in silence. They ride the perimeter of the property and stop at each unoccupied cabin. At the cabins, Officer Simon dismounts and checks all the doors and windows to make sure they are secure. He then mounts his horse, and they continue. Lily enjoys the relaxing rocking motion of her horse as he walks. Rounds take about an hour, and they finish back at the stables.

"Miss Lily, I'm going to relieve Officer Lambert at the hut. Do you need anything else?"

"No, I'm going to turn Sammy back out into the pasture. Thanks for letting me tag along. That was very relaxing."

"Any time. Have a great rest of your day." Simon tips his head and touches the brim of his hat. He turns his bay horse and trots toward the hut at the entrance of the property.

Lily takes off Sammy's bridle and puts on his halter. She gives him some grain as she takes off the saddle and pad and puts them in the tack room. She runs the brush over Sammy's soft fur while Sky lies watching. After Lily gives Sammy a carrot, Sky gets into position. Lily takes the halter off Sammy, and Sky herds him back into the pasture to join the other horses. Lily laughs. She knows that Sammy doesn't really need to be herded, but that's one of Sky's jobs, and she loves it.

When Lily gets back to the house with Sky, Sky drinks from her water bowl. Lily makes herself a tomato and cheese sandwich and eats it as she sips a cool glass of lemonade. After eating, she puts her dishes in the dishwasher and heads upstairs with Sky.

Sky leaps onto the bed. Lily joins Sky and snuggles in close to her. She picks up her journal and opens it. Taking in a deep breath and letting it out, she begins to write.

> *Really, I'm reduced to riding around my home ranch with a guard. I'm a grown woman! How can this be happening? As much is I appreciate the security, I can't live like this forever. And my parents, they went to my home. They saw how I was living. I'm so ashamed.*

Lily tosses her journal and rests her head against Sky, crying into Sky's soft fur. After several minutes, Lily sits up and reaches for her journal again.

> *I don't want to ever live there again. I think I want to start fresh. I've saved money over the last few years. I'll put it on the market, and when it sells, I'll look for another location. Fresh start—that's what I need. I'll need to write to all my students and let them know I'm moving. I'll miss them.*

Lily wipes tears from her eyes as she thinks of her students.

> *I don't care where he is or if he's watching. And I don't want to care or think about where he is or if he's watching. I want to move on. Well, OK, maybe security for a little while longer.*

Lily yawns, stretches, and lies down with her arm around Sky. After a few sighs, she's asleep.

Lily wakes and looks at the clock. It's 5:00 p.m.—she has slept for two hours. She gets up and heads downstairs with Sky.

Lilith is in the kitchen chopping vegetables. She looks up when she sees her daughter. She tips her head to the side, and her lips quiver. As she moves around the kitchen island, her arms go out, and Lily runs into them. The two hug and cry.

"Oh, sweetie, being in your place gave me a visual of what you've been going through. I saw all the locks on the door, and the lamppost where he watched you."

"Mom, I don't want to ever go back there again."

Lilith pulls back and looks at her daughter. "I don't want you to ever feel like that again."

"I don't want to live there anymore. I'm going to sell it and start new somewhere else. I need a fresh start. I want to be a different person than I was when I lived there."

"Are you sure? You don't have to go back any time soon."

"I'm sure. I want a fresh start."

"OK, I'm available to help in any way you need. I have a friend who's a realtor in the Denver metro area. I could give you her name if you like."

"Thanks, I would like that."

Lilith gives Lily's back a quick rub and releases her. "Want to help me make dinner? I have the vegetables but haven't planned the rest."

Lily smiles at the wonderful distraction and change of topic. "How about stir-fry?"

Lilith smiles. "That would be great."

Lily opens the refrigerator and gets out some chicken, mushrooms, and garlic. She chops them up and then browns them in a large pan. Lilith puts on some rice to cook and then hands Lily the vegetables, which she adds to the pan. Lily stirs them frequently.

Roy enters the room and hugs his wife and daughter. "There're my girls. Something smells wonderful! I'll set the table." Before he turns, he puts a wad of cash in front of Lily.

Lily looks up. "What's this?"

"I sold your car. The dealer just asks that you sign over the title and scan it to them. You should probably mail it as well."

Lily's eyes get big as she notices the amount of money. "But it was an old car."

Roy shrugs. "That's what they wanted to give me, so I didn't argue."

"Well, keep it, Dad—my down payment on the security you're providing."

Lilith and Roy both shake their heads, and Roy says, "That's your money. Don't you worry about the security."

Tears leak out of Lily's eyes. "Thanks, you guys."

"We picked up your mail." Roy sets the bundle of mail on the kitchen counter.

Lily glances at the bundle and gasps. She drops the spoon she's holding and grabs one of the letters. "Adam! That's his handwriting."

Roy steps close to his daughter. "Are you sure?"

"Yes, and it's postmarked the day of his memorial." Lily tears the envelop open. After seeing the contents, she drops the letter. Sky moves in close to her.

Roy picks it up and reads, *"I'm coming for you. Be ready."*

Lily shakes her head. She reaches down and strokes Sky's head. "He's doing it again. I'll not stand for it."

Roy puts his arm around Lily. "You're safe here. We can let the police and our officers know about the letter."

Lilith wipes the tears that stream down her face. "Why don't we try and eat."

Roy and Lily nod.

They eat, clean up, and then sit at the table with big bowls of ice cream. Lilith and Roy sit on either side of Lily.

Lily feels their eyes on her. "I'm ok, you guys. I think this situation makes me more determined to break away from his attempts at controlling me." Lily tries to give them a brave smile.

The next day, after a dreamless sleep, Lily and Sky head to the studio. Lily takes her toe shoes, which her mom had collected from the apartment.

After unlocking the door and putting on a Chopin CD, Lily sits and tapes her toes. She flexes her toe shoes back and forth—it has been almost a month since she has been up on pointe.

"This might hurt," Lily says to Sky.

She slips off her clothes, which cover her tights and leotard, and puts them on the chair near the stereo. Sitting on the floor, she puts on her toe shoes, wraps the ribbons around her ankles, and ties them. While still sitting on the floor, she does some stretches—touching her hands to her toes with her legs in front and touching her toes with her legs in a split, arms arched over her head, and rotating her shoulders and head. She rises and goes to the barre. She goes through the five ballet positions to the music. Then, placing her leg on the barre, she stretches her leg as she leans down with her arm and then switches legs on the barre.

Holding onto the barre, she rises on pointe. She can feel the ache in her toes and arches, but it feels good. She glides down the wall on pointe, with her hand sweeping gently across the top of the barre in case she needs it. Then she lets go and glides across the floor, back and forth, swaying to the music. Her mind is alive and floating as she dances. She does pique turns across the diagonal and then does a pirouette. She can feel the fatigue in her toes and ankles. She does an arabesque on pointe and then a curtsy. Sky is at her side, yelping. She laughs and ruffles Sky's fur. She stretches for a cooldown, sits on the floor, and gently takes off her toe shoes. She rubs her sore toes and makes circles with her ankles. As she sits there, she looks around her studio.

"Hmm…maybe I could teach here. I could get a van with my name on it and bus the students from the school to here and back. Well, maybe that wouldn't work. This might be too far for them to come, but it's fun to think about."

She pulls her clothes back over her tights and leotard and slips her feet into her boots. She locks the studio door before heading back to the main house. She plans to journal, rest, and walk in the afternoon and then repeat the same tomorrow and the next day. Exercise and journaling will help her move forward.

The wind is picking up, and it blows Lily's red curls. Sky is, as usual, running up and back to her. She remembers that on Thursday she and her mom are going to make a cake for Kit's birthday. And then she remembers Thursday night: burgers and dancing.

Anxiety wells up inside her. "What am I thinking?" Lily says out loud. "I haven't been out at night in years." She can feel her heart speed up, and her breath comes in short gasps. She stops and taps on her sternum. "I'll have Ben, Sky, and Charlie there with me." Lily sighs. "I have to start living." She sighs again. "Oh, my God! What will I wear?" She laughs at the ridiculousness of the difference in her worries. Something clicks inside her, changing her mood, and she jogs back to the house.

Thursday morning, Lilith, Lily, and Sky drive to the store to get supplies for Kit's birthday. Ben follows behind them. They get the ingredients for a cake and the snickerdoodles and pick up balloons and cards. Lily buys Kit a new journal—one the size that she had seen her using. Back at home, they make up the guest room, which is down the hall from Lily's room. They place a vase with fresh flowers on the bedside table.

"Mom, I'd like to make Kit's cake, if that would be all right."

"Sure, honey. I'll make the snickerdoodles afterward, or while you're on your date."

Lily swings around. "Mom, it's not a date. We're friends going out to dinner and maybe dancing…" Lily covers her face with her hands. "Do you think Charlie thinks it's a date?"

Lilith tries to hide her smile. "Charlie knows you've been through something. He's a good friend. But he's always been fond of you. You probably need to talk with him and tell him how you feel."

"Well, right now I don't feel anything, other than appreciation for the friendship. I'll tell him. I don't even know what to wear."

Lilith hugs her daughter. "Just be comfortable. But I have something you might want to look at." Lilith runs down the stairs to her room.

Lily walks down to her room, and Sky runs and jumps up on their bed. Lily walks into her closet. "Maybe a nice pair of jeans, my boots, and a blouse." She holds them out toward Sky. "What do you think, girl?"

Sky lies down. "Is that a yes or no?" Lily laughs as she talks to Sky.

Lilith comes in holding something behind her back. "Now, this is mine. You're shorter, but I think it could work." Lilith pulls out a black suede skirt with fringe.

Lily touches the soft fabric and holds it up to her waist. It hangs to midcalf. "It's beautiful. Are you sure you don't mind me wearing it?"

"Of course not. It's rare that I wear it—only occasionally, when we have a dance here at the ranch for the guests. I think it'll be beautiful on you."

"Oh, Mom, I have a red blouse that'll be perfect with it."

Lilith claps. "And with your red boots!"

Lily hangs the skirt in the closet. She gives a big sigh as she sits on her bed. Lilith tips her head and furrows her brow as she sits down next to her daughter.

"Mom, I haven't gone out at night in years. What am I thinking?"

Lilith puts her arm around her daughter. "Lily, you deserve to have some fun. You'll have Charlie, Sky, and Ben with you. You don't have to worry. And if you feel uncomfortable at any time, Charlie will understand, and they'll bring you back home."

"I guess you're right. I have to start living again. I just don't know how that looks." Lily rests her head on her mom's shoulder.

After a while, they head downstairs. It's a busy afternoon of baking. The house is filled with the smell of freshly baked cake and then cookies. Lily and Lilith eat bites of lunch while baking and talking. Lily is reminded of times when she was a young girl, baking with her mom. When the cake is cooled, Lily ices it and writes, "Happy Birthday, Kit."

"Mom, I'm going to take Sky for a walk and then get cleaned up and maybe rest before Charlie arrives."

"OK, I'm about done. I think I'll go read and maybe nap too."

Lily and Sky head out the door and walk down to the stables. Lily leans on the fence, watching the horses in the distance, scavenging for something to eat among the dried weeds. Sky runs out to bark at the horses, and then she runs back. After a while, they head back to the house. Lily sees dark-gray clouds moving in over the mountains.

"Maybe a storm tonight," Lily says out loud.

After a shower and a nap, Lily gets dressed. She lets her red curls hang down to her shoulders. She puts Sky's therapy vest on her dog. Then she hears voices downstairs. Her heart rate quickens.

She laughs. "I feel like I'm in high school, though I didn't really date in high school."

She calls to Sky, and they head down the stairs. She finds Charlie chatting with her mom and dad in the den.

Charlie looks up when Lily enters. His face broadens with his smile. "Wow, you look beautiful."

Lily flushes. "Thanks, you look nice too." Lily sees that Charlie is wearing dark blue jeans and polished brown cowboy boots. He has on a cream-colored western snap shirt and a brown vest. His curly red hair is damp.

Charlie notices that Lily is looking at his hair. "Yeah, I'm a bit damp. It's starting to rain—should have put my hat on. Maybe we should get going. Ben is waiting outside."

Lily and Charlie say good night to Lilith and Roy and head to Charlie's truck. Lily has grabbed an umbrella, and Charlie holds it as she gets in. He then secures Sky in the backseat. Once in the truck, Charlie puts on his seat belt. He looks over at Lily. "Are you doing OK?"

Lily sighs. "Yes, thanks for asking. I've been looking forward to going out tonight. I do so appreciate your kindness."

Charlie turns to Lily. "I understand something happened to you. I hope you'll share it with me when you're ready. But just know I care for you, and there's no pressure. I'm your friend. And if at any time tonight it becomes too much or you're uncomfortable, we can come right back to the ranch."

Lily lets out a shuddering breath. She reaches over and squeezes Charlie's hand. "You have no idea how much what you said means to me. Thank you." Lily smiles through damp eyes.

Charlie starts the truck, and the two vehicles head to the Blue Jay Bar. Lily doesn't know what to expect as they pull into the parking lot. The rain has stopped. They park, and Lily smiles as Charlie puts on his cowboy hat and runs around to open her door. After Lily is out, he unbuckles Sky so she can jump out. Ben follows behind them. It's a log building with a wraparound porch. To the right of the entrance, the porch is enclosed with canvas drapes, and Lily can see heating oil lamps. Lily can hear voices, so she assumes it's warm enough to eat outside.

Charlie holds open the door so they all can enter the bar. A slight young woman with auburn hair that falls to her shoulders greets them. "Do you want to sit in the bar, dining room, or outside? And is it three?"

"No, just the two of us and our service dog." Charlie looks at where the dance floor is in relationship to the dining area. It's located on the south side of the dining room. There are a few musicians warming up.

He looks to Lily. "Which would you prefer?"

Lily sees that the dining room is dimly lit, and it's brighter on the patio. "Why don't we sit outside if it's warm enough?"

"If you get chilly, just tell your server. They'll turn up the gas lamps," the hostess says.

Charlie smiles. "OK, patio it is."

The hostess takes them to a table on the patio where they have a view of the band in the dining room. Sky curls up at Lily's feet. The hostess returns a moment later and seats Ben at a table a few yards away. They peruse their menus.

Charlie looks over at Lily. She catches him smiling at her.

She smiles. "What?"

"Just glad we're here."

Lily touches his hand. "Me too."

"All the burgers are great. If you prefer chicken or fish, they do a good job with those as well."

The waiter comes by to give them glasses of water. "My name's Warren. Would you like something from the bar?"

"Not for me, but I'll have a Coke. How about you, Lily?"

"No, thank you. But I would like some lemon for my water."

"I'll give you a few minutes to decide on dinner, and I'll be right back with your Coke and some lemon."

Lily looks around the room. She can feel her skin tingling with anxiety. The other customers are chatting quietly. Then she sees a shadow on the other side of the drape. Her breath catches until she sees that it's a young couple heading toward the entrance. She lets out a sigh. Sky rises to stand at her side. Lily leans over, strokes her fur, and whispers into her ear. "Good girl. I'm just nervous. So glad you're with me." Lily takes in a slow, deep breath and lets it out slowly as Sky lies back down at her feet.

Warren returns with the Coke and lemon. "Are you ready to order?"

Lily looks up. "Yes, I'll have the avocado and mushroom burger, medium well-done."

"Would you like fries or a salad?"

"No just the burger, thanks."

Warren looks to Charlie. "And you, sir?"

"I think I'll have the same, but with fries. And the burger cooked medium."

The waiter nods and leaves. The band starts playing, and the music is piped in over the patio. They're playing a Garth Brooks song, "Unanswered Prayers." Lily finds she's swaying to the music.

Charlie laughs. "So you like Garth Brooks?"

"Who doesn't?" Lily grins.

The burgers arrive, and Lily's stomach growls as she smells the grilled aroma. Warren sets some catsup, mustard, barbecue sauce, and relish on the table. Lily grabs the barbecue sauce and pours a puddle next to her burger. The burger is so big that she cuts it in half. Then she steals a fry from Charlie and pops it in her mouth.

He laughs. "I knew you couldn't resist my fries."

Lily smiles and then takes a big bite of her burger. She closes her eyes as she chews slowly. When she opens them, Charlie is staring at her.

"I told you—great burgers."

"You're right."

They chat about their childhood as they finish their meal. After their plates are cleared, they listen to the music in silence. Charlie pays the bill.

Charlie looks over at Lily. "Do you want to dance?"

Lily hesitates, and then says, "Sure."

She rises and takes Sky over to Ben. "I think she'll need to stay with you. There isn't a place for her near the dance floor.

Ben waves at the waiter. "I'll pay my bill and get a table near the dance floor."

Lily sighs. "Thanks, Ben."

They wait until Ben has taken care of his bill, and then the four of them enter the dining room. Ben finds a table near the dance floor. Sky sits at Ben's feet and watches Lily move onto the dance floor.

The band calls out, "Line dance."

The dancers on the floor get into a line, as do Charlie and Lily. The band starts playing Brooks and Dunn's "Boot Scootin' Boogie." Lily's laughing hard as she tries to remember the steps and follow the other folks dancing. When the song is over, the band changes to a waltz—Reba McEntire's "I'm Not That Lonely Yet."

Charlie puts out his hand to Lily, and she takes it. They start waltzing around the floor as the singing begins. Lily's pleased that Charlie is such a good dancer because it helps her remember the steps. She hasn't waltzed in a long time. He moves her all around the floor. She realizes she's relaxing and having a great time. Lily also notices that Charlie looks handsome under his brown cowboy hat.

Suddenly, there's a loud noise of breaking glass. Lily falls against Charlie, hiding her face as he encircles her in his arms. Ben and Sky are immediately at their side, moving them off the dance floor. The music stopped with the noise.

Just then, one of the band members says, "It's OK, folks, just a tray of glasses that took a dive. Let's give them a minute to clean up the mess and we'll start up again."

Charlie takes Lily by the shoulders. "You're shaking. Are you OK?"

Ben motions for them to go outside. Ben and Charlie stand next to Lily, with Sky herding behind her. They sit her down on a bench outside.

Lily is shaking and weeping. In a shuddering voice, she says, "I'm sorry."

Ben kneels in front of Lily and takes her hands. "Lily, you did nothing wrong. You've experienced a terrible trauma, and there are triggers, like the crashing glasses, that take you right back to your terrifying events. Your reaction is normal. And you're safe. Take some slow, deep breaths." Ben reaches into his pocket, takes out a tissue, and gives it to Lily.

Lily wipes her eyes and does as he asks. She looks into Ben's eyes. "You're good at this."

"Just doing my job." He smiles and squeezes Lily's hand. "Do you want to go back in or head for home?"

Lily looks over at Charlie, who is sitting silently next to her with his arm around her shoulders.

Charlie gives her a squeeze. "Why don't we head for home?"

Lily nods, stands up, and gives Ben a hug. Ben hugs her back and then walks with them to their truck. Lily climbs in, and Charlie closes the door. He shakes Ben's hand and thanks him before securing Sky in the backseat. He climbs in the cab and looks over at Lily, who lets out a big sigh. Charlie starts the truck and pulls out of the parking lot, with Ben close behind.

As they drive, Lily looks out at the night. She feels like a limp rag, rung out and blowing in the wind. She shakes her head as she thinks how ridiculous it is to have one thing, the breaking glass, cause her to shrink and crumble. She's angry but too exhausted to feel the emotion.

When they pull into the ranch drive, Ben honks and waves. Charlie and Lily wave back and then wave at Lambert in the hut as they pass. Charlie pulls into the drive of the main house and parks.

Lily looks over at him. "Would you like to come in for some coffee or tea? I think we have decaf of both. And I want to tell you my story if you're up for it."

Charlie squeezes Lily's hand. "I'd like that."

They both climb out of the truck. Lily opens the back and releases the seat belt so Sky can jump out. Sky whines, and Lily takes off Sky's work vest.

"You go, Sky." Lily encourages Sky to run back and forth and do her business. She leans into Charlie. "I had a really nice time until..."

"You don't have to say anything. It was great getting out together. It's a start. As I suspect, it was new going out at night, and maybe not my best choice."

"Now don't apologize. You were wonderful. Let's get Sky inside and get something to drink. Then we can talk."

The three enter the house. It's dark except for a small light on the stairs and in the kitchen.

"Mom and Dad must be asleep. Let's go in the kitchen."

Lily leads the way as Sky and Charlie follow. She gets out two mugs, and they both decide on decaf coffee. After the mugs are full of hot coffee, Lily puts out the cream and sugar, and they sit down at the kitchen island.

Lily tells Charlie about her marriage and all the troubles the followed. She tells him how it isolated her.

"Is that why you didn't come home for so long?"

"Well, at first it was because my folks didn't like him, but later it was to protect them. I didn't want him to hurt them. He terrorized anyone who got near me."

"That's why all the security?"

"Yes, and there's more." Lily tells him how she thought Adam had died, and then he appeared at the funeral. Lily shares how she got sick, was hospitalized, and was having trouble coping. She tells him about HRC and her progress.

"So here I am, trying to put my life back together, but always wondering if he's lurking out there. He hasn't harmed me physically, just my property. But he says things that indicate he might. I have a restraining order, and he stays the ordered feet away, except at the funeral. But I was never able to prove he cut my phone lines, broke my windows, slashed my friends' tires, or was responsible for the multitude of silent phone calls."

"Has there been any indication of him trying to call or come onto the ranch?"

"No." Lily sighs. "But I know that I can't have security follow me around forever." She takes a sip of her coffee. "Mom says to give it some time and not worry about the security for now."

"That sounds like good advice."

Lily laughs. "I'm a mess, Charlie. You should stay clear."

Charlie reaches over and takes Lily's hand. "I'm your friend. I'm not going anywhere. You'll get stronger with time. You went out tonight."

Lily rolls her eyes.

Charlie laughs. "Now that's the Lily I remember. You're getting back to your old sassy self."

Lily laughs and punches him in the arm.

"Ow! I see you're learning self-defense tactics."

Lily stands and takes her friend into a hug. "Thanks for tonight."

Charlie hugs her back and then steps away as he releases her. "You're welcome. We'll do it again soon. Now you better get some sleep. Don't you have a friend coming tomorrow?"

"Yes, my friend Kit. You'll like her. She's even sassier than me."

"Oh, boy. Thanks for the warning." Charlie winks as he turns to leave.

Lily walks him to the door and latches it after he has left. She takes in a big breath and lets it out slowly. Sky sits near the stairs, ready to head up to bed. She gives a big yawn.

"Well, girl, you better go to sleep quickly. I'm afraid it might be a rocky night. Maybe if I do tapping before going to sleep, it'll ward off the dreams. I also read somewhere that if you drink a big glass of water before bed, you have good dreams." Lily laughs as she climbs the stairs with Sky. "That will probably just make me need to go to the bathroom in the middle of the night."

Sky looks over at Lily's chattering and yawns. She jumps up on the bed and lies down. Lily gets undressed and slips on her nightgown. She washes her face and brushes her teeth. After turning off the light, she snuggles next to Sky.

Lily strokes Sky's soft fur and realizes she's fatigued. She thinks of Kit and smiles. Soon, she's asleep.

KIT'S SURPRISE

Lily and Kit start off on the trail, with Sky taking the lead. Their horses, Kit on Sammy and Lily on her mom's horse Willow, are neck and neck as they move from a slow trot into a gallop. Lily checks that Kit is OK with the transition, and she nods. The sun warms their backs as the wind cools their faces and tears their eyes. They pull their horses up when they get to the ridge. Kit looks over the ridge at the ranch below.

"I can't believe you grew up here. That must have been amazing. You must have great stories to tell."

Lily looks over at her friend. "I'm sorry that you didn't have good memories of your childhood."

"Well, there are good memories, but they're drowning in the bad. I think that's normal when you're processing and healing from your trauma."

"I guess so. Sometimes it would be nice to have a vacation from the bad ones."

Kit pulls her horse around to face Lily. "Isn't that what we're doing now—vacationing?" Kit laughs.

Lily laughs with her. Then it starts to rain, drenching their faces. They head back, still laughing. Lily tries to wipe the wetness from her eyes so she can see. She wakes to Sky licking her face.

She ruffles the fur at Sky's neck as she sits up and stretches. "Now that was a fun dream. Bet you're surprised to have me laughing in my sleep." Lily gives Sky a kiss on the side of her face.

Lily jumps out of bed and checks the clock. It's 6:00 a.m. She washes her face and gets dressed. Lily and Sky head downstairs. Her dad is already up and gone, but Lily can smell the coffee. She pours herself a cup and adds cream. She puts on her boots and jacket, and she and Sky step out the door into the cool morning air. The sun has not yet risen, but the sky is lighter and shows twinkling stars. Lily and Sky walk down the drive. Sky runs up and back, finds a rabbit to chase, and then she circles back to Lily. Lily sips her coffee as the smell of cinnamon wafts up to her. Lily and Sky make their way to the stables, and Lily sees her dad throwing the horses some hay. The horses are nickering softly.

"Morning, Dad."

Roy looks up as Sky runs out to see if the horses need herding. "Hi, sweet pea, you're out early."

"It's so peaceful out here."

"Yeah, I know. I love the early mornings. And there isn't much grass yet for the horses, so they appreciate the hay. Jake, one of the ranch hands, is giving hay to the cattle. Sky used to go with me when I did that early in the morning."

Lily looks over at her sweet dog, who is lying down at attention and watching the horses. "Maybe I can go do that with you one morning and Sky can do her thing."

Roy smiles. "That'd be great." He brushes his hands on his pant legs and then walks toward Lily. He reaches out and puts his arm around her shoulder, and they head to the house. Sky comes bounding back to Lily's side and then races ahead.

"How was your night out with Charlie?"

"It was nice, though not easy. But a start."

Roy smiles at his daughter. "You'll get there."

After feeding Sky, Roy and Lily make breakfast while Lilith gets ready. Lily runs to the greenhouse with Sky and picks some fresh flowers to take with her to HRC. She wants Kit's birthday to be special, since she doesn't have family that cares about her.

Back at the house, Lily sits down with her mom and dad and has a bowl of oatmeal with blueberries. After eating and cleaning up, Lily runs upstairs to brush her teeth. She runs back down and sees her mom is already in her blue Toyota 4Runner. Lily leans down to Sky and clips on the therapy vest. The two run down the steps to the car as Roy waves. Lily secures Sky in the back and gets in next to her mom.

Lilith grins and raises her shoulders. "Ready to go get Kit?"

Lily laughs and touches the amethyst and hematite bracelet on her wrist. "You look as excited as I feel."

"I'm excited to meet one of your friends. And, honey, it's so nice to see you so excited."

Lily smiles as she looks out the window. "Yeah, I know."

"Your bracelet is beautiful."

Lily holds up her wrist. "Kit made it for me. She has one too."

Lily waves at Lambert as they exit the ranch, and Ben pulls up behind them. Lily doesn't remember how far HRC is from the ranch. She doesn't even remember what the outside of the building looks like. She's surprised that it doesn't look like a hospital or a psychiatric facility. It could be a hotel. *I was in my own zone. It's really amazing how the brain shuts down when you're sick or traumatized.*

Lilith pulls in and parks, and Ben pulls in next to them. Lilith goes over to his car as Lily lets Sky out.

Ben rolls down his window as Lilith approaches. "Hi, Ben, you can wait out here. It's a locked facility. I don't know how long we'll be."

"No problem, Mrs. Johnson. I'll be here if you need me."

Lilith, Lily, and Sky walk through the front entrance of Hope Rehabilitation Center and step up to the front desk. A young woman in her midtwenties with short blond hair and big blue eyes in a round face greets them.

"Hi, I'm Suzie. How can I help you?" She notices Sky on a leash at Lily's side. "And who's this?"

Lily steps forward. "This is Sky, my therapy dog."

"She's beautiful. So how can I help you?"

Lily hands Lilith the flowers she's holding. "My name is Lily Johnson. You have a client that's being discharged today, and we came to pick her up."

"Oh, what's her name?"

"Her name is Katherine Suffisant. She's on the fourth floor."

Suzie stares at her computer screen. "Well, I'll see what I can find in the computer." Suzie scrolls and taps. "I don't see anyone by that name."

Lily leans into the counter. "Are you sure? The last name is s-u-f-f-i-s-a-n-t."

"I'll check the discharges from the last few days." Suzie scrolls through the computer.

Then a voice from behind a back computer says, "I remember that name." Up pops a thin gray-haired woman with dark eyes peeking over her reading glasses. She pushes them back in place with her hand. "It's an author of a book of poetry. Let's see, I think I have it in a drawer somewhere here." She starts opening drawers. "Here it is." She laughs—her eyes disappear in the crinkles of her skin when she laughs.

Lily rubs her brow and bites her lip. She sees her mom shake her head as she touches her ears.

Suzi smiles as she motions toward the older lady. "That's Madeline. She's worked here her whole career. She gets so excited about books, and poetry in particular."

Madeline dusts off the book and flips through the gold-trimmed hardcover book. "I have a favorite. Here it is. 'The Guardian.' I love the last verse."

> I'm the guardian of the secret,
> But it's farther from my mind.
> I surround myself with love,
> With those that know the truth,
> And I don't have to hide.

Someday when Mother leaves this place,
Maybe, she will know,
And her learning will begin.

Lily closes her eyes and says,

Then she will understand
The guardian of the secret,
As the duckling becomes a swan.

Madeline looks up fast, startled. "How did you know that?"

"My friend read it to me." *Did Kit borrow the last name? Did I misunderstand? Did she copy the poem from the book? Maybe she's still registered by her old last name. I don't think she ever told it to me.* She feels a confusion pouring over her. Sky moves in close to Lily, rubbing against her leg.

Madeline holds the book up so Lily and Lilith could see it. It's titled *Poetry Memoir of a Forgotten Child* by Katherine Suffisant.

Madeline strokes the book. "She was such a sweet child—awful what happened to her."

"What happened to her?" Lilith says.

Madeline catches her breath and then lets it out. "I guess I can say. It was in the news." She takes a deep breath. "It was thirty years ago. This young girl, Katherine, was abandoned by her family after she confronted them about her father raping her. They made her a ward of the state, and she lived here. She wrote about her pain in the form of poetry." Madeline looks at the book. "Funny that she has the same name as your friend. Maybe she's a relative."

Lily pales. *No wonder Kit took her name. She experienced the same unspeakable trauma that Kit did.* She looks at Madeline and says, "What happened to her?"

"She died."

Lily gasps.

Madeline looks at Lily and frowns. "You OK?"

Lily straightens. "It's just so sad."

"Well, Katherine had been cutting herself, and the cut had gotten infected. No one knew, and I think Katherine was too embarrassed to show anyone. She got sick, and before she got treatment, she was already septic. That means the infection was in her blood and her organs were dying."

Lilith looks at her daughter and squeezes her hand. "How awful."

"After she died, her mom came to get her things and found her notebook of poetry. Her mom hadn't believed her until she read the poetry. She had it published in memory of her daughter." Madeline pushes her glasses up her nose. "Well, sorry, I didn't mean to go off on a sad story. I just really liked her poetry."

Lily swallows and looks at Suzi. "Any luck locating my friend?"

Suzi looks again at the computer. "We had three discharges yesterday. Maybe one of them was your friend. One of them was named Katherine Barnes."

Lily looks up. "That might be her. I think I had the last name wrong. And I must have gotten the date confused. She has my contact information, so she'll probably call me. Thanks for your help, and sorry to bother you."

Suzi smiles as Madeline stands behind her. "No problem. Hope she gets in touch with you soon. Take care."

Lilith and Lily walk with Sky to the exit, but then Lily turns. "If you don't mind my asking, where was she cutting herself?"

Suzi shrugs and looks back at Madeline. Madeline says, "It was her abdomen—her belly."

Lily gasps as she remembers Kit touching her belly. She looks at her mom, who puts her arm around her. They go out into the sunlight with Sky. Once outside, Lilith leads Lily over to a bench in the shade of a tree. They sit down, and Sky leans into Lily.

Lily looks over at her mom. "She's dead, isn't she?" Tears stream down Lily's face.

Lilith puts her arm around her daughter. "Yes, honey, she is." Lilith doesn't say anything else.

Lily looks at her mom. "I remember her touching her stomach. I didn't know she was sick. Maybe I could have done something."

"You did do something. You gave her friendship." Lilith rubs her daughter's shoulder as Lily continues processing.

Lily remembers her friend: their talks, their laughs, their secret handshake with palms open, and the hike where they walked like ancient Egyptians. Then she remembers Kit's funny style of clothes—old fashioned—and her love of music from her mom's era. Then she thinks of how when Kit snuck into her room, she gilded or almost floated across the floor, and she never got caught coming into Lily's room. And then she remembers how she got a tingling feeling throughout her body that only lasted a few seconds.

"Mom, she gave me two poems that she'd written about us. I have them in my journal at home." Lily sobs. "I...can't believe she's gone."

Lilith holds her daughter while she cries.

Lily feels a tingling sensation throughout her body, which dissipates within a few seconds. Lily takes in a quick breath and sits up. She looks at her mom as she wipes her tears away with her hands. "She didn't just die. She died many years ago." Lily stands up and starts hyperventilating.

Lilith reaches out to her, and Lily sits back down. "I...was talking to a ghost?" Lily looks at her mom, who nods. "But we touched and laughed. How is that possible?"

Lilith takes a slow breath. "Spirits can manifest in different ways. She obviously had a strong connection with you, so you could feel her."

"But I can't talk to ghosts. That's your thing."

"Honey, anyone can have or develop the gift of spirit sensitivity. It's not just inherited."

"But we went on a hike in the daytime. We were with a group, laughing and dancing. The other clients looked back at us because we were being silly. So everyone could see her?"

Lilith looks at her daughter. "Are you sure that they saw Kit? Or were they just looking at you?"

Lily laughs through her tears. "They must have thought it was part of my crazy—dancing and talking to myself." She gets up and stops in front of her mom. "So I can see ghosts?"

Lilith nods.

"I can talk to ghosts?"

Lilith nods again.

Lily sits down hard on the bench, and Lilith pats her knee. As Lily sits down, Sky puts her head on Lily's leg.

Lily looks over to her right and sees a shadow under a tree, near a rosebush. She squints and realizes she's looking at Kit in her nightgown. Sky is looking in the same direction as Lily. Lily points. "Mom, she's here, over there under the tree. Do you see her?"

Lilith looks in the direction that Lily is pointing. "No, honey, I don't see her. She's here for you. I'll wait here while you go and talk with her. Sky seems to see her too."

Lily stands and looks over and sees Kit smile. She heads toward Kit and then goes back to her mom and gives her a hug. "Thanks, Mom." She grabs the flowers that she had picked for Kit, and then she and Sky head toward where Kit is standing.

As she approaches Kit, Kit becomes brighter and easier to see. Sky sits at Lily's side. Lily holds out the flowers, and Kit takes them. Kit smells them and smiles and then sets them down next to the tree. As she looks at Lily, tears stream down her face.

Lily starts crying too and says, "Happy birthday."

"Thanks. I like your dog."

"This is Sky. She's a therapy dog."

"Is it OK if I pat her?"

"Sure." Lily pats Sky's head. "Sky, it's OK, go see Kit."

Sky stands and moves toward Kit. Kit puts out her hand for Sky to sniff and then pats the soft fur of her head. Sky circles Kit and then sits down next to her.

"She's lovely. I never had a dog." Kit looks up at Lily. "You know, I was so looking forward to coming to the ranch. I didn't know that I was dead." Kit wipes tears from her eyes.

Lily laughs through her tears. "I didn't know you were dead either."
Lily sniffs. "And I'm really bummed about that." She laughs. "Do you
know that your mom had your poetry published in a beautiful book?"

Kit smiles. "Yeah, shortly after you left, I started having angel dreams.
I think they were bringing me messages. It took a while to realize they
were my angels telling me what had happened. Then I saw my death, the
funeral, and my mom coming to get my things. I saw her read my poems
and weep. She called out that she was so sorry for abandoning me and not
believing in me."

Lily smiles. "That must have given you some comfort."

"Yes, it did. And my angels tell me that she's still among the living. I'll
go see her next. I was just waiting here to talk with you."

Lily bursts into tears. "You don't know how much your friendship
means to me. You helped me move through my darkness."

Kit wipes tears from her eyes. "You did the same for me. I was stuck
here, and you helped me heal and forgive. You made it possible for me to
play and laugh again. To have a friend that I could depend on helped me
believe in myself again. Even though I died, I wasn't done with my life lessons. You helped me finish the journey. I can go now."

"I'll miss you, but your sense of bravery stays with me. I'm continuing
to work on myself and figuring out how to start my life over. I have a lot
of work to do."

Kit smiles. "And you have a gift that you didn't know you had. Learning
about your gift should keep you busy as well."

"I don't know about that. I'm scared of the shadows, wondering if
Adam is there. Now I have ghosts to worry about too?" Lily gives a laugh.

"Have you seen any sign of Adam?"

"No, the ranch is well secured. And no one has seen him or had a
sense that he has been lurking around."

Kit moves closer to Lily. "Perhaps your gift will give you a sense of security. Maybe you might be more aware if he's near and be reassured when
there's no sense of him."

"Perhaps, and Sky's very intuitive and helps me. She wakes me from
nightmares."

"Like my knocking on your door?" Kit smiles.

Lily laughs. "Yeah, but her wake-up involves licking."

Sky gives a yelp.

Kit puts out her arms, palms facing up. Lily places her arms on top of Kit's, and they close their hands around the other's arms.

Lily looks down and sees the amethyst and hematite bracelet on Kit's wrist. She looks into Kit's blue eyes. "I'll never forget you."

Kit looks back into Lily's green eyes. "I'll never forget you."

Sky moves to Lily's side as Kit becomes transparent and then fades away. Lily puts her empty arms down, kneels next to Sky, and hugs her. Sky nuzzles into Lily's neck.

Lily walks back to the bench where her mom sits watching. She sits down hard, letting out a swoosh of air. Her puffy, swollen eyes look over at her mom, and she lays her head down on her mom's shoulder. "Let's go home and eat cake."

Lilith laughs at her daughter. The two get up, and with Lilith's arm around her daughter and Sky at Lily's side, they walk to the car. Lily takes off Sky's vest and secures her in the backseat and then climbs in the passenger side. Lilith goes over to Ben and talks with him a moment. She then comes back and gets in the car.

Lily looks over at her mom. "What did you tell him?"

"I told him that your friend passed away. He said to tell you how sorry he is for your loss."

Lily sighs. "I didn't think about what I would tell everyone at the ranch. I've been talking about her for two weeks."

"You can tell them anything you like. You are among family and friends. They know about spiritual gifts. You can tell them whatever you're comfortable with. But for the officers, I'll give them the same message that I gave Ben."

"Good idea. Mom, I have so much to learn. I don't know anything about this spiritual gift business."

"Don't worry about it. You kind of learn as you go. And you have me, your brother, and your father who can help. There are lots of resources:

books, seminars, and some trusted spiritual guides." Lilith taps the steering wheel. "You know you don't have to do anything with it. You can just go about your life, and if something unusual makes you question, you can explore the possibilities or ignore it."

"Kit wonders if the gift will help me feel more secure, because maybe I can sense when Adam is around and know when he isn't."

Lilith smiles. "Funny, I was thinking the same thing."

"I remember some of your stories about how hard it was when you told someone close to you about your gift and they didn't believe you."

"Yes, there will be nonbelievers. There are those who are scared of what they can't see, and some who'll be worried for your soul because they think it's evil."

"Oh, boy." Lily looks out the window and tears spring up in her eyes. "I'm going to miss Kit. I remember things about her that should have been clues, like her old-fashioned clothes, slang from the past, and old songs that were her favorites. But we laughed and touched hands, and she gave me physical presents that I still have. How can that happen?"

"Honey, ghosts can manifest in different ways. Some can have physical contact with the living."

As they pull up into the ranch entrance, Lilith waves at Officer Lambert. She sticks her head out the window and motions for Ben to go to the hut. They continue and park at the house.

Roy comes out on the steps to greet them. His smile changes to a frown when he sees they do not have Kit.

Lily and Sky approach him. Lily looks at her dad and thinks, *Oh, Dad, she's a ghost.* Lily falls into his arms, and her dad circles her with his love.

"What do you mean, she's a ghost?"

Lilith approaches, and nods her head.

Roy pulls Lily from him and looks into her eyes. "You mean your friend died?" He can see the tears streaming down Lily's face. "Oh, sweet pea, I'm so sorry." He pulls her into the house, and they sit down on the couch. Lilith sits in a chair across from them, and Sky curls up at Lily's feet. "Tell me what happened."

Lily looks up at her dad. "She died thirty years ago."

Roy shakes his head and looks over at Lilith, who nods. "What?" He runs his hand through his hair. "Are you talking about Kit?"

Lily takes her dad's hand. "Yes. For the eighteen days that I was at HRC, I saw and talked with Kit every night. But she was a ghost. She didn't know she was dead, and neither did I."

"Wait, you can see ghosts?"

Lily gives a small smile. "Apparently so." Lily tells him what happened when they got to HRC—about the poetry book, about hearing that Kit had died, and about when she realized that her friend was a ghost. She told him how Kit appeared in the garden and how she got to talk with her and say good-bye.

Roy's mouth hangs open as he listens. "So Kit didn't know she was a ghost?"

Lily shakes her head. "We were traumatized friends sharing our stories and helping each other. I don't know. I guess she had some earthly things she still had to work on, even though she was dead. I don't know how else to explain it."

Lilith smiles. "I think you're doing a great job explaining it."

Roy looks from Lilith to Lily. "So both my girls can see ghosts?" He smiles.

Lilith nods as she tips her head at Lily.

Lily stands up. "I think I want to go to my room for a while." She leans down and gives her dad a kiss on his cheek. She then goes over to her mom and kisses her cheek. She looks back and forth at both of them. "I'm so thankful for the two of you." She turns and walks slowly, grabbing the railing as she slowly pulls herself up the stairs with Sky.

"We love you so much."

Lily notices Lilith cross the room and snuggle into her husband. "Our poor girl has to mourn the death of her friend."

Lily stays in her room all day. Her mom brings up a sandwich for her lunch, but she hardly touches it. Lily takes out the two poems from her journal that Kit had written and given her. She moves her hand over the indentations of the printed words. Lily thinks it feels so surreal. She strokes her journal, but can't muster the energy to write. She sleeps off and on and cries in between. Lilith comes, takes Sky out for a while, and then brings her back.

"Honey, do you want to come down for dinner later?" Lilith asks.

Lily, who is lying on her bed, and opens her swollen, bloodshot eyes. "No, I'm just going to rest."

"I'll bring you a tray later. I love you."

Lily hears a knock on her door, and for a moment she thinks of Kit. Tears stream down her face. She sits up and wipes her eyes. "Come in."

Lilith opens the door and carries in the tray. "I brought some dinner." She hears Sky whine. "Why don't I take Sky downstairs and feed her and let her out for a while?" She sets the tray of food on Lily's lap.

Lily reaches over and strokes Sky's fur. "Sorry, girl, you must be hungry. Go with Mom."

Sky jumps off the bed and heads to the door. Lilith turns to leave with Sky.

"Thanks for making my favorite comfort food," Lily says.

Lilith turns and smiles. "I love you, honey."

"I love you too, Mom."

Lily takes some sips of her soup—it warms her down to her toes. She dips her grilled-cheese sandwich in the soup. She can't help but smile at the memories. Her mom has even made her some hot chocolate with marshmallows.

Lily finishes the soup and half the sandwich. She sets the tray aside and is sipping on the hot chocolate when her mom returns. Sky jumps back up on the bed.

Lilith smiles when she sees that Lily has eaten. She sits on the edge of the bed. "How're you doing?"

Lily looks at her mom. "I just can't believe that she's gone. I mean, I know now that she was already gone, but the ghost thing...I don't know. It's just all a lot. I miss her. It had been so long since I'd had a friend. I'd become so isolated with Adam. It was just great to be able to share with a friend. We talked for hours into the night, every night."

Lilith rubs Lily's leg. "She sounds amazing."

"She was. And she was so brave. She went through terrible, confusing years of sexual abuse by her father. And when she realized that it was wrong, she was so brave to confront him. But he denied it, and none of her family believed her. She was so alone."

"And she found you. You were a good friend to her, as she was to you."

"Yeah, you're right. We saved each other." Tears leak from Lily's eyes. "I know she's at peace now. But she never got to live."

"Actually, she did."

Lily looks at her mom. "What do you mean?"

"Well, think about it. She died thirty years ago. She's been stuck with unfinished business all this time, until you arrived at HRC. Through the friendship you shared, she worked on herself, as you did on yourself. And through sharing your stories, you each got to see a different perspective."

Lily's face brightens. "And it was our friendship that gave us strength. She'd been as isolated as I'd been."

"That's right. And it sounds like you had fun together."

Lily smiles as she remembers. "We did laugh a lot. It was fun. And on the hike, we kidded around and enjoyed eating, singing, and looking at the beautiful scenery."

"Honey, she needed to finish her journey before she left this world. And you helped her."

Lily's voice cracks as she says, "She helped me too."

"I know she did." Lilith touches Lily's journal.

"Yeah, that's a good idea."

Lilith hands the journal to Lily. She kisses her daughter on the forehead. After picking up the food tray, she leaves the room and quietly shuts the door behind her.

Lily opens the journal and writes.

Dear Kit, I'm grieving the loss of you and our friendship. I can't believe you're gone. And I can't believe you were a ghost and neither one of us realized it. I cry as I think about you. You didn't get to meet my family, ride horses, see my studio, or eat your birthday cake, and you missed your snickerdoodles! And you didn't get to go to France. There's so much you missed due to your torment. It isn't fair. You're such a kind soul. You did so much for me. You really listened to me and made me laugh. I'm stronger and braver because of what we shared. Thank you for trusting me enough to share your darkest thoughts and experiences. I'm so proud of you. You survived. And now you're in a better place. I believe that now. There is something beyond this life. I know I'll see you again someday. I love you, my dear friend.

"I love you too," a voice says. "I heard you talking to me through your writing."

Lily's head swings to the door. "Kit, you're here."

Kit approaches Lily's bed, and Sky looks up at her. "Yeah, this ghost thing is kind of amazing." She sits on the end of Lily's bed, just as she had at HRC.

"Did you see your mom?"

Kit smiles. "Yes, she's living in a retirement community with her sister. She sure looks older. I haven't seen her in thirty years. I tried to talk to her, but she didn't respond. I touched her face, and her hand came up to her face. She tipped her head as if she'd felt it. I know that she believes me now. She had my poetry published." Kit giggles and her shoulders come up. "I'm a published author."

Lily smiles. "Yes, you are. Will I get to see more of you?"

Kit frowns. "I don't know how all this works yet, but I'm getting an energy pull that it's almost time to go."

"Will you be able to come back and visit? My mom says she has friends who come back at Halloween."

Kit looks at Lily. "I really don't know. If I'm able, I sure will. I'll never forget you. You helped me get ready to move on. I'm happy."

Lily puts out her arms to her friend. "I'll never forget you."

Kit places her arms on top of Lily's, and they clasp their hands around the other's arms. Kit and Lily look into each other's eyes as Kit fades away.

Lily closes her journal and turns off the light. She snuggles against Sky and thinks of her friend. She takes deep breaths in and lets them out slowly. She melts into her soft bed and falls asleep.

REBUILDING

Lily wakes as the sun dances across her face. She stretches and opens her eyes. She does not remember opening the window; maybe her mom did. The breeze blows the lace curtains and makes the sunbeams dance. Lily laughs. Sky sits up, surprised by her outburst. She ruffles the fur at Sky's neck and leans over to give her a kiss on the side of her face.

"Sky, it's a new day." Lily jumps off the bed, dances to the shower, and turns on the water. Once the water is warm, she climbs in. Lily lets the warm water wash away her dried tears. She covers herself in suds and lets the water wash everything away. After toweling dry, she combs her wet curls and puts on her leotard and tights and then jeans and a shirt. She and Sky walk down the stairs and outside into the cool breeze. Sky takes off, chasing a rabbit. She races back and then does it again. Lily walks down the drive, looking at the mountains.

Lily looks up at the blue sky. "Lord, it's me, Lily, I'm thankful for this gift. I don't know what to do with it, but I'm so glad I was able to have time with Kit. Help me to grow, learn, be brave, and become independent. In the name of the Father, the Son, and the Holy Spirit. Amen." Lily makes the sign of the cross over herself.

She turns and heads back to the house. Sky is at her heels. Once inside, they go into the kitchen. Her mom and dad are sitting at the island, having coffee.

Lilith looks up. "I thought I heard you. How're you doing?"

Lily grabs a scoop of dog food and feeds Sky and refills Sky's water bowl. "I'm doing OK. I think I want some cake for breakfast."

Roy chokes on his coffee. "Cake for breakfast?"

Lily laughs. "Yes, cake with a side of eggs."

Lily moves to the stove and gets out a frying pan. She goes to get some eggs and butter from the refrigerator. "Anyone want scrambled eggs?"

Lilith and Roy look at each other. "Yes!"

Lily goes back to the refrigerator and gets out some mushrooms and spinach. She sautés the mushrooms in butter, and she adds some garlic and parsley. Once they are cooked, she adds the spinach. She beats the eggs in a small bowl and adds a bit of cream, salt, and pepper. She pours the egg mixture into the pan.

Lilith gets out some plates, and Roy pours Lily a cup of coffee. When the eggs are done, Lily sprinkles some grated asiago cheese on them. She gives everyone a heaping spoonful on their plates, and they sit around the island and eat. The cake stares back at Lily as she looks at it in the glass cake dish. Lily reaches out and takes the cover off and slides the dish toward herself. She slices a piece for herself and for each of her parents.

She takes a forkful and holds it in the air. "Happy birthday, Kit!" Lily eats the bite of cake. Lilith and Roy hold up their bites of cake and do the same.

After finishing her eggs and cake, Lily sits back to enjoy her coffee. "So I want to talk to you guys about a few things."

Lilith looks over at Roy. "OK, honey. What's on your mind?"

Lily takes another sip of her coffee. "Well, last night I was writing in my journal. I was writing a letter to Kit. And guess who came for a visit?"

Roy looks up. "Kit?"

Lily smiles. "Yes, she said she heard me talking to her through my writing. So this ghost stuff is interesting. Anyway, Kit and I had a nice chat until she had to leave." Lily laughs. "I can't believe I'm talking like this. I never thought this would happen to me." She sighs. "I was confused and sad yesterday. Thanks, Mom, for feeding me. Today, I want to put my studio with the apartment up for sale. I don't want to live or teach there anymore." Lily looks at her mom. "Did you tell me you knew a realtor that I could use?"

Lilith puts down her fork. "Wait, wait. Did you just say that Kit came here last night?" Lilith looks at her daughter, who nods. "That's wonderful. Did it help you?"

"Yes. I'm still a bit sad, but I'm excited to get on with my life."

"Yes, I know a realtor—a good friend of mine," Lilith says.

"Also, what would you think about me using the studio on the ranch to teach my classes? And I would want to expand it to add an apartment. I could buy it from you when I sell my place. I know this is your property. I don't know how you feel about me living here."

Lilith looks over at Roy, who nods. Lilith moves over to her daughter and gives her a hug. "We would love for you to live here. It's a family ranch. Everyone else lives here."

Roy wipes a tear from his eye. "I always hoped someday you would want to live here. But with your career, I didn't know if that would be possible."

"I don't know if it's possible either. The ranch is in a remote location, and I'm an unknown here. I thought I would drive around and see what other studios are offering students."

"You can use my computer to look them up," Lilith says.

"Thanks, Mom. I'll do that."

"You could develop a website. Charlie's great at doing that. He did one for their veterinary business and also for our ranch," Roy says.

"I can't do that. It's too public. And if Adam wants to cause trouble, the website gives him more information." Lily sighs. "And about that— don't you think it's time to scale back on the security around here? It must cost a fortune."

Roy reaches over and takes Lily's hand. "Do you feel ready for that?"

Lily thinks for a moment. "Yes, I do." She swallows hard. "I think I do."

Roy pats Lily's hand. "Why don't we scale back in phases and see how you feel?"

Lily sighs. "OK, how about not having an officer that follows me when I leave the ranch? And then the officers that make rounds."

"I like having the front entrance watched. Maybe we should put in a gate with a code and card access for night and have the hut staffed during the day so the gate can be open," Lilith says.

Lily smiles. "I like that idea. I have to admit, the security gives me comfort. I've really been able to relax, but I need to figure out how to move forward on my own."

Roy looks at Lilith and back to Lily. "We'll do it in phases. I'll give Ben two weeks' notice so he has time to get another assignment. And I'll alert the day and night officers who do rounds that we won't need them in a month. Hmm, let's see. I'll get some estimates on a gate. How does that sound?"

"Great. Thanks, you guys." Lily sighs as she shakes her shoulders. "We need to have a party for the security guys. They've been so helpful and respectful to me. I'm going to miss them. Can we have a barbecue in their honor as a thank-you?"

"That's a great idea." Roy and Lilith answer together.

"Well, back to my plan. I thought I would hold a few summer dance camps. That way the students can get to know me. I can advertise in the schools before they let out for the summer."

Lilith smiles. "That's a great plan, honey."

Lily looks at her parents. "Do you mind if I live here in the house until I get the apartment built?"

"Of course not. You can stay here as long as you want," Roy says.

Lily nods with a smile, jumps off her stool, and gathers the plates to wash. After doing the dishes while her parents talk, she heads toward the door with Sky.

Roy and Lilith look up. "Where are you going?"

"I'm going to the studio. See you later." Lily runs down the road, with Sky close behind.

Lily tips her head back and enjoys the sun on her face. The day is warm with a slight breeze. When she arrives at the studio, she walks around it, thinking about where to place the apartment addition. The studio has a bathroom at the back. She thinks that might be a good spot, due to the plumbing. She shakes her head. She will need some expert advice.

Lily unlocks the door to her studio. She and Sky enter, and she locks the door behind them. She opens some of the windows to allow fresh air to sweep through. After taking off her jeans and shirt, she sits and puts on her toe shoes. After putting on a Chopin nocturne, Lily goes to the barre and starts her warm-up before moving to the floor to continue the warm-up and stretches. Then she dances around the floor, swaying to the music. She gets up on pointe and moves across the floor. She loses herself in the dance and feels her heart swell. Sky is lying on the small rug near the stereo, when she sits up and watches Lily. Lily travels on pointe close to her and away as she says to Sky, "See, girl, this is what I do—dance. And soon I'll teach again."

The days fly by. Lily talks with a realtor and puts her old studio and apartment up for sale. She travels to her old place with her dad and Sky, and Ben follows them. It's his last week, and Lily is glad to have him there. When she opens the door to her studio and steps inside, she feels an oppressive weight surround her. Sky moves in close. Her dad brings in some boxes, and they pack her things from the studio, which include costumes and music. Then they move upstairs to the apartment. Lily packs her clothes, shoes, favorite pillows, and personal items, such as toiletries, books, and photos. She gets her computer, printer, phone, and answering machine. She places her files from the file cabinet into boxes and packs most of the kitchen supplies, but leaves some items for showing the apartment. She sets up the bathroom with towels and leaves the bed made as a staging for the sale. Her dad and Ben help her load the boxes, file cabinet, and electronics in the truck. They decide to come back for the rest once the place is sold.

Roy looks back at the studio as he stands near his truck. "Lily, would you like me to take down your studio sign? It's such a pretty painting of you."

Lily looks up at the sign with a mixture of pride, sadness, and hope. "Yes. I'm not sure I'll use it, but I'd like to have it."

Roy gets out his tools and a small ladder from the truck. Ben comes over to assist him. It doesn't take long before they have the wooden sign down and loaded in the back of the truck next to Lily's boxes.

Lily secures Sky in the backseat and climbs in next to her dad. "Thanks so much, Dad."

"This is your first time back. How're you doing?" Roy asks as he starts the car and heads toward the ranch.

Lily looks in the side mirror and sees her studio without the sign. "I felt a heaviness within my body when I was in there. It was like the energy was being sucked out of me. I know it's the right decision to start new somewhere else, but I'll miss my students. I had sent out messages that classes were cancelled due to an emergency when I heard Adam had died. I need to reach out to all of them and let them know how much I enjoyed teaching them. I'll tell them that I'm relocating." Lily slips into silence.

Roy pats her knee as they drive home.

Lily tells her extended family and friends that Kit has died, but she tells her brother and grandma the whole story. They're very sorry and comforting but are excited that Lily shares a spiritual gift that helped her friend and her to heal.

Lily busies herself with exercise, which includes dancing, hiking with Sky, and riding. She rides her mom's horse, Willow, when she rides with Charlie, or she rides Charlie's horse if she goes out with her mom. Sky loves the exercise.

Before Ben leaves, there is a barbecue party for the security officers. They eat and laugh and tell Lily how pleased and grateful they are that she's feeling better. Lily tells them how much they helped with her recovery. There is a new automatic gate across the entrance to the ranch that locks and has a keypad and card entry. The hut is occupied during the day by an officer. Lily is adjusting to having only one officer around during the day.

Lily and Roy meet with an architect and a contractor to talk about the addition of an apartment onto the studio and have some ideas drawn up. Lily finds it very exciting.

Lily puts up fliers in the schools, advertising her dance camp at the ranch. She's planning to hold four different sessions of a week-long camp. Interested children who come to the ranch with their families can join the classes as well.

One warm spring day, Lily and Sky go out for a walk. Lily is thinking of going for a ride and heads toward the barn. She runs into Charlie, who looks up as she approaches.

"Hi, Lily, I've been thinking about you. You've been very busy getting your studio ready. Do you want me to help you set up a website?" He smiles. "I'm pretty good at it, if I say so myself." He laughs.

Lily laughs. "Modest, aren't you?" She nudges his shoulder with hers. Then darkness falls over Lily's face, and she takes in a shuddering breath. "Actually, I can't be that public. It isn't safe."

Charlie looks up suddenly. "Because of Adam?"

Lily nods. "I can't risk him finding me. I mean, I don't want to make it easy for him. I don't want to advertise what I'm doing."

Charlie approaches Lily. "I'm so sorry. I didn't even think of that." He gives her a hug, and she lets him.

Lily feels his warmth against her. She closes her eyes for a second and then releases him. *I'm not ready for involvement.* She steps toward the fence, shielding her eyes with her hand. She tries to locate Willow and calls to Sky to go get her. Lily turns to Charlie. "Do you want to go for a ride?"

Charlie's smile lights up his face. "Sure, I was thinking about a ride myself."

Lily has a nice feeling of closeness with Charlie that makes her feel she can tell him what really happened to Kit. *I'll tell him on the ride.*

Willow comes trotting in, with Sky close at her heels. Her ears are back, and she doesn't seem happy. Lily steps up. "Good girl, Sky. And good girl, Willow." Lily approaches Willow with a carrot, and her ears perk forward.

Charlie looks at Sky. "Sky, go get Silver Knight." Sky looks at Lily, who nods, and then she takes off.

Silver Knight comes trotting up, with Sky close behind. Charlie puts on his halter and ties him up. Lily and Charlie brush their horses and saddle them up as they talk.

Lily looks over at Charlie. "You know about my brother's special way of communicating with animals, right?"

Charlie lets out a laugh. "I was working with another vet when John started his practice and asked if I'd like to join him. He told me about his gift at that time and wanted to see how I felt about what he said."

Lily is watching Charlie's expressions closely. "And how did you feel about it, if you don't mind me asking?"

Charlie smiles to himself as he cinches up his saddle. "I thought he was kidding at first. Then I really listened. I asked questions, and he had answers. I had no reason to doubt him. I just had never had the experience. But when we started working together, I saw how he talked with the animals. He listened as if he were getting a message and then responded. The animals really reacted to him. He could calm the most terrified horse or cow. I even saw it with a bull that had gotten himself wrapped up in wire." Charlie sighs. "We don't usually work together unless there are several animals that need our care. But I've asked him to use his gift a couple of times when I felt an animal could really benefit."

As Lily puts her foot in the stirrup and swings onto Willow, she says, "I've got a story to tell you."

"That sounds ominous." Charlie grins at Lily.

As Charlie mounts, he turns his horse to ride beside Lily. They head up the road to the trailhead, with Sky close beside them.

"Did John ever tell you that my mom and dad have gifts?"

Charlie tips his head and says, "No, I don't recall him saying anything."

"Well, my mom can talk to the dead and people who are in a coma. She does that with her patients at the hospital."

Charlie's eyes open wide. "Does anyone she works with know?"

"No. When she was a flight nurse, some of her partners suspected. But no, she keeps it a secret. Not everyone believes or thinks it's a good idea. Some even think it's evil. So to protect the integrity of her career, she keeps it quiet."

"Wow. And your dad, he can talk to ghosts?"

"No, he's telepathic."

Charlie laughs. "You're kidding, right?"

"No, I'm not kidding. He can hear your thoughts, but only the ones you put out to him."

Charlie's face flushes pink and then red. Lily notices and asks, "Are you all right?"

Charlie nods. "I remember your dad saying something strange to me about you." Charlie shakes his head. "Now I know why. He read my thoughts. How embarrassing is that?"

Lily smiles. "What did you think about me?"

Charlie's face reddens again, and he says, "Never mind that."

They ride in silence for a while, and then Charlie asks, "So how was that, growing up with a family that had all these special gifts?"

Lily smiles. "Well, I didn't have any gifts. Sometimes it made me feel like the adopted nobody. My brother was annoying, and I had to watch what I said to my dad. Sometimes I would trick my dad—that was fun. But as you know, I was busy dancing. I didn't pay too much attention. It was their thing." She looks over at Charlie and catches him looking at her.

Charlie grins. "When I was over for dinner that first Sunday, I thought to myself, 'Mr. Johnson, your daughter is hot.'" Charlie flushes red again.

Lily laughs loud and hard. "No wonder he spoke to you. What did he say?"

"He put his arm around me and said quietly, 'Lily has been through a lot. You're a good guy, but give her space.'"

"What did you say?"

"Nothing. I just swallowed and nodded."

They ride on in silence. Lily looks straight ahead and concentrates on her breathing. She realizes she's scared to tell Charlie what really happened with Kit. She likes Charlie and doesn't want to jeopardize their friendship. But she always hears her mom say, "If they don't accept you for who you are, they really aren't your friend." She thinks of Kit, and sadness surrounds her.

Sensing her mood and seeing a frown on her face, Charlie asks, "Are you thinking of Kit?"

Lily sniffs. "Yes."

"I'm so sorry for the loss of your friend, and so sudden."

Lily lets out a slow breath. "Well, not so sudden."

"What do you mean?"

Lily looks Charlie in the eyes. "She died thirty years ago."

"What do you mean, she died thirty years ago?"

Lily sighs and begins again. "She was a ghost."

"Wait, you can see ghosts? But I thought you didn't have any of the ghost gifts."

"I didn't. I didn't know she was a ghost. And she didn't know she was dead."

Charlie rubs his head. "So all that time you were talking with her and you couldn't tell?"

Lily shrugs. "I talked, danced, touched, sang, hiked, laughed, and ate with her. I had no idea. She even gave me two poems that she wrote. I have them at home."

"So did you find out when you went to pick her up?"

"Yes. It was awful and confusing. And then she appeared to me and we talked. She knew then that she had died." Lily feels tears well in her eyes. She reaches up and brushes them away. "We shared so much. Every night we would talk and share our trauma and how we were dealing with it. She helped me so much."

Charlie reaches over and touches Lily's arm. "You helped her too."

"I know. It just wasn't what I thought would happen. I lost a friend and found I can see ghosts."

Charlie sighs. "So it isn't inherited."

"Apparently not always, or sometimes it can be. Anyway, that's that."

They ride again in silence. When they get to the ridge overlooking the ranch, they pull up their horses and gaze out over the property.

Charlie snickers. "You have quite the family."

Lily smiles. "I know, right?"

Lily's glad she told Charlie. She knows he's processing the information. She smiles to herself—she's being brave. She's opening herself up, and she's proud of the person that sits here on this beautiful horse. She feels a chill and looks to the mountains. A storm is coming in, and it looks like it might contain snow.

Lily points. "I think we might get a May snowstorm. We'd better start back."

Charlie looks toward the mountains, where Lily is pointing. "You're right. And it's moving fast."

They turn their horses and trot down the trail. Sky seems to sense the storm and stays close to Lily. As they near the ranch, they bring their horses to a walk.

Charlie moves his horse close to Lily's horse and touches Lily's hand. "Thanks for telling me about Kit and your gift."

Lily nods.

Charlie squeezes Lily's hand and releases it, and then gives her a big smile. "And I'm not going anywhere."

Lily smiles as large snowflakes start to fall.

TENDER HEARTS

After returning home, Lily sits down to dinner with her parents, and they chat about their day.

"Mom, thanks so much for letting me ride your lovely horse."

Lilith swallows a bite of salad. "You're so welcome. I don't get to ride her as much as she needs. I'm glad we both can exercise her."

"Have you ever done dressage with her?"

"No, but she's bred for it. Her shire was shown at upper levels."

"I have heard of it, but what's dressage?" Roy asks.

Lily smiles. "It's ballet for horses. The horse does intricate maneuvers as the rider gives them cues that aren't visible. It teaches the horse to be supple, balanced, and responsive."

"And it's one of the best ways to build and tone any horse's muscles so they perform the best at whatever activity you ask of them," Lilith says.

Roy nods. "Huh, interesting. Lily, did you just look that up?"

Lily grins. "Well, I was thinking about it, so I did Google on my phone to see if there were any instructors in the area. I shared the jargon with you."

Roy smiles.

Lily sighs. "As an older ballerina, I can't dance as many hours as I used to. I think adding more riding, especially dressage, would help me. And it would be fun."

Lilith looks at her daughter. "I think it's a great idea. I'm sure Willow would enjoy it. You can use the truck and trailer to take her for lessons if the instructor can't come here. Willow loads well. And I can teach you the ins and outs of trailering." Lilith looks at Roy. "Or your dad can as well."

Roy looks up. "Sure."

Lily stands and starts clearing the table. She turns and looks at her parents. "I love living on the ranch. And I hope to be employed and pulling my own weight soon."

Roy takes Lilith's hand and says to his daughter, "We love having you here. And it will happen. If it doesn't, I'll just put you to work this summer when the family groups arrive." Roy grins.

Lily laughs. "Well, as great as it is to have a fallback plan, I think I'll let Sky out and then go upstairs to work on my strategies for building my business. And remember Grandma is coming over for breakfast in the morning."

Roy puts his hand to his head. "I forgot I have to be in town early tomorrow for an appointment."

Lilith smiles. "Well, then it will be just us girls, including Sky."

Lily smiles and blows her parents a kiss. She heads to the door, puts on her coat, and steps outside with Sky. The snow has accumulated to make about three inches of soft, fluffy whiteness. Sky runs out and rolls, turning this way and that. Lily breathes in the fresh, cool mountain air. *I do love it here.*

Lily calls to Sky, and the two enter the house and go upstairs. Sky jumps on the bed, while Lily heads to the bathroom and turns on the shower. She takes off her clothes and puts them in the hamper. After stepping into the shower, she lets the warm water run over her. She thinks about her plans and realizes that she has come a long way. Kit would be proud of her. She takes in a slow, deep breath as she thinks of Kit.

"I hope you're happy and at peace, wherever you are. You deserve it," Lily says out loud.

Lily turns off the water and towels dry. She slips on her nightgown and snuggles into bed next to Sky. Lily gives Sky a kiss and opens her book.

She reads until she is nodding off, and then she turns out the light and slips into sleep.

Lily and Sky run toward the stables as large flakes of snow fall all around them. Lily sees that Willow is in the arena. She is trotting around on her own, tossing her head as the snowflakes touch her. Lily climbs on the fence. She stretches out her leg and then hooks her leg through the fence, balancing herself. She leans backward as snowflakes land on her face. She does the ballet positions with her arms. She's laughing hard. Out of the corner of her eye, she sees Sky jumping up and trying to catch the snowflakes, and she laughs even harder. Then her face becomes wet with snow. She wakes to find Sky licking her.

She laughs. "Sorry, Sky. But that was a funny dream." She ruffles Sky's fur. "It's morning already."

Lily hears a soft knock on the door. "Come in."

Grandma opens the door and peeks her head in. "Are you awake? I thought I would come early so we could have a chat."

Lily sits up and pats the side of the bed for her grandma to sit down. They embrace each other, and Lily takes in her grandma's smell: Rosewater and cookies. Grandma sits down.

"How're you doing? It was quite a shock for you to find out Kit was dead and realize your gift."

Lily sighs. "I miss her. She was such a good friend. And I still can't believe this ghost thing. Mom helps me understand what doesn't make sense. I've been doing some reading about paranormal gifts. There're so many kinds." Lily takes in a deep breath and lets it out. "Mom says it's a journey of learning." Lily sighs and looks down.

Grandma pats Lily's leg. "Your mom told me of her challenges in the beginning. You'll learn. It's been a comfort to your mom to understand what happens after someone dies. You don't just end—it's another journey."

Lily looks at her grandma. "Is that how you felt when my birth mom died?"

Grandma looks up. "No, I didn't know about Lilith's gift at that time. I was lost. But Lilith had a way of talking to me that made me feel that Jess was in a good place and that she would be looking out for you. And then later, Lilith helped me talk to your birth mom. It was wonderful. And I realized the value of the gift that you share."

Lily sighs. "Well, it only happened to me with Kit. Maybe it was a one-time thing."

Grandma laughs. "I don't think it works like that. Your mom told me of times she put her gift out of her mind, but it never went away. It's always there, like her guides. She can access it whenever she wants. I think it's a comfort to her."

"I don't know. And I don't know about any guides that follow me around."

"Well, when you're ready, I'm sure your mom can help."

Sky is staring at Grandma Catherine. "Hi, Sky, I didn't mean to ignore you." Sky scoots closer to Grandma and rubs her head under Grandma's hand. "You're so soft. What a good girl, and such a comfort to Lily."

Lily leans down and gives Sky a kiss on her head. "She's the best."

Lily jumps out of bed. "I'll put on some clothes. You must be hungry. What would you like for breakfast?"

Grandma grabs Lily's hand and brings her back to sit on the bed. "I'm not hungry now. Tell me about your plans for your studio."

Lily tells her grandma about the summer camps and distributing fliers. She tells her how Charlie offered to develop a website for her, but she didn't want that much public exposure because of Adam.

Grandma frowns. "Have you seen him or heard that he's around?"

Lily shakes her head. "No, but I don't want to take any chances."

Then Lily tells her about the meeting with the architect and the contractor about expanding the studio with an apartment. She tells her that she shared with Charlie that Kit was a ghost and had died thirty years ago.

Grandma's eyes get big. "How'd he take it?"

"He was cool about it. He knows about John but didn't know about Mom and Dad. I think he likes me. He said he isn't going anywhere."

Grandma laughs. "He's always liked you. He's a good man. But are you ready to get involved?"

Lily flushes. "Grandma!" Then she laughs. "No, I'm not. And I told him so. We're just friends." Lily giggles. "For now."

Grandma shakes her head. "Just be happy, my sweet Lily." Grandma wipes a tear from her eye.

Lily feels a tingling sensation throughout her body, which dissipates in a few seconds. She shakes it off as she sees the wetness on her grandma's face. "Are you OK?"

Grandma smiles. "Yes, I'm OK. Now, do you remember your mom told you that I have an irregular heartbeat and am taking medicine for it?"

Lily frowns. "Yes, I think she said it was atrial something."

"Yes, atrial fibrillation. I take blood thinners, but sometimes you can develop clots in the heart chamber."

"You took your medicine, didn't you?"

Grandma touches Lily's hand. "Yes, I always take my medicine. But sometimes a clot develops anyway. And there's nothing you can do." Grandma looks deep into Lily's eyes. "Do you know how much I love you?"

Lily takes in a sharp breath. "Yes."

"And I hope you know how proud I am of you. You're pulling your life together after experiencing a terrible trauma with your former husband. You should be so proud of yourself. And you helped a troubled young woman who was stuck in between worlds due to her horrific trauma."

"Grandma, you're scaring me. What are you saying? Are you not well?"

Grandma smiles and touches Lily's red curls. "I love these curls. They're just like my Jess's."

Lily stands up and faces her grandma. She touches her paling face. "Are you sick? Should I get mom?"

"No, I'm going to be OK. And so will you. You know I have your mom's paintings in my house and the photos. They're all for you, as well as all my things."

"What are you saying?" Lily takes her grandma's hand.

Grandma stands, and Lily sees that she has a wavering light around her. "What's happening?"

"Lily, I went to bed last night, and I didn't wake up."

"What? No!"

Sky whines and comes to Lily's side.

"I love you, Lily." And Grandma Catherine disappears.

Lily screams, "Mom!" She and Sky run down the stairs to her parents' bedroom.

Lilith opens her door—tears are streaming down her face. She puts her arms out, and Lily falls into them.

"We've got to go to her house. We have to save her."

Lilith hugs her daughter tightly. "She's already gone."

Lily cries. "Did you see her?"

Lilith wipes tears from her face. "No, but I heard her."

"This gift sucks! I don't want to keep losing people I love!"

Lilith gives a shuddering sigh. "It's not the gift. It's losing people we love."

Lily leans back and looks at her mom. "But I didn't even know she was a ghost. We were talking and laughing. And I hugged her."

"She didn't want you to know until she was ready."

"I'm not ready. I just found her again."

Lilith hugs her daughter. "I know. Let's get dressed and go down to her house. I have to call and report what happened."

Lily goes into the kitchen and gives Sky her food. Then she runs upstairs and puts on her clothes. When she gets back downstairs, her mom and Sky are outside. Her mom is on the phone, notifying her dad and the rest of the family.

They start heading toward Grandma Catherine's house. Lily breaks out into a run, and Sky runs with her. When she gets to the house, she sees that the curtains are closed and the door is locked. She finds the key under a statue of an angel next to the red planter.

Lily opens the door, and calls out, "Grandma!"

She runs to the bedroom and freezes in the doorway. There's her grandma—she looks as if she's sleeping. Lilith and Sky come up behind Lily. Lilith walks over to the bed and feels Catherine's neck. Lily knows her mom is feeling for a pulse, and she holds her breath.

Lilith makes the sign of the cross on Catherine's forehead. She gives her a kiss on her cheek and says, "I love you, Catherine. My life is richer because of you." Tears fall down Lilith's face.

Lilith puts out her hand to her daughter and says, "Honey, she's gone. There's no pulse or breathing, and her skin is cold to touch. She's been dead for a while. Do you want to come closer?"

"Mom, I just hugged her and she was warm, before she got paler and cooler."

Lily approaches the bed and takes her grandma's hand. "It's cold and stiff. She's been gone for a while." Lily leans over, hugging her grandma, and she cries, "I love you, Grandma. I'm going to miss you so much."

Lilith steps out of the room. She takes a tissue from her pocket, wipes her eyes, and blows her nose. She dials her phone to report the death.

Roy arrives and takes his wife into his arms. He looks into the room and sees his daughter draped over Catherine's body, hugging her. Sky's head is lying on the bed next to Catherine's still hand, and Sky's body is wedged close to Lily.

"We should call Father Rod. I'll do that. And I'll call John, Steven, and Clark. They might want to see her before the coroner takes her," Roy says.

Lily comes up behind her dad and puts her arms around him. "Coroner? What are you talking about?"

Lilith puts her arms around her husband and daughter. "An unexpected death has to be a coroner's case."

"Oh." Lily hugs her parents.

Father Rod arrives as John's truck pulls up. Soon Steven and Clark arrive. Their wives stay with the children and explain what has happened. Then the police and coroner arrive. The coroner waits for the family to pray with Father Rod and give Catherine a blessing.

The week is a blur for the family. Catherine was a grandma to all of them, and she was a great-grandma to Steven's and Clark's children.

The coroner examines Catherine's body and finds that Catherine had a blood clot in her lung that stopped her breathing and then stopped her heart. He notes that it was probably related to her atrial fibrillation. She died in her sleep.

The family has a viewing of the body at St. Agnes so that family and friends can say good-bye. Catherine's body is then cremated, according to her wishes.

Once the family receives her ashes, Father Rod comes out to the ranch for the memorial and the dispersing of the ashes. Roy has two wagons hitched to horses. Family and friends get in the wagons and ride up into the woods to the ridge that overlooks the ranch. Father Rod leads the memorial, and then family members speak.

Lilith comes forward first. "I first met Catherine when I was the nurse taking care of her daughter, Jessica, who was pregnant with our Lily. Jessica was dying, and after Lily was born, Catherine asked if I would adopt Lily. We became a family. Catherine moved in with me and baby Lily until she found a house nearby. And we've been family ever since. She became a mom to me, and she was a wonderful grandma to Lily and John, as well as Steven and Clark. And the family grew to include Missy and Ali and then great-grandchildren: Mac, Ben, Sam, and An. We were blessed to be able to love her and be loved by her. I'll miss her so very much. She's now with her husband and daughter, Jessica." Lilith sniffs and catches some of the tears that are streaming down her face.

Roy puts his arm around his wife. "I met Catherine when she was already a family with Lilith and Lily. I had to be on my best behavior under her scrutinizing eye. Lucky for me, I won her over with my charm."

There are some chuckles from the family.

Roy continues. "I had no idea the richness that would come to my life when I married into this beautiful family. Catherine moved onto the ranch and fit right in." Roy laughs. "I have a great memory of looking out over the ranch on this ridge with my wife and two young children. Let's see—John was a baby, and Lily was two. We looked down, and Steven and Clark were driving one of the utility carts. Christmas, our cat, was sitting on Clark's lap with his paws on the dash. And Grandma Catherine was laughing as she sat in the back and waving up at us." Roy wipes a tear from his eye.

Clark and Steven smile at the memory.

John steps forward. "When I was still just dreaming of helping animals as a vet, I was about thirteen and was riding when I saw one of our cows limping. Grandma happened by—she was driving back from one of her meetings. I waved at her, and she stopped. I don't know what I thought I was going to do, but I was going to try. Grandma climbed through the fence in her dress and traipsed through the mud in her nice shoes to where I was standing, holding my horse. She held my horse and fed the cow grass as I lifted its left leg and saw a cactus barb. As I pulled out the barb, the cow lunged forward, knocking Grandma into the mud. Then the cow ran off happily. Grandma was laughing so hard she had tears running down her face. I got in trouble for putting her and myself in danger."

Everyone laughs.

Lily steps forward and waits for the laughing to stop. She takes a breath in through her nose and lets it out through her mouth. "I'm going to talk about the things for which I'm grateful. I'm grateful for my mom, who chose to have me even though she didn't have a partner. And I'm grateful to Grandma for encouraging my mom's nurse to adopt me after my mom died. I'm grateful that my mom married my dad and we lived on this beautiful ranch with Grandma and the rest of the family. I'm grateful that Grandma was around my whole childhood. I'm grateful that she supported my dream to dance." Lily sniffs and brushes away a tear. "I'm grateful that after several years of absence from the family, I was able to reconnect with my family and Grandma. She told me things I didn't remember about my birth mom and answered questions that had haunted me. One of the things she told me was that life is short. She said we must 'seize the day.'" Lily sees that her family is nodding. "Her words encourage me and give me strength." Lily looks up to the sky. "I'll miss you, Grandma. I love you. Thank you."

Father Rod steps forward and says, "Let us bow our heads and pray this prayer that Roy wrote."

God our Father,

You give us the gift of life in birth.
You guide us through our lives.
And welcome us as we return to you in death.

Lord, bless this family.
May their memories bring comfort
Until they are united again
In your kingdom.

Amen.

Lilith and Lily step to the edge of the ridge and release Grandma Catherine's ashes, which float down over the ranch where she has lived and loved well.

EPILOGUE—ONE YEAR LATER

It's been one year since Grandma Catherine died. "Seize the day" is Lily's continued mantra, which her grandma bestowed upon her, and she is taking it seriously. She's working hard to be the independent woman she was before she let fear cripple her.

Grandma's will was read, and Lily was named the beneficiary of her estate. Her mom and dad had known and had copies of her will. Lily received Grandma's house, all its contents, and her savings and investments, as well as her old 1995 white Toyota 4Runner, which she didn't drive much—it only has one hundred thousand miles on it and still runs great. Sky loves riding in it. Grandma also left her an eighteen-carat gold locket. It has a picture of Grandma, pregnant, with the grandpa Lily never met on one side and a picture of her birth mom on the other. And Lily has all the old albums to remind her of her history.

Lily redecorated the cabin with fresh paint, refinished the wood floors, put in wooden blinds, and bought some nice rugs, new bedding, and a new bed. She didn't want her old one that she had shared with Adam and didn't want to sleep in the bed where Grandma had taken her last breath. She loves having her birth mom's paintings around her, so she kept those. And she bought a large farmhouse table so that she can entertain. Lily loves to cook, and with the family greenhouse, which she helps weed and keep up, she gets lots of great vegetables.

Dad insisted on an alarm system for her cabin and the studio. She's the only one with a security system on the ranch, but after letting the security go last year and Lily living on her own, her mom and dad were worried. Lily realizes that it's nice to have someone worry about you. And Sky is always with her—she's her buddy. The security alarm helps her relax and especially sleep well at night.

The first summer, Lily had four summer dance camps at the studio, each a week long. The students were mostly girls, but she had a few boys.

She tried to separate them by age, but that didn't always work, so sometimes she had a group of all ages. They arrived at 8:00 a.m. and were with her until 3:00 p.m. She had them dancing all day. They did a combination of ballet, contemporary dance, and a little hip-hop. The students did a performance for the ranch families at the end of each week. They had a blast, and so did Lily.

Lily did connect with some serious dancers who wanted to continue taking classes with her during the school year. They love hearing her stories about Julliard and the NYC Ballet. If it's their dream to be professional dancers, Lily intends to help. She always appreciated the instructors who helped prepare her.

The classes are growing slowly, and she has a couple adult classes and a mixed class of adults and teens. She doesn't have enough students for a *Nutcracker* production, but she's working on it. She's proud of her dancers. Because she has a small group, they partner with another studio for the dance productions.

Lily dances every day—it feeds her soul. And she rides her mom's horse, Willow. Her mom says they have joint ownership of Willow. On Saturday mornings Lily travels to a farm about thirty-five minutes away and rides with the farm's dressage trainer. Both Willow and Lily are learning the dressage discipline. They practice some weekday mornings when Lily doesn't have a class.

Charlie is still present in Lily's life. They ride together and sometimes cook together. They go out dining and dancing at night with no trauma. Sky always goes along. They're taking it very, very slowly.

John and Amy are dating more seriously after he shared his gift with her and she didn't run off. They spend most nights at John's house. Lilith and Roy aren't pleased, but they know he's an adult. They adopted a short-haired black female kitten.

Lily hasn't seen a ghost since Grandma came to her in her bedroom after she'd died. She was hoping at Halloween that she might see Kit or Grandma, but nothing happened. She thinks that they must have been busy somewhere else. Lily has been reading and working on her gift. Her mom helps her, but Lily still has a lot of questions.

She feels good making her own money again, and she's thankful for what Grandma left her. It helped, especially before her place sold and before she got started with students. It took several months, but her place in Lakewood sold. The new owners turned it into a bakery, and they live upstairs.

When Lily goes riding, Sky always accompanies her. She usually rides Willow. Before she leaves, she tells the family her route and doesn't veer from it. Lily feels good moving around on her own, and she's gaining back her confidence. She has seen her therapist now and then, especially after Grandma died, and once so far this year. It's good to check in and make sure she's on track. She feels very proud of her progress.

Lily loves living on the family ranch. She has invited her friend Sasha and Sasha's daughter, Sam, to come visit during the summer. And even though the family members all have busy lives, they always go to Mass on Sunday mornings and then come together on Sunday evenings for dinner. Lily regularly invites Charlie, and she seems to laugh and smile a lot around him.

It's the end of May, and school will be getting out soon. Lily has had telephone calls from parents interested in signing their children up for the dance camp. It'll be a busy summer, and she may not get to ride Willow as often as she likes. So today, which is warm with a cool breeze coming from the mountains, Lily is going for a ride up to the ridge. She notifies her mom of her route. She remembers to take her phone and wear her helmet and orange vest because of the hunters.

Sky herds Willow out of the pasture and up to the stable. Sky's energy always makes Lily laugh. She brushes Willow as Sky looks on. Sky whines because she's so excited to go. After putting on the saddle with an orange saddle pad and then the bridle, she puts on her helmet and an orange vest and climbs up. She lets out a long breath. It's so relaxing to be up in the saddle on a powerful horse. They turn to the trail and start up at a walk. Once Willow is warmed up, they trot and then canter.

Up ahead, Sky comes to a halt. Lily pulls Willow up as they see a deer cross the path. It stops and looks at them and then bounds across and into the woods.

"Good girl, Sky. You're so smart. Thank you for alerting us. And thank you for staying with me." Lily's so glad that Sky is so well trained and doesn't leave her to have fun and run after the deer.

They continue and reach the ridge that overlooks the property. The trees are leafing out, and the grass is coming in green. Lily can see a flurry of activity as the ranch staff members prepare for the first group of families coming in June. She dismounts, pulls a collapsible bowl from her saddlebag, and takes out the cool bottles of water. She pours some for Sky, who drinks. Lily takes a sip of the cool water. After Sky drinks, she offers Willow some; she plays with it and then takes some sips. After they finish, Lily puts the bowl and bottles back in the saddlebag and climbs onto Willow's back.

They start down the trail toward home. As they enter the woods, Sky and Willow halt at the same time. Sky's growling, and Lily can feel that Willow's heart rate is elevated. The hair on the back of Lily's neck is standing up, and her heart is racing. She sees a shadow, and then the shadow steps forward. Her breath catches as she realizes its Adam.

"You bastard! Get out! Private property! Leave me alone!"

He approaches, and Willow rears up, kicking at the air. Sky moves at him, growling and barking as she shows her teeth.

Lily has a tingling sensation throughout her body that dissipates in a few seconds.

Adam stops and puts a hand up. "Lily, I just want to say that I'm so sorry for what I did to you." Adam tips his head to the side. "I didn't know what had happened when I approached you in the cemetery." Adam puts his hand down and backs up a few steps.

Willow has settled with all her hooves on the ground, but Sky is still at attention, growling. Lily notices that she can see through Adam—she can see the leaves and trees behind his body. Her heart rate slows. Adam nods, and he disappears as if he has evaporated. Sky runs to where he had stood and sniffs the ground as if making sure he's really gone. Sky looks back at Lily.

"Come, Sky. Good job, girl. You're the best."

Up in the saddle, Lily sighs. She rubs a hand down Willow's neck. She takes in a deep breath and lets it out slowly. She looks back at where she saw Adam.

Shaking her head, she says, "Well, girls, another ghost. Maybe Adam was a ghost at the cemetery and is still a ghost? And he's finally gone. Oh, my God!"

Lily turns Willow toward home, and they prance down the path as Sky runs ahead. Relief and confusion flow through Lily. She didn't want something bad to happen to Adam—she just wanted him to leave her alone. She had no idea that he was a ghost when she saw him at his memorial, and neither, apparently, did he.

After putting Willow away, Lily and Sky head to the main house to talk with her mom. She thinks back to what happened and wonders if she imagined it or if it really happened. She needs validation that she really saw what she saw. As Lily climbs the front stairs, she knocks on the door.

Lilith answers the door. "Honey, you don't have to knock." Seeing the confusion in Lily's furrowed brow, Lilith pulls her into the house as Sky follows her inside. "Tell me what happened."

Lily plops down on the couch. "Mom, Adam is dead."

Lilith sits next to her. "What? How did you find out?"

"I saw his ghost."

Lilith shakes her head. "Where did you see him? When you were riding?"

"He just stepped out of the woods. Willow and Sky saw him too. Sky growled and was ready to attack, and Willow reared up, kicking her feet in the air."

"Oh, my gosh, did you stay on Willow?"

"Yes, and I yelled at Adam to leave me alone and to get off the property."

"What did he say?"

"He said he was sorry for what he did to me and that he hadn't known what had happened when he saw me at the memorial."

"And then what happened?"

"I could see through him. He just stood there with this smile and then disappeared as if he had evaporated. Sky ran in to make sure he was gone, and then she came back to me."

"So he's really gone. You don't have to worry about him anymore."

Lily sighs. "But he's been gone over a year. He was a ghost at his memorial. Why didn't I know?"

"Honey, maybe you weren't ready to know. If you'd known at that time, you would never have gone to HRC and met Kit. You needed Kit as much as she needed you. And you both grew and healed with the help you got at HRC and with the friendship you shared. Sometimes things work out in their own time."

"But all the security you paid for, and we didn't need it. I'm so sorry."

Lilith takes Lily's hand. "You needed it at that time, whether Adam was alive or not. You needed all that time to finish healing and become the independent woman you are today."

"But Adam was so different from when he was at his memorial."

Lilith looks into Lily's eyes. "What I've learned is that right after someone dies, especially if it's sudden, they're the same in death as they were in life at that time. That's why Adam was so sinister and threatening at the memorial. He was just as he was in life, and of course he also didn't know he was dead. He wanted to torment you. But after a year, he's evolved enough to be remorseful for his actions. That's why he appeared to you and said he was sorry."

"So animals can see spirits?"

"Some have the sensitivity to be able to see or sense spirits. We knew that Sky did, and now we know that Willow does as well."

"So how can I tell the difference between a person and a ghost? They keep surprising me."

Lilith thinks for a moment. "Well, in Adam's case, I don't think you were ready to know, and with Kit, neither of you were ready to know. But with Grandma, she wanted to talk with you before disclosing what had happened."

Lily gets up and paces around the rug. "That didn't answer my question. How can I know?"

"The simple but confusing answer is when you're ready, you'll know. But it may be that it just takes practice and experience. You needed time to rebuild your confidence. And this gift is a lifelong journey. You'll learn from each experience."

Lily thinks a moment. "Actually, I get a tingling sensation throughout my body. It only lasts a few seconds. I felt it when I first met Kit, and then right before Grandma told me about her heart, and just before Adam apologized."

Lilith smiles. "Well, that must be your first clue."

Lily gives her mom a hug. "So my learning journey continues, right?"

Lilith hugs her daughter tightly and releases her. "Yes. We keep learning, and hope we learn something new every day." Lilith smiles at Lily.

Lily touches the soft fur on Sky's head as she sits next to her. "I suspect that Adam still has learning to do, wherever he is."

Lilith smiles. "I think you're right about that."

ABOUT THE AUTHOR

Poetry and short-story writer and nurse Karen Steur is the author of the novel *Lilith Whispers Back*. She'll soon graduate with an MA in creative writing. She lives and works in Boulder County, Colorado.

Made in the USA
San Bernardino, CA
07 February 2018